Publisher's Note

Purchase of this book entitles you to a free trial membership in the publisher's book club at www.rarebooksclub.com. (Time limited offer.) Simply enter the barcode number from the back cover onto the membership form on our home page. The book club entitles you to select from millions of books at no additional charge. You can also download a digital copy of this and related books to read on the go. Simply enter the title or subject onto the search form to find them.

Note: This is an historic book. Pages numbers, where present in the text, refer to the first edition of the book and may also be in indexes.

If you have any questions, could you please be so kind as to consult our Frequently Asked Questions page at www.rarebooksclub.com/faqs.cfm? You are also welcome to contact us there. Publisher: Books LLC™, Memphis, TN, USA, 2012. ISBN: 9781153726016.
Proofreading: pgdp.net

✂ ✂ ✂ ✂ ✂ ✂ ✂ ✂

THE WOMAN'S WAY

BY CHARLES GARVICE

AUTHOR OF "JUST A GIRL" "TWO MAIDS AND A MAN" ETC.

HODDER AND STOUGHTON LONDON NEW YORK TORONTO

Printed in 1914

CHAPTER I

Celia climbed up the steps to her room slowly; not because she was very tired, but because her room was nearly at the top of Brown's Buildings and she had learnt that, at any rate, it was well to begin slowly. It was only the milk boy and the paper boy who ran up the stairs, and they generally whistled or sang as they ran, heedless of feminine reproofs or masculine curses. There was no lift at Brown's; its steps were as stony and as steep as those of which Dante complained; the rail on which Celia's hand rested occasionally was of iron; and Brown's whitewashed corridors, devoid of ornament, were so severe as to resemble those of a prison; indeed, more than one of the inhabitants of the Buildings spoke of them, with grim facetiousness, as The Jail. Without having to pause to gain her breath, for at twenty-two, when you are well and strong, sixty steep steps do not matter very much, Celia unlocked a door, bearing the number "105," and entered her room.

It was not large; to descend to detail, it measured exactly ten feet by fifteen feet; but scantily furnished as it was, it contrasted pleasantly with the prison-like corridor on which it opened. Like that of the Baby Bear, everything in the apartment was small; a tiny table, a diminutive armchair, a miniature book-case; the one exception was a wardrobe, which was not in reality a wardrobe; it served a double purpose; for when the doors were opened, they disclosed a bed, standing on its head, which came down at night and offered Celia repose. The room had a cheerful air; there was a small fire in the tiny grate, and the light of the flickering coal was reflected on one or two cheap, but artistically good, engravings, and on the deep maroon curtains—"Our celebrated art serge, *1s. 6d.* a yard, double width"—which draped the windows looking down on Elsham Street, which runs parallel with its great, roaring, bustling brother, Victoria Street.

There were few prettier rooms in Brown's than Celia's; but then, compared with the other inhabitants of The Jail, she was quite well-to-do, not to say rich; for she earned a pound a week; and a pound a week is regarded as representing affluence by those who are earning only fifteen shillings; and that sum, I fancy, represented the top income of most of Celia's neighbours.

You can do a great deal with a pound a week. Let us consider for a moment: rent, which includes all rates and taxes, five shillings a week; gas, purchased on the beautiful and simple penny-in-the-slot system, say, one shilling and three-pence, and firing one shilling and six-pence—at Brown's you only have a fire when it is really cold, and it is wonderful how far you can make a halfpenny bundle of wood go when you know the trick of it. Now we come to the not unimportant item of food. It is quite easy; breakfast, consisting of an egg, which the grocer, with pleasing optimism, insists upon calling "fresh," one penny; bread and butter, per week, one shilling and sixpence; tea, milk, and sugar, per week, one and fourpence. Lunch, a really good, substantial meal, of savoury sausage or succulent fish and mashed potato, and a bun. If you are a lady the bun is indispensable; for if there is one faith implanted firmly in the feminine breast, it is that which accepts the penny bun as a form of nutrition not to be equalled. Thrones totter and fall, dynasties stagger and pass away, but the devotion of Woman to the Penny Bun stands firm amidst the cataclysms of nature and nations. This substantial lunch costs sixpence. On Sundays, you dine sumptuously at home on a chop, or eggs and bacon, cooked over your gas-ring, and eaten with the leisure which such luxury deserves. Tea, which if you are in Celia's case, you take at home, consists of the remains of the loaf and the milk left from breakfast, enhanced by a sausage "Made in Germany," or, say, for a change, half a haddock, twopence. Of course, this meal is supper and tea combined.

If you tot all this up, you will find it has now reached the not inconsiderable sum of fifteen shillings and tenpence. This is how the rich person like Celia lives. There still remains a balance of four shillings and twopence to be expended on clothing, bus fares, insurance and amusement. Quite an adequate—indeed, an ample sum. At any rate, it seemed so to Celia, who, at present, was well set up with clothes, and found sufficient amusement in the novelty of her life and her surroundings; for, only a few months back, she had been living in comfort and middle-class luxury, with a larger sum for pocket-money than had now to suffice for the necessaries of existence.

The kettle was boiling, she set the tea; and while she was arranging in a vase—"Given away with every half-pound of our choice Congo!"—the penny bunch of violets which she had been unable to resist, her lips were moving to the strains of the hackneyed but ever beautiful intermezzo in "Cavalleria Rusticana," which floated up from the room immediately underneath hers; but as she drew her chair up to the fire, the music of the violin ceased, and presently she heard footsteps ascending the stairs slowly. There came a knock at the door, and she opened it to an old man with a frame so attenuated that it appeared to be absolutely fleshless. His hair was white and almost touching his shoulders, and his face so colourless and immobile that it looked as if it were composed of wax; but the dark eyes under the white, shaggy brows were full of life, and piercing.

"Oh, good evening, Mr. Clendon!" said Celia, in the tone a woman uses when she is really pleased, and not affecting to be pleased, at the advent of a visitor. "Come in."

"Thank you, Miss Grant," said the old man, in a peculiar voice that was quite low and yet strangely vibrant, like the note of a muted violin. "I have come to ask you if you could oblige me with a couple of pieces of sugar. I have run out, and somehow—one has one's foolish weaknesses—I dislike my tea without sugar."

"Why of course," said Celia, with a touch of eagerness. "But—but won't you come in and have your tea with me?"

The old man shook his head; but his eyes, taking in the comfort of the tiny, fire-lit room, the aspect of home, grew wistful; besides, there was a note of entreaty in the invitation; and "Thank you," he said, simply.

With a nod of satisfaction Celia insisted upon his taking the easy chair, gave him a cup of tea—"Three lumps, please," he said—and seated herself opposite him and smiled on him with the sweetness that is as indefinable as it is irresistible. Mr. Clendon, who played in the orchestra at the Hilarity Theatre of Varieties, just below Brown's Buildings, being a gentleman as well as a broken-down fiddler, was conscious of, and appreciated, the subtle manner. He sat quite silent for a time, then, as his eyes wandered to the violets, he said:

"They smell of the country."

Celia nodded. "Yes; that is why I bought them. It doesn't often run to the luxury of flowers; but I could not resist them."

"You are fond of the country?" he said.

"Oh, yes!" she responded, turning her eyes to the fire. "I have lived there all my life, until—until quite recently—until I came here." She was silent for a moment or so. This old man was the only person she knew in Brown's Buildings; they had made acquaintance on the stairs, and they had now and again borrowed little things—sugar, salt, a candle—from each other. She liked him, and—she was a woman and only twenty-two—she craved for some companionship, someone on whom she could bestow the gentle word and the smile which all good women and true long to give. At this moment she wanted to tell him something of her past life; but she hesitated; for when one is poor and alone in the world, one shrinks keenly from speaking of the happiness that is past. But the longing was too much for her. "I used to live in Berkshire."

She paused, and stifled a sigh.

"My father bought a house there; we had plenty of money—I mean, at that time." She coloured and was silent again for a moment. "My father was a business man and very lucky—for a time. Then luck changed. When he died, nearly six months ago, we found that he was ruined; he left very little, only a few pounds."

The old man nodded again.

"I understand," he said, with neither awkward sympathy nor intrusive curiosity.

"I was an only child, and suddenly found myself alone in the world. Oh, of course, there were relatives and friends, and some of them were kind, oh, very kind"—once more Mr. Clendon nodded, as if he understood—"but—but I felt that I would rather make my own way. I dare say it was foolish; there have been times when I have been tempted to—to accept help—throw up the sponge," she smiled; "but—well,

Mr. Clendon, most of us dislike charity, I suppose."

"Some of us," he admitted, dryly. "You found it hard work at first? Sometimes, when I hear stories like yours, Miss Grant, when I pass young girls, thin, white-faced, poorly-clothed, going to their work, with the look of old men on their faces—I mean old men, not women, mind!—I ask myself whether there is not some special place, with a special kind of punishment, appointed for selfish fathers, who have consigned their daughters to life-long toil and misery. I beg your pardon!"

"No, I don't think my father was selfish," said Celia, more to herself than to her listener. "Not consciously so; he was sanguine, too sanguine; he lived in the moment——"

"I know," said Mr. Clendon. "Some men are born like that, and can't help themselves. Well, what did you do?"

"Oh, it was what I tried to do," said Celia, with a laugh. "I tried to do all sorts of things. But no one seemed inclined to give me a chance of doing anything; and, as I say, I was on the point of giving in, when I met in the street, and quite by chance, an old acquaintance of my father. He is a literary man, an antiquarian, and he is writing a big book; he has been writing it, and I think will continue to write it, all his life. He wanted, or said he wanted, a secretary, someone to look up facts and data at the British Museum; and he offered me the work. I—well, I just jumped at it. Fortunately for me, I have had what most persons call a good education. I know French and one or two other foreign languages, and although I have 'little Latin and less Greek,' I manage to do what Mr. Bishop wants. He gives me a pound a week; and that's a very good salary, isn't it? You see, so many persons can do what I am doing."

"Yes, I suppose so," Mr. Clendon assented; he glanced at the slight, girlish figure in its black dress, at the beautiful face, with its clear and sweetly-grave eyes, the soft, dark hair, the mobile lips with a little droop at the ends which told its story so plainly to the world-worn old man who noted it. "And you work in the Reading Room all day?"

"Yes," said Celia, cheerfully, and with something like pride. "It is a splendid place, isn't it? Sometimes I can scarcely work, I'm so interested in the people there. There are so many types; and yet there is a kind of sameness in them all. One seems to lose one's identity the moment one enters, to become merged in the general—general——"

"Stuffiness," he said. "I know; I have been there. Do you manage to keep your health? I have noticed that you are rather pale."

"Oh, I am quite well and strong," she said, with a laugh. "I always walk there and back, unless it rains very hard; and I take long walks, sometimes in the early morning; sometimes at night, when it is fine. I think London is wonderful in the moonlight. You know the view from Westminster Bridge?"

"Yes," he said. "And you are always alone?"

"Why, yes," she assented. "I know no one in London, excepting yourself; for Mr. Bishop lives in the country, in Sussex, and we work by correspondence. Oh, yes; I am lonely sometimes," she added, as if he had asked a question. "But then, I am very busy. I am very much interested in what I am doing, and besides—well, when one is poor, after 'seeing better days'"—she laughed apologetically—"it is, perhaps, better—one can bear it better—to be alone."

He gave another nod which indicated his complete comprehension.

"And there is so much to interest one in the people one sees and lives amongst. Now here, in Brown's Buildings, in The Jail, one finds quite a large amount of amusement in—well, in noticing one's neighbours and fitting a history to them. There is the young girl who lives on your floor; the girl who, you told me, is in the chorus of the 'Baby Queen'; I am sure she is dreaming of, and looking forward to, the time when she will be—principal lady, don't you call it?—and there is the lady who lives opposite her; the old lady who always wears a black silk dress, a satin cloak, and a crape bonnet. I am sure she has been 'somebody' in her time. I met her one day on the stairs, carrying a milk-can. I should have been cowardly enough to put it under my jacket or behind me; but she held it out in front of her and stared at me with haughty defiance. And there is my opposite neighbour"—she jerked her head, with a pretty, graceful motion, towards the door fronting her own—"that handsome, good-looking young fellow who comes up the steps two at a time and bangs his door after him, as if he were entering a mansion."

"I know the young man you mean," said Mr. Clendon. "Have you fitted a history to him?"

"Well, no; he puzzles me rather. I am sure he is a gentleman, and, of course, he must be poor, or he would not be here. Sometimes I think he is a clerk looking for a situation; but he has not the appearance of a clerk, has he? He looks more like an—an engineer; but then, his hands are always clean. He is well groomed, though his clothes are old."

She paused a moment.

"Do you know, Mr. Clendon, I fancy that he has been in trouble lately; I mean, that something is worrying him. Yesterday, I heard him sigh as he unlocked his door. He used to sing and whistle; but, for the last few days, he has been quite quiet, and as I came in last evening I heard him walking up and down his room, as men do when they have something on their minds. Do you know his name?"

"No," said Mr. Clendon, shaking his head; "he is a comparatively new-comer. I could find out for you, if you like."

"Oh, no, no!" she said, quickly, and with a touch of colour. "I am not at all curious. I mean," she explained, "that knowing his name would not increase my interest in him; quite the reverse. You know what I mean? But I fancy I am interested in him because I think he may be in trouble. You see, when one has suffered oneself——"

"Yes, that is the way with you women," said the old man. "In fact, I suppose that, until you have suffered, you do not become women." He glanced at the sheets of paper which lay on the little writing-desk and added, "I am afraid I am keeping you from your work. It was very kind of you to ask me to stay to tea—and to tell me what you have told me. I wish I could help you——. But, no, I don't; for, if I could be of any assistance to you, you would not let me; you are too proud, Miss Grant. I like you all the better for the fact."

"Oh, but you have helped me, more than you know," Celia said, quickly. "You don't know what a delight it is to me to hear the violin you play so beautifully; but, of course, you are an artist."

"Thank you," he said, his voice almost inaudible, and yet with that peculiar vibrance in it. "I was afraid I worried you."

"No, no," said Celia; "I am always sorry when you leave off. You play me to sleep sometimes and—and keep me from brooding. Not that I have any cause to brood," she added, quickly; "for I count myself lucky."

"Yes," he said; "you are lucky; for you have youth, beauty—I beg your pardon," he apologized with a little bow and a gesture which were strangely courtly. "And best of all, you have hope; without that, one is indeed unfortunate."

He rose, and Celia accompanied him to the door; it was only a few steps distant; but the old man moved towards it as if he had been accustomed to traversing apartments of a larger size. As Celia opened the door, the one opposite hers opened at the same moment, and a lady came out. Judging by her figure, for her face was thickly veiled, she was young; she was plainly but richly dressed, and wore a coat and muff of sable. Her appearance was so strangely different from that of the residents and visitors of the Buildings that Celia could not help staring at her with surprise. As if she were conscious of, and resented, Celia's intent regard, the lady turned her head away, and, keeping as near the wall as possible, descended the stairs quickly.

Celia and Mr. Clendon neither exchanged glances nor made any remark. With a gesture of farewell and thanks, he went down. Half-unconsciously, she stood looking at the door which the lady

had closed after her; then Celia shut hers and went back to clearing away the tea.

When Mr. Clendon had asked her if she had fitted a history to the young man who had interested her so much, she had replied in the negative; but now, involuntarily, she began to do so. Of course, he was in trouble; probably in debt; this beautifully-dressed woman was his sister, or, perhaps, his sweetheart; she had come to help him, to comfort him. Something in the idea was pleasant and welcome to Celia; he was such a good-looking young fellow; that voice of his, which used to sing but had become silent lately, had a good, true ring in it; yes, it was nice to think that his sister—or his sweetheart—had come to bring him comfort.

She sat down to her notes; but she could not concentrate herself upon her work. The imaginary history of the young man obtruded upon her; she decided that she would go out for a walk, and take up her work again when she returned. She was getting her coat and hat when Mr. Clendon began to play; she changed her mind about the walk and went to the door to open it an inch or so, that she might hear more distinctly the soft strains of the Beethoven Sonata which came floating up to her. As she opened the door, she heard a strange sound rising above the notes of the music; it was that, perhaps, most terrible of all sounds, the unbidden, irresistible groan, rising from a man's tortured heart; and it came from the young man's room.

Startled, chilled, by the sound, she wondered that she could hear it so plainly; then she saw that the door opposite was slightly ajar; evidently the visitor had failed to close it. Celia waited, with the familiar horror, the tense expectation, for a repetition of the groan. It came. Obeying an impulse, a womanly impulse, to fly to the call of such poignant distress, Celia crossed the corridor softly and opened the door.

By the light of a single candle, she saw the young man seated at a table; his head was resting, face downward, on one arm; his whole attitude was elo-

quent of despair; but it was not this abandonment of grief which caused her to thrill with quick terror; it was because the hand held clenched in its grasp a revolver.

Most women have a horror of firearms; Celia stood motionless, her eyes fixed on the shining, deadly weapon, as if it were a poisonous snake. She wanted to cry out, to rush at the beastly thing and snatch it from the hand that gripped it; but she felt incapable of speech or movement; she could only stare with distended eyes at the revolver and the head lying on the arm.

So quick, so noiseless had been her entrance, that the man had not heard her; but presently, after a few moments which seemed years to her, he became conscious of her presence. He raised his head slowly and looked at her with vacant eyes, as if he were half-dazed and were asking himself if she were a vision. The movement released Celia from her spell; a pang of pity smote her at the sight of the white, drawn face, the hopeless despair in the young fellow's eyes; her womanly compassion, that maternal instinct which the youngest of girl-children possesses, gave her courage. She leant forward, loosened the stiff, cold fingers and took the revolver from them. He submitted, as if he were still only half-conscious of her presence, and her action; and he glanced at his empty hand, at the revolver in hers, and then at her face. Guided once more by impulse, Celia closed the door, then went back and seated herself in a chair on the other side of the table; and so, face to face, they regarded each other in silence.

The man broke it.

"How—how did you know?" he asked. He spoke almost in a whisper, as a man speaks who is recovering from an anæsthetic.

"I heard you—groan," said Celia, also almost in a whisper.

"You did?" he said, more clearly, and with disgust. "I must have groaned pretty loudly." His self-contempt was evident.

There was a pause, then he said: "You are the girl who lives opposite?"

A flicker of irritation and impatience shone in his eyes. "Why do you interfere? It is no business of yours!"

"Yes, it is," she said, and there was something like a note of anger in her voice; for it seemed to her that he was extremely ungrateful. "It is the duty of anyone to prevent a man making—a—a fool of himself. You ought to be ashamed."

Unwittingly, she had used the right tone. He leant back in the chair and stared at her with a mixture of resentment and amusement.

"You have plenty of confidence, anyhow, young lady," he said.

"And you have none," retorted Celia, with a dash of colour. "Fancy a man of your age trying to—to kill himself!"

"My age!" He laughed mirthlessly, ironically. "You talk to me, look at me, as if I were a boy."

"You are not much more," said Celia; "and a foolish one into the bargain."

He pushed impatiently the short lock of hair from his forehead, which was dank with sweat.

"Be that as it may," he said, "you have interfered most unwarrantably in a matter which does not concern you. All the same, I suppose you expect me to say that I am obliged to you. Well, I'm not; I don't like being interfered with, especially—by a woman. You come into my room——" He tried to rise with an air of dignity, but he sank back, as if he were weak, and with his arms extended along those of the chair regarded her with a grim smile of whimsicality. "Well, I suppose I ought to say I am obliged to you. Consider that I have said it and—pray, don't let me keep you."

Celia rose, the revolver still in her hand.

"Good night," she said.

"Here!" he called out to her, wearily; "give me back that thing; put it down."

"Certainly not," said Celia, with decision. "You are not fit to be trusted with it."

"Oh, am I not?" he said, sarcastically.

"You know you are not. What were you doing with it, what were you going to do with it, when I came in?" she demanded.

"What an unnecessary question," he retorted. "I was going to shoot myself, of course."

"Exactly. That is why I am taking it away from you."

"You are very clever," he said, with an attempt at sarcasm. "I can go out and buy another. No, I can't"—he laughed rather quaveringly—"I haven't the coin. Put that revolver down, young lady, and leave me alone."

"I shall do nothing of the kind," said Celia, her eyes bright, her lips drawn straight. "I mean, that I am going to take the revolver. And I am not sure that I ought to leave you alone. If I do, will you promise me——"

"That I won't try to kill myself in some other way? I will promise you nothing of the sort; you don't know what you are asking. But, as I said before, I don't want to detain you. In fact, if you knew—what I am——" his voice faltered for a moment—"you would clear out without any urging on my part."

There was a pause, then: "What are you?" asked Celia, in a low voice.

"I am a forger," he replied, after another pause.

The colour left Celia's face, her lips quivered for a moment, but her eyes did not turn from him; and his eyes, after an attempt on his part to keep them steady, drooped before her intent gaze.

There was a silence which could be felt; then Celia said, very slowly, very quietly:

"I don't believe you."

CHAPTER II

The colour rose to the young man's pallid face; he leant back and, with narrowed eyes, regarded her, for the first time, with curiosity and interest. It may be said that, up to that moment, he had not realized her personality; she was just a something, a nuisance in the shape of a girl, which had come between him and a shameful death. Of course, he had seen Celia in the corridor now and again, had noticed vaguely that his opposite neighbour was young and graceful and pretty—no man, especially one of his age, could fail to notice such

palpable facts—but he had been too absorbed in his own affairs to take any interest in her. Now, surprised by her courage, he regarded her curiously, and he saw that she was not only pretty, but quite beautiful. He took in the clear oval of her face, the soft waves of dark hair which garlanded the low forehead, puckered now by lines of decision, the blue-grey eyes almost violet in the intensity of her gaze, the lips which, he felt, could smile with infinite tenderness, though now set tightly.

Yes; this young woman who had come at the sound of his groan of despair, who now sat opposite him, gripping the revolver which she had forced from his hand, was very beautiful, and, obviously, very brave; he saw, too, that she was a lady, that she was different from most of the girls who lived in the Buildings. In that flash of scrutiny, he took in even the details of her dress, and knew that, plain as it was, it had come from a good house, probably from Paris itself; there were no cheap rings on the well-formed, but not too small, hands; he realized that he was confronting the embodiment of the three qualities most desirable—youth, beauty, strength; and he was conscious of a reluctant thrill of admiration. His eyes sank, and, involuntarily, he sighed. For he was thinking of another woman.

"Did you hear what I said?" asked Celia, in a low voice, one a trifle more gentle, though it was still firm. "I said that I don't believe you."

"Yes; I heard," he responded, with a listless smile of irony; "but I am afraid twelve good men in a box—the jury, you know—would not be so incredulous. May I ask why you refuse to accept my plea of guilty? Not that it matters!"

Celia's brows drew together, and she looked as if she were somewhat embarrassed and puzzled by the question; at last, after a pause, she replied, womanlike,

"You don't look like one."

"Quite so," he said, with deeper irony. "That is essentially a feminine reason. Of course, your idea of a forger is the theatrical one; the gentleman with a Mephistophelian face, a sardonic sneer, evening dress, with a big cloak, and a cigarette in the corner of his mouth; the villain who looks every inch the part and says 'Curse you!' whenever it is possible to do so. My dear young lady, your ignorance of the world spoils your compliment. The worst man, the biggest criminal I ever saw in the dock, looked as innocent as a baby."

"All the same, I don't believe you," Celia declared, doggedly.

"I am sorry to say the court is not with you," he said, with a smile that did not hide his bitterness. "The cheque was cashed by the prisoner—myself, my lord.—You see, I accept you as judge. —When he was asked to give an account of it, he refused to do so; I am speaking in the past tense, but I am merely forecasting the course of the trial. A man who cashes a forged cheque and declines to say where he got it, how it came into his possession, is quickly disposed of by a British jury, than which there is no body of men more acute and intelligent."

"Why do you refuse to tell the truth and clear yourself?" asked Celia, in a low voice, her lips parted now, with a perplexity, a vivid interest.

He rose, strode up and down the room for a moment or two, then came back to the table, and, with his hands pressing hard on it, looked down at her upturned, anxious face.

"Your belief, your persistent, unreasoning belief in me, upsets me," he said, with a smile, and evidently still making an effort to retain his assumption of cynical indifference and levity. "I am strongly tempted by it to tell you 'my story,' as the bores on the stage say; but I can't. However, I will admit that you are right. I did not forge the accursed thing—I beg your pardon! No, I didn't sign the cheque; but the case, so far as I am concerned, is just as black as if I were guilty. Hold on a minute! I know what you are going to say; that I am sacrificing myself——"

"You have no right to do so," Celia broke in, in a voice that trembled, not only with pity, but with indignation. "Oh, don't you see! I am only a girl,

and I know so little of the world; but I know, I am as sure as I am that—that I am standing here, you have no right, no one has any right, to make such a sacrifice, and certainly no one would be justified in accepting it." She pushed the hair from her forehead with a gesture of impatience. "Oh, you must be mad! You—you look so clever, you take it all so calmly; you are not excited, bewildered—don't you see yourself that, in consenting to ruin yourself, to go to—to prison, an innocent man——? Oh, you have not realized——"

"Have I not?" he broke in, grimly, and with a significant glance at the revolver. "Oh, yes; I realize it clearly enough; it was because I did that I decided to—slip out of it. I am sorry that you prevented me. It was good of you; it was brave of you; you meant well. And you have succeeded. It is a case of the interposing angel; but you have placed me in a terrible fix. I don't know what I am going to do."

His hands fell to his side with a gesture of helplessness and despair, and he turned his head away from the searching gaze of the clear eyes regarding him so intently.

"Tell the truth," said Celia, in an urgent whisper. "Why should you screen the guilty? Why should you suffer in his place? Oh, I don't want to hear the story, it does not concern me. But if you told it to me, it would make no difference, it would not alter my opinion that you intend to do a very wicked things—and a very foolish one."

"Foolish! That hits me rather hard," he commented, with a wry smile.

"Well, it is foolish," said Celia, emphatically. "Why, look how young you are!"

"Why, how young do you think I am?" he interrupted, looking down at her with a grave smile. "As I said just now, you seem to regard me as if I were a boy. I think I am as old as you—older. How old are you—you look like a girl?"

"I am twenty-two—but what has that to do with it? How can you turn aside, trifle——"

"And I am twenty-five," he said, with an involuntary sigh. "So you see I am

your senior. But they say a woman is always ten years older than a man of the same age. I suppose that is why you always have us under your thumbs. No, I'm not trifling. Don't you see that I am fighting for time, that I am trying not to *think*, that I am putting the thing from me as far as I can, even for a few minutes. Immediately you go, I shall have to face it all again, and—alone. You have been very good to me; you don't think I am ungrateful, because I—I play the fool?"

"Don't play it any longer, then," said Celia, earnestly. "Make up your mind to do the right thing. Why should you ruin yourself? But I have said that before. You know I am right; you say you are grateful because I have stopped you from——" She shuddered, and her hand closed still more tightly on the revolver. "Promise me——"

He looked at her wistfully; but he shook his head.

"I can't do that," he said, in a low voice. "Here, I see I shall have to put the case to you." He sank into the chair and leant his head on his hand, and, still with his eyes covered, he continued, in little more than a whisper: "Supposing there was someone you cared for more than anything else in the world, more than life, more than honour. Is there someone?"

Celia did not blush, and without a sign of embarrassment, shook her head.

"I beg your pardon for asking. I am sorry there is not; because, you see, you would understand more readily. Well, there is someone I care for like that, and I am doing this to save her—I mean him," he corrected quickly, "from all that I should suffer if I stood up and faced the music, as you want me to do."

"Whoever she is, she is not worth it," said Celia, her voice thrilling with indignation and scorn.

"I said 'him,'" he corrected, almost inaudibly.

"You said 'her,' first," retorted Celia. "Of course, it's a woman—and a wicked, a selfish one. No woman who had a spark of goodness in her would accept such a sacrifice."

"You wrong her," he said. "There are

always exceptions, circumstances, to govern every case. In this case, she does not know. I tell you that, if I take your advice, I should blast the life of the woman I—I love."

"Then you are screening a man for her sake?" said Celia.

"That's it," he admitted; "and you would do the same, if you stood in my place. Oh, you would say you would not; perhaps you think at this moment you would not; but you would. You're just the sort of girl to do it." He laughed again, bitterly. "Why, one has only to look at you——"

For the first time, Celia coloured, and her eyes dropped. As if ashamed of having caused her embarrassment, he bit his lip, and muttered, "I have been offensive, I am afraid. But you see how it is? And now you know the truth, have guessed something of it, you will see that I have either to face the music, plead guilty to the charge and go to prison, or get out of it by the only way."

It was she who hid her face now. He saw that she was trembling; he knew that she was struggling with her tears; he went round to her and laid his hand on her shoulder, very gently, almost reverently. "Don't cry," he said. "I'm not worth it. I am sorry you should be so distressed. I wish—for your sake, now—that you had not come in. Hadn't you better go now?"

Celia rose; her cheeks were wet, her lips were quivering.

"What—what will you do?" she asked, fighting with a sob.

He met her eyes moodily. Celia held her breath; then, with a sudden tightening of the lips, a flash of the eyes, he said, grimly, as if every word cost him an effort,

"I will face it."

With a gasp of relief, and yet with infinite pity and sorrow in her eyes, she flung out both hands to him.

He took them in his, which were burning now, and gripped them tightly.

"My God! what a woman you are," he said, with a sudden uplifting of the brows. "Someone else will find that out some day."

Celia drew her hands away and moved to the door. As he opened it for her, his glance fell on the revolver she had laid on the table.

"You have forgotten," he said, with a mirthless smile. "Hadn't you better take it with you?"

She looked straight into his eyes, not in doubt, but with infinite trust and confidence.

"No," she said; and with the word, she passed out.

CHAPTER III

Celia went back to her room and sank into a chair. She had been upheld during the scene by the excitement and the strain; she had been strong and purposeful a few minutes ago; but now the reaction had set in and she felt weak and exhausted. It was difficult to realize that the thing was real; it was the first time in her life that anything dramatic, tragical, had touched her. She had read of such incidents in novels, and even then, presented in the guise of fiction, with all its licence, such a self-sacrifice, so absolutely illogical and immoral, had seemed incredible to her; and yet here was a case, under her very eyes.

When she was able to think clearly, one or two points in the affair stood out from the rest. If the forgery was detected, and the young man under suspicion, how was it that he was still free, still unarrested? Perhaps they had not yet been able to trace him; but, no doubt, they were on his track, they might discover him and capture him any moment. She shuddered, and crouched over the fire as if she had been struck by a sudden chill. The pity of it, oh, the pity of it! He was so young—he still seemed to her little more than a boy—and he was so good to look upon, so frank, so honest; and what a noble, generous nature he must have to sacrifice his future, his career, for the woman he loved; why, he had been going to face death itself!

Not a word had been said by either Celia or he of the graceful, richly-dressed woman she had seen leaving his room. Of course, she was the woman who had wrecked his life. Celia began to piece the story together; they had loved each other—at any rate, he had loved her—probably for years; he had loved her with all his heart, and she with, perhaps, a small half; she had thrown him over to marry a wealthy man—and yet, that theory seemed scarcely consistent; for a wealthy man would not need to commit forgery. It was a mystery and a puzzle; but the grim fact remained that the young man was going to take upon himself the terrible stigma of a convict for the sake of a woman—perhaps utterly unworthy of him.

She stared at the fire, and it gave her back a picture of the young man dressed in the hideous prison garb, with the wavy hair cut close; with the prison look, that indescribable look of degradation and despair, stamped on his young, handsome face.

She sprang to her feet and moved about the room restlessly. He was sitting there, alone, waiting for the touch of the detective's hand on his shoulder, waiting for his doom. It was her fault; she had held him back from the release of death, had made him promise to live, to drag through a life of shame and humiliation, an outcast, a pariah, a creature from whom such women as herself would shrink as from something loathsome.

The thought was intolerable. Surely he could escape; they had not got upon his track yet. Oh, why had he not gone, while there was time?

Then she remembered that he had said that he had not enough money even to buy another revolver; of course, he could not hope to get away without money. A blush rose to her face; she sprang to her desk; with a trembling hand she unlocked it and took out a five-pound note—it was the only one she possessed, and she had been keeping it for the day, that might so easily come, when she should lose her work and have to fall back upon her resources. Often enough she had regarded this five-pound note as a barrier against the dread wolf that prowled about so many of the doors of The Jail, against absolute destitution. But, without a moment's hesitation, she folded it and put it in an envelope; but now she did hesitate; she stood, biting her lip softly, her brows knit. At last she wrote on a sheet of notepaper:

"I was wrong; you ought not to wait here. There is time for escape. I would send you more than this; but it is all I have. Don't refuse it, or I shall feel as if I were to blame for anything that may happen to you. Oh, please go at once. Good-bye."

She was about to sign her name, but did not do so; it was better that they should remain strangers to each other.

She went out softly, crossed the corridor on tip-toe, pushed the envelope under his door, then knocked very gently and darted back to her own room. Listening, with a heart that beat like a sledge-hammer falling on an anvil, she heard him open the door, heard it close again; she waited almost; breathlessly, and presently his step crossed the corridor, and a piece of paper slid to her feet. She picked it up and read:

"To refuse your generous gift, to disobey your command—for to me it is an absolute command—would be ungrateful; would be worse. I feel as if you had taken my life into your hands and had the right to dispose of it. I am going. If I escape——Oh, I can't write any more; but I know you will understand. You are the most wonderful girl, the bravest, the most generous, in the whole world Good-bye."

Celia sank into the chair and, with the scrawl tightly clenched in her hand, burst into tears. She sat and waited and listened; a quarter of an hour dragged by; footsteps, some dragging and stealthy, some light and free, passed up and down the stairs, and every step made her heart leap with apprehension. Had he gone? Oh, why had he not gone? There was danger in every moment. Presently she heard a faint, almost inaudible knock at her door; she rose quickly and opened it a little way; no one was standing outside, the corridor was empty; but she heard someone descending the stairs below her. She took a few steps out and looked down.

It was he. At the bend of the stairs, he paused and looked up; the light of the murky, wire-globed gas-jet fell on him and she saw the pallor of his face; saw something else, something that remained with her while life lasted—a look, that expression in his eyes, for which many a woman has been willing to give body and soul. He gazed up at her in silence for a moment; then, with a gesture of the hand which conveyed farewell and gratitude, he moved on and disappeared.

Celia stood there until his footsteps had ceased to sound, and she heard the outer door close softly, then she went back to her room and covered her face with her hands; perhaps she was praying; if so, it was unconsciously; but she still listened for the detectives, the police-officers who might be coming. The strain was almost unendurable, and it was with a strange, inexplicable relief that her suspense was brought to an end by the sound of someone approaching the opposite door and knocking. She rose, trembling, and listened, as she had listened so many times that eventful night. The knock was repeated three times; she heard the visitor—a detective, she didn't doubt—try the handle of the opposite door. Then, to her horror, she heard him move across the corridor and knock at her door. The horror was so great that she felt as if every limb were benumbed and paralyzed; her mouth felt so dry as to be incapable of speech. The knock came again, and, with a great effort, she managed to say:

"Who is there?"

"Pardon me. I wish to speak to you," came the response in a man's voice.

What should she do? The detective would be made suspicious by her agitation, would question her, in all probability would drag from her some information which would enable him to track and arrest the fugitive. And yet she could not refuse to speak to him. Clenching her hands and setting her teeth hard, she forced herself to an appearance of self-composure and opened the door; an elderly man, scrupulously dressed, after the fashion of a solicitor or well-to-do City man, confronted her. He raised his hat and, in a grave and apologetic manner, said:

"I beg your pardon. I am sorry to intrude upon you, trouble you. Can you tell me, madam——? Do you know your opposite neighbour; a young man who lives at No. 106 there?"

Every woman is an actress; every woman will show fight for the thing she is protecting, whether it be a man or a dog. Celia's nerves were highly wrought; she was herself again, for that moment, at any rate; for she was on the defensive, and when a good woman is on the defensive, she is full of innocent guile.

"No," she replied. "I have seen him, of course; seen him going in and out of his room——"

"Thank you," he said. "I am much obliged to you, and I apologize again for my intrusion."

He was turning away; but suddenly he paused and, with a most deferential air, said:

"May I ask you one question? The gentleman I wish to see, particularly wish to see, is not at home. I have knocked several times and have got no answer. May I ask if you happen to know whether he is likely to return; I mean, do you think he has gone away?"

Celia did not hesitate for a moment; it seemed to her as if she were inspired by an abnormal acuteness; instantly, she said:

"I believe he has gone away. The room is to let."

She had spoken the truth, and it was evident, by the old gentleman's face, that he accepted her statement, for he regarded her with an expression of profound disappointment, combined with one of anxiety.

"Oh!" he said, thoughtfully. "Indeed. Thank you very much." He turned away, but again he paused. "You would be doing me a very great favour, madam," he said, "if Mr. ——" He checked himself and looked at her with sudden keenness. "Do you happen to know his name?"

"No," replied Celia. "It is not unusual," she explained. "I mean, that very few of us in the Buildings know each other's names. It is a large place, and the tenants come and go——"

"Quite so," he said, blandly. "I lived in the Temple for several years, and did not know the name of the man on the floor below me, because the name was not painted on the doorpost. London is a city of strangers. Yes, yes. But may I trespass upon your kindness to the extent of asking you to give a simple message to my young friend, if he should return?"

"Yes, I will do so," said Celia.

"Thank you, thank you. If you will, please, say just the four words, 'It is all right.'"

Celia inclined her head; she could not speak; the blood surged to her face, then left it white; her eyes closed, she felt as if she were going to faint; the revulsion from terror to relief had been almost too great for her.

The old gentleman saw the effect his words had upon her; he looked at her curiously, his eyes piercing in their keenness.

"Tut! tut! What is the matter? Are you ill?" he asked, compassionately.

"No," Celia managed to enunciate. "I am tired. It is very hot—I was resting when—when you came, I am not very well."

"Oh, I am sorry, very sorry that I should have disturbed you," he said. "Pray forgive me. Is there anything I can do? Are you alone—I mean, is there anyone to take care of you?"

Celia was touched by the kindly, paternal note in his voice; the tears—they were those of joy and relief—rose to her eyes.

"No, I am alone," she said. "But I am all right; it was only a momentary faintness. I will deliver your message."

He bowed, murmured his thanks and, with another glance of pity and concern for her loneliness and weakness, turned away—this time for good.

Celia leant against the table, her hands closed tightly. "It is all right," rang in her ears, thrilled in her heart.

"Oh, thank God, thank God!"

But the cry of thanksgiving changed to one of dismay.

The words evidently meant that the young man's innocence had been proved or the charge had been withdrawn; but, whichever it meant, the message had come too late. Oh, what had she done! She had saved his life, but she had made him a fugitive, had condemned him to the cruellest of fates, that of a doomed man flying from justice. Instinctively, mechanically, she flew for her hat and jacket; then she realized, with bitterness, the hopelessness of any such quest as that which, for an instant, she had thought of undertaking. If she had known his name, anything about him, the search would have been difficult; with her complete ignorance it was an impossible one. She flung aside her outdoor things with a gesture of despair.

CHAPTER IV

The young man whose life Celia had saved crossed the courtyard of the building, and walked quickly into Victoria Street. Though he was a fugitive, there was nothing furtive in his gait, and he looked straight before him with a preoccupied air. As a matter of fact, he was not thinking at that moment of his own escape, but of the face which had looked down on him over the rail of the corridor. If Celia had been moved by the expression in his eyes, as he looked up at her, he was still more impressed by the tender, womanly pity in hers; and he was so lost in the thought of all that she had done for him, of her courage and compassion, that there was no room in his mind for any anxiety on his own account.

But presently the sight of a policeman recalled Derrick Dene to the peril of the situation. He fingered the five-pound note in his pocket and stood at the corner of a street hesitating; then, with a little gesture of determination, he walked on again quickly in the direction of Sloane Square, reached it, and turning into one of the streets leading from it he entered one of the tall buildings of expensive flats. Declining the porter's offer of the lift, he went quickly up the stairs, which, unlike those of Brown's Buildings, were carpeted and well-lit, and rang the bell of a flat on the second floor.

"Lord Heyton in?" he inquired of the servant. "Yes, I know he is," he added quickly, as he caught the scent of a cigarette. "Is he alone? All right, don't trouble to announce me." He walked quickly across the passage, entered a room and, closing the door behind him, turned the key in the lock.

A young man was sprawling in a low chair before the fire. He was a good-looking young man, very fair, with rather thin hair, parted in the middle; his eyes were blue and somewhat prominent, his mouth weak and sensual; he was in evening-dress, and presented a definite type of the young man about town.

As he turned his head at the click of the lock and saw his visitor, his face flushed hotly, his under-lip drooped, his eyes opened widely, and he clutched at the arms of the chair. Fear was written all over him in large letters. There was silence for a moment or two; then, with a catch of his breath, he rose and involuntarily muttered the other man's name. He also held out his hand; but Dene, ignoring it, seated himself on the table and, pointing to the chair, said, curtly, but without anger:

"Sit down, Heyton. Sit down. Yes; I've come. You didn't expect to see me. You thought you had got rid of me? Well, I'm going right enough; but I wanted a word or two with you first."

Lord Heyton dropped back into the chair and, covertly wiping the sweat from his face, which was white now, glanced from Dene to the fire, then back again; but his eyes could get no higher than Dene's waistcoat.

"I—I suppose you've come to kick up a row, to bully me?" he said, sullenly.

"Not at all," retorted Dene, coolly. "If I had wanted to kick up a row, to bully you—in other words, to round on you and show you up, I should have come before, the moment I knew how you had—sold me. Yes, that's the word; sold me."

"I—I was hard driven," said Heyton, almost inaudibly. "I tell you that, if I hadn't been able to put my hand on the money, I should have been ruined. A man in my position can't stand being declared a defaulter. I—I thought it would be all right; that my father would have stumped up; but he left England for some beastly place abroad; where, I don't know even know, and there was no getting at him. And there wasn't a penny to be got out of those cursed lawyers——"

"Oh, you needn't trouble to explain," said Dene, grimly. "I understand it all—Miriam has been to see me."

The young man in the chair started, his face flushed, and he looked savagely, yet fearfully, at Dene.

"Miriam been to see you!" he repeated, huskily. "Why—what——!"

"When you told her that I was a forger, that I'd passed a false cheque, you didn't think that she would go to me. You thought she would accept your statement, as she has accepted your other lies about me, and just drop me. Oh, yes; I know how you managed to get her away from me. Poor girl! Unawares she let out a great deal in the few minutes she was with me to-day. You blackened my character pretty considerably; and, by George! you must have done it very well, or you would not have got her to believe you. I've met some bad 'uns in my time, Heyton; but, upon my word, I think you're the very worst of the lot. You're black rotten, through and through. And yet you've got a decent girl not only to believe in you, but to marry you—a liar, a coward, and a scoundrel."

The other man rose, his hands clenched. Dene jerked his head towards the chair.

"Sit down," he said, as he sought in his pockets for a cigarette, found it, and began to smoke. "I'm glad to see that I've touched you on the raw. I didn't think there was a tender spot on you. Oh, sit down, man, and put your fists in your pockets; you haven't the pluck to strike me. I wish you had"—his eyes flashed ominously—"for I might be tempted to give you the thrashing you deserve and I'm longing to give you. And yet—no, I shouldn't; for I wouldn't defile my hands by touching you."

There was a pause, then, with a gesture, as if he had mastered himself,

Dene went on:

"Well, I have bullied you, after all, haven't I? And, upon my soul, I didn't mean to; for I knew it would be only waste of breath. Nothing can really touch you; and you'll forget every nasty thing I've said as soon as you've got rid of me safely. No; what I came to say was this: I'm not going to show you up. I'm going to take this thing upon me; you know why well enough."

Heyton shot a glance at him, a glance full of hate and jealousy.

"Yes, it's for Miriam's sake," said Dene, quietly, without any sign of emotion. "She and I were pals; nothing had ever come between us until you turned up. She would have married me but for you. Oh, I'm not blaming her; poor girl, there's a weak streak in her; she comes of a bad lot. Of course, the Earl of Heyton, the son of a marquess, was a better match than Derrick Dene, a nobody, with his fortune to make, his bare living to get; but, on my soul, I think she would have stood by me, and would have resisted the temptation, if you had not told lies about me and persuaded her that I was an utter blackguard. And, by the way, you did it rather well. I was quite astonished how she let things out just now when she came to me. You did it very well. And I thought you were an utter fool!"

The other man glanced wickedly under his brows and set his teeth, but he said nothing; he was afraid to utter a word lest he should rouse his victim from his state of calm and quiet.

"It was clever of you to saddle poor little Susie Morton's trouble on me, while you were really the man—the scoundrel, I should say; it was clever of you to rake up all my little sky-larkings and turn them into something worse. Well, they say that 'all is fair in love and war.' You won, you took her away from me—and it's about Miriam that I've come to talk to you."

Heyton moistened his lips and, with his eyes fixed on his patent leather boots, he said, thickly:

"Did you tell her that—the truth?"

Dene laughed shortly. "No; I didn't. Nine men out of ten would think I was

a fool for not doing so; certainly you would. But most men wouldn't understand, and most assuredly you wouldn't, why I didn't. No; I didn't tell her that I was innocent and that you were guilty; that you had forged a cheque and got me, like a fool, to present it. I didn't even tell her that it was you, you blackguard, who had ruined poor little Susie. You look surprised."

Heyton swiftly withdrew his eyes, in which astonishment, amazement, and something nearly approaching contempt, had shown, and Dene laughed with bitter scorn.

"You can't understand that a man who has once loved a woman loves her for always——"

He paused; for, at that moment, it was not the face of his old love, the woman who had jilted him for a better match, that rose before him, but that of the girl at Brown's Buildings who had stepped in between him and death, talked him back to reason, given him her last five-pound note.

"—And that even if he has ceased to love her, he'll stand a lot to save her from trouble; that he'll make any kind of sacrifice to keep disgrace and shame from her. That's how I feel towards Miriam. I thought of you being dragged off by a couple of bobbies to quod, and of how she would suffer; and I remembered—which was a precious lucky thing for you—that there was no one to suffer on my account. I thanked God—for the first time—I'd no one belonging to me. That thought made it easier for me to do what I am doing."

He tossed the end of the cigarette into the fire.

"I am going to make a bolt for it; and I looked in just to say a few words to you, Heyton. I'm standing between you and a complete bust-up. I'm doing it for Miriam's sake, not yours; and I want you to bear this in mind: that if ever I hear of your treating her badly—oh, you needn't look so virtuously indignant; I know your sort; you'd treat her badly enough presently, if you hadn't a check on you. And I'm going to be that check. Let me hear even a whisper of your acting on the cross with her, and

I'll come back, if it's from the other end of the world, to denounce you. I've proofs enough. Oh, I'm not such a fool as you think; and, if you don't treat Miriam fairly, I'll show you up, and probably give you, into the bargain, the thrashing that's owing to you."

"You needn't talk about Miriam like that," said her husband, sullenly, and with an affectation of righteous resentment. "I'm fond of her; I shouldn't have done—well, what I have done, if I hadn't been. You needn't insult me."

"My good man, I couldn't," said Dene. "One word more and, you'll be relieved to hear, I'm off. For some reason or other the police, the detectives, have been slow, or have failed to track me."

As he spoke, Heyton turned his head and looked at him curiously, with a furtive, cunning expression; but he said nothing; indeed, his lips closed tightly, as if in repression of speech.

"I shall leave England to-night," continued Dene; "and I may succeed in giving them the slip. I know one or two out-of-the-way places—but I needn't trouble you with my plans. All I want to say is that if I'm caught I shall continue to hold my tongue. And you hold yours, as much as you can; for, though you think you're pretty clever, you'd make a silly kind of ass in a witness-box."

He got off the table, buttoned his coat, and took up his cap. The other man rose and stood, fidgeting with a silver cigarette-box on the table and looking from Dene's pale, haggard face to the floor.

"You're—you're behaving like a brick—you're doing me a good turn, Dene——" he muttered, hoarsely.

"Oh, for God's sake, don't do that!" broke in Dene, with contemptuous impatience. "Clear your mind of that idea. I'm playing the giddy-goat not for your sake, my man; but—but for your wife's, for Miriam's."

"You're crossing to-night?" asked Heyton, hesitatingly, fearfully. "If there's anything I can do to—to prove my gratitude——"

"You couldn't prove what doesn't exist," said Dene, with a laugh. "You're incapable of gratitude. You hate me like poison, and, if it wasn't for the risk to yourself, you'd like to throw up that window, call for the police, and give me away." He paused a moment, and looked the bent, cowardly figure up and down, from toe to crown. "You don't mean to say that you were going to offer me money? Not really?" He laughed, and at the laugh Heyton's face crimsoned with shame and rage. "That would be too funny. I'm off. Remember what I've said. Treat Miriam well, and you've seen and heard the last of me; let me hear a word—But I've told you that already; and you're not likely to forget it. A coward like you will think of his skin before anything else."

Heyton's teeth closed on his underlip and he glanced at the window; Dene saw the glance and understood it; with a gesture of infinite scorn he sauntered slowly to the door, Heyton following him with clenched hands, the veins swelling in his forehead, his face livid.

As the door closed behind Dene, Heyton sprang towards the bell; his finger touched it, but he did not press it, and, with an oath, he sank into his chair and mopped his face.

Five minutes later, the woman whom Celia had seen in the corridor entered the room. She was a pretty, graceful woman, little more than a girl; but the beauty of the face was marred by a weak mouth and chin. She was exquisitely dressed, her fingers were covered with rings, and diamonds glittered on her snowy neck. Her face was pale, and her eyes were swollen with weeping; and it was with something like a sob that she said, as she stood at the table and looked down at the sullen, ghastly face of her husband:—

"Someone has been here—just gone; I heard a footstep; I know it. Derrick has been here."

He would have lied to her if he had thought she would have believed the lie.

"Yes," he said. "He has just gone. He—he came to say good-bye."

"Good-bye!" she repeated, her brows knitting with perplexity and trouble. "Is he going? Where? Why? Didn't you tell him that Mr. Brand, the lawyer, had—had paid the money and settled everything? Oh, if I had only known it when I went to Derrick; if the letter had only come before, so that I could have told him there was no need for him to fear any—any trouble! But you told him, Percy?"

"Yes, of course I told him," he said, staring at his boots; "but he had made up his mind to go abroad; and—and, 'pon my soul, I think it's the best thing he could do."

She looked down on him with a face still showing trouble and doubt.

"But—but, Percy, he hadn't any money; he admitted as much to me. And I couldn't give him any."

"That's all right," he said, clearing his throat. "I—I saw to that. I couldn't give him much, unfortunately; but I scraped together all I'd got. It will leave us pretty short of coin for a bit, Miriam."

She went to him quickly, put her arm round his shoulder, and, bending, kissed him. "You did! That was good of you; it was like you, Percy—after all that he has done, and the trouble he might have got you into. I'm glad you gave him all you'd got; and I don't mind running short."

Her cheeks were wet and wetted his; he drew his hand across his face with barely-concealed impatience and annoyance.

"That's all right," he said. "Of course, I had to do the best I could for him, poor devil! for the sake of—of old times. I didn't forget that you were once fond of him—well, rather taken with him; that you were old friends. Look here, Miriam, we don't want to harp upon this affair; it's a beastly bad business, and the sooner we forget it the better. For Heaven's sake, let's drop it here and now. I shan't refer to it, shan't mention Derrick Dene's name again; and don't you. Just push that tray over, will you? I've had a deuced unpleasant scene with him, I can tell you; and it's upset me deucedly. But there!" he added, with a jerk of the head, as he mixed a stiff soda and whisky, "there's an end of him, so far as we're concerned. What?"

CHAPTER V

Celia lay awake half the night, and was up and dressed early in the morning, waiting for the cry of "Pipers! Daily Pipers!" and when the newsboy came bounding up the steps she almost sprang out on him in her eagerness and anxiety.

"Give me—which of the papers has the best police news?" she asked, trying to speak casually.

"Oh, the *Wire*, o' course," replied the boy, promptly; "they don't let nothing escape them, you bet, miss!"

She bought the halfpenny paper and eagerly scanned its columns, forgetting that there could be no report of the case until the appearance before the magistrate; but the absence of any mention of an arrest, following the message which the old gentleman had given her, confirmed her relief and encouraged her. Notwithstanding, she found it almost impossible to eat; but she drank a cup of tea, gathered her papers together, and went down to the Museum. For the first time she found her work difficult; for she could not dismiss the young man and his tragic fate from her mind. Staring at the blank paper, she went over all the details of the strange scene, and, standing out from them all, was the expression in his face, in his eyes, as he had paused at the bend of the stairs and looked at her.

Something in that expression haunted her as she had never been haunted by anything in her life before, and she was weighed down by the sense of a burden, the burden of a man's life, destiny; she could not forget that she had sent him away, that if she had waited and he had remained, he would have learned that he had no longer reason to fear, that "it was all right."

She was disturbed in her reverie by the arrival of a young man, who seated himself in the next chair at her desk; she turned to her book and papers and began to work; but now a fresh difficulty arose in the conduct of the young man beside her; the attendant had brought him a pile of books, and the young fellow was turning them over, in a restless way, thrusting his hands through his hair, fidgeting with his feet and muttering impatiently and despairingly.

Celia glanced at him involuntarily. She saw that he was young and boyish-looking; there was a look of perplexity and worry in his blue eyes, and muttering a word of apology he rose and went quickly to the inner circle, the rotunda, where the patient and long-suffering superintendent stands to be badgered by questions from the readers needing the assistance of his wonderfully-stored brain. In a minute or two the young man came back, accompanied by an attendant bearing another pile of books.

"I don't know whether you'll find what you want," he said; "but it's all I know of it." He looked at Celia as he spoke, and added, "Oh, perhaps this young lady can help you; she does antiquarian work."

The young man coloured and raised his eyes appealingly to Celia.

"Oh, I couldn't trouble you," he said, humbly.

"What is it?" she asked. "I shall be glad to help you, if I can."

He took up some slips of paper on which were "pulled" impressions of blocks, and Celia saw that they were pictures of ruined castles, abbeys, and similar buildings.

"This is the trouble," said the young man. "The man I work for—he's the proprietor of the *Youth's Only Companion*—is a rum sort of chap, and fancies he has ideas. One of them was to buy up a lot of old blocks in Germany; these are they, and he's given me the job of writing them up, fitting them with descriptive letterpress—history, anecdote, that kind of thing, you know."

"That should not be very difficult," Celia remarked.

"Oh, no!" he assented; "but"—he grinned, and his whole face lit up with boyish humour—"the beastly things have no names to them! See? I've tried to hunt them up in all the old county histories, and books of that kind; but I've succeeded in getting only two or three, and there's a couple of dozen of the wretched things. I've driven the superintendent pretty nearly mad, and— But look here, I don't want to drive you mad, too. You mustn't let me bother you about it; you've got your own work to do."

"That's all right," said Celia, bending over the slips with the literary frown on her young face. "Oh, I can recognize some of them; that's Pevensey Castle; and that's Knowle House, before it was rebuilt; and, surely, this one is meant for Battle Abbey."

"I say, how clever you are!" he exclaimed, gazing at her with admiration.

"Oh, no, I'm not," said Celia, with a smile; "I just happen to remember them because I've come across them in the course of my own work. Let us go over the others."

She turned to his pile of books and, still with knit brows, tried to find the counterpart of the other pulls; and the young fellow watched her, his eyes growing thoughtful and something more, as they dwelt upon her face.

"You mustn't worry any more," he begged her, presently. "You're losing all your own time; I feel ashamed; I'm most awfully grateful to you."

"Not at all," said Celia. "I'm afraid I've been of very little help to you; and I don't see that I can do any more——"

"No, no," he said, quickly; "don't take any more trouble. It wouldn't matter so much if I had plenty of time; but I haven't. You see"—he coloured—"one doesn't get too well paid for this kind of work, and can't afford——"

He coloured still more deeply, and his voice dropped below the regulation whisper in which one is permitted to speak in the Reading Room. Celia glanced at him, and saw that he was poorly dressed, that his shirt-cuffs were frayed, and that he had the peculiar look which is stamped on the countenances of so many of the frequenters of the Reading Room.

"Just tell me what you would do if you were in my fix," he said.

Celia hesitated for a moment, then a smile broke over her face which transfigured it and made it seem to the young fellow absolutely lovely.

"I should invent histories for them," she said. "It would be so much easier—and, perhaps, ever so much more interesting."

"Oh, that's stunning!" he exclaimed, in a whisper. "Of course, that's the way. I say, what a brick you are! Would you mind telling me your name?"

"Grant—Celia Grant," she told him, without hesitation.

"Mine's Rex—Reggie Rex," he said. "I've often noticed you and wondered what kind of work you did—But I beg your pardon; I mustn't disturb you any longer."

They both fell to work, and Celia heard his fountain-pen racing over the paper; once or twice he chuckled, as if he were enjoying a joke; but very soon Celia forgot him; and when, at last, she looked up from her work, she found his place empty; but on going out for her lunch she saw him standing by one of the pillars of the portico. He blushed at sight of her, moved forward, hesitated, then approached her.

"You're going to an A.B.C. for your lunch?" he said, with a mixture of a man's timidity and a boy's audacity. "May I—will you let me come with you? I feel as if I hadn't thanked you enough; I couldn't do it in that stuffy old hole, where you can't speak above your breath."

He took Celia's silence for consent, and they went together to the big shop in Oxford Street, and seated themselves at a table. They both ordered a cup of tea and a roll and butter; Celia would have liked to have added the omnipotent bun, but refrained; for, somehow, she knew that he could not afford one.

"Do you like the life, in there?" he asked, jerking his head in the direction of the Museum. "Dreadful grind, isn't it? But, somehow, it gets hold of you; there's a kind of fascination in literature." He spoke the magic word with the air of quite an old, old man of letters. "I ought to have been a grocer. My father's got a shop in Middleswick; he calls it The Emporium. I think that's why I couldn't stick it. Pity, isn't it? for it's a rattling good business. Another thing; I couldn't stand the apron. Guv'nor insisted on the apron; 'begin from the beginning' sort of thing, you know. And then I felt the call of literature. Fond of reading, and all that. You

know?"

Celia nodded. That tender heart of hers was quite ready with its comprehension and sympathy.

"I hope you will succeed; but if you don't—Ah, well; you can go back," she said, half-enviously.

"No; one doesn't go back," he said, with a gravity that sat curiously on his boyish face. "Once you've got the fever, you've got it for life. Tiger tasting blood, you know. I'd rather be a literary man than—than the German Emperor. Of course, I'm hoping to do better things; but even the stuff I do makes me—oh, well, kind of happy. Every time I get a proof something runs through me, something grateful and comforting—like the cocoa. I mean to get on to fiction presently." He blushed like a girl, and looked at her timidly, with the appealing look of a dog in his eyes. "I've tried my hand already at a short story or two." He paused. "I say"—hesitatingly, his eyes still more dog-like—"you are so awfully kind, I wonder whether you'd mind looking at one of my things. Oh, of course, it's too much to ask! You're busy—you work hard, I know; I've watched you."

"Why, I shall be very pleased to read something you have written," said Celia, smiling encouragement.

"You will! Oh, that's stunning of you! I'll send you a short story to-night, if you'll give me your address. But perhaps you'd rather not," he added, quickly.

"Why not?" said Celia. She gave it to him.

"I'll send it," he whispered; but as he spoke, his hand went towards his breast-pocket.

Celia tried not to smile; for she saw what was coming.

"To tell you the truth," he said, with a burst of candour, "I've got one with me. I'll give it to you now. But for Heaven's sake don't look at it here! I should see by your face what you thought of it, and you're likely to think precious little of it; you'll think it tommy-rot; though, of course, you won't say so. Look here!" he went on, as he drew out the precious manuscript slowly, "don't

tell me that it 'shows promise'; I can bear anything but that. That's fatal; it's what all the beastly editors say when they don't mean to have anything to do with you."

"Very well," said Celia. "I will tell you exactly what I think of it."

"Honest Injun?" he queried, his blue eyes twinkling.

"Honest Injun," repeated Celia. "And I think I shall be able to say something very nice; for I am sure you are clever."

He blushed, and his eyes danced.

"You've said something very nice already," he said, gratefully; "and when you say it like that—well, upon my word, it makes me feel that I am clever. And that's half the battle, Miss Grant. A man is just what he feels himself to be; that's why nothing succeeds like success; to feel that other people know you can do your job. Oh, well!"

Celia nodded. "I must go back," she said. "I was not able to begin my work so early as usual this morning."

"Not feeling well?" he said, anxiously, and with a glance at her face which, he had noticed, was paler than usual. "I suppose you've got the Reading-Room headache. Everybody gets it; it's the general stuffiness of the place. They can't help it—the officials, I mean; they've tried all sorts of dodges for ventilation; it's better than it used to be; but it's still crammed full of headache."

"No; I've been worried this morning," said Celia, more to herself than to him.

"Oh, I'm sorry!" he said, in a voice full of a boy's ready sympathy. "Look here! Is it anything I can help you with? I mean——" He grew red, and stammered. "Oh, of course, you'll laugh; and it's like my cheek, but—you helped me, you know—and we're brothers and sisters in misfortune, working on the same treadmill—I'd do anything for you—it would be a pleasure——"

Celia sighed as she smiled, and wondered idly how he would respond if she said, "Well, find a man for me, a man whose name I don't know, to whose whereabouts I have not the slightest clue." She shook her head.

"It is very good of you," she said;

"but you could not help me; no one could."

"I am sorry," he murmured. "I should have loved to have done something for you; perhaps I may some day—lion and the mouse, you know. It's a rum world. You'll find my address on the manuscript," he added, shyly, as she rose.

He did not follow her; but later in the afternoon Celia caught sight of him seated at the farther end of the Reading Room. He was looking in her direction, but, as his eyes met hers, he dropped them and bent over his work. It was evident that he had changed his place lest she should think he was intruding on her.

As she entered the courtyard of Brown's Buildings, Celia bought an evening paper. If she had mistaken the significance of the old gentleman's message and the man who haunted her thoughts had been arrested, the case might be reported. She scanned the police news anxiously; but there was no report, and she was laying the paper down when her eye caught a familiar name in a paragraph. She read the few lines in a kind of stupor, with a sense of unreality; and when she had finished reading she stood with the paper gripped in her hand, and staring stupidly before her.

The paragraph ran thus:—

"We regret to announce the death of Mr. William Bishop, the well-known antiquarian, which occurred suddenly at his country residence early this morning." Slowly through her stupor broke the realization that she had been thrust back into the ranks of the unemployed, that only a few shillings stood between her and utter destitution.

CHAPTER VI

Strangely enough, Dene's spirits seemed lightened by the scene with Heyton; perhaps he had found that peculiar satisfaction which comes to all of us when we have relieved our minds by telling a man who has behaved badly and injured us what we think of him. But this hypothesis does not altogether account for the uplifting of Dene's mind. He had been going to commit suicide, because he was assured that everybody would regard him as one of the meanest of creatures, a forger and passer of a "stumer" cheque; but suddenly, at the tragical moment, an angel, in the guise of a young girl, had appeared, snatched the revolver from his hand, and saved him by just telling him that she believed him innocent.

It seemed to him that this guardian angel of his was hovering about him still; that it was incumbent upon him to carry out his pact with her, and to escape the fate that had threatened him, and, indeed, threatened him still. So centred were his thoughts on this girl, whose very name he did not know, so buoyed up was he by her wonderful goodness to him, that he had to remind himself he was still in danger. Perhaps, after all, that fact was not without its compensations; for Youth, when it goes with strength, and a clear brain, loves adventure, and enjoys pitting itself against any kind of foe. Here was he, an innocent man, flying from Injustice; he was to find out, perhaps for the first time in his life, what his wits were worth.

As he walked quickly, but not too hurriedly, through the shady streets towards the river, he considered the situation. If they were keen on the pursuit, the police would no doubt already have set a watch at the various ports; and it would be useless for him to attempt to reach the Continent; besides, he had not sufficient money to carry him far enough from England; for, in addition to the five-pound note, which had assumed already the character of a talisman, there were only a few shillings in his pocket.

It occurred to him that he would go down to the docks and see if he could obtain a berth on one of the small trading vessels; he had the quickness of hand and foot which comes of football and cricket, and he had done some sailing in a friend's yacht; enough, at any rate, to make him useful on board a ship. He took the train to Mark Lane Station, and suddenly reminded by the inward monitor that he had eaten nothing for some hours, turned into one of the numerous old-fashioned coffee-shops near the quay.

The place was crowded with ship hands and dock labourers, and reeked with that indescribable odour which is peculiar to the locality. Without receiving an order, a one-eyed waiter slammed a cup of thick coffee and two hunks of bread and butter before Dene; and Dene, eating and drinking the rough fare with an enjoyment which amused him, looked round him with the keenness of a man who is watching for an opportunity to seize upon the extended hand of Chance.

At the same table were seated two men whom he found it rather difficult to place; they did not look like dock labourers or sailors; and there was a mixture of the artist, the actor, the cheap-jack about them which stirred his curiosity; he found himself listening to them involuntarily.

"About time we were moving, isn't it?" said one. "The whole caboose will be down there by now; and it will be a devil of a job getting it on board in the dark. Why the old man didn't go by the regular line I can't think."

"'Thrift, Horatio, thrift,'" responded his companion; "he'll save a lot of money by hiring this old tramp; and he won't care how we have to pig it, so long as the blessed animals are all right. I had a look at her just now, and if ever there was a jumping, rolling, sea-sick old tub, she's one."

"A nice prospect," grunted the first man; "and we're short-handed, too; catch the old man taking a single man more than he wants."

Dene pricked up his ears. Was the hand of Chance being extended already? He waited for more, but the men ceased talking, and presently rose and walked out, with a gait which was as curious as everything else about them. Obeying an impulse, Dene rose and followed them. They joined the crowd going down towards the docks, and, keeping them in sight, he merged into a group of excited persons who were moving about in a scene which struck Dene with amazement.

On the quay, beside which a steamer

was moored, towered a couple of huge elephants, surrounded by camels, horses, and mules, while on trollies stood cages of wild beasts, lions, tigers, jackals; one of the elephants was trumpeting, the camels were groaning, the carnivora roaring; mixed with their din were the voices of a motley crew, men and women, having the same appearance in dress and manner as that of the two men he had followed. Dene saw that it was a travelling menagerie and circus, and he looked on it with an amusement which predominated over his self-interest. Presently there darted into the conglomerate mass an extraordinary object—it might have been one of the monkeys escaped from its cage and miraculously raised into imitation of a man's stature. The diminutive figure was enveloped in a fur coat, much too large for it, and crowned by a ridiculous sombrero hat. An extinct cigar was held in the clenched teeth, and as the thing waved its hand Dene caught the glitter of innumerable rings.

At the appearance of this strange creature a momentary silence fell on the crowd. Without a word, he darted to and fro, always waving the beringed hand and biting harder on his cigar. But though he did not speak, and there seemed to be no meaning in the waving of his hands, the movements of the crowd began to take to themselves something of purpose and order, and the animals fell into line and began to pass along the broad gangway as if they were under the command of Noah and going into the Ark. The little man in the fur coat was evidently the controlling spirit; he seemed to be everywhere at once, and the gesticulating paws were like those of a conductor conducting a band; wherever a difficulty cropped up, the fur coat and the sombrero hat were beside it, and the glittering paws smoothing it away.

The more docile of the beasts were on board. The cages had been hoisted by the crane, and the horses were following; one of them grew restive, and slipped from the grasp of the man in charge of it. It would have made a bolt for it, but Dene, who happened to be standing quite close, caught hold of the bridle. As he did so, the hands waved before his face; somehow or other, Dene understood that the gesture meant "Go on!" and he led the horse over the gangway on to the ship.

The grotesque figure had followed him, and, with another gesture, ordered Dene to lead the horse to the rough stables which had been set up on deck. He did so, and was at once seized upon by one of the men, who badly needed assistance; and for half an hour Dene was kept hard at work. There was a fearful din; but presently he heard the warning whistle, and was making his way for the gangway when he was stopped by the fur coat and waved back again.

"No time to go ashore, my man," said the dwarf, speaking for the first time in Dene's hearing.

Dene paused for just one moment, then, with a shrug of the shoulders, he turned and went back to the horses. He heard the snorting and panting of the tug, felt the vessel move, heard some cheers from the deck, and knew the tug was towing the vessel from the quay.

For the next hour Dene was convinced that he was the most-needed man on earth; for everybody wanted him. He helped to get the horses into their stables; he bore a hand in putting the cages into position; he carried hay to the elephants and shins of beef to the lions; and while he was doing these and innumerable other tasks, someone was perpetually shouting in his ear, "'Ere, matey, lend a hand, will you?" But at last the confusion simmered down, and, wiping his face, Dene went with the other men below, where a meal had been hastily prepared for them.

The insufficient light of a waving lamp fell upon a group of men and women he had seen on the quay. They were of the usual types which go to make up a circus company, and they all seemed merry and bright, and utterly indifferent to the noise and the discomfort. There were some nice-looking girls amongst them, and they were laughing and talking excitedly, their eyes flashing merrily as they crowded round the trestles which bore the steaming coffee, the chunks of bread, and the slabs of meat.

With a not-unnatural shyness, Dene stood aside for a moment or two; but feeling that, at any rate, he had earned his supper, he drew near the board. As he did so, one of the men he had seen in the coffee-house caught sight of him, scanned him curiously, and said:—

"New hand, eh? What's your line?"

This was a somewhat awkward question, and Dene temporized.

"Well, I don't quite know," he said. "I've been lending a hand generally."

The man looked at him with an increased interest, as if struck by the tone of Dene's voice.

"Oh!" he said, thoughtfully. "Engaged at the last moment? Well, you'd better go and see the guv'nor."

"Gentleman in the fur coat?" asked Dene.

"The same," said the man, with a grin. "You haven't met him yet? Engaged through an agent, I suppose? Well, you've got a novel experience awaiting you. Better look him up at once; he's in his cabin at the present moment."

"Thanks. I will," said Dene.

"My name's Sidcup," said the man, in a friendly way. "What's yours?"

This was another staggerer.

"Oh, mine's—Sydney Green," said Dene.

Mr. Sidcup smiled and winked. "Good name," he said. "Short; descriptive; good professional name."

Dene coloured, but passed off his embarrassment with a laugh.

"You'll find you've not joined a bad lot, Mr. Green," said Sidcup, with a jerk of his head towards the collected company. "It's a good show, and some of us"—he passed his hand over his smooth chin, and pulled down his waistcoat complacently—"are not without talent."

"I'm sure of that," said Dene, with an air of conviction. "I'll go and see—what is the proprietor's name?"

"Bloxford. Bloxford's Mammoth Circus; the largest on Earth; see Press notices. But, of course, you know," replied Mr. Sidcup, with some surprise.

"The old man's all right, as you'll find. Curious customer; but knows his business. He's not much to look at; but he's a devil to work, and he's a born manager. What I mean is, that he sees what a man's worth, in the—er—twinkling of an eye. And here's a tip for you: never argue with him; don't contradict him; just let him have his say and keep your mouth shut. If he says the moon's made of green cheese—ask him for a biscuit to eat with it. I've been with him for five years, and I understand him."

"Thank you very much," said Dene. "I'll take your tip. I'm not fond of arguing myself."

When he had disposed of his supper, he made his way to Mr. Bloxford's cabin and knocked at the door. He was bidden to enter in a sharp, falsetto voice, like that of a phonograph when it is on the high note. The manager was still enveloped in his fur coat, but his hat had been thrown aside, revealing a head apparently completely hairless. A lighted cigar was now between his teeth, and a bottle of champagne stood on the table. Mr. Bloxford looked up from a paper that he was reading, and eyed Dene with that suppressed impatience which is peculiar to all managers of theatres and circuses.

"Well, what do you want?" he demanded. "Tub isn't sinking already, is she?"

"I've come to ask you to take me on, to let me join your company, Mr. Bloxford," said Dene, going straight to the point.

The manager stared at him. "Take you on! Why, aren't you one of the hands? Then what the blank are you doing here?"

"No, I'm not engaged at present," replied Dene; and he explained how he had been caught up in the turmoil and had remained on board. While he was speaking, Mr. Bloxford had been eyeing the tall, well-made figure, the pleasant, handsome face, and, being a man of the world—and a circus manager to boot—he had no difficulty in seeing that the young man, standing so modestly, and yet so easily, before him, was a gentleman.

"I suppose you know that you're a stowaway, that I could have you chucked overboard, or put into irons or something," he said, furiously, his eyes snapping.

Dene smiled merely.

"Well, now you're here, I'll have to take you on, I guess," said Mr. Bloxford. "You seem to be handy with horses."

"I'm fond of them," said Dene.

"That's all right," rejoined Mr. Bloxford. "I suppose there's nothing you can do in the professional way? You'd make a good acrobat, or—well, you'd shape into several things." He looked the figure up and down again, just as he would have examined an animal offered for his inspection. "But we'll see about that later on. Thirty bob a week. How will that suit you?"

"It will suit me very well; and I'll try to earn it," said Derrick.

Mr. Bloxford stared at him. "Here, don't startle me; I've got a weak heart," he observed, with a grin. "You say it as if you meant it. Here, what's your name?"

"Sydney Green," replied Dene, with a promptitude acquired by his recent experience.

"Right!" said the manager. "Have a drink?"

He poured out a liberal quantity of champagne for Dene, and, filling his own glass, raised it, eyeing Dene keenly over the edge of it.

"Here's to us! I rather like the look of you; but just listen to me, young fellow. I don't care who and what a man is when he joins my company, he's under my orders. See? And look here, I don't ask any questions; I take a man for what he says he is. You say your name's Green. *Dark* Green, I expect, eh? Well, it's no business of mine. You know where we're bound for, I suppose? Well, we're bound for South America. We're going to do it thoroughly; if ever we get there, which seems doubtful, for this infernal old tramp is more rotten than I thought. But she's cheap, anyhow; and economy is my motto. Thirty shillings a week." He wrote down Dene's new name and the

amount of his wages. Then, suddenly, his manner changed; with an impatient gesture he waved his beringed hand, and Dene felt himself swept outside.

He stood in the gangway and looked straight before him for a minute or two. His brain was whirling somewhat, but he realized that he had escaped. His hand went to his breast pocket, where reposed the five-pound note his guardian angel had given him. It was still intact. He felt that it was proving itself a talisman. God bless her!

CHAPTER VII

A week later Celia was crouching over her fireless grate. The Wolf was no longer outside the door, but beside her, his red eyes watching her balefully, his cruel teeth showing between his mowing jaws. The hunger, for which the overfed rich man longs in vain, was gnawing at her; she was penniless and well-nigh starving; no longer did she regard the little chorus girl in the floor below her with tender pity and sympathy, but with envy; she knew now how rich she had been with her pound a week.

For days she had tramped the streets, in the intervals of reading the advertisements in the free library, in search of some employment, any employment, which a woman could take up; and her last few pence had been spent in one of those advertisements which tell their own tale of despair. She was willing to do anything; she would have taken a situation as a housemaid; would have gone out charing; for life is precious to all of us, and scruples of refinement disappear when there is no bread in the cupboard. But her applications, for even the lowliest place, were turned down; she had no experience, no character; the persons she interviewed saw, at a glance, that she was a lady, and that was fatal: a lady willing to sink to the position of a housemaid—well, there is something suspicious in it.

As she sat, with her hands tightly clasped, the cold of the early, so-called, summer day chilling her to the marrow, she was cheerfully employed in picturing her death; the discovery of the body, the coroner's inquest, the leader which would be written in the *Wire*, the properly indignant, stereotyped leader, dwelling with righteous indignation on the "terrible poverty in our midst." She raised her head and looked round the room. No, there was nothing left to sell or pawn—for her dire necessity had driven her to the pawnshop, that last refuge of the destitute, that dire rubicon which, having passed it, a girl like Celia feels is the last barrier between her and self-respect.

A letter lay on the table; it was one from the Museum lad, Reggie Rex, thanking her, with all the fervency of youth, for the words she had written in praise of his story; the hope, the encouragement she had implanted in his breast. She envied him, as she envied everyone who had enough to purchase a loaf, a glass of milk. Then the incident in which he had figured passed from her mind. The strains of Mr. Clendon's violin stole up to her; but that brought no peace, no joy; to enjoy good music when one is starving is an impossibility; the sounds irritated her, and she was glad when they ceased.

Presently she heard the sound of footsteps on the stairs, and a knock came at her door. She rose, painfully, wearily, and moved with difficulty; for the floor seemed to rock under her, the room to swing round. It was Mr. Clendon.

"I'm sorry to trouble you——" he began; then he saw her face, and, closing the door behind him, took her hand in his. "You are ill," he said.

To attempt concealment she felt would be impossible; worse, ridiculous.

"Not ill; but very hungry," she said, forcing a smile.

He led her to the chair, and she sank into it, turning her face away from him. He glanced round the room quickly, took in its emptiness, the black, cheerless grate, her attitude of utter dejection; then, without a word, he went downstairs. To Celia, hours seemed to elapse after his departure, but it was only a few minutes before he came up again, with bread and other things; but it was the bread only that Celia saw. With all her might and main, she strove to eat slowly, indifferently, the food he pressed up-

on her; and as she ate, the tears of shame and of relief coursed down her wan cheeks. He had brought fuel also; and, while she was eating, he seemed to devote all his attention to the making of the fire; when it was burning brightly, and she was leaning back, with her hands covering her face, he said, gently, reproachfully:

"Why didn't you come to me—why didn't you tell me?"

"I was ashamed," she said. "I knew you, too, were poor." She tried to laugh, but the laugh was choked in her throat.

"Not too poor to help a friend," he said. "I think you have been very wicked." He tried to speak sternly; but the "My poor child!" that broke from him declared his sympathy. "You have lost your situation?"

"Yes; he died. And I can't find anything else," said Celia, trying to speak calmly. "I've tried—oh, everything. I've spent all my money advertising and answering advertisements. Look! That's my last." With a laugh, she pushed a paper towards him. He glanced at the advertisement and slipped the paper into his pocket. "It's modest, humble enough, isn't it?" she said. "You see, I'm ready to do anything, secretary, companion, housekeeper—oh, anything; even for no salary, just for bed and board."

"I know," he said, with a nod. "It's very rarely that such an advertisement is of any use. Everybody specializes nowadays."

Celia rose and went to the window, that he might not see her face.

"I am stony-broke," she said. "I haven't a penny; and I'm friendless—no, not friendless. How can I thank you, Mr. Clendon! The sight of you—to say nothing of the food—has—has put fresh life into me. Tell me, what do you think I had better do? I'm not proud—why, I'm willing to be a domestic servant, to go to one of the factories to fill match-boxes; but I've no experience. And there are thousands in my plight, thousands of girls who are worse off—well, no, I suppose they couldn't be worse off; and yet—I haven't paid this week's rent; and you know what that means."

"I know," he said, in a low voice.

He was sitting over the fire, looking into the burning coals, with a curious expression on his pallid, wrinkled face; an expression of hesitation, doubt, reluctance; for the moment it seemed as if he had forgotten her, as if he were communing with his own thoughts, working at a problem.

"I have a little money," he said. "I'll go down and pay the rent."

"No, no!" she protested; but he waved his hand, the thin, shapely hand of the man of good birth.

"You'll get something presently; it is always when things are at the worst that they turn. I blame you for not coming to me; it was unkind. But I understand. You are proud; charity comes hard to people like you and me——" He checked himself and rose, buttoning his coat as he did so with the air of a man who has come to a decision. "Yes; I'll pay the rent, and I'll send them up with some coals. Oh, don't be afraid; you shall pay me when things come right. Don't you see, my good girl, that I am glad to be able to help you—that it gratifies *my* pride? There, sit down and warm yourself, and try to eat some more food. I wish it were better worth eating: but we shall see."

He laid his hand on her shoulder as he passed her on his way to the door, and Celia, blinded by tears, took the hand and carried it to her lips.

Mr. Clendon went down to his own room, almost as barely furnished as Celia's had become; and he stood for a moment or two looking round it with a sigh; then he took up his worn hat and stick, and went out. With bent head, and eyes fixed on the pavement, he made his way to Grosvenor Square; and, mounting the steps of one of the largest of the houses, rang the bell. A dignified hall-porter opened the door leisurely, and eyed the thin, poorly-clad figure and pallid face with stern disfavour.

"Is Lord Sutcombe at home?" asked Mr. Clendon, quietly, and not without a certain dignity.

"His lordship the Marquess is within; suttenly; but——" The man hesitated, with unconcealed suspicion.

"Will you tell his lordship, please, that a gentleman wishes to see him?" said Mr. Clendon.

The porter looked beyond the bowed figure, as if he expected to see someone else, the "gentleman" referred to; then, as he failed to see anyone, he said, severely:

"'Ave you an appointment? 'Is lordship don't see promiskus visitors."

Mr. Clendon seemed to consider for a moment; as if he had expected this difficulty. He wrote the single letter "W" on a piece of paper he found in his pocket, and handed it to the man.

"Please give this to his lordship," he said, still with that quiet air of dignity and composure which had impressed the porter, against his will.

The man eyed the piece of paper doubtfully, and the applicant for admission still more so; then, signing to the bench in the hall, by way of permitting rather than inviting the old man to take a seat, he went slowly up the broad stairs, lined with pictures and statuary, and carpeted with thick Axminster. Mr. Clendon seated himself, leant both hands on his stick and looked around him, not curiously, but with a thoughtful, and yet impassive, expression. Presently the man came down, with evident surprise on his well-fed countenance.

"Please follow me," he said; and Mr. Clendon followed him up the stairs, and was ushered into a small room on the first floor. It was a library, handsomely furnished and luxuriously appointed; a huge fire was burning in the bronze grate, and, as its warmth went out to meet him, Mr. Clendon thought of the fireless grate over which the young girl had crouched. By the table, with one hand pressed hardly against it, stood a middle-aged man, with a pale, careworn face; his hair was flecked with grey; his thin lips drawn and drooping at the corners, as if their possessor was heavily burdened by the cares of the world. That he was agitated was obvious; for the lids flickered over his almost colourless eyes, and the hand he held against his side was clenched tightly.

At sight of the old man he uttered a cry, the kind of cry with which one might greet a ghost.

"Wilfred! You! You! Alive! I—we—thought you were dead."

"I am sorry," said Mr. Clendon. "Yes; I knew that you thought me dead. It was just as well; I wished you to do so. Don't be alarmed; there is nothing to be alarmed at. Permit me to sit down; I have walked some distance."

The Marquess of Sutcombe, with an air of desperation, motioned to a chair, and fell to pacing up and down the room. "I swear that I thought you were dead, Wilfred! When you disappeared, father—all of us—did our best to find you; we searched for you everywhere. We were in the greatest distress, perplexity; for we did not know why you had gone—I don't know even now—I can't, no, I can't believe that it is you! Why did you—disappear?"

"There is no need why I should tell you, Talbot," said Mr. Clendon, calmly. "It is my secret; it must remain so."

"But—but, consider my position!" exclaimed the Marquess, with agitation. "You *must* do so! Here am I, bearing the title and—and the rest of it, under the impression that my elder brother has died. Wilfred, you must explain. We all believed the report of your death——"

"I know," said Mr. Clendon, quietly, but not apologetically. "I took care that the evidence should satisfy you. Once more, there is no cause for alarm——"

"No cause for alarm! You talk—absurdly! You forget that the fact of your sitting there proves that I am a—a usurper; that I have no right to the title, the estate; that everything belongs to you. By Heaven, Wilfred, I can scarcely believe that you have done this thing, that you could have found it possible to do me—and Percy—such a wrong! Put yourself in my place. How would you like to discover that you were living under false pretences, that you had no right to—everything you hold. Yes; put yourself in my place!"

"That is exactly what I have refused, and still refuse, to do," said Mr. Clendon, quietly. "I see that you think I have come to disclose my identity, to displace you. You are mistaken. To do so

after I, of my own free will, have effaced myself all these years, and allowed you to step into my place, would be unjust, would be impossible for—well, one of us, Sutcombe."

"And—and there's Percy, my son," went on the Marquess, as if he ignored, or had not heard, the other man's assurance. "It's hard on me, but it's harder on him; for I—well, I am well-nigh weary of everything, of life itself. My wife died—you may have heard of it—there was nothing left but Percy, and—yes, perhaps you know it—he's a bad lot. He has given me a great deal of trouble, will give me more. He has married beneath him. I had hoped, much as I disapprove of the match, that it might steady him; but I fear——All the same, bad as he is, it's hard on him——"

The Marquess wiped the sweat from his brow and stifled a groan.

"You distress yourself without cause, Talbot. I am sorry to hear that you are not happy, that your son is not—satisfactory. I have not come to add to your unhappiness. Believe that."

"Then why *have* you disturbed me?" demanded the Marquess, desperately.

"I will tell you," said Mr. Clendon. "Will you not come and sit down? Be calm, and listen to me quietly. Accept my assurance that I have no intention whatever, and never shall have, of taking my proper place, of depriving you of all I resigned. If I ever had any desire to do so, that desire would have died since I entered this house. Are you any happier, Talbot, for the burden which I laid down, resigned to you? I am poor, as you see,"—he glanced at his old, worn clothes—"but——"

The Marquess broke in impatiently.

"Oh, I see that. You look—look as if you'd had bad times; you look old enough to be my father. You look—are dressed—in rags. Do you think that doesn't worry me, and add to my misery? Do you think that, ever since you entered and I recognized you, I haven't been saying to myself, 'This is my elder brother; this old, haggard-looking man, clad like a beggar, is the Marquess of Sutcombe and you are an impostor'?"

"Grant the case as you put it. I am

poor, but not unhappy. I will venture to say that I am far happier than you, Talbot," said Mr. Clendon, his dark eyes scanning the careworn face of the Marquess. "I have my niche in the world; I earn my living, such as it is; I am free from care; I have enough laid by to save me from a pauper's grave, while you——"

"Oh, I'm unhappy enough, I'll admit," said the Marquess, with a deep sigh. "I hold your place, and all that it means in the way of money and power; but I'm alone in the world, worse than alone; for Percy, my only son, I tell you—by Heaven, there is not a morning I wake that I do not dread to hear that he has done something to disgrace the name he bears. Wilfred, if you've a mind to take it all back——"

He stretched out his hands with a gesture of renunciation, almost an eager, anticipatory relief.

Mr. Clendon shook his head. "No," he said, resolutely, "you must continue to bear the burden I have imposed upon you, Talbot; and I beg you to believe me, fully and undoubtingly, that I shall never relieve you of your responsibilities, which you have borne so well. Oh, of course, I have watched. I know how admirably you have filled your place, and where I should have failed. Fate, Providence knew better than I what was best for me, for all of us, when it drove me out of the world."

"Tell me, why can't you tell me, why you disappeared?" demanded the Marquess. "Surely you owe it to me!"

"No, I have buried the past," said Mr. Clendon. "Let it lie. But I will tell you why I have forced myself to come to you—yes, forced myself, Talbot, for I knew that it was better that I should remain as one dead."

"Yes, tell me," said the Marquess, with feverish eagerness. "If there is anything I can do, if you have decided to stick to your resolution, if there is nothing I can say that will persuade you to come forward——"

"There is nothing," Mr. Clendon assured him calmly.

The Marquess sighed heavily. "Then you must let me—how shall I put it?—

provide for you, take care of your future. You must want money. Oh, it's absurd; it drives me mad! To think that nearly every penny I possess is yours. But tell me what I'm to do, Wilfred."

"Nothing for me—that is directly," said Mr. Clendon. "Don't say any more about myself. I am touched by your generosity—yes, generosity, Talbot; for I feel that you have every reason, every right, to turn upon me and upbraid me for presenting myself after all this time, for harrowing you with the knowledge of my existence. You can do nothing for me in the way of money. I have all I need. I have grown so used to the poverty of my surroundings that, if I were raised out of them I should feel like the prisoner released from the Bastille, and weep for my cell and the prison rations. But you can do something for someone in whom I am interested."

The Marquess looked up, with something like a gleam of apprehension.

"Someone belonging to you? Your son—daughter?"

Mr. Clendon was silent for a moment, then he said: "No, I have no son or daughter. I am childless. The person of whom I speak is a young girl, no relation of mine, scarcely a friend, save for the fact that I have been of service to her, and that she regards me as the only friend she has. We live in the same block of buildings—have met as ships pass in the night. She is a poor girl who has been working as a kind of secretary, but her employer has died suddenly, and she is now penniless and helpless."

The Marquess started to his feet and paced the room again.

"I feel as if I were in a dream, a nightmare," he said. "Here are you, suddenly springing to life, poor, almost destitute, and you come to me, not asking for all that is yours by right, not even for money for yourself, but for someone, for some girl who is not even of your kith and kin, has no claim on you. I always thought you mad, Wilfred, in the old days when we were boys together. I still think you're mad. How could I think otherwise?"

"We are all mad, more or less, Talbot," rejoined Mr. Clendon, with the

flicker of a grim smile on his thin lips. "But this young girl—I have taken her misery to heart. If you had seen her as I have seen her—but you haven't, and I have to try to impress her case on you, enlist your sympathies, as well as I can. She is a lady, not by birth, perhaps, but by instinct and training. She has been well educated. That's been against her, of course. It always is with persons in her position; anyway, it makes her lot a still harder one."

"Well, well!" broke in the Marquess. "You want me to give her money. Of course, you can have what you want, any sum; you have but to ask—*Ask!* it is all yours; you have but to *demand*!— No, no, I don't mean to be angry, brutal; but, surely, you can understand what I am feeling. How much do you want?"

"Nothing," said Mr. Clendon, with another flickering smile. "My dear Talbot, you don't understand. But I don't blame you; how should you? All the same, we poor people have our little pride; the girl of whom I speak—well, I found her starving in her miserable little room, because she was too proud to descend a flight of steps to mine, to ask for the bread for which she was dying."

The Marquess stared. "Is it possible that such cases can exist?"

"Oh, yes, my dear Talbot," responded Mr. Clendon, with grim irony. "There are more persons die of starvation in London every day than the Boards of Guardians wot of. The doctor calls them 'heart-failure' in his certificate; and he is quite accurate. But let me tell you what I want you to do. This girl has been a secretary; she has been advertising for some similar post; any post, indeed."

He took out the paper and pointed to the advertisement. The Marquess took the paper, passing his hand over his eyes, as if he were dazed, and read the few lines which had cost Celia her last penny.

"Got it?" asked Mr. Clendon. "Well, now, I want you to write an answer to it, Talbot, and offer her a situation."

Lord Sutcombe dropped into his chair, his head sunk in his hands.

"What kind of situation?" he asked,

looking up. "Of course, I'll do it—I feel, confused. Little wonder!—What kind of situation? I suppose you have planned it all? I am trying to follow you, to interest myself; but I can only think of *you*!"

"Yes; I have formed some kind of plan," said Mr. Clendon, in his low, vibrant voice. "There is the library at Thexford. It is a great library, a fine collection; it has been neglected for years; I suppose you have not looked after it?"

"No," said the Marquess, shaking his head. "I seldom go to Thexford. I have been in the Cabinet, as you may know; am still interested in politics—it has been something to do—and, in consequence, I have to live in London most of the time. I have not been to Thexford for two years; the house is kept up, of course; I have often intended going there; but there are the other places."

"Pity!" said Mr. Clendon, looking straight before him, as if he were calling up a memory. "It is a beautiful place; perhaps the most beautiful you've got——"

"*You've* got," muttered Lord Sutcombe, bitterly.

Mr. Clendon ignored the interruption.

"It is time the library was taken in hand, set to rights, and catalogued, and the rest of it. She will do it very well. Give her a good salary—but not too large a one, or she will suspect; and I do not wish her to know how she obtained the post. You need not see her; she can obtain testimonials from the executors of her late employer. She will give you no trouble; she will do her duty; for she is a lady, and a pure, high-minded girl. Will you do this for me, Talbot?"

"You know that you've no need to ask," said the Marquess. "Do you mean to tell me this is all I can do, that you will permit me to do?"

"That is all," said Mr. Clendon, quietly. "I am much obliged to you. Yes; I am sincerely, unaffectedly grateful. Do you think I don't realize how badly I've treated you, Talbot, not only in allowing you to believe I was dead, but in turning up again? Well, do this for me, help this young girl, and try to persuade yourself that we can cry quits."

"Quits! It is absurd! You are going?

By Heaven, I feel that I ought not to let you go. That, in justice to myself, my own sense of right and honour, I ought to detain you, proclaim that——"

"It would be of no use," said Mr. Clendon. "You could not detain me, the disclosure could not serve me. Remember that I am—that I have no child; and that it is only a question of time, a short time, before all you hold will be really, legally yours. Have patience. Let me go my way—it is the only one for me——"

"But you will tell me where you live, where I can find you?" interrupted Lord Sutcombe.

Mr. Clendon smiled, gravely. "I think not, Talbot. To tell you the truth, I am so enamoured of this life of mine, of its solitude and independence, that I cannot run the risk of having it broken in upon. Good-bye. Don't bear me ill-will. And don't be afraid. I am going back to the grave again."

The Marquess stretched out his hand, as if to detain him; but, with a gesture, full of dignity and command, as well as imploration, the bent figure passed out.

CHAPTER VIII

Four days after Mr. Clendon had rescued her from the Wolf, Celia, who had been listening daily for his footsteps, heard them on the stairs. She ran down, and caught the old man by the hand.

"Oh, come in!" she said, excitedly. "I have something to tell you."

He looked at her flushed face, her eyes all alight now; but without a smile, and with his usual impassiveness, he went to her room.

"The most wonderful thing has happened!" she exclaimed. "Oh, but first, let me try to thank you! The people who brought the things would not tell me who had sent them, but they insisted that everything was paid for, and, of course, I knew the milk and the bread, and the groceries and the rest of it, came from you."

"That is nothing," he said, with the simplicity of good breeding. "Tell me of this wonderful news."

"It's the most extraordinary, the most miraculous news," she said, with a long

breath. "You remember that advertisement I showed you? Well, there came an answer to it—an answer! Here it is. " She handed him one of several letters she had snatched up from the table. "It is from a very great man, you see; but, of course, it is one of his secretaries who writes. It is from a real live marquess!—Lord Sutcombe. Of course, you have heard of him?"

Mr. Clendon nodded affirmatively.

"He is well known."

"Though I had no hope of getting the situation, I sent some letters of poor Mr. Bishop's as testimonials, and this morning—oh, it is almost incredible—I received this letter, informing me that my testimonials were satisfactory, and that I had obtained the post. And what do you think it is? Oh, the most delightful of all work—the very thing I would have chosen! It is to arrange, and catalogue, and generally take care of a large library. And the salary—this is the most wonderful part of the whole fairy tale—is to be £150 a year. Think of it! One—hundred—and-fifty—pounds a year!"

"It is a very good salary," said Mr. Clendon. "I congratulate you."

She laid her hand on the wrinkled one which rested on his stick.

"But don't you think it is quite extraordinary? Surely one does not usually get such a post as this so easily as I have done! There is a kind of magic in it. You"—she looked at him keenly, searchingly—"Mr. Clendon, have you had any hand in this?"

He looked up at her and shrugged his shoulders.

"Do you think it is likely that I consort with marquesses or have any influence with them?" he asked, with a smile.

"Anyway, it is you who have brought me this great good luck," she said, as gratefully as if he had admitted the truth. "You have been my mascot. A very dear, generous mascot. But you will let me pay you back? But I am almost ashamed to speak of payment, when no money could repay."

"Certainly you shall pay me, my dear young lady," he said, quietly. "I am poor, and you are proud. But you will wait until you draw the first instalment of your salary."

"No need," she exclaimed, triumphantly. "See here!" She held up a cheque. "The Marquess—what a kind, good sort of man he must be!—has sent me a cheque to pay my fare and other expenses."

Mr. Clendon took the cheque.

"I see it is an open one. The bank will pay you when you present it," he remarked, in a matter-of-fact tone.

"Yes, I am going presently. In the last letter he says that I can go down to the place—Thexford Hall, it is called—as soon as I please; and, of course, I shall start to-morrow. It is in Devonshire, and all my life I've longed to see Devonshire. And now I'm to be *paid* for going there! Mr. Clendon, I have been living in a dream since this letter came. I've read it fifty—oh, a hundred times! Sometimes I've held it tightly in both hands, afraid that it should turn to a withered leaf, as the paper did in the fairy story, or that I should wake up from my dream and find my hands empty. Do you know Thexford Hall?"

"It is a large place, I believe—quite a famous one," he said. "I hope you will be happy there."

"I should be quite happy if it were not so far from Brown's Buildings, and—and one who has been so good to me," said Celia, her eyes suddenly moist. "But I may come up and see you some day, on my first holiday? Yes, and it's not only you, but—Well, strange as it may sound, I have grown fond of the Buildings. You see, it was my first home; I mean my own home. And I've got to like the people, though I know so little of them. Oh, Mr. Clendon——"

She paused a moment, and the colour stole to her face and she looked hard at the fire. She went on hesitatingly, almost shyly:

"You remember the young man who lived opposite? He has gone; but I think—I mean, it is just possible that he may come back."

She was silent for a moment or two, as she asked herself whether she should tell this good friend of hers all that had happened on that fateful night; but she felt that she could not do so. The secret did not belong to her.

"He may come back," she continued, in a low voice. "And if he should, and you see him, will you give him a message that was left with me for him. It is just, 'It is all right.'"

"Certainly," said Mr. Clendon, without the least sign of curiosity, though his piercing eyes had been watching her face. "Will you write to me, and tell me how you get on at—what is the name of the place?—ah, yes, Thexford?"

"Why, of course I will. I will write and tell you everything," said Celia, promptly, gratefully.

"And if it should not suit you, and you are not happy there, you will tell me frankly?"

"Oh, yes; for you will still be my mascot, will you not? But I am sure to be happy. I love books. I shall be in Devonshire, and I shall be earning all this money. Mr. Clendon, I am the very luckiest girl in the world."

"And the best, I am sure," he said, gently. "Now, I will go down to the bank with you, if you will let me, and see that you get this money all right."

This was the last straw. She could not keep back her tears. She hurried into her coat and hat, and they went out together. As they descended the stairs, they happened to pass the little chorus girl and the grim old lady, and Celia could not help nodding and smiling at them. The chorus girl smiled back, and even the grim old lady's frown relaxed as she bowed in stately fashion.

"I'm so happy, that I could shake hands with everybody," said Celia. "I feel as if I must make friends with everyone I meet."

Then suddenly the happiness fled from her face, her eyes grew dark and sad; for at that instant she thought of the young man, the fugitive flying from justice. Where was he? What was he doing? Oh, if he would only come back and get the message!

The polite and amiable cashier at the bank handed over ten bright sovereigns, and with these in the purse clasped in her hand Celia returned to the Buildings, to engage in a fight with Mr. Clendon over the sum which he declared was all that was due to him. But it was settled at last, though scarcely to Celia's satisfaction.

"I'd come to see you off to-morrow," he said, as he held her hand at parting, "but I have an early rehearsal. Goodbye, and God bless you," he added, in a very low voice.

When he had gone Celia mopped her eyes and finished her packing, and the next morning a taxi bore her from the Buildings. She looked out of the window as long as the huge and grimy place remained in sight, and she sighed when it had disappeared. In a sense she still belonged to The Jail; for there had been no time to dispose of her furniture, and she was so rich that she felt justified in keeping on the room for a while. The rent was only a few shillings a week, and she could well afford to pay it, at any rate until she had decided to sell the furniture. At the bottom of her heart was the desire to keep it, for the sake of its association: perhaps they would let her have it at Thexford Hall?

The journey, which no doubt most of the passengers considered a long one, was to Celia a delightful experience, for she had been immured in London long enough to enjoy the change. Her heart beat fast and her breath came quickly, with suppressed excitement and a touch of anxiety, as the train drew up to the small station of Thexford. On the platform stood a tall footman, and as she alighted he came up, touched his hat, and spoke her name. The station-master and the porter were in attendance also, and all three received her as if she were a person of consequence. The footman led the way to a landaulette car, touched his hat again as he closed the door on her, and the car glided off, carrying Celia still nearer to the unknown.

They ran through a beautiful, undulating country, dotted here and there with farms. Then the way grew wilder. They passed across a stretch of moorland, turned into an avenue guarded by huge iron gates, and, mounting quickly, stopped before an old red brick mansion, the size and grandeur of which filled Celia with awe. The great door opened, and a footman, behind him a middle-aged lady in a black silk dress, stood ready to receive Celia.

"I am the housekeeper—Mrs. Dexter," said the lady, pleasantly. "I am afraid you have had a wearisome journey, Miss Grant. Let me take you to your room at once."

They crossed a large hall, lit by the afternoon sun, which, streaming through a window of stained glass, poured flashes of vari-coloured light on the antique furniture, the men in armour, the trophies and pictures on the wall. Mrs. Dexter led the way up a broad flight of stairs to a room on the first floor, a room so large and beautiful that Celia had difficulty in repressing an exclamation.

"Is this for me?" she could not help asking.

"Yes," replied Mrs. Dexter, "unless you wish to change it. There are plenty of rooms vacant, unfortunately."

"Does no one live here?" asked Celia, with astonishment.

"Only myself and the other servants," replied Mrs. Dexter. "The Marquess is enormously rich, probably one of the richest noblemen in England. Of course, some of the rooms, the state-rooms, are kept shrouded; but they could be prepared almost at an hour's notice—though we might not get that," she added, with a smile. "I hope you will not feel dull and lonely. You have come from London, where everything is so bright and gay."

Celia thought of the Jail and smiled.

"We are rather isolated here," continued Mrs. Dexter. "There is the village, of course; but we have very few neighbours. The nearest house of any consequence, Lensmore Grange, is nearly two miles away. Didn't you know that you would be alone here? Oh, I hope you won't mind, for I had so looked forward to having someone in the house."

"No, no," said Celia, quickly, and she smiled again, reassuringly. "I think I rather like it; and if I didn't, I should remain, for I am quite poor, and this situation means so much to me."

This little speech completed Celia's conquest of the good-natured house-keeper.

"We must try to make it as cheerful as we can for you, my dear—I mean, Miss Grant," she corrected herself.

Celia shook her head.

"No, no," she said. "I think it is very kind of you to speak to me so nicely, to be so good to me, before you know I'm worth it. I am sure that we shall—like each other, and that I shall be very happy here."

"I hope so. I'll do all I can," said Mrs. Dexter, evidently moved by Celia's warm response. "Now I'll send you up some tea, and if you're not tired I will show you the house when you have rested."

In a very short time a maid, neatly dressed in black alpaca, with cap with white strings, brought up the tea. Celia noticed that the salver and the service were of silver. It was a very luxurious tea; the maid was respectful, but pleasantly sympathetic. Said she:

"Shall I put away your things after tea, miss, or now at once? I am to wait on you."

"Oh, that's very nice," said Celia. "You will not have much trouble, at any rate, with my things," she added, with a laugh. "For I have very few."

"Yes, miss," said the maid. "Fashions change so soon, don't they?"

It was beautifully done, and Celia laughed again, appreciatively. The place had seemed to her a kind of Paradise, and certainly it was inhabited, judging by the specimens she had seen, by persons of angelic amiability. She was so excited that she could scarcely drink her tea, and when Mrs. Dexter reappeared, she sprang up all eagerness. For half an an hour she went from room to room, almost speechless with admiration and a delighted awe. It was her first experience of a house of the size and grandeur of Thexford Hall, and almost at every step she took she was trying to realize that she was actually going to live there. And to be paid £150 per annum for doing so!

"Now I'll show you the library," said Mrs. Dexter. "Naturally, that will interest you more than anything else, though our state-rooms are considered to be very fine. Indeed, the drawing-room, with the Inigo chimneypieces, is said to be unique. This is the library."

She opened a thick mahogany door, and as Celia crossed the threshold an exclamation of ecstatic delight escaped her lips. And not without cause; for the Thexford library is a famous one. Celia was not unduly impressed by the number of the books, though the collection is by no means a small one, for she had spent weeks and months at the British Museum Reading Room; but the subdued splendour of the room, its vaulted roof, its ebony bookcases, enriched by Wedgwood plaques, the great fireplace, with its marble mantelpiece rising to the very ceiling, kept her for a minute or two dumb with amazement.

"No doubt you will spend a great deal of your time here," said Mrs. Dexter. "I have had the fire lit; we burn wood only in the larger rooms." She nodded towards the great logs glowing between the brazen dogs and giving the room not only warmth but an air of comfort and homeliness. "I hope you will find everything you want; but if not, you have only to ask for it. His lordship sent me special instructions that I was to provide you with everything you required."

"As if anyone could want anything more than there is here," said Celia, with a smile and upraised brows. "The Marquess must be a very kind man; he has been so good and thoughtful."

"He is," said Mrs. Dexter. "But people of his rank always are kind to those in their service. At least, that is my experience. You have not seen his lordship?"

"No," replied Celia. "I should like to do so. I should like to try to thank him for his kindness to me."

Mrs. Dexter smiled.

"I don't think he would like that, my dear. Great people don't like being thanked. At least, that's my experience," she repeated. "I will show you his lordship's portrait, if you like," she said, as they passed into the hall. "It is growing dark here; that painted window keeps out the light."

She switched on the electric light, and directed Celia's attention to the row of family portraits.

"I'll tell you who they all are some day," she said. "That is the present Marquess, at the end there."

Celia went to it and looked at it with interest.

"He has a nice face," she said.

"Yes, it is a good-looking family, as you see," said Mrs. Dexter, with a smile.

Celia's eyes wandered from the portrait of the Marquess to the one hanging next to it. It was the picture of a young man dressed in riding kit. He was a handsome lad, with a dare-devil look in his dark eyes, a hint of wildness, of recklessness and defiance, in the carriage of his head, the curve of his lips.

"That is a very beautiful picture," said Celia.

"Yes; it is one of the best in the gallery," said Mrs. Dexter. "It is the portrait of the Marquess's brother—his elder brother. He was very wild, and caused the family much trouble. He is dead, of course, or he would have been the marquess instead of his present lordship."

"He is very handsome," said Celia. "I suppose that is why one feels so sorry for him."

She moved away from the picture as she spoke; but presently, as if drawn by it, she returned to it.

"The picture interests you?" said Mrs. Dexter, with a smile. "That is always the way with us women, my dear. It is always the wild and wicked men who attract us."

"Oh, but that's a libel, surely," said Celia. "No; I think you are right. But how foolish of us, if it is true."

She turned away and went towards the great fireplace where the logs were now burning; but after a moment or two, as she stood with her foot on the fender, she looked again over her shoulder at the picture.

"It is very strange," she said, "but I have a curious feeling that I have seen someone very like—no, not very like, but bearing a faint likeness to that portrait."

"Yes, my dear? One often has that feeling when looking at a portrait. Can't you remember who it was?"

"No," said Celia, "I've been trying to think; but I can't remember ever meeting anyone resembling that face. I suppose it is only my fancy."

"I dare say," assented Mrs. Dexter. "You will dine at the usual hour, eight o'clock, I suppose? I am going to have your dinner served in the little room behind the library. You will not feel so lonely as you would in the big dining-room; but, of course, if you prefer——"

"What, sit there all by myself, in that great big room! I should die of fright. I should feel as if I had been wrecked on a desert island. Oh, the little room, please, by all means."

CHAPTER IX

Celia was awakened the next morning by the singing of the birds. For a few minutes she was confused by her strangely luxurious surroundings; but she soon realized her good fortune, and she leapt out of bed, ran to the window, and peeped out on the wonderful view. She might have stood openly at the window, for no building, no human being were in sight. It seemed to her that she was the only person in that vast solitude of umbrageous park and wide-stretching heath.

Immediately beneath her lay the velvet lawns of the splendid gardens; they were irresistible; she had her bath and dressed quickly, and, to the amazement of the housemaids who were at work in the hall, went out bare-headed. She felt as if every moment in which she was not enjoying this wonderful new experience of hers were a lost one; and she wandered about, stopping occasionally to examine the noble façade of the house, a quaint sundial, an antique fountain of bronze, some particularly tasteful arrangement of the flowers.

There was an Italian garden, with marble benches, fawns and dryads, which was exactly like those depicted in *Country Life*: and here it was, and she was free of it! Oh, marvellous! Presently a huge deerhound, graceful as the forest from which he sprang, came bounding to her; he stopped and eyed her critically for a moment, then he came forward in stately fashion and laid his beautiful head in the hands she outstretched to him. She went down on her knees and hugged him; and he submitted to the embrace, with his great, loving eyes fixed on hers approvingly. When the big bell in one of the towers rang for breakfast the dog followed her into the little room behind the library and flung himself down at her side, as if he belonged to her.

While she was eating her breakfast Mrs. Dexter looked in, inquired how Celia had slept, cast an examining eye over the bountifully furnished table, with its gleaming silver and dainty china, and asked if Celia had everything she needed.

"Oh, yes," said Celia, with a laugh. "I have never seen such a breakfast in my life; there are so many things that I don't know which to choose."

Mrs. Dexter smiled, with an air of satisfaction. "I see you have got Roddy," she said.

At the sound of his name the big dog rose and went to the housekeeper, then returned to Celia.

"Yes; isn't he a beautiful dog?" said Celia. "We made friends outside. I am flattering myself that he has taken a fancy to me; I hope he has."

"It certainly looks like it," assented Mrs. Dexter. "He will be company for you on your walks."

"Oh, may I have him?" cried Celia, delightedly. "I've fallen passionately in love with him."

Mrs. Dexter assured her that Roddy, as well as everything in and about the place, was at Celia's service, and, explaining that she was very busy, hurried away. Immediately after breakfast Celia began her delightful work, and for the next two or three days stuck to it so persistently that Mrs. Dexter remonstrated.

"Oh, but you don't know how much I love it," pleaded Celia. "The moment I leave the library I want to get back to it. You see, I'm mad on books, and this work of mine is a labour of love; the very touch of some of these old volumes thrills me. And there are so many of them; sometimes I feel that I shall never get through my task, if I live to be ninety."

"You'll soon look like ninety, my dear, if you don't take more exercise," observed Mrs. Dexter, wisely. "I am sure his lordship would be grieved if he knew you were working so hard. Now, come, take Roddy and go for a long walk; or perhaps you would rather drive?"

Celia declared that she preferred a walk, and a little later she started out, somewhat reluctantly, with Roddy close at her heels. It was a delicious morning; the feeling of the coming summer was in the air, the larks were singing joyously above the moorland, as if they, too, were revelling in the bright sunlight, the clean, keen air, the scent of the gorse with which it was perfumed. Celia could scarcely refrain from singing; she walked quickly, and sometimes, to Roddy's delight, she ran races with him. She came to the end of the moor at last, and swung down to the high road, followed it for some time and presently came to two cross-roads. She was hesitating which to take, when a small phaeton, drawn by an Exmoor pony, came rolling towards her.

In the phaeton was an old lady with white hair and a pleasant countenance; she had very sharp eyes and a smile that was a trifle cynical. At sight of the young girl, with the brilliant eyes and the healthily flushed cheeks, she stopped the pony and looked at Celia curiously. Celia felt as if she must speak to everyone that morning, so she went up to the tiny carriage and asked how far it was, by the road, to Thexford Hall.

"Oh, I see," said the old lady. "I was wondering who you were. You are the young lady who has come to the Hall as librarian. Let me see, what is your name?"

Celia told her.

"And a very pretty one, too," said the old lady, with a short nod. "I'm called Gridborough. You've walked six miles, and must be tired," she continued. "You ought to have a rest. Get in and I'll drive you to my house; you can have some lunch with me."

As they entered a long drive, bordered by tall elms, Celia saw a small cottage set back a little way from the road. A young woman, with a pale face and sad-looking blue eyes, was standing at the gate with a baby in her arms. As the phaeton drove up, a faint colour came to her white face; she dropped a little curtsy and was turning away, but stopped when the old lady called to her. The young woman approached, with an air of timidity, of passive obedience, which was as pathetic as her eyes.

"Well, how is the baby, Susie?" asked her ladyship.

"He is quite well, now, my lady," replied the girl, in a low, toneless voice.

"That's right. I thought he'd soon pull round; it's the wonderful air. Let me look at him." She took the baby from the young woman's arms, which yielded him slowly and reluctantly. "Oh, yes, he is looking famously."

"What a pretty baby!" Celia exclaimed, bending over the child with all a young girl's rapture. "It's a darling."

The young mother's pale face flushed, and the faded blue eyes grew radiant for a moment, as she raised them gratefully to Celia's face; but the flush, the radiance, vanished almost instantly, and the face became patient and sad again.

"You must try to get some of the baby's roses in your own cheeks, Susie," said her ladyship, peering at the girl.

"Yes, my lady," came the passive response. She took the child into her own arms, pressing it to her with a little convulsive movement, then, as the carriage drove off, dropped a curtsy.

"That's a sad business," said Lady Gridborough, speaking rather to herself than to her companion. "It's the old story: selfish man, weak woman."

"She is a stranger here?" asked Celia.

"Yes; she was born in a little village where I live sometimes. I brought her here—was obliged to. They were harrowing the poor child to death, the toads! She was dying by inches, she and the child, too, and so I carried her away from her own place and stuck her into this cottage."

"That was very good of you," said Celia, warmly.

"Oh, well, whenever I see Susie, I think of my own girlhood and its temptations, and say to myself, like the man whose name I can't remember, 'but for the grace of God, there goes Constance Gridborough.' Here we are!"

They had covered the long drive, and reached a house almost as grand as the hall. As at the Hall, there was a superfluity of servants, and one would have thought the little Exmoor was an elephant by the way in which a couple of grooms sprang forward to his diminutive head. The old lady, leaning on a stick and the arm of a footman, led Celia into the house.

While lunch was in progress the old lady talked in the same friendly and familiar way, as if she had known Celia for years.

"I suppose you're a college girl? Wiggins, help Miss Grant to some chicken. You must make a good lunch, for I am sure you must be hungry. Father and mother living?"

"No," said Celia, quietly.

"That's sad," commented her ladyship. "And so you're thrown on your own resources. Well, they look as if they'd stand by you. I'm glad you've come to the Hall, now I find that you're not a blue-stocking and don't wear spectacles. Yes, I'm glad, for I've rather taken a fancy to you. I like healthy young things, and you look as if you were a part of the morning. Sounds like poetry out of one of your wretched books."

"And now," said Celia, after a while, "I must be going, Lady Gridborough. I have been away quite a long time."

"You must come again," said the old lady.

"Do you think," said Celia, hesitatingly, as she slipped on her jacket, "that the young woman, Susie, as you call her, would let me go to see her sometimes? I should like to."

"Yes, my dear," said her ladyship, with a nod which showed she was pleased. "Go and see her, by all means. You're a girl of about her own age, and she may open her heart to you. A sad business—a sad business," she murmured. "And what makes it more sad for me is that I knew the young man."

She paused and appeared as if she were hesitating, then she said:

"Look here, my dear, it's scarcely a story for your ears; but I've no doubt it will come to them sooner or later, and so I may as well tell you. This place, where I have another house, where Susie Morton lived is called Bridgeford. She was in service with me, and a young gentleman who lodged in the village— he was studying engineering—made her acquaintance. I suspected nothing. Indeed, he was supposed to be in love with the daughter of the rector, Miriam Ainsley. I thought it was going to be a match, but they were both poor, and the girl suddenly married a young nobleman, a man I disliked very much, a wastrel and a ne'er-do-well. But there were stories about this other young man who was supposed to be in love with her, and perhaps they came to her ears, and drove her to the other man, though it was a case of out of the frying-pan into the fire. The young engineer left the place suddenly, and disappeared, and everybody attributed poor Susie's downfall to him."

There was silence for a moment, then she went on musingly:

"Strange how even the most timid of our sex can display firmness and determination when they have made up their minds to do so. Though Susie has been implored to disclose his name, she has refused to do so. Those childish little lips of hers close tightly whenever one approaches the subject, and she has absolutely refused to say one word that would lead to a clue."

"Perhaps—perhaps the young man was not guilty after all," said Celia.

Lady Gridborough shook her head.

"I'm afraid he was, my dear," she said, with a sigh and a shrug. "She was very pretty, is so still, and I took a fancy to her and let her help me when I was pottering about the garden. I used to like to have him near me, and so they were thrown together. The old story. And yet I found it hard to believe that Derrick Dene was a scoundrel, and a heartless one to boot. There! That's enough of it. But as I say, you would have heard of it sooner or later. Put it out of your head,

my dear; it's not the kind of story to dwell upon; though I suppose nowadays young girls read and hear about these sort of things every day. Now mind! you're to come to see me whenever you feel inclined."

Celia promised warmly, and the childless woman stood in the doorway and sighed as she watched the girlish figure going lightly down the drive. Celia was feeling very happy; she would try to make a friend of Susie, and forget the story of her ruin and the name of Derrick Dene.

CHAPTER X

It was a pity that Derrick Dene was not a descriptive writer, instead of a struggling engineer, for had he been, he might have got some copy of quite a purple hue out of the "tramp" and its temporary denizens. We often hear of a literary production which is without a dull page, but it may be said with truth that Dene's life on board the *Angelica* was without a dull moment. And without an idle one; for he had accepted the position of general utility, and the man-of-all-work is expected to do everybody else's as well as his own. So it happened that while Sidcup, for instance, who was the principal acrobat and trapeze man, lolled through his day with a pipe in his mouth, and only lending an occasional hand, when necessity compelled him, Dene was in request everywhere.

Fortunately he was as strong as a modern Hercules, quick and alert in his movements, and, now that he was free from the terror which had overthrown him at Brown's Buildings, was of his wonted cheerfulness. Fortunately, also, he was a good sailor, and did not go under with the sea-sickness which soon prostrated nearly all the other members of the company. For they ran into bad weather, and once or twice, when the storm was at its worst, scenes occurred which would need the pen of a Joseph Conrad or a Morley Roberts to describe adequately; I will not attempt to do so.

The rickety old tub, straining in every plate, rolled and pitched and tossed all ways at once, like an hysterical cat, and the discomfort in which they had started

rose, or rather sank, to absolute misery. Like most strong men, Derrick had the heart of a woman towards anyone in pain or trouble. There was no doctor; the so-called stewards were quite unable to cope with the well-nigh general suffering, and Derrick, in some marvellous way, found time to bear a hand. There is no doubt that, in any case, he would have been popular; but in the present circumstances he stepped at once into the position of first friend with the men, and became a hero and a little tin god in the regard of the women; and as to the children—for there were three or four in the company, young acrobats and riders—they watched for his coming, and clung to him and adored him with their pathetic eyes, as if their present and future safety and happiness were dependent on him. Often, in the middle of the night, he would be awakened by the wail of a child, and with eyes still half closed, and his mind only half awake, would make his way to it, give it a drink, and sometimes fall asleep with the poor little thing nestled up against him. To them he was no longer "Mr. Green," but "Syd," or "Dear Syddie," and they fought for a word and schemed for a smile from him.

Among the women were some who were quite young. Many of them were pretty, and not a few of them, naturally enough, fell in love with the good-looking young man who befriended them. Like the children, but with a different kind of ardour, they waited for his coming, and laid feminine snares for him. Two girls, to particularize, thought of little else than Sydney Green as they lay in their bunks, recovering from that horrible malady at which we all laugh, and all quail. One was a fair girl, named Alice Merton. She was one of the riders, and was extremely pretty, with blue eyes and a complexion like cream and roses. She was very slight and dainty, and looked fragile; but she was a very good equestrienne, and when on a horse displayed extraordinary nerve.

The other girl—her name was Isabel Devigne, a stage name, no doubt—was tall, dark-eyed, with the regular features and blue-black hair of a Spaniard. She also was a rider; she had been in the business—pardon! profession—since she could walk, and her experiences of life were many and peculiar. Perhaps because of their contrasting character-istics, she and Alice Merton had been drawn towards each other, and were fast friends. They occupied opposite bunks, walked and talked together, and were both in love with Sydney Green, who ministered to both, in his capacity of amateur ship doctor, with strict though unconscious impartiality.

Derrick was not of the susceptible genus, and, if he had been, he was too much driven by the incessant work to spare time for even the mildest flirta-tion. Besides, whenever he found time for thought, his mind always went back to a certain room in Brown's Buildings, far away in London, to a girl's face looking down at him from over the balustrade. He thought of her only; scarcely once had his mind wandered from her to Miriam, the girl he had loved, the girl for whom he had sacri-ficed himself. Sometimes, when he put his hand in his breast pocket, he could feel the five-pound note; and whenever he did so, back came the scene, and his heart grew warm.

The bad weather lasted for a week; then the storm abated, the sea grew calmer, and one morning the invalids began to crawl up to the deck.

Derrick, busy with the horses, some of which had suffered terribly, paused for a moment and looked at the wretched folk as they emerged from the companion-way. One of them was Alice Merton, and he was moved to such pity by the sight of her white face and evi-dent weakness that he put down his cur-ry-comb and brush and went to help her. Her face was flooded with colour as she raised her piteous blue eyes to him, and her hand shook as he drew it through his arm.

"You'll be as right as a trivet—I don't know what a trivet is, by the way—before very long," he assured her. "It's wonderful how you pull round, es-pecially in such air as this. Here, I'll rig up a little nest against the warm side. That's what you want—warmth."

"You're very good to me," she fal-tered. "But you're good to everyone, and we all know how busy you are."

"That's all right," he said, cheerfully. "Nothing like plenty of work."

While he was making the nest, the tall, supple figure of Isabel Devigne came on deck; she too was weak, but she walked firmly and held her head erect. At sight of Derrick and his em-ployment she also coloured, a rich, pas-sionate red, and she drew a long breath, her white, even teeth clenched tightly. Informed by the direction of Alice's eyes, Derrick turned and saw the other girl.

"Plenty of room, Miss Devigne," he said, cheerfully. "You two snuggle up together; keep each other warm. Halloa! here we are. Let 'em all come," he added, as a cry of welcome and joy rose from the children, who appeared now and rushed at him as if for refuge and comfort.

The two girls watched him hungrily as he caught up the smallest of the group, gave her a playful shake, and chucked her softly into the nest. They shrilled their thanks and their love, and clamoured to him to remain; but Derrick wiped them off gently, as one wipes off a bunch of clinging bees, and promising to look them up as soon as he could, re-turned to the horses, which needed him quite as badly as did these humans.

"He's almost too good to be a man," murmured Alice, involuntarily, as her gaze followed him wistfully.

Isabel's dark eyes flashed, and her full and sensuous lips curved contemp-tuously.

"He's a man, every inch of him," she said. "He's the first man I've ever met in this god-forsaken world. You—like him, because he's been playing the nurse to all of us women; you're the sort that always wants some man to be fuss-ing about you. I'm different. I like to see him when he's fighting it out with, and mastering, one of the horses, or holding his own with one of the men-swine who give him trouble sometimes."

"You and I are different," sighed Al-ice.

"I should hope so," retorted Isabel,

scornfully; but the next moment, with a kind of rough tenderness, she drew the shawl closer round Alice's shoulders. "Yes, we're different; perhaps that's why I like you. And I do like you still, though sometimes, when you look up at him with the eyes of a sick calf, and make excuse to touch him——"

"Oh, don't, Isabel!" murmured Alice, in a low voice. "He—he never thinks of me."

"You idiot! He never thinks of any of us," breathed Isabel through her teeth. "That's why he gets such a hold of one; we're just a parcel of helpless, miser-able wretches, who've got on his nerves and forced him to help us. Do you sup-pose, if this beastly old tramp went down this minute, that he'd shed a tear for any of us? Not he!" She paused a moment; then she said, with a kind of snarl, "He's got his girl. He's left her behind there, and his heart with her. Oh, don't cry! But, yes, do; your sort of woman can always find relief in tears. I can't."

An hour later, when Derrick returned to the group with a big can of soup, he found Alice asleep, with her head pil-lowed on the bosom of Isabel.

"Don't wake her," said Derrick.

Instantly Isabel, with a flash of the eyes, pushed the other's girl's head away from her.

"Here, wake up!" she said, roughly. "You want as much petting as a baby."

Derrick dealt out the soup, waited for a minute or two to see the children start on it, then went down below to feed the elephants. One of the huge beasts was troublesome, and as Derrick came up the man who was the cause of it gave the animal a jab on the trunk with a hay-fork. Derrick had already warned the fellow, one of the men-swine of whom Isabel had spoken; consequently Der-rick wasted no further words, but dropped the truss of hay and gave the man a blow which sent him sprawling. He got up, seized the hay-fork, and with murder in his eyes lunged at Derrick; but Derrick, too quick for him, struck up the fork, snatched it from the man's grasp, and hit him on the head with it.

"Get out of my sight," said Derrick,

without raising his voice. "Let me see you, or let me hear you, ill-treating one of the animals again, and I'll lay you up for the rest of the voyage. You may take that as a promise, and I've a knack of keeping my promises."

The man swore vilely, but suddenly stopped and slunk away, wiping the blood from his face, and Mr. Bloxford's voice, from behind Derrick, demanded shrilly:

"Who appointed you general chucker-out of the establishment?"

"I've no direct appointment," said Derrick, coolly, patting the elephant's soft trunk, which was wandering caressingly and gratefully over his body. "But, unfortunately for me, I'm so made that I can't stand by and see any animal ill-treated. It's a weakness of mine that has caused me no end of trouble."

"I guess so," said Mr. Bloxford, dryly. "That waster Jackman, for instance, won't forget that tap you've given him. He'll lay for you some day, mark my words. I've wanted to go for him many times myself; but"—he was going to say, "I'm not big enough," but he drew himself up to the top of his few inches and expanded his chest—"I haven't the time. Here! The business seems to come handy and easy to you. I'll appoint you chucker-out; in other words, I'll make you deputy-manager, Mr. Green. I've had my eye on you, and I'll tell you, in strict confidence, that it's very little that escapes this eye of mine." He twisted both glittering eyes till they looked like those of an acute monkey. "You seem as if you could hold your own, and it wants holding with this gang. Deputy-manager—two pounds a week. How will that suit you?"

"It suits me very well, thank you, Mr. Bloxford," said Dene, and away went his hand to the talisman in his pocket.

"Then fix it so," said Mr. Bloxford. "And mind and keep your eye on Jackman," he added, as he trotted off.

Derrick's new and exalted position relieved him of a great deal of the drudgery he had previously performed, but it kept him on the continual spring, and burdened him with fresh responsibilities; for it was necessary that he

should be all over the ship at once, so to speak. All the details of the daily life on board passed under his supervision; all the multitudinous cares, disputes, arrangements, were referred to him; and, strangely enough, though most of the men in the company must have envied him, their envy was not accompanied by ill-feeling, for Derrick's value was admitted by all of them.

One of the first things he did was to rearrange the women's and children's quarters, and render them more comfortable, for which the benefited ones blessed him and loved him all the more intensely. Then he set to work to cleanse the ship, which during the spell of bad weather had become almost unendurable. The crew, and some of the company, grumbled at the increased work and Derrick's drastic regulations, but they all enjoyed the results of his despotism.

Derrick had less time than before to spend in friendly interchanges with those who had become attached to him, and the two girls, Isabel and Alice, watched him wistfully as he moved rapidly within their sight, and hungered for a word, a smile; and presently they taught the children, when they were with them, to waylay him, and had to be content with the scraps of kindness which fell from the children's table.

Fortunately for Derrick's *régime*, the weather continued fine, and three weeks later the *Angelica*, much battered and straining still most piteously in every plate, was steaming up the La Plata river to Buenos Ayres.

The disembarkation shall not be described. Several times during it Derrick wondered how Noah had managed the same business.

CHAPTER XI

The two days that followed their arrival seemed to Derrick to be a succession of hours born of delirium and nurtured by frenzy. Mr. Bloxford, still in his preposterous fur coat, was everywhere at once, and waving his hands as usual; Derrick, who had begun by shouting, soon became hoarse, and discovered why it was that Mr. Bloxford relied, on such occa-

sions, entirely on gesture.

Derrick followed his example as well as he could, and by dint of expressive pantomime, and sometimes forcible persuasion with a fist which had acquired an astonishing readiness, got the motley crew of quadrupeds and bipeds on dry land, formed up his column, marched it to the spot outside the handsome city, and then sank on an upturned box, wiping his brows, and wondering, while he watched the experienced baggage hands deftly erect the monster tent, whether he should ever get his voice back.

It was summer in England, but it was like winter here, a bland and mild winter, with, fortunately for Bloxford's circus, no rain—at any rate, at present—and all through the day the scene had been lit up by a brilliant sun which, shining through a singularly clear atmosphere, seemed to destroy distance and to bestow sharp outlines on every object. There was something exhilarating in the air, and the bustle and excitement, and Derrick, having rested, went to his canvas quarters feeling his blood stir within him, and his past life stretching away behind him as if it had belonged to another man.

They opened to a big "house," comprising an audience of all classes, and it might be said all nationalities; for in the din that arose from the crowd Derrick caught scraps of Italian, Spanish, and French, the thick, soft tone of the Mexican, the brogue of the Irishman; it was a veritable Babel. As he passed behind the opening through which the performers entered, Isabel Devigne stepped out from the women's dressing-room, and Derrick could not suppress a start of surprise and admiration.

As a kind of compliment to the country, she was made up to represent a queen of the Incas, and was the personification of barbaric splendour. Her superb figure glittered and scintillated with silver and gold tinsel, which, in the garish light, would look like a plate of precious metal. A scarlet cloak partially draped her. The effect of her height was increased by a head-dress of waving plumes, and her dark brows and the natural scarlet of her lips were intensified by her make-up. Of course, she saw him start and the frank admiration in his eyes, and she smiled as she drew herself up with a proud consciousness of her beauty.

"Shall I do?" she asked, knowing well what the answer would be.

"You're simply splendacious," Derrick assured her. "That costume suits you down to the ground. You're magnificent."

She flushed beneath her paint, and her lids drooped.

"I'm glad you like it," she said. "Yes, I think I shall knock them."

"You'll knock them silly," said Derrick, confidently.

Then Alice stepped out from the dressing-room, a very different figure, in her conventional short skirt and silk-clad legs. She looked very slight and fragile, very fairy-like, against the gorgeous figure of Isabel, and she glanced down at herself deprecatingly, then raised her eyes appealingly to Derrick, who responded promptly.

"You look too beautiful to be real, both of you," he said. "If the rest are as good as you are, this show's going to be the biggest success on earth."

The band was now blaring away with all its might; the two clowns had rolled into the ring, the master was cracking his whip, the horses, awaiting their turn impatiently, were pawing and breathing loudly. Mr. Bloxford, still in his fur coat, with a big cigar in full blast, was seated in a coign of vantage from which he could see everything, his Simian eyes darting everywhere, his jewelled hand ready to wave on the various items of the programme. The huge audience received the opening turns with a kind of judicial silence; but as Isabel, on a big black horse, came sweeping into the ring, a shout of admiration greeted her, and as she completed a really clever performance a roar of applause filled the big tent. Sidcup, who was standing beside Derrick, nodded two or three times with an air of satisfaction.

"Show's going well," he said. "We're making a good start. I shall give 'em my double somersault act to-night; that

ought to fetch 'em," he added, glancing down his perfectly-formed figure, clad in its skin-like tights.

"I'm sure it will," said Derrick, who had learned the value of a word of encouragement. "Give 'em the best you've got. They've taken to Miss Devigne immensely, haven't they? And no wonder."

Sidcup glanced at him sharply.

"You admire her? She's a great friend of yours, Mr. Green," he said, with a hint of significance in his tone.

"Oh, yes," assented Derrick, in a matter-of-fact way. "No one could help admiring her. She's one of the most beautiful women I've ever seen. And her performance was wonderfully clever. Here she comes!"

The black horse, with its magnificent rider, came through the opening, and Derrick, as he caught the bridle, looked up and nodded his congratulations. Sidcup approached also, and began to praise her; but she merely glanced at him. Her eyes fixed themselves on Derrick, and she rested her hand on his shoulder for a moment as she slipped from her horse. Sidcup noticed her little action, and his face darkened. At this moment Mr. Bloxford's hand waved towards him; his turn had come, and he sprang into the ring with the acrobat's conventional bow and gesture. After trying his ropes carefully, he swarmed up to the trapeze; the music of the band slowed down, and became impressive. In almost breathless silence, Derrick and the audience watched the man as he went through his performance. It was an extremely clever and daring one, and he brought it to a close by turning a double somersault as he left one trapeze and caught the other, a feat which made all who watched it hold their breath.

The audience roared at him, Mr. Bloxford waved him on twice to bow his acknowledgments, and Derrick, as Sidcup came tripping out of the ring, met him and held out a hand.

"Simply stunning!" said Derrick. "Cleverest thing of the kind I ever saw. You must have the pluck of the devil. You made my heart turn over. Wonderful, wasn't it, Miss Devigne?"

She took her eyes from Derrick for an instant, and smiled at Sidcup, but her gaze returned to Derrick's face, and Sidcup's smile vanished as he passed them without a word.

Alice, too, got her share of the applause for her very pretty and refined act of horsemanship. The rest of the company, heartened by the previous successes, did their best, and an evidently well-pleased audience streamed out into the cool, clear air. Sent for by Mr. Bloxford, Derrick went to the manager's tent or office.

"Congratulations, sir!" he said.

"Here, help me count this," commanded Mr. Bloxford, nodding to the heap of notes and coin. "Yes, it's been a good start, and a jolly good thing for us that they were pleased. I've heard since I've been here that if they don't ketch on, if they don't cotton to the show, they're apt to cut up rough. A man at the hotel told me that the last circus was wrecked, clean wrecked. Something they didn't like got their monkey up."

"Oh, we're all right, anyhow," said Derrick. "Our people are all very pleased. They're going to have a kind of beano over the supper. You'll come along, Mr. Bloxford; they'll want you."

"All right," said Mr. Bloxford. "But it seems to me that you're the popular man of this crowd. Oh, I don't walk about in my sleep, young man. I can see as far as a blind horse. You've got through your bit like a little man; and no nonsense, neither—no side and no frills. And no fooling about with the women, eh?"

He shot a glance at Derrick who shrugged his shoulders, and Mr. Bloxford, after another glance, appeared to be satisfied with the shrug.

After they had counted the money as best they could, for some of it was strange to them, and had locked it in the safe, they joined the company. Their appearance was hailed with a cheer. Mr. Bloxford was conducted, with theatrical pomp, to the head of the trestle-board which served as a table, and Derrick, after some protest, was installed at the bottom. The simple, almost child-like, folk enjoyed themselves amazingly.

Bloxford's and Derrick's health was drunk, and it was with unfeigned reluctance that Derrick at last broke up the party and ordered them off to the rest they had so well earned.

On the second night there was another packed audience; but there was a larger proportion of the rougher element, and Mr. Bloxford remarked on the fact somewhat anxiously to Derrick.

"There's always a lot of cowboys in the city," he said, "and there's a good many of them here to-night. They come in from the plains for a lark, and they generally see that they get it."

"Oh, they'll be all right," said Derrick. "They're bound to be pleased."

"Well, keep an eye on things," remarked Mr. Bloxford, who was evidently still rather uneasy. "It there's any disturbance, turn on the band. Make them play like blazes, the louder the better."

Derrick nodded, and hurried off to overlook things. He found that the women were rather nervous, for they had heard of the fate of the last circus; but they, too, were encouraged by his cool and easy manner and the few words of cheer which seemed to come so easily to him. The early turns went well, especially those of Isabel, Alice, and Sidcup. Sidcup's was followed by an exhibition of bareback riding by two men. One of them on this occasion was Jackman, who was taking the place of a rider who had strained his ankle on the previous night. Jackman had been drinking, not heavily, or Derrick would have noticed the fact, but just enough to make him unsteady and uncertain, and in attempting to leap from the ground to the horse while it was in motion he missed and sprawled on the tan.

A roar of ridicule rose from the cheaper part of the house. Jackman sprang to his feet, ran across the ring, and made another attempt; and failed again. The roar of mockery rose now like one vast derisive cheer. Jackman, glaring round the audience, his lips drawn from his teeth in a snarl, waited till the horse came round, then struck at it, as if to show that the animal and not he was in fault.

The laughter, derision, gave place suddenly to a yell of objurgation. Two young men, obviously cowboys, sprang over the low barrier, and Jackman, after a moment's hesitation, turned and ran. One of the cowboys caught the horse, and the audience, breathless and silent now, waited for events. Derrick, who had been watching the scene closely, came slowly, almost saunteringly, across the ring to the two young men.

CHAPTER XII

"What is the trouble?" Derrick asked, in a perfectly calm, almost casual way.

The man who was holding the horse turned to him with a grin.

"We're going to show your man how to do the trick, mister," he said. "He's a fool-man, to think he can come over here and teach us boys how to ride."

Derrick had not been to a public school for nothing. He caught the spirit of the thing in a moment, and with that readiness which makes the Britisher the master of circumstance wherever he goes, he nodded and smiled, and clapped the cowboy on the shoulder.

"Right you are! Go ahead," he said, cheerfully, and the cowboy, evidently surprised by Derrick's complaisance, stepped back.

The horse was set going, the cowboy walked slowly in the proper direction, the audience watching him in intense silence, then, with a run and a bound, he alighted on the horse's back, performing the trick to perfection. The audience thundered its applause, and Derrick, to round off the thing properly, took the cowboy's rough hand, shook it, and whispered,

"Bow, bow, and get back to your place at once. Off with you!"

Amidst cheers and laughter, the now shy and confused amateur obeyed, and Derrick, with his hands in his pockets, strolled across the ring, as if the whole incident had been planned.

A group of persons awaited him; men and women who had paled beneath their paint, for they had expected trouble. But they were flushed now, and the women's eyes were sparkling with admiration. Isabel, in all the glory of her costume, was the first to greet him.

"It was splendid," she said, in her deep contralto, and, as if involuntarily, she held out her hand. "You saved the show."

Derrick, with the wholesome red of modesty mantling in his cheeks, gently pushed by them.

"Nonsense! There was no danger, not a bit. Keep it going; we're all right."

And so it proved; for the audience, highly pleased with itself and the member who had distinguished himself, received the rest of the bill with marked satisfaction and pleasure.

"The guv'nor wants you, Mr. Green," said Sidcup, who had not joined in the congratulations and admiration of the rest.

"All right," said Derrick. "Be with him in a moment."

He went in search of Jackman, and found him, with a bottle of whisky, just outside the men's quarters. He looked up and snarled as Derrick approached him. Derrick took the bottle from him, and then looked down at him with an air of doubt and uncertainty.

"I'm trying to make up my mind whether I should give you your discharge or a good hiding. I don't like sacking a man in a strange land, and you're not in a condition for a fair fight. What do you think I ought to do?"

Jackman staggered to his feet and glared at him.

"You've hit me once before, Mr. Green," he said. "Hit me again—just lay your hand on me, and it'll be the last man you ever bash. You're an upstart, that's what you are. You think, because you can come over that old fool, that you're going to lord it over everybody. You can play that sort of game with the women, but you can't with me. I'm engaged for this trip, and you can't sack me because I made a slip of it in the ring just now. I know the law, Mr. Green. You think I'm drunk. I'm sober enough to best you, anyhow."

Thinking to take Derrick unawares, the foolish man aimed a blow at him; but Derrick caught the arm, and almost gently forced Jackman into his seat again.

"If you hadn't gone for me I'd have

sacked you; but I see there's some good left in you, anyhow. Pull yourself together, man, and don't be an idiot. Cut this stuff"—he tapped the bottle—"and do your job properly. I'll talk to you in the morning. No, I won't; but if I find you playing the giddy goat again, I'll give you your choice of a hiding or a discharge."

As Derrick hurried off to the manager's office he asked himself why he had been so merciful, for the man had deserved all with which Derrick had threatened him. But Derrick knew, for as he had stood looking down at the man, he had remembered a certain young man who had been saved from playing the fool by a girl; and the remembrance would never leave him, would always make him merciful towards the folly of other men.

Mr. Bloxford was not wearing his fur coat, but he nodded to the garment, where it hung on a chair behind him.

"Help me on with it, will you? Took it off—thought there was going to be a row," he said, with the air of a man who is quite able alone to quell a disturbance. "You managed that very well, Mr. Green." This was the first time he had honoured Derrick with a prefix. "The neatest thing I've seen. Yes, you're a cool hand, young man. At first I thought you were going to come the high and mighty over that cowboy, and if you had, you'd have raised Hades and Thomasus. We should have had the rest of them on us and the show wrecked, like they did that other one. I tell you I was out of that coat before you could say Jack Robinson. But before you were half across the ring I twigged your game. And you played it for all it was worth. You're made of the right stuff. Yes, you're the sort of man I've read about in the silly story books; but I little thought I should ever come across him. Now, I wonder why it is?"

He cocked his bald head and peered at Derrick thoughtfully.

"Of course, they'd say in the books it's because you're a 'gentleman.' Well, up to now, I've always given the grin to that highfulutin notion; but—I dunno. Anyhow, I'm much obliged to you."

He held out a grubby paw and shook the now very much embarrassed Derrick by the hand.

"Of course, I'm going to raise your screw. We'll say, double it, and no palaver."

Derrick expressed his thanks, but Mr. Bloxford waved him away.

"As for that pig Jackman, we'll fire him out, of course."

Derrick pleaded for the man, and Bloxford yielded, but with a shrug of the shoulders and a dissenting shake of the head.

"All right," he said, grudgingly. "It's up to you, of course. But don't you forget what I told you when you and he had a shindy on board. He's the kind of man who'll wait and lay for you when he gets a chance."

Derrick laughed easily as he proceeded to count the money.

They drew good audiences for the whole of their stay, and then prepared to move on. As before, the heaviest of the responsibility fell on Derrick's shoulders, but it was made as light as possible for him by the good will the company bore him, which it expressed by rendering prompt obedience and willing assistance. Jackman had given no further trouble, but had gone about his work with a sullen demeanour, and he markedly avoided any meeting with Derrick, who treated him exactly as he treated every other member of the company.

On the morning of their departure Derrick was standing in the centre of the tent, superintending the displacement and packing up of the seats and other properties. He was immediately beneath a large and heavy circular lamp which afforded the principal light, and up above him was Jackman, who had been sent to lower it. He was waiting for the word from the chief baggage man, who was standing at a little distance from Derrick.

Derrick was moving away, when suddenly he heard a warning cry. He looked up and saw the mass of metal descending, though the baggage man had not given the word. It was a swift upward glance, and as swiftly he swerved

aside. Then he felt a sharp but heavy pain on his shoulder, and fell. He was conscious of a number of voices shouting, of vague forms hurrying towards him, then all became a blank.

When he recovered consciousness he found himself lying in one of the living vans. He tried to move, but the upper part of his body felt as if it were made of lead. He opened his eyes and looked round him. Someone, a tall figure, bent over him, and laid a hand on his forehead. He looked up and, with a struggle for consciousness, saw that the face above him was Isabel's.

"What's the matter—what is it?" he asked, and, to his surprise and consternation, his voice sounded hollow and weak.

She dropped on her knees beside him, her hand still on his brow.

"You've been ill," she whispered. "Don't move. I don't think you ought to speak. Stay quite still."

"But why?" he asked, with gentle impatience. "Why am I lying here, and what's the matter with me?"

"You've been hurt," she said, in a voice that was trembling as well as low. "It was the lamp. Don't you remember?"

Derrick knit his brows and tried to recall the past just before he became unconscious.

"The lamp—Jackman!" he said, with a frown that turned to a grin; for even at that moment he appreciated the neatness of Mr. Jackman's revenge.

"Don't think of it," Isabel said, her hand becoming caressing, as she passed it over his forehead. "You needn't be afraid; the beast has disappeared. Yes, he bolted, or it would have been the worse for him. The men——" Her eyes flashed, her white, even teeth clenched together. "It was a wonder you weren't killed; if you hadn't moved, just at the moment you did——"

"Am I badly hurt?" asked Derrick, anxiously. "Am I going to be laid up? Awful nuisance!"

"No," she said; "it was your collarbone. It is all right now. It struck your head, too. That's why you were unconscious. We brought a doctor along with us. He'll be here presently. They wanted to take you to the hospital, but Mr. Bloxford—all of us—couldn't leave you behind."

"I'm glad you didn't," said Derrick. "I shall be all right presently. I feel better already. And you have been nursing me?" he asked.

A blush rose to the clear olive of her face, and she smiled, a heavenly smile, for this was a very beautiful woman, and when a beautiful woman smiles the gods nod approval.

"You see, I was used to it. I was a nurse once; but I couldn't stick it—too quiet. Alice has been helping me," she added, as if forced to make the admission.

"I say, you have been awfully good to me," said Derrick, gratefully.

"Oh, that's all right," she said. "I—I like it. Like old times, you know. I must go and tell Mr. Bloxford; he's been like a sick monkey fretting over its young."

She stood beside the bed, her eyes downcast, her face pale now, but an expression on her proud and haughty lips which would have befitted a schoolgirl.

"Let me give you some broth. The doctor said you might have it, if you came to."

She brought him a cup, but to Derrick's disgust he could not grasp it, and she held it to his lips while he drank.

"You're an angel," he said; "yes, an angel. You look pale; you've been nursing me all this time. How long is it?"

"Four days," she said, in a low voice. They had been the happiest four days of her life.

"Good lord!" he muttered. "Four days! Oh, here, I say, I wish I could thank you properly, but I can't."

"There's no need," she said, in a low voice. "I'll go and tell the doctor and Mr. Bloxford."

She smoothed the clothes about him, her eyes still downcast, but as she went to the door she turned and looked at him. Derrick met the gaze of the dark eyes full blank, and as he did so the colour rose to his face, and it was his turn for his eyes to become downcast.

He had learned her secret, and his heart was heavy within him, for, though they were unlike, the eyes of that other girl, who was always in his thoughts, flitted between him and Isabel.

CHAPTER XIII

Celia hurried back from Lady Gridborough's, ran up the great stone steps and entered the hall. Catching sight of Mrs. Dexter coming from the dining-room, Celia began,

"Oh, Mrs. Dexter, I've had quite an adventure——" But she stopped as she saw that the hitherto placid housekeeper was evidently in a state of agitation, and, instead of continuing, Celia broke off with: "Oh, is anything the matter, Mrs. Dexter?"

"Matter! I should think so," responded Mrs. Dexter, throwing out her hand, which grasped a telegram. "I've just had this from his lordship the Marquess, saying that he is coming down. And to dinner! I'm sure I don't know what I'm going to do."

"But everything is in readiness?" said Celia, remembering Mrs. Dexter's vaunt.

"Of course it is, my dear; but the dinner——! All the staff seems to have lost its head; and I, myself, am so flurried——"

Celia laid her hand upon the plump arm and pressed it, encouragingly.

"It will be all right," she said, soothingly. "Surely there will be enough in the house for one man!"

"My dear young lady," retorted Mrs. Dexter, solemnly, "you have to prepare a regular dinner, with all the proper courses, whether it's for one man or a party. Like enough, his lordship will only partake of one or two dishes, but you have to provide them all, and serve them properly."

"I see," said Celia, who was beginning to understand the exigencies of rank. "Can I help you? Surely there must be something I can do!"

"Well, you can arrange the flowers for me, if you will be so good, my dear," said Mrs. Dexter. "Mr. Douglas, the head gardener, will cut you some from the conservatory."

"All right," said Celia eagerly. "You run away and see to the dinner; and if I

can help you in any other way, after I've done the flowers, let me know."

Herself not unexcited, she interviewed the dignified and extremely capable head gardener, who, departing from his custom, did not utter any complaint, but sacrificed his choicest blossoms to the beautiful young lady to whom he had not yet spoken.

Celia thanked him, and ran off to get the receptacles for the flowers from the stately Mr. Smith, the butler, and set about arranging the exquisite blossoms. As she was doing so, she remembered a certain bed of beautifully-grown pansies on one of the lawns. She picked a great bunch, and arranged them by themselves in a flat bowl; and when the table was laid, her floral decorations made a brave show amidst the glittering plate and old English cut-glass.

"Oh, you've done them beautifully, my dear!" exclaimed Mrs. Dexter; and even the impassive Smith nodded his head approvingly. Celia was able to render assistance in various other ways, following Mrs. Dexter everywhere, and venturing to give a hint now and again. Then, her excitement increasing, she tried to settle down to her work in the library; but all the while she was writing down titles in her draft catalogue she was listening for the sound of the motor, and presently she heard it buzzing up the drive, followed by hasty footsteps and the murmur of subdued voices.

When Celia's dinner was brought into the little room behind the library, which was now recognized as her own, Mrs. Dexter appeared for a moment. She was quite calm now, but looked rather tired.

"Everything is all right?" said Celia, sympathetically.

"Yes, my dear," responded Mrs. Dexter, with a little sigh of relief, as she smoothed her black silk dress. "It's as well that we were all ready; though this is the shortest notice we've ever had."

"I hope the Marquess is well," said Celia.

Mrs. Dexter shook her head, and sighed again. "I'm afraid not," she said, gravely; "indeed, he is looking ill; though not so much ill as tired and worried. He has changed greatly since he was last here, and looks years and years older. When I last saw him, his lordship was in the Government, which means, as I dare say you know, a great deal of work and responsibility; but he was quite cheerful then, and strong; now——" She paused, and added, "He ought not to be so worried; but perhaps it's Lord Heyton—he's always been a trouble to his father, I'm sorry to say. But now he's married, I should have thought that he would have settled down and not have caused his father any further anxiety. The Marquess tells me that Lord Heyton is coming down with his bride in a day or two."

As Mrs. Dexter was departing, Celia said, a little shyly:

"Is there any way out of this room except through the library and the hall? I don't want to disturb the Marquess."

"There is no other door but this one," replied Mrs. Dexter. "You see, it's only a kind of ante-room. But you need not be afraid of disturbing his lordship; he will be sure to go to the drawing-room or his own sitting-room, after he has had his dinner. Though there's no cause for you to be nervous at meeting his lordship, for he's one of the kindest of men, especially to anyone in his service."

Celia ate her dinner and returned to the library, where she worked for a couple of hours to make up for the time she had lost in the afternoon; then she took up an exquisitely-bound copy of Spenser's "Faerie Queene" and settled herself in a chair for half an hour's quiet reading. But the great masterpiece could not hold her attention; she let it lie on her lap and thought of her adventures of the day; she tried not to dwell on Susie's tragedy, though it was difficult not to do so; and presently her mind reverted to Brown's Buildings, to Mr. Clendon and the young man she had rescued. And yet "rescued," she thought, with a sigh, was scarcely the word, for, unwittingly, she had made him a fugitive and an outcast.

The great house was quiet, and, relying on Mrs. Dexter's assurance that she ran no risk of intruding upon the Marquess, she turned out the lights and went into the hall. On the threshold she drew

back, with a little flutter of excitement, for in the dim light of the great fire, which was always burning, she saw a tall, thin figure in evening dress standing with its hands clasped behind it. It was the Marquess. She saw distinctly the pale, worn face, the thin, almost colourless lips, drawn into a line that indicated profound sadness and a deep anxiety. He was standing before the portrait of the lad, his elder brother, of whose history Mrs. Dexter had told her; the elder brother who, if he had not died, "in foreign parts," would have been the Marquess instead of the man who was gazing at the portrait.

Celia stood quite still, her eyes chained to the haggard face; she did not know whether to withdraw into the library or to pass softly behind him and reach the stairs; and while she was hesitating, the Marquess heaved a deep sigh, made a gesture as of a man beaten by some insoluble problem, and, turning, saw her.

He did not start—men of his class are taught to repress every sign of emotion—and he stood quite still, looking at her gravely, as if the sudden interruption of his train of absorbing thought had caused him to forget whom she might be; then, as if he had remembered, he came towards her and said:

"You are Miss Grant, the librarian, I suppose?"

Even as she answered, "Yes, my lord," Celia noted the dull, toneless melancholy of his voice, the voice of a man to whom all things save one, whatever that might be, are but trivial and of no consequence.

"I am glad to see you," he said, with a little courtly inclination of his head, but certainly with no gladness in his voice. "I hope you are comfortable here; that you find your work congenial?"

"Oh, yes, my lord," said Celia, and, unconsciously, her voice was pitched low, like his own; for, somehow or other, she felt as if she were in the presence of a deep grief, of an unnamed trouble.

"I am very glad," he said again. "You are fond of books, I was told—I heard—I was given to understand. The collection"—he nodded towards the li-

brary—"is a good one, is it not?"

"A very good one," assented Celia; "it seems to me a magnificent library. But, then, I am not qualified to express an opinion. I have not much experience; I mean, of private libraries; I am used to the British Museum one only."

"My great grandfather was an enthusiastic collector," said the Marquess; "but I fear I have not inherited his taste, and have neglected the library."

In an absent-minded kind of way, he passed into the superb room, and looked round, reflectively.

"You are making a catalogue, of course? It must be a very heavy task, especially for one so young."

Celia began to tremble; and at that moment she realized fully how precious the work and position were to her.

"I am not so very young, my lord," she said, with a little, nervous smile. "I am twenty-two."

He looked at her with a suspicion of a smile on his lips.

"Youth has much in its favour," he said. "It is rich in energy and in strength. All the same, one must not abuse either. You are working late to-night; that is not wise."

"I was out, took a holiday, this afternoon, and was making up for it; but I enjoy working at night; it is so quiet—but it is always quiet here, in this great place."

"You have no father and mother?" he said, after a pause, during which he was trying to remember what Mr. Clendon had told him of her.

"No, my lord," said Celia. "I have no one belonging to me."

"That is sad," he said, more to himself than to her. "Mrs. Dexter looks after you, I suppose? I must tell her to see that you do not work too hard."

"She is more than kind to me," said Celia, warmly.

There was another pause; she did not know whether to remain or stay; but, as he had taken up the draft catalogue, she paused, standing by the table and waiting to see if he would speak to her again.

"Do you not feel lonely here?" he asked.

"Oh, no," she replied, promptly. "Not the very least. There is Mrs. Dexter, and the books and——" She laid her hand on the head of Roddy, who strolled in at the moment, and, after wagging his tail in response to her caress, moved slowly to the Marquess and thrust a wet, cold nose against the long, thin hand. "Besides, I made an acquaintance this afternoon; a lady, a dear old lady, Lady Gridborough, at Lensmore Grange, you know."

"Yes, I know," he remarked, with a nod. "That is well. She is a good soul. Warm-hearted, but eccentric. By the way, the house will not be so dull presently; for my son, Lord Heyton, and his newly-married wife are coming to stay."

As he made the announcement, he checked a sigh and turned away. Celia waited for a moment or two; the Marquess had sunk into a chair, his eyes fixed on the great dog, which had thrown itself at his feet. It seemed to Celia that his lordship had forgotten her.

"Good night, my lord," she said, softly.

He looked up with a start, rose, and opened the door for her, and, with a courtly inclination of the head, bade her good night.

Now a strange thing happened. As Celia was crossing the hall, she stopped and looked at the portrait before which the Marquess had been standing; and she remembered how she had been struck by a fancied resemblance to someone whom she could not trace. Her pause before the picture was scarcely more than momentary, but she was startled by the sound of footsteps, and, looking up with a half-frightened gaze, found the Marquess standing beside her. His face was almost stern, his dark eyes, so like those of the picture, were fixed on her, questioningly; and there was just a suspicion of anger in the keenness of his regard.

"You are interested in that picture?" he said, in a dry voice.

"I—I——Yes," said Celia, telling herself that she had no cause for fear, seeing that she had committed no crime.

"Why?" he demanded, curtly, and his tone was still dry and harsh.

Celia was silent for a moment; then she raised her eyes to his, calmly—for what was there to fear, why should he be angry with her for looking at the portrait?

"It is a very beautiful picture," she said.

The Marquess's brows lifted, and he bent his head as if apologizing for his curtness.

"That is true," he said, more gently. "It is one of the best in the collection. And your interest is only an artistic one?"

Celia had only to say "Yes," and to escape; but she was not given to equivocation; moreover, her high spirit had resented the anger and suspicion in his manner, for which, she felt, he had no justification.

"Not only, my lord," she said, as quietly as before; "but the first time I saw it, I thought that the face of the portrait was like that of someone I knew."

She was startled by the sudden change in his demeanour. His brows came down again, his eyes grew piercing, his lips stern.

"Like whom?" he demanded, shortly.

"I don't know," she said, with a slight shrug; "that is why the portrait interests me so. If I could trace the resemblance, I should—well, not be so bothered by it."

The Marquess paced to the fire and held his hands to it, as if he had become cold suddenly.

"Strange!" he said, musingly, and with an air of indifference, which Celia felt to be assumed. "Is the man you think resembles the portrait young—or old?"

As he put the question, a sudden flood of light seemed to illumine Celia's mind; it was as if she had been gazing perplexedly on a statue swathed in its covering, and as if the covering had been swept away and the statue revealed. She knew now that the face in the portrait resembled that of the young man on whom her thoughts were always dwelling. The resemblance was faint; but it existed in her mind quite plainly. The revelation brought the blood to her face, then she became pale again. The Marquess, looking over his shoulder, waited for her answer.

"I remember now, my lord——" she began.

"Young or old?" he said, not loudly, but with a quiet insistence.

"Young," replied Celia.

To her surprise and relief, the Marquess gave a little dry, almost contemptuous, laugh; and as he turned to her, with his hands folded behind his back, there was a faint smile on his face.

"Who is he?" he asked.

"I don't know," replied Celia.

"You don't know!" said his lordship, raising his brows. "Pardon me, I don't understand."

Celia stood before him, her hands clasped together in a clasp that, light at first, became tighter; her eyes were downcast, a slight fold came between her brows; for an inappreciable second or two, she lost consciousness of the great hall, the tall, bent figure silhouetted against the fire; she was back in Brown's Buildings, in that poverty-stricken room, and she saw the young man's head lying on his outstretched arm, a revolver in his hand.

"I don't know," she repeated, returning, suddenly, from that vision of the past. "It was someone I met, saw, for a short time——"

"But his name?" said the Marquess, with a subdued impatience.

"That I don't know," Celia replied, raising her eyes, in which the Marquess could not fail to read truth and honesty. "I saw him once only, and for a short time, and then—then he passed out of my life. I mean, that I did not see him again; that it is unlikely I shall ever see him again."

"Where was this—this meeting of which you speak?" inquired the Marquess, in a conversational tone. "Pardon me if I seem intrusive—it is your affair and yours only—but you have excited my curiosity. The portrait is that of my brother."

"I know," said Celia. "I do not mind your asking me; but I cannot tell you. What passed between me and him—— " She stopped; she was on delicate ground; this man, with his worldly experience, his acute intelligence, might lead her on to disclose what had happened that night; she could not cope with him. "I do not know his name."

The Marquess bowed his head, and smiled slightly, as if he scented the aroma of a commonplace romance.

"Quite so," he said. "A casual meeting. Such occurs occasionally in the course of one's life, and I dare say the resemblance you noticed was only a fancied one. It must have been," he added, looking on the ground, and speaking in an absent way; "for as it happens, my brother"—he nodded towards the portrait—"was unmarried, had no relations other than myself and my son." He turned away to the fire again. "Oh, yes; only a fancied one. Good night."

This was a definite dismissal, and Celia, murmuring, "Good night, my lord," went up the stairs. At the bend of the corridor she glanced down involuntarily. The Marquess had turned from the fire again, and was looking, with bent brows, at the portrait.

CHAPTER XIV

As Celia undressed slowly, going over the scene that had taken place in the hall below, recalling the changes in the Marquess's expressive face, his strange manner, with its suggestion of anger and impatience, she sought in vain for an explanation. Had he actually been annoyed and irritated by her admission that she had noticed a resemblance in the portrait of his dead brother to someone whom she had met? He had said, emphatically, that it was only a fancied resemblance, and she accepted his decision. It certainly could be only a freak of imagination on her part, seeing that the Marquess's brother had not married—indeed, it was ridiculous to suppose that there was any connection between the noble family of the Sutcombes and the unknown man in the poverty-stricken room at Brown's Buildings. Woman-like, her mind dwelt more on him than on the Marquess's impatience and annoyance. There was something strange, mysterious, in the fact that, not only was

she haunted by the memory of the young man, but that here, at Thexford Hall, she should fancy a portrait of one of the family resembled him.

It did not need much to recall him to her mind; for it may be said that in no idle moment of hers was her mind free of him. Now she asked herself, for the hundredth time, not only what had become of him, but what was her duty to him. She had not tried to find him, had not endeavoured to communicate with him. At the moment it occurred to her that she might have inserted a carefully-guarded advertisement in the Personal column of one or more of the newspapers, and she felt ashamed that the thought had not struck her before. She almost, but not quite, decided to insert such an advertisement at once; but, as she pondered, she questioned the wisdom of such an action. Her mind swung, like a pendulum, from one side to the other, and at last she fell asleep, still undecided, but still thinking of him.

The next morning she went out with Roddy for her usual before-breakfast run. It seemed that the Marquess also was an early riser; for she saw his figure, pacing one of the walks, his eyes fixed on the ground. She was going in his direction, and Roddy, catching sight of him, bounded towards him. The Marquess saw her, raised his hat, and turned. It seemed to Celia that he wished to avoid her, and she went on her way—the dog returning to her—and re-entered the house. She did not know whether to expect a visit in the library from the Marquess; and every now and then, when she heard his footstep or his voice, she paused in her work with something like apprehension. But he did not come. In the afternoon he went out in the motor, and presently Mrs. Dexter came into the library.

"The Marquess tells me he saw you last night, my dear," she said. "I hope you liked him."

"Yes," said Celia; "he was very kind."

"Oh, his lordship is kindness itself," said Mrs. Dexter; "and he seems quite interested in you; he is anxious that you should not overwork yourself, and he

told me that I was to look after you and see that you went out and took plenty of exercise every day. He's like that; no one could be more kind and considerate to those in his service. And now, my dear, it's a beautiful afternoon and you must go for a run, or I shall get into trouble with his lordship."

"Anything rather than that," said Celia, with a laugh. "Indeed, I'm just going out. Won't you come, too, Mrs. Dexter?"

"Oh, my dear, it's quite impossible," said the housekeeper, "Lord and Lady Heyton are coming this afternoon. No, you can't help me, thank you very much; everything is ready. I've given her ladyship the best south room, and I hope she will be pleased. I hear that she is a very beautiful young lady. She's a clergyman's daughter, and it was a love-match. It is a good thing that Lord Heyton is married and settled; a good thing for everybody," she added, with, perhaps, unintentional significance.

Remembering her promise to Lady Gridborough, Celia decided to go to see Susie; and, with Roddy scampering about her, she walked briskly in the direction of the cottage. As Celia came up to it, Susie was at the gate with the child in her arms, and the pale-faced girl-mother turned as if to avoid her; but Celia, with shyness in her soft, clear voice, said:

"Oh, mayn't I see the baby? Mayn't I come in?"

"Yes; you may come in, if you wish, if you want to, miss," said Susie, in her low voice, and after a moment's hesitation.

Celia followed her into the little sitting-room. It was a tiny place, but it was scrupulously clean and neat. Susie placed a chair for the visitor, and stood, with her baby pressed close to her, her eyes downcast. Her girlish face, pretty, notwithstanding the lines and hollows graved by sorrow, was like a mask in its impassivity. It was as if she were saying, "You have come, but I did not ask you to do so; I do not want you. I have all I want here, lying on my bosom."

"Let me have him for a moment," begged Celia, who, young as she was, comprehended the girl's feelings. "How sweet he looks!" she exclaimed, as she took the child and kissed it.

The mother's face twitched as she noted the kiss, and her eyes softened a little.

"He is very good," she said, as if she were speaking to herself rather than to Celia. "He is never any trouble; he is very healthy."

"He looks like a strong little cherub," said Celia, touching, with a forefinger as light as a feather, the dimple on the child's chin; "and, of course, he isn't any trouble. And you wouldn't think he was, if he were, would you? What is his name?"

Susie turned away to set a vase straight.

"He hasn't any name," she said, not suddenly, but in a dull, toneless voice. "He hasn't been christened yet."

"Oh, but you must have him christened," said Celia, speaking lightly, to conceal the embarrassment of the subject. "Haven't you decided on a name for him yet?"

Susie shook her head. "What does it matter?" she asked, in a whisper.

Celia fought the growing embarrassment womanfully.

"Oh, I think it matters a great deal," she responded, in the same light tone. "If I had a beautiful boy like this, I should like him to have a nice name— a manly name. But, of course, you've thought of one?"

Susie shook her head again.

"No? Will you think me very—well, cheeky—if I suggest some? Now, let me see! He is fair, isn't he? Some names are appropriate to fair men, while others are more suitable to dark ones, don't you think so?"

She laughed; but there was no smile in Susie's eyes, as she turned and looked, moodily, at the baby, one of whose chubby hands was clasping Celia's finger.

"Let's think of some names," said Celia. "James! I don't like that, do you? Richard; no, that's a dark name. Percy; how would that do?"

It was almost impossible for the pale face to grow paler, and yet, for a mo-

ment, as the blue eyes fixed themselves on Celia, Susie's pallor increased. Her arms went out as if she were about to take the child; but Celia looking up, smiled beseechingly.

"Oh, let me have him a little longer," she pleaded. "You have him all the time, you know. Let me see, what was the last name—Percy! Do you like it?"

With an effort, Susie said, slowly, and in almost a whisper:

"My—my father's name was Gerald:—will—will that do?"

"Oh, the very thing!" cried Celia, earnestly. "Gerald. Of course, you will call him after his grandfather. Do decide on that, Mrs.—Morton," she added, with a sudden nervousness.

"I'll call him Gerald, if you like," Susie said, phlegmatically. "Her ladyship was saying that he ought to be christened."

"Of course," said Celia; "and I'd like to be his godmother, if you'll let me?"

Susie swung round, her lips parted, her brows bent, and her eyes fixed on Celia's upturned face.

"You!" she said, as if she were panting. "You'll be a godmother to—him? And you know what he is—what I am? Her ladyship has told you?"

"Yes," said Celia, in a low voice.

"And you come here to me: you offer to—to do this! Don't you know that I was driven from my place, the place in which I was born, that every woman I've met, excepting her ladyship, would like to throw a stone at me? Why are you different from the others?"

"I don't know," said Celia, simply. "Perhaps it's because Lady Gridborough told me the whole story. But I'm—you see, I'm young, like yourself; and though I've mixed in the world, perhaps I haven't learnt to feel hardly as some of the folks you speak of do. I was going to say that I pity you, Susie; but I won't say that. I like you, I like to see you when you're looking at the child."

Susie turned away, her bosom heaving; there were no tears in her eyes, she had already wept them dry.

"And you mustn't look at me as if I were a stranger, as if I had come to see you out of impertinent curiosity only; I

want to come to see you very often. I'm in love with Gerald—it is to be Gerald, isn't it?—already. And it will be such a pleasure to me to run in and see him as often as I can; indeed, I must look after him; I shall be his second mother, you see; and between us, we'll train him up in the way he should go, and make a good man of him."

She was smiling now; but there were tears in her eyes, though Susie's were still dry.

"I can't resist you," said Susie, at last. "I know it's wrong that you should be mixed up with one like me. Your friends——"

"Haven't any friends," said Celia, lightly. "I mean, friends that would interfere with me; and if I had, I should not let them do so. I'm alone in the world, like yourself, Susie; and I'm my own mistress. Come, say 'Yes.'"

"I must. It's not in me to resist you, miss," said Susie, with a little gesture of yielding. "But, mind me! the people hereabouts, the grand folk up at the Hall, will take offence——"

"Let them!" said Celia. "But I don't think they will. They are all very kind, even the Marquess."

Susie looked up swiftly.

"Is—is he here, at the Hall?" she asked.

"Yes," said Celia. "He came last night. I saw him; he is very kind, though a very sad, melancholy man. You shall have the baby now. It's cruel of me to have kept him so long. But I must hurry back; for I have so much work to do. I shall come again as soon as I can; and I'll speak to Lady Gridborough about the christening, and arrange everything."

Susie went out to the gate with her, and was saying the last good-bye, when the stillness was broken by the humming of a motor-car. In a cloud of dust, an automobile came up the road; it was upon them almost in an instant.

"That's the big car from the Hall," said Celia. "Why, it must have come from the station, and that must be——"

As she spoke the car came abreast of them. In it were seated a fair, good-looking man, with prominent eyes and loose lips, and beside him an extremely pretty woman, clad daintily in a fashionable and expensive travelling costume.

"——Yes, that must be Lord and Lady Heyton," finished Celia; and her attention was so engrossed by the occupants of the car that she did not see the sudden pallor which had fallen on the face of the girl beside her, nor the swift gesture with which she drew the shawl over the child's face and pressed it to her bosom, as if to hide it. She uttered no cry, but a look of something like terror transformed her face; and, with a quick movement, she turned and fled into the cottage. Celia opened the garden gate and went on her way, half-suffocated by the dust of the rapidly disappearing car.

As Celia entered the Hall, she was met by the odour of an Egyptian cigarette. There was something unpleasantly pungent about it, and, coming out of the fresh air, she, unconsciously, resented the too obtrusive perfume; it recalled to her the atmosphere of a cheap Soho restaurant, and shady foreigners with shifty glances. Such an atmosphere was singularly inappropriate in that great hall, with its air of refinement and dignity. She was making her way to the stairs, when the man she had seen in the car came out of one of the rooms. The objectionable cigarette was between his lips, his hands were thrust in his pockets, there was a kind of swagger in his walk. He looked like a gentleman, but one of the wrong kind, the sort of man one meets in the lowest stratum of the Fast Set. Celia noted all this, without appearing to look at him; it is a way women have, that swift, sideways glance under their lashes, the glance that takes in so much while seeming quite casual and uninterested.

Lord Heyton stared at her, curiously and boldly; her youth and her beauty brought a smile to his face, the smile which is very near to an insult, and he removed his cigarette and opened his lips, as if to speak to her. But, as if unconscious of his presence, Celia went up the stairs quickly and looking straight before her. She had seen the smile, and knew, without looking back, that he was standing in the hall and staring up at her.

Instinctively, she felt that Lord Heyton was a man to be avoided.

CHAPTER XV

Somehow or other, Celia was relieved that she was not asked to dine with the family; for she had feared that she might have to do so. She had her dinner in her own room as usual, and afterwards went into the library to do a little work; but she had scarcely commenced when she heard a knock at the door, and a fashionably-dressed young woman entered. As she rose, Celia knew that it was Lord Heyton's wife, and she regarded the beautiful face and exquisitely-clad figure with all a woman's admiration for a lovely specimen of her own sex.

"Oh, may I come in?" said Lady Heyton. "I shan't disturb you, Miss Grant? I do so want to see you. The Marquess has been telling us about you. What a handsome room! May I sit down—you're sure I shan't disturb you, be a nuisance?"

"Oh, no," replied Celia, pushing forward one of the antique but comfortable chairs.

Lady Heyton seated herself, looked round her, and then fixed her eyes on Celia's face, curiously.

"And so you are the lady librarian; and this is where you work? How charming! Why didn't you come in to dinner to-night?" she asked, abruptly.

"I dine alone, in that room," replied Celia, colouring slightly.

"How quaint!" remarked Lady Heyton, with a little shrug. "I shall ask the Marquess whether you can't dine with us; you will be company for me. It was rather dull this evening, and I was terribly bored. It's the first time I've been here, you know; the first time I've seen the Marquess, in fact. Don't you find this great big place rather—rather depressing?" She gave a little shudder, and held out her ring-laden hands towards the fire. "I suppose it's because the house is so old, and there are so few people in it.—But tell me about yourself. You're very young, and—yes, you're exceedingly good-looking. Do you mind my telling you so?"

"Not at all," said Celia, with a smile. "I wish the information was as accurate as it is candid. No, I don't find the house dull. I'm very busy, you see."

"Ah, that makes a difference, I suppose," said Miriam, leaning back and barely concealing a yawn with her hand. "I'm afraid I shall be bored to death if we stay here long. You know, I've only been married a short time, and I hate being bothered."

Celia noted the petulant droop of the almost perfect lips, the faint lines of weariness which trailed from the corners of them, noted the weakness of the chin, the restlessness of the blue eyes which shone like amethysts in the firelight; it was evident to Celia that this beautiful, graceful young creature was not a happy woman. She did not know how much, since her marriage, Miriam had deteriorated, mentally and spiritually. One cannot touch pitch and escape undefiled.

"Oh, I've no doubt you'll find plenty to amuse you," she said. "The country is delightful——"

"Oh, I'm rather fed up with the country," said Lady Heyton. "I've lived in it all my life, you see—one of a poor country parson's superfluous daughters. Oh, I've had enough of muddy lanes and stupid local people. Give me London—and life. One doesn't *live* in the country, one only exists, like a vegetable. Do you like my dress?" she asked, with her irrelevant abruptness; and she cast a complacent eye down her exquisitely-clad figure.

"It is a very beautiful one," said Celia.

"Paris. The worst of Paris is that, once you have had it, everything else seems dowdy. By the way, that's a very pretty frock you're wearing," she added, with an appraising glance.

"I'm glad you like it," said Celia, laughing. "I made it myself."

"Really! How clever you must be! Oh, of course, in the old days I've made dresses myself; but they were always sights. Yes; you must be very clever;

you have good taste, evidently. I've got a maid who's a perfect fool; perhaps, sometimes, you won't mind giving her a hint or lending her a hand?"

"Why, I should be very pleased to do so," said Celia; "though I'm afraid she will not consider my advice or assistance of any great value, Lady Heyton."

"How nicely you said that!" said Miriam, again looking up at Celia, curiously. She possessed intelligence enough to discern, at the first glance, that Celia was not the common, ordinary type of girl she had expected to see; but the repose of Celia's attitude, the timbre of her voice, were making their due impression. "But, of course, you would speak nicely, having to do with books and all that sort of thing. Do you like the Marquess?" she asked, slipping off to another subject, with her usual irrelevance. "He is very stern and grim; and I must confess I'm almost afraid of him. He is quite different from Percy; they're scarcely like father and son—I mean my husband, of course."

"I don't think the Marquess is very stern or hard," said Celia, musingly. "I have only spoken to him once, but he seemed very kind," she added, with a certain hesitation; for she remembered that he had been somewhat stern in the matter of the portrait.

"Oh, I dare say it's only his manner," said Lady Heyton; "and I suppose I'm not a favoured person. You see, he was opposed to our marriage: poor parson's daughter, you know."

Celia coloured with embarrassment; it seemed to her that this beautiful young woman was without reserve, and that her remark had been in very bad taste; but Celia was always ready to make allowances and look on the best side of people, so she said, gently:

"I dare say you will grow to like him. He is sure to like you."

"Think so?" said Miriam. "Well, I hope he will; he ought to like his daughter-in-law; and I mean to make him, if I can. I want to keep the peace between him and Percy; they haven't been the best of friends, as I dare say you've heard. Did you cut that dress from a paper pattern, or how?"

"You've guessed correctly," said Celia, laughing. "It was cut from a paper pattern, given away with a popular magazine."

"Well, it fits awfully well. And there's a style about it; it's quite *chic*. Oh, you really must give a hint or two to that idiot of a Marie. What society is there here? I thought, as we drove from the station, that the place looked awfully dull and quiet. By the way," she went on, without waiting for her question to be answered, "didn't I see you standing at one of the cottages as we drove past?"

"Yes," said Celia. "I had been calling on a friend."

"A friend," repeated Lady Heyton, raising her brows, languidly. "Do you mean the woman with the baby? I thought she looked quite a common, ordinary sort of person."

"I should scarcely call Susie common," said Celia, with a smile. "I like her very much."

"Do you? How quaint! This fire is very jolly. Do you always have one here?" asked her ladyship, as if her volatile mind had forgotten the last subject of the conversation.

Celia told her that the fire was lit every evening, and Lady Heyton, rising with a yawn, remarked that she should often drop in for a warm; the rest of the house seemed to her chilly. Celia gave the required invitation, and Lady Heyton stood looking about her vacantly, and as if she were waiting for the volition to go.

"I say; do tell me your name?" she said, languidly.

Celia told her.

"Awfully pretty name. Mine's Miriam; ridiculously unsuitable, don't you think? So hard and cold; and I'm anything but that. Pity one can't choose one's own name! Do you mind if I call you 'Celia'? 'Miss Grant' is so stiff."

"Oh, not at all," said Celia.

"Thanks very much. What's that?" she asked, starting, her hand going to her bosom, her brows coming together nervously.

The sound of voices, not in actual altercation, but something very near it, came from the hall.

"It's the Marquess and Percy," said Miriam, in a low and frightened voice. "Oh, I do hope they're not quarrelling. I warned Percy. Hush! Listen!"

She stole to the door and opened it slightly, and Celia heard the Marquess say:

"I have promised. The money shall be paid; but I warn you, Percy, there must be an end to this wicked and foolish extravagance. I say there must be an end to it. I do not want to threaten you, but——"

"Threaten!" came the younger man's voice, which was almost insolent and rather thick, as if he had been drinking too much wine. "No, I don't suppose you do. After all, I've got to live. I'm your son——"

"Do not hesitate," said the Marquess. "You would add, my heir. I do not forget it. But do not count too much on the fact. I say to you, do not count too much on it. Percy!" His tone changed to a pleading one. "For Heaven's sake, take heed to what I say. Do not try me too much. There are reasons——"

His voice broke and ceased; with a glance at Celia and a shrug, Lady Heyton opened the door widely, and went into the hall.

"I have been making the acquaintance of Miss Grant," Celia heard her say, with an affectation of casualness. "Are you two going into the smoking-room; may I come with you? I shall feel so lonely in that big, solemn drawing-room."

"Miss Grant in there?" said Lord Heyton, with a nod towards the library. "I should like to make her acquaintance, too."

He took a step towards the door; but Celia closed it and went quickly into the room beyond; and soon afterwards, when the coast was clear, went up to her own room.

CHAPTER XVI

Not only on her own account, but on that of the Marquess, Celia regretted keenly the advent of Lord and Lady Heyton at the Hall. Of the man, Celia had formed a most unfavourable opinion, and she could not but see that his wife, beautiful as she was, was shallow, vain, and unreliable, the kind of woman who would always act on impulse, whether it were a good or evil one. Such a woman is more dangerous than a deliberately wicked and absolutely heartless one.

The coming of these two persons had broken up the quiet and serenity of the great house; she felt sorry for the Marquess, who had been forced almost into an open quarrel with his son on this first night; and she felt sorry for herself; for she had taken an instinctive dislike to Lord Heyton, and knew that she would have hard work to avoid him. There are men whose look, when it is bent upon a woman, is an insult; the touch of whose hand is a contamination; and Celia felt that Lord Heyton was one of these men. She shut herself up in the library the next morning, and though she heard him in the hall, and was afflicted by the pungent cigarette, which was rarely out of his lips, he did not intrude on her; but as she was passing through the hall, on her way for a walk, she met him coming out of the smoking-room. His was a well-groomed figure, and save for the weak and sensuous lips, and the prominent eyes with the curious expression, he was, physically, by no means a bad specimen of a young man; but Celia was acutely conscious of the feeling of repulsion, and she quickened her pace. With his hands still in his pockets, he almost intercepted her.

"Good morning, Miss Grant!" he said, with the free-and-easy manner of a man addressing a dependent. "First-rate morning, isn't it? Going for a walk?"

"Yes, my lord," replied Celia, giving him his title with a little emphasis, and speaking coldly, with her eyes fixed on the ground, her hands touching Roddy, who had not offered to go to Lord Heyton, but gazed up at Celia as if he were saying, "I don't like this man. Let us go for our walk and get away from him."

"Not a bad idea, a walk; tip-top morning," said Heyton. "I'll come with you, if you'll allow me."

Celia bit her lip, and flushed angrily; for the request for permission was so evidently a mere matter of form.

"I would rather go alone, my lord," she said. "I am going to call on a friend."

"Oh, but I can go as far as the door with you, surely," he said, with the smile of a man too self-satisfied to accept a woman's rebuff seriously. "Two's company and one's none."

"But there are already two," said Celia, forcing a smile and glancing at Roddy. "It is very kind of your lordship, but I would rather be alone." She moved on quickly, her heart beating rather fast with resentment, her face crimson. Heyton followed her to the door, and stood looking after her, an evil smile on his face.

"Pretty high and mighty for a typewriting girl," he muttered. "By jove! she's pretty. I like that swing of hers. All right, my girl; I'm not taken in by that mock shyness. You wait awhile. Yes; she's deuced pretty. I wonder how the old man picked her up!"

Celia had gone some distance before she recovered her equanimity. Certainly, this son of the Marquess was a hateful creature, and she could not help wondering how even so shallow and frivolous a woman as his wife could have married him. She had reached the bend of the road, when she stopped short and stared with amazement at a group which presented itself a little farther down.

On the bank adjoining the pathway was seated Lady Gridborough; her hat was on one side, her face was flushed, her mantle dusty and disarranged; but her good-natured face was wreathed in smiles as she watched a young man, standing beside the Exmoor pony and attempting to keep it from rearing and plunging.

"Oh, whatever is the matter?" demanded Celia, as she ran forward.

Lady Gridborough looked up, laughed, and wiped her eyes.

"Good morning, my dear," she said; "you've come just in time to enjoy a little comedy." She nodded at the young man and the frisking pony. "Turk took it into his head to bolt just now, coming down the hill there. I suppose it was only his fun, but we ran up on to the path, the cart overturned——"

"Oh! Are you hurt?" demanded Celia, anxiously.

"Not a bit," replied Lady Gridborough; "but I might have been, for I was mixed up with the cart in some extraordinary fashion. I don't know what might have happened if it hadn't been for that young man there. He appeared on the scene as if he had dropped from the clouds; he disentangled me somehow, set the cart up again, and is now trying to persuade that fool of a pony that this isn't a circus."

At the sound of Celia's voice, the young man had turned his head and uttered an exclamation, and now that Celia saw his face, she, too, uttered a cry of astonishment; for she recognized Mr. Reginald Rex, the young man of the British Museum.

She sprang up and went to him with a hand extended; he grasped it, and they stared at each other for a moment in astonished silence; then Celia burst into laughter.

"Why, how ridiculous!" she said. "To think of meeting you here, and in this way!"

"It's—incredible!" he retorted. "What are you doing here?"

"I may ask you the same question," said Celia.

"I'll tell you directly," he replied, "as soon as I've persuaded this pony that we've finished the trick act."

"Celia!" called Lady Gridborough from the bank. "Come here at once. What does this mean? Do you know that young man? You greet each other as if you were life-long friends!"

"Well, we're not quite that," said Celia, laughing. "We've met at the British Museum. He is a novelist."

For an instant Lady Gridborough looked slightly disappointed; but it was for an instant only.

"Well, he's a plucky young man all the same, my dear," she said. "He really did show great presence of mind, and has been awfully nice throughout the whole business. Fancy your meeting here in this way! What is his name?"

As Celia told her, Reggie, having secured the harness sufficiently, brought the now placid and subdued Turk to his mistress.

"Oh, is it all right?" said her ladyship. "Well, Mr. Rex, I'm very much obliged to you. And so you know this young lady, my friend, Miss Grant! Dear me, how extraordinary. My dear, is my hat straight?"

It was resting on one ear; and Celia, laughingly, but gently, put it straight.

"I was going into the village," said Lady Gridborough; "but I suppose I'd better go home."

"Yes, yes; of course you had!" said Celia. "You must be very much shaken, if you are not actually hurt."

"Very well, then," said her ladyship. "Get in, my dear. And you, too, Mr. Rex, if you've not already had enough of me, and Turk."

"I'll come, and drive," said Rex, with marked promptitude.

"Yes, do; though a child might drive him with a match and a piece of cotton now. This is a very interesting meeting for you two. May one inquire what you are doing in this locality, young man?"

"I'm taking a bit of a holiday—well, scarcely a holiday; for I'm thinking out a new novel," said Reggie, modestly, and with a little blush.

"Dear me, you don't say so," said the old lady, opening her eyes wide. "Wonder how you do it! Come in search of character, I suppose? Well, here's your heroine, anyway."

"Yes, she is," said the boy, now blushing outright and nodding at Celia. "She's been my heroine ever since I first saw her—in the British Museum Reading Room, you know."

"That's a candid avowal," observed her ladyship, dryly, as Celia laughed.

They chatted in this pleasant fashion, and, in due course, reached the Grange. It was quite a merry little lunch, through which Reggie talked incessantly, to the increased amusement of his good-natured hostess, and confirming her good opinion of him.

"Now, you two children can go and sit on the terrace while I have my nap. Wiggins, give Mr. Rex a cigar."

The two went out on the terrace; and scarcely waiting for him to light a cigar,

Celia demanded "his story."

"Oh, well; I've had a stroke of luck," he said, with a long breath. "And it's all owing to you."

"To me!"

"Yes. You remember that 'short' I sent you? But, of course, you don't."

"Oh, yes, I do," Celia assured him. "It was an awfully good story."

"Well, backed up by all the fine things you said, I sent it to the editor of the *Piccadilly Magazine*. He accepted it—perhaps he wasn't well at the time—and more than that, he sent for me. I thought, perhaps, he wanted to shoot me; but, bless you, no! He liked the thing so much that he commissioned me to write a 'long, complete,' twenty thousand words; so I thought I'd kill two birds with one stone, run down into the country for a holiday and business combined. But, look here, before I say another word, you've got to tell me what you're doing here."

Celia told him as briefly as she could.

"Oh, but that's splendid!" he cried, seizing her hand and shaking it, just as if she were another boy. "I say, you *are* a swell; and amongst such swells; marquesses and lords and ladies of high degree! But, I say, I am glad. How happy you must be!"

"I am," said Celia. "But go on, tell me about your novel; what kind of a novel is it to be?"

"Do you remember my telling you, that afternoon at the A.B.C. shop, how, if ever I got a chance, I meant to go in for character, psychology? Good word, psychology! Well, I've got my chance, and I'm going for it bald-headed. Since I saw you, I have been studying Lavater; the physiognomy man, you know—wonderful book!—and I've been fitting imaginary histories to everybody, man or woman, I've met."

"I used to do that," said Celia, dreamily; and back came Brown's Buildings.

"Yes? Of course, one may make an awfully bad shot sometimes; but I'm inclined to think that, as a rule, one is pretty accurate. I mean, that you can judge the character of a man from his face—not so often that of a woman, because she's more difficult, she knows

how to mask her feelings——"

"Thank you," interjected Celia.

"Oh, you know what I mean! She's been the slave of the man for centuries, and she's been obliged to deceive him."

"Thank you very, *very* much!"

"Oh, but she's getting past that, now; she's coming into her own, whatever that may prove to be; and presently she'll go about with an open countenance, and it may be easier for me to study her."

"It's to be a detective story, I suppose?" said Celia.

"Right the first go off!" he assented, admiringly. "Yes; but something out of the ordinary, I hope. I've been through a course of Gaborieau, and the rest of the detective-story men, and I want to come out with something fresh. Of course, what I need is real experience. I suppose I ought to have served my term as a criminal reporter; do murders and forgeries, and all that kind of thing. But, then, I haven't. I must trust to luck and chance. You don't happen to know whether a nice little murder I could sleuth down has been committed here?"

"I'm afraid there hasn't," replied Celia, laughing.

"Rather a pity, isn't it? Never mind! Oh, are you going?"

"Yes, I must go," said Celia. "I won't disturb Lady Gridborough. Will you say good-bye to her for me?"

"Oh, but I'm coming with you," he said, decidedly. "I'll walk with you as far as your place and then come back and make my adieux to her ladyship."

They set off, laughing and talking; and presently, as they came to Susie's cottage, Susie herself, with the baby in her arms, was standing at the door. At sight of Celia's companion, Susie drew back; but Celia called to her and ran up to her.

"Oh, Susie, I'm so sorry!" she said, remorsefully; "but I meant to speak to Lady Gridborough to-day about the christening. I have seen her; but she met with an accident; she is all right, quite all right. I will go up to the Grange again to-morrow, and come in to tell you what we have arranged."

She had taken the child in her arms

and was hugging and kissing it; then, seeing that Susie wanted to retreat, she gave her the child and returned to Reggie, who had been standing by the gate, his eyes fixed on them. He drew a long breath as they turned away, and exclaimed, in a low voice:—

"I say! What an awfully pretty woman! Was that her baby? She looked quite a girl."

"Yes," said Celia, gravely. "Susie is only a girl."

"She must have been married very young," said Reggie, with, evident interest. "What beautiful eyes! But, I say, why did she look so sad? Isn't—isn't her husband good to her?"

Celia was silent for a moment, her eyes fixed on the ground, a faint colour in her cheeks. If he were staying in the neighbourhood, he must inevitably learn something of Susie's story. Would it not be well for her to tell him?

"She is not married!" said Celia, in a whisper.

"Oh, lord," said Reggie, "I'm sorry! Poor girl!"

There was no more light-hearted chatter; he became absent-minded; indeed, they were almost silent till they were close upon the lodge gates.

"You must go back now," said Celia.

"Must I? I say, when can I see you again; and how soon? May I write to you and fix up an appointment, or will you write to me? You will, won't you, Miss Grant?"

"Yes," said Celia. "I want to hear how the novel goes on. Perhaps Lady Gridborough will let us come to tea at the Grange, if I ask her."

They were shaking hands, when they both saw Lord Heyton crossing the lawn. Reggie looked at him in silence for a moment; then he said:—

"That one of the swells of the house?"

"That is Lord Heyton, the Marquess's son," said Celia.

"Friend of yours?" Reggie inquired.

"No!" escaped Celia's lips.

Reggie turned his eyes to her quickly.

"Glad of that!" he said. "Because, if there's anything in the science of physiognomy, that gentleman is a decidedly bad lot."

Celia turned away from the gate and walked slowly beside Reggie.

"You jump at conclusions," she said. "You have only seen him for a moment or two, and at a distance."

"I've got very good eyes," said Reggie; "and a moment or two's long enough; it's the first impression that's valuable; and, as I say, if there's any truth in the theory that you can read a character by facial characteristics, that gentleman is about as bad as they make 'em."

"But—forgive me—that you should be able to judge so swiftly sounds absurd."

"Well, it may be," admitted Reggie, grudgingly. "But I'll bet my last dollar that I'm right. Why, don't you see," he went on, earnestly, insistently, "the man's got all the wrong points; the low, shelving brow, the weak chin, the—the wrong lips. Did you notice the trick he has of looking sideways under his lids? You know what I mean, the furtive 'does-anyone-know' look?"

"I have noticed it," said Celia, reluctantly. "I have only seen him once or twice. I—I agree with you partly, and I don't think he's a good man."

"*Good* man!" retorted Reggie, with a laugh of derision. "You take it from me that he's as bad as they make 'em. It's my belief that he's done something already—something he's ashamed of; something he's afraid may be found out. Oh, laugh if you like; but, look here, Miss Grant, you take my advice and keep clear of that man."

"I mean to," said Celia, as lightly as she could. "And so, as he's in the front of the house, I'm going in at this side door. Good-bye; I'll write to you."

Reggie walked on towards the Grange, and as he approached Susie's cottage, his step grew slow, so slow that, when he came to the gate, he almost stopped; and his eyes searched the door and the window eagerly; but he was not rewarded by a sight of the sad, pretty face which had moved him so deeply.

CHAPTER XVII

To return to Derrick Dene. When Isabel had left the van he lay, with a frown on his face, thinking sadly and troubled by a somewhat unreasonable remorse. He was not a vain man, but he knew that, all unwittingly, he had gained the love of this dark-browed, passionate girl. She was very beautiful; she had nursed him with the tenderness of a sister, a mother, a wife. Why should he not accept the gift which the gods were offering him? Why should he not make her his wife? Even as he put the question, the answer rose to confront him. He was in love with another woman, a girl he had seen once or twice only in his life— the girl at Brown's Buildings.

It was absurd, of course. He might never meet her again; it was more than probable that by this time some other man had discovered so great a prize; she might be engaged, married. The chances were that, though he had thought of her every day since he had left her, she had well-nigh forgotten him, or, at the best, thought of him as a foolish young man who had sacrificed himself for a mistaken sense of chivalry, the man whom she, a slip of a girl, had saved from suicide. Why, he told himself, any feeling she must have for him must be that of contempt. All the same, he loved her, and therefore this other woman could be nothing to him.

The doctor and Mr. Bloxford came to see him; Bloxford full of impish delight and satisfaction at Derrick's recovery, and full also of threats of what he, Bloxford, would do if ever he came across the cause of Derrick's "accident."

An hour later Derrick had another visitor. It was Sidcup. Derrick liked the man; for, notwithstanding his harmless vanity, he was a decent sort, and the courage he displayed in his performance won Derrick's admiration. Sidcup came in and stood beside the bunk, and looked down at Derrick with a grim countenance, and he did not offer to shake hands.

"You're better, Green?" he said. "Do you think you're well enough to have a little talk? Don't say so, if you're not; but I want to have a word or two with you rather badly."

"I'm all right," said Derrick. "Fire

away! It's awfully good of you to come and see me."

"I dunno," said Sidcup, moodily. "I came on my own account—and another's. Look here, Green; it's about Isabel. I want to have it out with you."

Derrick had raised himself on his elbow, but at this he dropped back and his eyes fell, for he knew what was coming.

"Of course you know how it is with her," said Sidcup. "You're not blind, and you must have seen for some time past that she's—sweet on you. I don't say it's your fault; in fact, I'll go so far as to say that you haven't led her on, encouraged her, as another man might have done. That's just the worst of it. Perhaps, if you had, she wouldn't have been so taken with you. It's the way with some women to go after the man that draws back or doesn't meet 'em half-way."

"Look here——" said Derrick. But Sidcup shook his head.

"Better let me finish," he said; "no doubt you'll have something to say when I've done. Of course, you'll deny it, but what's the use? All the company know it. And I—well, I've the best reason for knowing it. Oh, yes, I've come to speak out. I'm sweet on her myself—no, that's not the word, for I *love* her. It's no new affair with me; it's been going on ever since she joined us. She's the one woman in the world for me, and I want her, want her badly. But it's love with me, the real thing, and I tell you straight, Green, that if you care for her, if you'll marry her, I'll stand aside, and I'll do all I can for you and her. That's how it is with me."

Derrick, with his brows drawn straight and his lips shut, held out his hand, for his heart went out to this man who was in the same case as himself. But Sidcup disregarded the proffered hand.

"Wait a bit!" he said. "I want to hear what you're going to say, what you're going to do; for I tell you plainly that, if you don't mean the straight thing by Isabel, you've got to reckon with me, and I shan't miss it, as that fool of a Jackman did. Will you marry her?"

"No," said Derrick, in a low voice,

but decidedly. "Mind, I don't admit the truth of your—your statement; but, if I did, there are reasons——"

"There's another woman," said Sidcup, drawing a long breath.

Derrick's pale face flushed. "There are reasons why I can't marry any woman, Sidcup," he said. "No, I can't tell you them, but you can take it from me that they exist. No, I'm not married already," he added, with a grim smile, as he saw the question in Sidcup's eyes. "The fact is, I'm an outcast and a pariah. Sounds melodramatic, doesn't it? But it's the truth. And you can tell Isabel so, if you like."

Sidcup laughed bitterly.

"Do you think that would make any difference to her?" he retorted. "You don't know much about women——"

"I don't!" interjected Derrick.

"——If you think that would put her off. It would make her more gone on you than ever. She's that sort. And if you don't, or can't, marry her, what are you going to do?"

"The Lord knows," groaned Derrick, desperately.

"Look here, Green, you're a gentleman," said Sidcup.

"Am I? Thank you. But I'm not so sure. I don't know that I've any claim to the title."

"You're a gentleman, right enough; we all know that," said Sidcup. "But you haven't traded on it, I'll say that for you. And there's only one thing for a man to do who is a gentleman——"

"And that is?" asked Derrick.

"To cut and run; to clear out," replied Sidcup. "Oh, don't make any mistake! If you stay on with the company, things between you and Isabel will grow from bad to worse."

"I tell you that it's your fancy, that you exaggerate——"

"She's one of the most beautiful women God ever made," said Sidcup, ignoring Derrick's remonstrance, "and no man could resist for long such a woman, especially when she's gone on him, as Isabel is on you. Yes, there's only one thing for you to do, and that is to clear out as soon as you're able. And if you're the straight man I think you,

you'll do it, for her sake—I won't say for mine."

Derrick rose painfully on his elbow.

"By Heaven, Sidcup," he said, in the stifled voice of a man who is deeply moved, "you're a good chap; and, if I go, it will be for *your* sake. I'd rather cut this hand off than come between a man and the girl he loves."

"Yes, and there's another reason," said Sidcup, with a shake of the head. "Isabel's not the only one; there's Alice."

Derrick's eyes shone angrily now.

"Oh, go to blazes!" he said. "You're out of your mind; you'll be telling me that all the blessed women in the company——"

"Well, we'll let her go," said Sidcup, "though it's the truth. What are you going to do?"

Derrick lay still for a moment or two; then he heaved a sigh. He had found an occupation which, if it did not exactly suit him, provided him with a living, and it was hard to be compelled to surrender it. It seemed to him that he was doomed to be a wanderer, a fugitive; he had flown from man's judgment; now he was told that he must fly from a woman's love.

"I suppose I'll have to go," he said. "I can't stay and make trouble between you and the woman who has been so good to me. God bless her!"

At this Sidcup took Derrick's hand and pressed it.

"I said you were a gentleman and would do the right thing," he said. "God knows whether it will be any good to me, your going; but it will be good for Isabel. Look here, you'll have to pad the hoof without any 'good-byes.' Yes, you will"—as Derrick stared at him. "Why, man, do you suppose she'd let you go if she knew you meant it? You don't know Isabel; you see, you don't love her as I do. She's the sort to go off with you——"

"Oh, stow it! You make me tired," implored Derrick. "But if I must, I must. Seems to me you're having it all your own way, Sidcup. I'm to go off without saying 'good-bye' to all the people who have been so kind to me. Oh, dash it!"

"The only way," said Sidcup, firmly. "And look here," he added, after a pause. "I know I'm doing you out of a good berth, and one that would have been better still if you could have stayed, for the old man's clean gone on you, and in time you'd have been the boss in reality, as well as in name, which you are now. And I don't forget that you're stranded in this outlandish place. Oh, I know how much I'm asking of you, and—and I'm not ungrateful."

"For goodness' sake, say no more about it," said Derrick.

"Only this," said Sidcup, colouring and hesitating nervously. "You may not be very oofish; you'll want some coin. I've saved a few quid——"

"That puts a finish to it," broke in Derrick, flushing angrily, and yet with something very different from anger in his heart. "Get out, or—or I'll throw you out!"

"You couldn't throw out a mouse," retorted Sidcup, with a mirthless smile. "All right. I was afraid you wouldn't accept my offer; but there it is. You've played the part of a gentleman, Green——"

"Oh, go and be hanged!"

"Is there anything I can do for you?" inquired Sidcup, with a friendly and admiring look in his eyes, which, though they were rather too fond of viewing themselves in the looking-glass, were honest and true.

"Yes, you can go and get the property pistol and shoot me," said Derrick. "But leave me alone now, there's a good fellow. I've given you my word."

"And you'll stick to it, I know," said Sidcup, shaking hands with him.

Isabel sat beside her patient that night, as she had sat for the four preceding ones; but few words passed between them, for Derrick seemed to be sleepy—at any rate, he lay with his eyes closed. The next day it was Isabel who was silent; for, woman-like, she felt that a barrier had risen between them, and she was wondering what it could be. Derrick was a strong man, and he recovered quickly. In a day or two he was able to get about, and on the morning of the fifth he sought Mr. Bloxford and, as gently as he could, informed him that he, Derrick, would have to leave his employment.

Mr. Bloxford stared, grew red and exceeding wrath.

"What the deuce does this mean?" he demanded, throwing open his fur coat and sticking out his chest. "Look here, if you're not satisfied——"

Derrick made haste to assert not only his entire satisfaction with, but his gratitude for, Mr. Bloxford's confidence and generosity.

"Then what is it?" shrilled Mr. Bloxford. "Has anybody been roughing you? If so, out he goes. Oh, I can't part with you, and that's the long and short of it. Here, what is it?"

"That's just what I can't tell you," said Derrick, colouring under the sharp, gimlet-like eyes.

Mr. Bloxford scratched his hairless head and looked despairingly at Derrick. From the first he had expected that there were grave reasons for the young man's presence in the company; a man of Derrick's breeding does not join a travelling circus for the mere fun of it.

"Some trouble, I suppose, eh? Got to clear out? I'm sorry, I'm sorry. Look here, can't something be done—can't it be squared? if it's money—well, say the amount"—he threw out his chest again—"and it shall be forthcoming. I'll own up that I've taken a fancy to you, that I'd plank down a biggish sum to keep you with me. No?"—for Derrick had shaken his head.

"Thank you with all my heart," said Derrick. "I must clear out without any fuss. I've got a bundle packed, and I'm going straight off directly I leave you."

Mr. Bloxford's countenance fell, and he whistled.

"Bad as that, is it? Whatever have you done? Well, well, I won't ask any questions. I've met some of your sort before; there's always something shady—though it goes against the grain with me to think that you've done anything low down and mean. But I see there's no use talking."

He thrust his hand in his breast-pocket, in which, with his love of ostentation, he always carried a bundle of notes and some loose gold, and, as he held out his hand to Derrick, there was something crisp in it.

Derrick shook the hand and pressed back the note; he could not speak for a minute; then he said, rather huskily:

"It's all right, Mr. Bloxford. You paid me on Friday night, and I've plenty to go on with."

With that he went out, heavy-hearted, and Mr. Bloxford stood at the door, his extraordinary face drawn into a thousand wrinkles and his lips shaping strange oaths.

CHAPTER XVIII

A week later Derrick was tramping along a dusty road which led to the little town of San Leonardo, where, he had been told, he could find a night's lodging. He was tired and footsore; in addition to the English five-pound note, he possessed but very little of the money with which he had left the circus; though, during his tramp, he had been able to get an occasional job, helping some herdsman rounding up his cattle or assisting timbermen to adjust their loads, and he was hoping that he would find some permanent employment in one of the big towns. He had the road to himself, and was feeling rather down on his luck, as a friendless man in a strange land must do; and, worse than all, he was, at that moment, terribly home-sick. Not for the first time, he had realized how much he had given up when he decided to sacrifice himself for Miriam Ainsley—no, Miriam Heyton, as she was now—the Miriam who, strangely enough, troubled his thoughts but little. Indeed, when he did think of her, with the remembrance was mixed a kind of amazement that he had ever loved her; for the illusion had now left him, and he knew that she had not been worth, at any time, all that she had cost him.

"What a fool I have been!" was the thought, the bitterness of which so many men have felt. But for Miriam, and the villainy of the man who had stolen her from him, he might have been still in England, might—who knows?—in better circumstances, have met the girl at Brown's Buildings. He would have been free to love her and to tell her so.

With a shake of the head, and a setting of the lips, he tramped on, every step giving him pain; and at last he neared the town.

It was a small place, with a few scattered 'dobe houses, one of which bore the sign indicating an inn. Outside the door, with their cigarettes between their lips, their whips lying beside them, sat and lounged a group of cowboys. Derrick had made the acquaintance of many of their kind since the night on which he had checkmated the specimens in the circus, and he had got on very well with them; for your cowboy is an acute person, and knows a "man" when he sees him. As Derrick limped up they stopped talking, and eyed him with narrowed lids.

Derrick saluted them in Spanish fashion, for he had picked up a few phrases, and one of the men made way for him on the rude bench, greeted him with a nod, and slid a mug and a bottle of wine towards him. Derrick drank—it was like nectar in his parched mouth—and the cowboy, with a grunt of approval, tendered him a cigarette and inquired curtly, but not unkindly, where he was going. Derrick replied, in broken Spanish, that he was looking for work.

The cowboy said, "Inglés," and nodded to one of his companions, who, with a sudden flush, said—

"Thought you were a fellow-countryman. On the tramp, mate, eh? Well, I've done that myself, and, between you and me, there's many a better job." He filled up Derrick's mug and eyed him with friendly questioning. "What's your line?"

"Oh, anything," said Derrick, with a smile. "Tramps can't be choosers. You have a ranch here, I suppose?"

The other Englishman nodded.

"Yes, we're on Donna Elvira's ranch, three miles out." He jerked his head in a westerly direction, then looked round at his mates. "Do you think there's any room for him?"

"Might be," replied one. "He'd better go up and see Don José."

The English cowboy translated this for Derrick, adding:—

"That's the overseer. Better go up and see him when you've rested and eaten. My name's Tom Dalton; they call me Tomas, of course. What's yours, and what's your county?"

Derrick said, "Sydney Green," and added, "London."

"Big county that," said Tom, with a grin. "Know anything about cattle? Not much use your going to Don José if you don't."

"I've worked with them on the road a bit," replied Derrick; "and I'm accustomed to horses."

The young man thought that Derrick might stand a chance, and again advised him to eat and rest; and, having proffered more wine, the cowboys presently moved off and left him alone. He engaged a bed of the landlord, got something to eat, and was dropping off to sleep in the moist, warm evening air, when he saw a cloud of dust rising down the road, and presently a carriage, drawn by a pair of magnificent horses, came tearing towards him. At the sound of the carriage the landlord hurried out, and stood beside Derrick, waitingly. The vehicle was of Spanish build, but had a touch of something English about it, and seated in it was an elderly lady, dressed in the local fashion.

There was something in her appearance so arresting that Derrick woke up fully and leant forward to peer at her; as she came nearer he saw that she was not so old as he had thought; for though her hair was snow-white, her dark eyes were bright and lustrous; she was very pale and there were deep lines on her face, which must, in her youth, have been exceedingly beautiful, and was even now handsome, though thin and careworn. She was leaning back, almost reclining, with an air at once graceful and haughty; it was evident to Derrick that she was a personage of some importance, and he was not surprised to see the landlord whip off his hat and bow low, with a gesture of extreme deference.

"Who is that?" asked Derrick, with an interest and curiosity which surprised himself.

The landlord lifted his swarthy brows and, extending his huge hands with an expression of pitying surprise, demanded of Derrick where he had come from that he did not know Donna Elvira.

"The lady of the ranch?" said Derrick, excusing his deplorable ignorance by explaining, as well as he could, that he had come from a distance.

"Donna Elvira of—all the señor sees!" exclaimed the landlord, with a sweep of his hand which included all the earth in view. "The rich, the all-powerful señora. Her *estancia* is on the other side of the hill. It is magnificent, superb, worthy of so great an Excelencia. The señor should trouble himself so far as to view it. It was probable that her Excellency might consent to see the señor, for it was well known that the Donna Elvira was good to all strangers—especially foreigners," he added, nodding encouragingly at Derrick.

Derrick declared himself grateful for the suggestion, and, with greater interest, asked if he could be permitted to wash himself. With the courtesy of his nation, the landlord led him to an outhouse provided roughly with means of ablution, and Derrick enjoyed a thorough good wash; then, feeling quite another man, he set off towards the ranch and the house of the overseer.

José, the overseer, received Derrick with Spanish politeness, and listened phlegmatically to his request for employment; and, in response, informed Derrick that his experience was insufficient; and Derrick, receiving the verdict, was limping away, when a little dog came bounding down the road which wound from the great house to the overseer's lodge. It yapped round Derrick's legs; then suddenly its bark turned to a squeal and it held up one paw and regarded, with an eye of entreaty, the face of the man at whom it had been yapping.

Derrick knew what had happened, and sought for the thing which had run into its foot. He found the thorn, and, not being able to extract it with his fingers, seated himself on the bank, and took out his pen-knife. As he did so, the white-haired lady came, with stately step, round the bend; she glanced at Derrick, but passed him and went to Don José.

"I want to speak to you," she said. "But who is that man, and what is he doing with Pepito?"

Don José explained. Donna Elvira spoke for a few minutes longer; then she turned and walked towards the house. By this time Derrick had performed the surgical operation on Pepito, and was about to set him down, when the lady stopped and said:

"What is the matter with my dog, señor?"

"It was,"—began Derrick, in Spanish; then, as he did not know the Spanish word, he concluded, in English, "a thorn."

Donna Elvira started, but so slightly that the involuntary movement of surprise was unnoticed by Derrick. "You are English?" she said, in his own language.

"Yes, my lady," replied Derrick.

Pepito's foot still hurt him, and, with extreme sorrow for himself, he turned over on his back.

"He is still in pain," said Donna Elvira. "Will the señor oblige me by carrying him to the house?"

Derrick picked up Pepito and followed the tall and stately figure up the drive. Presently they came in sight of the *cása*. Donna Elvira ascended slowly the broad steps of the verandah and seated herself in a satin-cushioned rocking-chair. She was silent and immovable for so long a space that Derrick was inclined to think that she had really forgotten his presence; then, slowly, she turned her head and looked at him, with a kind of masked scrutiny.

"What is your name, and whence do you come, señor?" she asked, in a voice which was low and grave.

Derrick told her that his name was Sydney Green, and that he came from London.

"To seek your fortune here, as so many English do?" she inquired.

"For that—and other reasons, my lady—I mean, señora," replied Derrick.

"And you have not found it?" she said, with a glance at his worn clothes and haggard face.

Derrick shrugged his shoulders; there was no need for words.

"It is often so," remarked Donna Elvira. "There are many English here in this country. Was it wise to leave your native land—your parents, for all the ills that might befall you in a strange country?"

"It was not," admitted Derrick, with a smile.

At the smile, which transformed his face, Donna Elvira's long, exquisitely-shaped hands closed spasmodically on the arms of the chair and a strange expression flashed for an instant across her face; it was an expression almost of fear, of the suddenly-awakened memory of a thing painful, poignant. The expression lasted only for an instant; the next, her face was quite calm again.

"Had you quarrelled with your parents?" she asked, with a kind of polite interest.

"I have no parents," said Derrick; "they are dead."

She was silent for a moment; then she said:

"That is sad; but death is the common lot." There was another pause; then she said: "Don José tells me that you are seeking employment, but that he could find you none. Will you tell me what it is that you have done, the work you were accustomed to do?"

"Well, I've been all sorts of things," said Derrick, reluctantly enough. "By profession I'm an engineer, I suppose; but——" He paused. "Well, I had a stroke of bad luck in England, and I had to leave it and chuck up my profession. Since then I've been a jack-of-all-trades."

"What you have told me has interested me," Donna Elvira said. "Besides," she added, "I have been in England—I had friends there. It is because of this that I desire to help you, señor. You say that you are an engineer. I think there should be work for you here on the *estancia*; there is machinery." Derrick sat up with a sudden lightening of the heart. "We have to send to a distance, sometimes as far as Buenos Ayres, when we

need repairs. Do you think you can undertake this work? Besides—you are well educated, of course, as is the English fashion for gentlemen?"

"I'm afraid not," said Derrick. "Unfortunately, it is not the fashion to give the English gentleman a good education. The other fellows at the Board school get that; but I can read and write, and keep accounts—at least, I think so," he added.

"It is sufficient," said Donna Elvira. "Consider yourself engaged, señor. As to the salary——"

"Pardon!" interjected Derrick, with a grin. "Wouldn't it be better to see whether I'm worth anything more than my board and lodging before we speak of salary, señora?"

"We will consider," rejoined the Donna Elvira; then she looked straight before her again, with an impassive countenance, with so vacant a gaze that Derrick felt that she had forgotten him once more. While he was waiting to be further addressed or dismissed, he studied the pale and still beautiful face. He was so lost in conjecturing the past of this stately lady, living in solitude in this vast house, mistress of a great estate and enormous wealth, that he almost started when, waking from her reverie, she said:—

"I will talk with you further, señor. Meanwhile, will you go to my major-domo?"

Derrick bowed and turned away; but as he was descending the steps she spoke again, and in a voice that, as it seemed to him, quavered slightly.

"You will be good enough to return to me in an hour, señor?"

Derrick bowed again, and went in search of the major-domo. A servant led him through the hall of the house to a small room, where sat the individual of whom he was in quest; but, before he had begun to try to explain his presence in broken Spanish, a servant came hurrying in and, with a muttered apology, the major-domo sprang up and hastened off. He returned after awhile, and, beckoning to Derrick, led him to a bedroom.

"Yours, señor, by her Excellency's instructions." He disappeared, but presently returned and laid a pile of clothes on the bed with another, "Yours, señor. I will await you."

With a feeling of bewilderment, of unreality, Derrick changed into the fresh clothes slowly, eyeing and touching them as if he suspected something of magic in them.

A little while afterwards the major-domo appeared and led him into a luxuriously-furnished room. Donna Elvira was reclining in a chair; she inclined her head slightly and motioned him to be seated opposite her. At his entrance she had shot one swift glance at him, her brows had drawn together, and her lips had quivered; but now she sat calmly, her hands clasped tightly in her lap. Derrick was the first to speak.

"I want to thank you, señora, for your great kindness to me," he said, with all a man's awkwardness. "It is all the greater because I am a stranger, a man you know nothing about——"

He paused at this, and his face grew red, for the story of the forged cheque flashed across his mind.

She raised her eyes and looked at him.

"It is nothing," she said, in a low voice. "One in my position learns to judge men and women by their faces, their voices. Besides, I have told you that I have been in England, and I know when one is a gentleman. But, if you wish, if you think you would like me to know more, you may tell me—just what you please." There was a slight pause. "For instance, your father—was he an engineer, like yourself?"

Derrick leant back and crossed his legs, and looked, not at the pale face before him, but at the floor, and his brows were knit.

"It will sound strange to you, señora," he said, slowly, "but I don't know what my father was—not even what kind of a man he was. I never saw him—to remember him."

"He died—when you were young?" asked Donna Elvira.

"Yes," assented Derrick, "and my mother, too. They must have been fairly well off—not poor, I mean—for they left me, or, rather, the people in whose charge they placed me, sufficient money to bring me up and educate me, and enable me to gain a profession."

A shaded lamp stood on a table at the side of Donna Elvira's chair. As if she found the light oppressive, she moved the lamp farther back, so that her face was completely in the shade.

"You lived in England; you were brought up there?" she said, still in the same impassive voice.

"Yes," said Derrick. "I lived in London, with my guardian—with the people who took care of me—until they died. Then I went to a place in the country, a quiet place where I could study with less interruption than one gets in London."

"You were all alone—I mean, you had no relatives?" asked Donna Elvira.

"No," said Derrick, gravely; and, after a pause, he added: "You will think this strange, too, señora—I know nothing, literally nothing, of my family. It is just possible that I have no relations. There are such cases. Anyway, though of course I asked the usual questions of my guardians, they could, or would, tell me nothing. Perhaps they didn't know. All I could learn was that they had known my mother quite slightly—and that they had been much surprised when I was brought to them with the request that they would adopt me."

"Do you desire to tell me, señor, why you left England?" asked Donna Elvira.

"Yes; I want to," said Derrick, after a moment or two's silence. "I feel as if I wanted to confide in someone. Perhaps it's because you've been so kind to me, have—well, taken me on trust. But I'm afraid I can't tell you, señora. You see, other persons are mixed up with the affair. Let it go at this—I beg your pardon, I mean I hope you will be satisfied if I confine myself to saying that I got into trouble over there in England."

"Trouble?" She knitted her brows. "You mean—what do you mean?"

"There you are!" said Derrick, with a shrug of despair. "I was accused of—well, something that I didn't do, but to which I couldn't plead innocence."

Donna Elvira regarded him closely.

"You shall tell me no more," she said, "but this: You have no other name than the one you have given me?"

Derrick's thoughts had wandered to the little room at Brown's Buildings, and he answered, absently:—

"No; just Derrick Dene."

The stately figure leant forward swiftly, almost as if it had been pulled towards him by an unseen hand. Then Donna Elvira rose, and, in rising, her hand struck and overturned the light table; the lamp fell, the room was plunged in darkness. She uttered a cry; Derrick sprang towards her and caught her in his arms, for he feared that the falling lamp might have set fire to the dress of lace and muslin. He swung the slight figure away from the point of danger, and she seemed to collapse in his arms and cling to him.

"It's all right," said Derrick, in the tone he would have used to an Englishwoman of his acquaintance. "Don't be frightened. You're not alight; you're all right."

As he spoke, still holding her, he reached forward and caught hold of the old-fashioned bell-rope; the major-domo rushed in, calling for lights. When they were brought by the startled servants, Donna Elvira was standing away from him, gripping the back of the chair. Her face was as white as the driven snow, her lids drooped as if she had recovered from a swoon, her lips were quivering. As Derrick, horribly frightened by her death-like pallor, made a movement towards her, she stretched out her hand and her lips formed, rather than spoke, the words, "Go! Go!"

Her woman in attendance hurried towards her mistress; and Derrick, seeing that he could be of no further use, obeyed the command and left the room.

CHAPTER XIX

Derrick was awakened the next morning by a servant-man who brought him a cup of fragrant coffee and the accompanying cigarette. Derrick dressed quickly and went in search of Don José, to get some information which would enable the newly-appointed engineer to set about his duties; on the way, he met the major-domo, and inquired after Donna

Elvira. The man said that her Excellency's maid had told him that her mistress had spent a bad night and was now trying to get some sleep. The major-domo was extremely respectful in his manner towards Derrick, and Don José, when Derrick met him in the patio, greeted him with marked consideration.

In response to Derrick's inquiries, Don José shrugged his shoulders and, twisting his lips into a smile, intimated that, so far as he was concerned, Derrick was free to do, or not to do, anything he pleased; but he led the young man to a shed which he designated as the machine room, and opening the door, with a wave of his hand, presented to Derrick's view a mass of machinery very much out of date and in exceedingly bad order, and intimating, with another shrug and wave, that Derrick was free of the concern, walked off. Derrick strolled round the antiquated engine and rusty pump and chaff-cutters, then took off his coat, turned up his sleeves and proceeded to make a detailed examination; wondering why the worn boiler had not burst and blown the whole kit, and anyone who happened to be near, into smithereens.

It was some time since he had had the handling of machinery, and, for several hours, he enjoyed himself thoroughly, emerging at lunch-time, very hot, and as grimy and soot-laden as a chimney sweep. On his way towards the house he looked up at the windows, and at one of them he saw, or fancied he saw, through a partially-drawn curtain, the face of Donna Elvira; but the curtain was drawn so swiftly that he could not be sure that it was the Donna who had been looking down at him.

She did not appear that day, and Derrick went about his work with a sense of satisfaction and enjoyment which he had not experienced during the execution of his duties at the circus: to the engineer the handling of machinery is as sweet as is the touch of a brush to an artist, the pen to an author. He was interested not only in his work, but in the strange and novel life going on around him. It was unlike anything with which he had come in contact hitherto; not on-

ly was the place overrun with servants, but, on every side, were evidences of a wealth and state which were almost regal and yet barbaric; the magnificent mansion itself was at some distance from the farm building, and the serenity of the house and its surroundings was not intruded upon by the business of which Donna Elvira was the head.

Derrick could not help being struck by the fact that his favourable reception and appointment had aroused no surprise and very little curiosity on the part of the household; and he concluded that Donna Elvira's rule was so despotic that her law passed unquestioned, and that no action of hers was received with astonishment. His position was accepted by everyone without question or remark; the man who had brought him his coffee had evidently been told off as his body-servant, and he served Derrick's meals in a little room adjoining the bedroom, or on the verandah; as the young fellow showed some intelligence, Derrick took him on as an assistant, much to the peon's delight and pride, and initiated him into the elementary mysteries of machinery.

Long before his examination had finished, Derrick had come to the conclusion that it would be necessary to scrap the existing machinery and set up new in its place; and he was anxious to consult Donna Elvira; but though he learnt that she had sustained no injury from the accident in the salon, she did not make her appearance until three days had elapsed. On the evening of the third, as he was sitting on the verandah, smoking a cigarette after an excellent dinner, and dreaming, as the exile must dream, however flourishing his position, of the land he had left, he saw her coming towards the verandah. He sprang to his feet, and, bare-headed, hastened to meet her and give her his hand to ascend the steps. She was dressed in black, and her lace mantilla, worn in Spanish fashion, half-shrouded her face, which was paler and even more worn than when he had first seen it.

"I hope your Excellency has quite recovered?" he said, as he led her to a chair and set a cushion for her feet; and

he performed the little act with a courtesy which was as genuine as strange in Derrick, who, like most men of his class, was not given to knightly attentions; but, every time he had seen this proud and sorrowful woman, some tender chord had been touched in his heart and given forth a note of pity and respect. "I can't blame myself enough for not keeping an eye on that lamp. I hope you were not burned?"

"No, it was nothing," she said in a low voice, her eyes covered by their lids, her lips set. "It was the shock, nothing more. I came to speak to you here because it is cooler, and I wished to see that you were—comfortable; that is the English word, is it not?"

"Yes," rejoined Derrick, with a laugh. "And it's the most important one in the language nowadays. Comfort is the one thing everybody goes for; we've made it our tin god, and we worship it all the time; it's because money means comfort that we're all out for it."

"And yet you are poor," said her Excellency, musingly. "And you are happy?"

There was a note of interrogation in her voice, and Derrick checked a sigh as he shrugged his shoulders, a trick which everybody about the place possessed, and he was acquiring unconsciously; he was dreading that, in time, he should come to spread out his hands and gesticulate like the rest of them.

"Count no man happy till he's dead," he said, a trifle wistfully; and, at that moment, the scene before him, fair as it was, assumed a dreary aspect, and he longed for the grimy London streets, the hustle of the crowd, the smell of the asphalt; and, above all, the stone staircase and the gaol-like corridors of Brown's Buildings. "At any rate, if I'm not happy, it is not your fault, Donna Elvira. Owing to your kindness, I have fallen on clover—pardon! I mean that I've got an excellent situation. And, speaking of that, I'm very glad to see you. I'm afraid you'll think I'm a nuisance, and that, like a new broom, I want to sweep everything clean; but I'm obliged to tell you that the machinery you've got out there is played out, and that it is absolutely necessary to have a new plant. It will cost you a great deal of money, and I don't know where it is to come from—straight from England, I suppose."

She made a movement of her hand, indicating what seemed to Derrick sublime indifference.

"It shall be as you say," she said. "You have been working very hard, is it not? Oh, I have seen you coming from the shed; you looked tired and so——Is it necessary, señor, to get so dirty?"

"'Fraid it is," said Derrick, with a laugh; "the worst of it is, the machinery is even dirtier than I am. 'Pon my word, I don't believe it's had a good over-haul for years."

"Possibly," said Donna Elvira, absently. "The last man who had charge of it was too fond of the wine."

"I can believe it," said Derrick; "anyway, he kept his machinery thirsty enough. What shall I do about it?"

She pondered for a moment or two; then, with a sudden raising of her sad eyes, she said, slowly,

"It must come from England, you said. It is possible to order it from thence?"

"Oh, yes," said Derrick, hesitatingly. "Of course, it would be better if one could buy it on the spot."

"That is so," she agreed. There was silence for awhile, then she said slowly, "Are you content to remain here—Mr. Dene?"

It was the first time she had addressed him by his name, and she did so with an hesitation that Derrick attributed to her uncertainty of the pronunciation.

"Well, I am as content as I should be anywhere out of England," he said, with a candour compelled by her kindness.

She glanced at him with an earnest regard, and said softly, but suddenly,

"It means that you have left your heart there?"

Derrick coloured and lit another cigarette. Again, he felt as if he were obliged to open his heart to this sorrowful, sympathetic woman.

"That is so," he said, gravely.

"You have no father or mother," she murmured, her eyes downcast; "then it must be the girl you love—a sweetheart?"

Derrick nodded.

"Yes, it's a girl I love," he said, with a thrill as he made the confession, and was impressed by the spoken words with the depths of his love for that girl. "Oh, don't misunderstand! It's true that I—love her; but she doesn't love me; it's all on my side, she doesn't even know that I care for her. You'll be surprised to hear that I saw her only once in my life, and then only for a few minutes."

"That is the Spanish way of loving, not the English," she said, with a long breath like a sigh, as she looked at him. "No; I am not surprised. Love is a strange thing, Derrick—pardon!—Mr. Dene; and it comes sometimes, more often than not with the people of my nation, at first sight. Will you think me curious, if I ask her name?"

"Not at all. I don't know it," said Derrick, with a grim laugh.

She looked at him with surprise in her mournful eyes.

"Oh, look here!" said Derrick, more to himself than to the listener whose sympathy affected him strangely and forced his confidence. "I've got to tell you everything, if you care to hear it. You are so clever, 'cute—I beg your Excellency's pardon!—that you will have guessed, as old Bloxford guessed, that I had good reason, or, rather, bad, for leaving England; besides, I hinted it the other night. I'll tell you what that is, if you care to hear it."

"Tell me," she said, in a low voice. "I—I am a lonely woman; I have neither husband nor child; you have interested me"—her voice sank for a moment—"Yes, tell me. I—I may help you——"

"I'm afraid I'm beyond even your help," said Derrick; "but this is how it is."

He told her the story of the forged cheque, suppressing all names, and Donna Elvira listened, as immovable as a statue, looking straight before her, her brows drawn, her lips set. She sighed as he finished, and said,

"The woman you did this for—you cared for her?"

"I did, at one time—or, I thought I did," said Derrick; "but, when I met that other girl, the girl who stepped in like an angel and saved me from suicide, I cared for her no longer. It was as if she had gone out of my life, out of my heart, and another woman had stepped into her place. Do you understand, Donna Elvira?"

"It is not difficult," she said, with a faint smile. "The woman for whom you made so foolish, so wicked a sacrifice was not worthy of you. It is well that you should have forgotten her. This other girl—I do not know her; but I think she must be good and true."

"She's all that," said Derrick, fervently. "If you had seen only just as much of her as I have, you'd know that you were right. She is not a girl who would jilt a man who cared for her, to marry another man for his rank. She's good and true, as you say; as true as steel. Why, think of it: a slip of a girl, scarcely out of her teens, facing, alone, a madman, with a revolver! The sight of the thing gave her the horrors, I could see; but there she stood, firm as a rock, pleading, arguing, insisting, until she'd saved the silly fool. A girl like that is—oh, I can't talk about her. And, what's it matter? I shall never see her again. Besides, it isn't possible that a girl so beautiful, so charming, should be free for long. I may meet her again; but it's long odds that, when I do, it will be to find that she's married, got children—I beg your pardon, your Excellency; you've been very kind to listen to all this and very patient. You see how hopeless it is. I must try to forget her. But that's impossible." He laughed ruefully. "I think of her every day: I fall asleep thinking of her. But that's enough! About the machinery?"

"We will talk of it some other time," she said, rising. "Good-night."

For several days Derrick saw Donna Elvira at a distance only; but, somehow, he was conscious that she was watching him; for now and again, when he was going to or from the shed, he caught sight of the pale face, with its white hair, at a window, or saw her moving across the court; but he did not venture to intrude upon her. While he was waiting for her decision, respecting the new plant, he employed himself in making a kind of survey of the house and the buildings; and he drew up a schedule of the repairs that were necessary and made some suggestions for various alterations. But though her Excellency did not grant him another interview, it was evident that she had not forgotten him, and he knew that it was to her he owed several comfortable additions in and about his rooms, and the increased respect and attention of the servants.

One evening, about a week later, his servant came to him with a message: he was to attend her Excellency in the salon. With a sense of relief, and of pleasure, Derrick hastened to obey the summons. The frail, yet proudly-erect figure was seated in the big chair; she looked thinner and more haggard; and Derrick, as he stood before her, feared that she was still suffering from the shock of the overturned lamp. She held out her hand, for the first time; and as Derrick took it, he felt it tremble under the pressure of his.

"You sent for me, your Excellency?" he said.

"Yes," she answered in a low voice, as she waved him to a chair which had been placed, either accidentally or by her orders, near her. "I have arrived at a decision—about—the machinery. I wish you to go to England for it."

Derrick could not repress a start, and he stared at her, somewhat aghast.

"Want me to go——?" he said, changing colour. "But I'm afraid—have you forgotten what I told you about—about the trouble of the cheque?"

"No, I have not forgotten," she said, in the same low voice. "I do not think you have any need to fear. I think that you were unwise to fly England. And yet I am glad; for—for, if you had not done so, I should not—you would not have come here."

"I'm glad enough that I did come here, your Excellency," said Derrick, warmly. "And I shall be very sorry to leave you, putting aside this question of my safety."

"You will be quite safe, or I would not ask you to go. I have been thinking over your story. I have not always lived in this out-of-the-way part of the world. I have had experience; and I see more clearly than you. I do not think you would have been prosecuted. They are clever, these lawyers, and they would have got the truth out of you. A word or a look on your part would have given them the clue. Besides, this other man; they would have questioned him, and he would have exposed himself."

"That's true enough; that's what I told Heyton——" began Derrick; in his eagerness, unwittingly letting slip Heyton's name, as he had the other evening let slip his own. He broke off and looked down, biting his lip. If he had still kept his eyes on the face of the woman beside him, he could not have failed to see the sudden change which came to that face, the expression of amazement, of fear, of intense excitement. She did not speak, she did not utter a word, but her lips writhed and her thin, long white hands closed and opened spasmodically.

"I'm sorry," muttered Derrick, regretfully, and frowning at his boots. "The name slipped out before I knew it." He laughed ruefully. "It seems as if I were unable to conceal anything from you."

"There is no cause for fear," she said in a tremulous voice. "You may speak to me as you would to a father confessor; as you would to a—mother."

"Oh, I know that," said Derrick, and his own voice shook a little. "Strangely enough—I'm afraid you'll think I'm pretty impudent—but ever since I saw you I have felt——Oh, well, I can't explain." He leant forward with profound respect and a warmer feeling he could not understand. "I suppose it was because you were so good to me; perhaps because you were so lonely, here amongst all these people——Oh, I can't explain, and I'm afraid I'm distressing you," he went on remorsefully; for the frail figure was trembling, and the tears had gathered in the dark eyes. "I'm a blundering kind of idiot, and I'm worrying you with my tuppenny-ha'penny affairs. Forgive me!"

She drew her hand across her eyes; then slowly, hesitatingly, laid the hand on his arm.

"There is nothing to forgive," she murmured. "But tell me. I too have felt—I am a lonely woman; you—you are young enough—you might be— shall we say that I have been drawn to you as you say you have been drawn to me—you said so, did you not?—that I have felt as if I were—your mother."

"I wish to God you were!" said Derrick, huskily, and feeling, with amazement, and an Englishman's annoyance, that his own eyes were moist.

"Let us pretend that we are—mother and son," she said, in so low a voice as to be almost inaudible. "Therefore, as a son, you need conceal nothing from me. Tell me, who is this man whose name escaped you?"

As she asked the question, she made an evident effort to control her agitation, and her voice and manner were well-nigh calm, and infinitely tender and persuasive.

"Oh, Heyton!" said Derrick, feeling that he would be quite safe to tell her everything. "He is the eldest, the only, son of the Marquess of Sutcombe; and, of course, he will be the next Marquess; and, of course, that's the reason why Miriam—Miriam Ainsley—chucked me and married him."

"This Lord Heyton, what manner of man is he?" she said.

"Oh, I'm afraid he's a bad lot; you'll see that, or he wouldn't have played this low down trick on me. He's a weak sort of fellow who has played the fool pretty thoroughly. I met him at the place where the Ainsleys lived, a little village called Bridgeford; and though—it's easy to be wise after the event—I didn't like him much, we got to be kind of friends. He's full of low cunning and I'd no idea he was after Miriam until it was too late. You see the sort of man he is."

"And he will be the Marquess," she said, musingly.

"Oh, yes, nothing can prevent that," assented Derrick, with a short laugh.

"It is a pity," she said.

"A thousand pities," agreed Derrick; "but there you are! It's our system of primogeniture, eldest son, you know."

"If you go to England, you will keep

out of his way," she said.

"Rather!" said Derrick, grimly. "If I go to England—and, of course, I shall if you wish it—I shall keep out of everybody's way. I shall use my assumed name, Sydney Green."

"It will be well to do so," she said, gravely. It was evident that she was considering the matter with all a woman's acuteness. "Yes; I wish you to go to England. There are other reasons—it will be better for you to see the machinery."

"All right, your Excellency," said Derrick, promptly; for he felt as if he had placed himself in her hands. "When would you like me to start?"

"To-morrow," she said. She raised her eyes and looked at him wistfully. "If you are to go, it is better for me—for you—for affairs, that you go at once."

As she spoke, she opened a despatch-box lying on the table beside her and took out two packets. She held one out to him.

"In this you will find some money; sufficient, I hope, to pay all expenses; if it is not, if you should need more, you will address yourself to the branch of the Bank of Spain in England, where I shall place some to your credit. Do not hesitate to use the money; I do not mean for the machinery only, but for any purpose for which you may want it. It is at your entire disposal. You will write to me——"

"Of course," said Derrick. "I shall send your Excellency a regular report at frequent intervals."

"The carriage is ordered, and you will be driven to the station to-morrow. Write to me as soon as you arrive."

Derrick rose to bid her good-bye; but she stayed him with a slight, hesitating gesture and held out the second packet.

"Take this," she said. "It contains instructions for your conduct in—in certain events."

"Sealed instructions," said Derrick, with a smile, as he noticed that the package was thus secured.

"Yes," she said. "You will break the seals and read the enclosed instructions if, at any time, during your absence, you should be in any great difficulty or danger. Do you think this is very strange—mysterious?" she asked, her eyes fixed upon him with a half-apprehensive regard.

"I've not the least doubt you have good reasons for giving me this," said Derrick; "I will not open it unless, as you say, I am in a fix."

"That is well," she said. "You have good reason—a reason I cannot explain," she added hurriedly, and with some agitation, "for trusting me."

"I'd trust you with my life," said Derrick, impelled to the burst of fervour by something in her manner and voice.

She held out her hand, and Derrick took it and pressed it; there was something so melting in the tenderness of her gaze that again he was impelled by a strange influence, and he bent and kissed the hand. As he did so, she laid her other one upon his bent head; it was a touch soft as thistle-down, as caressing as that of a mother; and as he felt it, something tugged at Derrick's heart-strings. He turned away and left the room quickly.

Some time after he had reached his own quarters, and had pondered over the singular emotion which had been aroused in him during the scene, he opened the first packet. It contained a large sum of money, greatly in excess of his possible needs. The generosity of this great lady was amazing. He stowed the notes in his belt and then turned to the other packet. This he sewed up inside his waistcoat; it was too precious to be committed to so commonplace a depository as the purse of a belt.

The following morning, as he stepped into the carriage—Donna Elvira's own carriage of state!—he looked round on the chance and in the hope of seeing her. She was nowhere in sight as the carriage started; but when it was turning the bend of the road, still looking back earnestly, he saw the tall figure standing on the steps of the patio. From the black mantilla which shrouded her, she waved a hand.

CHAPTER XX

Derrick reached London on one of those mornings when she is at her very best, and he felt his heart grow warm within him as he strode the familiar pavements, and inhaled the air which seemed to him laden, not with smoke but with the flowers which were blooming bravely in the parks and squares. He had seen some beautiful places during his wanderings, but it seemed to him that none of them could compare with this London which every Englishman, abuse it as he may, regards sometimes with an open and avowed affection, sometimes with a sneaking fondness.

Derrick was so full of the love of life, so thrilling with that sense of youth and health for which millionaires would barter all their gold, that it seemed to him difficult to believe that he was the same man who, only a few months ago, had paced the same streets, weighed down by misery and despair; indeed, as he thought of all that had happened, the events took to themselves the character of a phantasmagoria in which Mr. Bloxford, the circus people and Donna Elvira moved like insubstantial shadows. But, standing out clearly in his mind, was the fact that he was in London, with his pockets full of money and with one desire predominating over all others, the desire, the hope of seeing the girl at Brown's Buildings.

He would have made straight for "the Jail"; but Derrick's sense of duty had not deserted him, and with a sigh of resignation, he betook himself to an engineering firm, whose offices were in that Victoria Street down which he had almost slunk the night he had left London, a fugitive. He presented his credentials, transacted his business, and then, with a fast-beating heart, walked—he could not have sat in a taxi, though it should exceed the speed limit—to the Buildings.

So great was the emotion that assailed him as he stepped into the cool shadow of the stone passage, that he actually trembled. The whole scene of that eventful night rose before him so plainly that it might have been the preceding one, instead of months ago; in imagination, he could see her face, as she bent over the rail and whispered her good-bye.

It was the hour at which the Buildings is most quiet, and as Derrick went up the stone stairs, he did not meet any one; he stood for a moment or two opposite Celia's door, actually afraid to knock; for, though he had said to Donna Elvira that the girl might be married, that he might have lost sight of her for ever, he had always pictured her as behind that door, and always cherished the conviction that, if ever he should return, he should find her there. At last, he knocked. No response came. He knocked again, and the sound of the diminutive knocker echoed prophetically amidst the stone walls; still there was no response. His heart sank within him, and he leant against the iron hand-rail, gnawing at his lip with a keen disappointment, a blank dismay. He tried to tell himself that her absence might be only temporary, that she would return: it was ridiculous to suppose that she should not go out sometimes, that she should be sitting there within the room, waiting for him: absolutely ridiculous!

He lit a cigarette and waited on the merely improbable chance of her return; the minutes grew into half an hour before he realised that he might wait hours, and that it would be easy to inquire if she were still living there. All the same, he lingered, as if he were loath to take his eyes from that door through which she had come to him as an angel of rescue—no, far better, as a pure, a brave woman.

Presently he heard the sound of slow footsteps ascending the stairs. They paused on the floor beneath him, and Derrick, descending quickly, saw the thin, bent figure of an old man; he held a violin-case and a small parcel of grocery under his arm, and was on the point of unlocking the door immediately beneath that of the girl. The old man turned his head as Derrick came down upon him, and Derrick, notwithstanding the state of his mind, was struck by the nobility and dignity of the thin, wasted face and the dark, penetrating eyes.

"I beg your pardon," said Derrick. "Can you tell me——?"

He stopped, for the old man had dropped the parcel and stood looking, not at it, but at Derrick. Derrick hastened to pick it up, and, instinctively, raised his hat as he handed the small package.

"I'm afraid I startled you, sir," he said, with that note of respect and deference which came into Derrick's voice when he was addressing women and the aged: it was just one of those little characteristics which attracted people to the young man, and made them take to him at first acquaintance. "I wanted to ask you a question about a young lady, the young lady who lives in the room above this." For the life of him, he could not bring himself to ask the question straight out.

Mr. Clendon regarded him with a calm and courteous scrutiny, which, for all its courteousness, had a note of guardedness and caution. "What do you wish to ask about her?" he inquired. He unlocked the door as he put the question, and waving his long, white hand towards the room, added, "Will you not come in?"

Derrick stepped into the plain, meagrely-furnished room, and took the seat to which Mr. Clendon motioned him. The old man set the parcel and violin-case on the table and, taking a chair, sat with his back to the light and waited in silence.

"I am afraid I am intruding," said Derrick, still with that deferential note in his voice. "I shall be glad if you can tell me if the young lady is still living above you."

"Why do you ask?" said Mr. Clendon. "Forgive me, you have not yet mentioned her name."

"I don't know it," said Derrick; "but I may say that I am a friend of hers. I have every reason to be, for she did me a great service. One moment, sir"— as Mr. Clendon opened his lips—"this must seem rather extraordinary to you, but I am sure that she would be glad to see me."

Mr. Clendon's eyes seemed to pierce Derrick through and through; then, removing his gaze, as if he were satisfied, Mr. Clendon said:

"The name of the young lady is Grant—Celia Grant; she is not now living in the Buildings."

Derrick's eyes dropped, and he drew a long breath; his disappointment was so obvious that Mr. Clendon said:

"Is your business with Miss Grant one of importance, may I ask?"

"The greatest importance—to me," said Derrick, who felt somehow inspired to confidence; there was something in this old man's manner and attitude, in the low, rhythmic voice, that harmonized with Derrick's mood and influenced him in a fashion strange and puzzling.

"I am afraid I can't tell you the whole—well, you may call it 'story'; but I may say that I am deeply indebted to Miss Grant, and that I am very desirous of paying that debt—no; I can't do that!—but of seeing her and telling her that her kindness, her goodness, to me were not thrown away."

"An amiable sentiment," said Mr. Clendon, with dignified simplicity. "No doubt, Miss Grant would be glad to hear it from your lips; but she is not here, she has gone."

"I am sorry, sir," said Derrick, rising, and the genuineness of his assertion was attested by the deep sigh which accompanied it. "I don't like to ask you——" he hesitated—"but you would be rendering me a very great service, greater than you can imagine, if you would, if you could, tell me where to find her."

There was a silence. Mr. Clendon sat perfectly immovable; but his eyes were searching Derrick's face, and the young man stood meeting the gaze honestly, candidly, unshrinkingly.

"I do not know whether I should be doing right in giving you Miss Grant's address," said Mr. Clendon at last. "But I will admit that I am tempted to do so."

"If you would——" began Derrick; but Mr. Clendon stopped him with an upraised hand.

"You say that you are a friend of Miss Grant's—I seem to remember you, though I have only seen you at a distance, and then indistinctly. Are you not the young man who lived in the flat opposite hers?"

Derrick's face grew red. "I am, sir," he said. "It was while I was living there that Miss Grant did me the service of which I speak. I was in great trouble; in about as bad a trouble as a man could be; in fact, I had come to a point beyond which it seemed to me—I was a fool!—that it was impossible to carry on. At that moment of folly and madness, Miss Grant came to my aid, and saved me—you will think me extravagant if I say—from death; but that's the real fact. I did not know her name until you told me just now; I saw her for only a few minutes; those few minutes, and her angelic goodness, changed the whole current of my life. Isn't it only natural that I should want to see her, to tell her——"

He broke off abruptly and turned away to the window. As the piercing eyes followed him, they grew troubled, the thin lips quivered and the wasted hand that lay on the table closed and unclosed spasmodically.

"Will you tell me your name?" asked the low voice. "Mine is Clendon."

Derrick hesitated for a moment; then he remembered Donna Elvira's injunction that he should bear his assumed name while in London.

"Sydney Green, sir."

"And you have come from abroad?" said Mr. Clendon. "I can see that by your tanned face, by the character of your attire."

"From South America," said Derrick. "I am here on a mission, on business for an employer. I am afraid I cannot tell you any more; I've only just arrived and am staying at the Imperial in Western Square. If you think I have told you sufficient, if you can trust me, I shall be very grateful if you will give me Miss Grant's address. I wish I could convince you that I am asking it from no unworthy motive."

"You have already done so," said Mr. Clendon, quietly. "I will give you her address. Miss Grant is acting as librarian at Lord Sutcombe's house, at Thexford Hall."

"Lord Sutcombe!" muttered Derrick, with an imperceptible start. The colour again flooded his face; his gratitude, his joy were so great that, for a moment, they rendered him speechless, and his voice was broken when he could command it.

"I don't know how to thank you, sir," he said, and, impulsively, he held out his hand.

Mr. Clendon took it after a moment's pause; and they stood, the old man and the young man, looking into each other's eyes, and Derrick's—no shame to him—were moist. For, think of it! he feared that he had lost the girl on whom his heart had been set ever since the first moment he had seen her; and now this old man had put him in the way of finding her. They stood with clasped hands for longer than is usual; and Derrick was too absorbed in his own emotion to notice the tremor in the thin fingers which grasped his.

"I see that you will go to Miss Grant at once," said Mr. Clendon, with a flicker of a smile, that was not one of irony, but of sympathy.

"By the first train, and as fast as it will take me," said Derrick, with the note of youth and hope ringing in his voice. "Look here, sir," he went on, impelled by a strange feeling, "I may as well tell you that which you have no doubt guessed already. I—I love Miss Grant. It would be very strange, if I didn't, considering that she's the most beautiful girl I've ever seen, and all she did for me. All the time I've been away I've thought of her and longed to see her again. Not a moment of the day or the waking night——But I beg your pardon, sir, I'm afraid you'll think me—rather mad."

"Yours is a madness common to youth, and befitting it well," said Mr. Clendon. "That you should love her is not strange; she is all that you say of her. Are you sure that you are worthy of her?"

"Good lord, no!" exclaimed Derrick, impetuously. "No man that ever was born could be worthy of her; no man could see her, be with her five minutes——Why, do you know, all the while I was talking to you, before you called her 'Miss' Grant, I was tortured by the dread that has made many an hour miserable for me, since I saw her last—the dread that some other man—that she might be married——"

"She is not married," said Mr. Clendon, with a faint smile, "though it is probable that many men have wanted to marry her."

"I've been thanking God that she is free, ever since I gleaned the fact from your words," said Derrick. "I'm going down to her at once. May I tell her that I have seen you, that you gave me her address?"

"You may," said Mr. Clendon. "Miss Grant honours me with her friendship; I hope, I trust, her affection."

After a pause, he added:

"You are staying in England for some time?"

"For some little time," said Derrick, stifling a sigh at the thought of ever again leaving the girl of his heart.

"May I ask you to come to see me when you return to London?" asked Mr. Clendon; and his tone, though courteously conventional, was fraught with a certain earnestness.

"Of course, I will, sir," replied Derrick, promptly. "You have been very kind to me; you might have answered my question with an abrupt negative, have refused me the information; instead of which, you have—well, you have been awfully good to me; you have relieved my mind of a load of apprehension, and set me in the way of finding Miss Grant. Yes; you have been very good to me, and I hope you will let me see you again. Besides, you are a friend of hers, and that's quite enough to make me want to know more of you."

"Then come to me when you return," said Mr. Clendon. "But do not let me trespass on your time, Mr. Green; you must have other claims, those of your people, your parents."

"Haven't any, sir," answered Derrick, gravely. "I'm all alone in the world—for the present," he added, his eyes shining with the hope that glowed in his breast.

"That is a strange statement," said Mr. Clendon, his brows raised, his eyes fixed on Derrick's face.

"But it's true, unfortunately," said Derrick. "I must be going now, sir. Let me see, Waterloo is the station for Thexford. I'll go there and wait for the first train."

He held out his hand and the two men shook hands again; and Mr. Clendon stood at the door and watched the young man as he went swiftly down the steps, as if his life depended on his haste; the old man went back to his room and, sinking into his chair, covered his eyes with his hands and sat as if lost in thought—and memories. And, strangely enough, it was not of the young man he was thinking, but of a very beautiful woman, half woman, half girl, with black hair and brilliant eyes, with the blood of the South mantling in her cheeks, with the fire of the South, passionate, impetuous, uncontrollable, in eyes and cheek; a woman of fire and strong will, hard to understand, impossible to control; a woman to make or wreck a man's life. The woman whose vision rose before the old man, who sat, a bowed and desolate figure, in his chair, had wrecked his. Strange that the meeting with this young man had called up that vision, strange that his face and voice had revivified the memory of the past. With a sigh, a gesture of the flexible hand, as if he were putting the matter from him, Mr. Clendon took his violin from its case and began to play.

CHAPTER XXI

Derrick's mind was in a condition of joyous confusion as the train bore him in a slow and leisurely fashion towards Thexford. Predominant, of course, was the thought that he was on his way to see the girl of his heart. But presently he began to think of the strange old man who had set him that way. Naturally enough, Derrick felt curious about him; for he had been much struck and interested by the old man's appearance and manner. Derrick knew a gentleman when he saw him, and he knew that Mr. Clendon was a gentleman and one of a very fine type; seen in befitting surroundings, Mr. Clendon would have filled completely the part of a nobleman; and yet he was poor and living in Brown's Buildings. Derrick felt strangely drawn towards the old man, but told himself that it was because Mr. Clendon was a friend of Celia's—Derrick had already learned to call her 'Celia' in his mind.

Then the fact that she was librarian to Lord Sutcombe recurred to him. It was a strange coincidence, one of the strangest; and as he faced it, Derrick's intention to go straight to the Hall and ask for Celia became changed. He did not want to meet the Sutcombes: it was just possible that Heyton and Miriam would be there; and most certainly he did not want to meet them. He uttered a groan of impatience: he would not be able to go to the Hall; he would have to find some means of meeting her elsewhere; every moment of delay, every moment that stood between him and the sight of her, assumed the length of years. With his brows knit, and his heart in a state of rebellion, he got out at the little station and looked round him wistfully, irresolutely.

There was a fly at the station steps, but he was in too much of a fever to ride in a crawling vehicle, and he inquired of a sleepy porter the direction of the nearest inn.

"There's no inn here, sir," said the man. "You see, this is really only the station for the Hall; but you'll find a small kind of place in the village farther on; it's called Fleckfield; it's rather more than a couple of miles."

Derrick gave his small portmanteau to the flyman and told him to drive there, and he himself set out walking.

Climbing a hill at a little distance from the station, he caught sight of the tower of a big house and knew that it must be Thexford Hall. And, within those walls, was the girl he loved! He set his teeth and strode on, resentful of every yard that took him from her instead of to her.

A signpost directed him to Fleckfield, and presently he came to the village and to the little inn in the middle of the single street. It was a rustic looking place, with the usual bench and table outside it; and on the former was seated a young fellow in a knicker-bocker suit. He was writing busily on a pad which rested on his knee, and he looked up with an absent, far-away expression in his eyes as Derrick strode in upon his solitude.

"Good afternoon," he said, pleasantly, when he had come down from the clouds; for it was Reggie Rex, busy on the outline of his novel.

Derrick returned the salutation and sank on to the bench beside him; and Reggie, after a comprehensive glance, and one of distinct approval, said:

"You look hot, sir. Have a drink. I can recommend the local ale. It is good though not particularly intoxicating."

"Thanks," said Derrick; and he made short work of the tankard of home-brewed which the landlord brought him. "Are you staying here?" he inquired. "I ask, because I want a room for a night or two."

"That's all right," said Reggie. "They'll be able to give you a room, I think. Your portmanteau has arrived already. Is your name Grey?"

"No," replied Derrick, staring at him with pardonable surprise. "Sydney Green."

"Oh, well, it wasn't a bad guess," said Reggie, complacently. "I saw 'S. G.' on your portmanteau, and 'Green' seemed so obvious that I hit on Grey."

"Are you a detective?" asked Derrick, with a laugh.

"Wish I were!" responded Reggie, with a groan. "No; I'm an author, novelist; and I'm engaged on a big detective story. That's why I get all the practice I can. You come from South Africa?"

"Wrong; guess again," said Derrick, with a smile.

"Then what do you mean by that tanned face?" demanded Reggie, indignantly.

"You can get tanned in other places than South Africa," said Derrick. "I'd tell you where I come from, but I've a feeling that I should spoil your enjoyment in finding out for yourself. Besides, if I did tell you that much, you'd want to know why I have come here."

"Quite right," assented Reggie, approvingly. "That's just what I should want to know. But don't you trouble; I shall find out quick enough. And don't be offended," he added. "You see, I'm obsessed—that's the new word, you know—by this detective business. I want to find out everything about everybody. But there's no harm in me; it's a kind of monomania; and if you don't want me to be inquisitive, just say so."

There was something so inoffensive in this young man's eccentricity, that Derrick found it impossible to be affronted; he leant back, filled his pipe, and smoked in silence for a minute or two; then, driven by the ardour of his desire, by that longing to talk round about, if not directly of, his heart's idol, which obsesses—as Reggie would say—every lover, he said, half-ashamed of his impulse,

"Have you been staying long in these parts; do you happen to know a place about here called Thexford Hall?"

Reggie surveyed him through half-closed eyes for a moment or two; then he said:

"Now, I wonder why you asked that. If you were a friend of the people there, or had business with them, you would have gone straight to the house; instead of which, you come away from them, and ask the first person you meet if he knows it. You will excuse me if I say that I scent a mystery, Mr. Green. By the way, let me introduce myself—it's evident that you have little of the detective in you, or you would have asked me long ago. My name is Reginald Rex, a name with which you are probably unacquainted, but which, I trust, will some day be known to the whole world." He expressed the hope with bland simplicity.

"I am sure I hope it will," said Derrick. "I am sorry to disappoint you, but there is no mystery in the case. I have come here to see a young lady——"

"Miss Celia Grant," broke in Reggie, with an air of quiet triumph. "How did I guess it? My dear fellow, it's as easy as shelling peas! There is only one young lady at Thexford Hall, and she is the one I have mentioned. And you want to see her without coming in contact with the other persons who reside at the Hall. I need not ask if I am right, because your extremely candid countenance confirms my assertion."

"Upon my word, you're a most amusing young man," said Derrick, biting his lip to prevent himself from colouring.

"But I am bound to admit that you are quite right."

"Thanks to your candour. I will now place myself at your service," said Reggie. "The young lady of whom we speak is a friend of mine—Mr. Green, when I rise in the morning, and return to my virtuous couch at night, I never fail to thank a beneficent Providence that I *can* claim her as my friend. Now, what you wish me to do, though you would rather die than ask me, is to arrange a meeting between you and Miss Grant. I will do so, without a moment's hesitation, because of Lavater."

"Because of *what*?" demanded Derrick, staring at him.

"Lavater, Mr. Green, is the author of the best-known work on physiognomy, and physiognomy teaches us whom to trust and to distrust. Informed by my knowledge of the science, I know that you are a man to be trusted, and with this knowledge, I am prepared to befriend you. What time this evening would you like to meet Miss Grant?"

Derrick regarded the strange youth with a mixture of amusement and surprise, not untinctured by jealousy.

"You speak, Mr. Rex, as if you held the copyright of Miss Grant," he said.

"Don't be offended; I'll explain," said Reggie, leaning back and folding his arms, and returning Derrick's gaze with one of extreme candour. "You see, Miss Grant once did me a service——"

"I don't find it difficult to believe that," said Derrick, under his breath.

"No," said Reggie. "There are a certain number of angels in woman guise who pace this wicked and weary old world of ours, and you and I happen to have had the extraordinary luck to meet one. Of course, I see how it is with you; and I might say that I am in the same boat. It's easy enough to fall in love with a star in the blue heavens, the Koh-i-noor diamond, or the second folio of Shakespeare. But I happen to be one of those few men who realise that the treasures I have spoken of are not for them. In the words of the poet, 'I worship Miss Grant from afar.' I kneel at her feet, metaphorically, in the adoration that has no hope of response or re-

ward. If I am any judge of character—which I beg you to believe I am—you, my friend, are not placed in the same category; judging by the salient characteristics of your countenance, I should say that you hope most considerably."

"You certainly are a most extraordinary young man," said Derrick; "and your candour is somewhat overwhelming. But you have hit the nail on the head; and I may as well confess that I am particularly anxious to meet Miss Grant as soon as possible, and that I accept your proffered aid. As you have divined, I do not want to go to the Hall, for reasons——"

"Which you are perfectly at liberty to keep to yourself," said Reggie, blandly. "If, at any time, I should want to learn them, I give you my word I shall have little difficulty in discovering them. Just at the present moment, I am impelled by the sole desire to do Miss Grant a service—and you too; for, if you will permit me to say so, I have taken a physiognomical fancy to you. Will you shake hands?"

With a feeling akin to bewilderment, but without any resentment against his strange companion's eccentricity, Derrick went through the ceremony; and Reggie, rising, said:

"I am now going to the Hall; if you will be in the little wood in the hollow behind the Hall at seven o'clock this evening—but I need not continue."

He rose, settled his cap, and took two or three steps; but stopped suddenly and, coming back to the table, leant his hands on it and regarded Derrick thoughtfully.

"One conjecture, if you will allow me. May we say that the person at Thexford Hall you most particularly wish to avoid is—Lord Heyton?"

Derrick, speechless for a moment, stared at him; then he nodded.

"Quite so," said Reggie, with an air of satisfaction. "Oh, I don't want to know the reason; I just wanted my surmise confirmed. And, by George! I commend your judgment; for, if there was ever an individual in this world an honest man might wish to avoid, it is the gentleman I have mentioned."

With this, he walked off; and Derrick sat for some time in a state of amazement at the quaintness—and, be it added, the acuteness—of his new acquaintance. Presently the landlord served him with a nice little meal, which it is to be feared Derrick did not appreciate; for he scarcely knew what he was eating.

The time lagged intolerably; and long before seven o'clock, he had found the little wood, and was pacing up and down it, his heart beating furiously, as he listened for footsteps; they came presently, and he drew behind a tree, that, for a moment or two, unseen himself, his eyes might rest on the girl he had seen but once, but whose form was enshrined in his heart.

And presently she came; a slim, graceful figure in a plain white dress. The evening was warm, and she had taken off her hat, and was swinging it idly in her hand. When he saw her face distinctly, he noticed that it was calm and serene; there was no expression of expectation in it; she looked as if she were just strolling without any object. Pale beneath his tan, Derrick stepped forward and raised his hat. Celia stopped dead short, and looked at him for a moment with the ordinary expression of surprise at the sudden appearance of a stranger; then she recognised him and, all in a flash, her face changed. First, it was flooded with colour; then it grew pale and her wide-open eyes held a look of astonishment and some other emotion which went straight to Derrick's heart and struck him dumb, so that he stood before her in silence. She was the first to speak.

"You!" she murmured, with a little catch in her voice, her hand going to her heart unconsciously.

"Yes," said Derrick, unsteadily. "Didn't he tell you?"

She shook her head.

"You mean Reggie Rex? No—he asked me to come here, and I thought it was to meet him. I—I am rather startled."

She sank on to the bank, looking straight before her, and, still bare-headed, Derrick stood beside her, speechless. If he had ever had any doubt of the completeness, the intensity of his love for her, that doubt would have been dispelled at that moment. The desire to take her in his arms, to crush her to him, was almost overwhelming; but he remembered that, though he had been loving her all these months, had been thinking of her so constantly that it seemed as if they had been in actual communication, she did not know this. He must go gently with this beautiful creature; he must not frighten her by word or look.

"I'm sorry he didn't tell you; I'm sorry you were so startled," he said, very softly, very gently. "I thought he would have done so."

"I am ashamed," she said, blushing, and forcing a smile to her lips, which were not yet quite steady. "It is very foolish of me; for—for why should I be startled, why should you not be here, anywhere?"

She made as if to rise; but he put out his hand, as if to stay her, and she sank down again.

"Well, there are reasons why I should not come back, as you know," he began; but she looked up quickly and broke in.

"Oh, no, there are not! Don't you know, have they not told you? You have no cause now for—for concealment."

"I've heard nothing," he said. "I have only just returned from abroad. Will you tell me what you mean?"

With a barely-suppressed eagerness, and an unconcealed gladness, she told him of the appearance of the old gentleman a few minutes after Derrick's flight, and gave him the lawyer's message.

Derrick nodded once or twice. "If I'd only known that!" he said in a low voice, "I should have come back at once; come back to tell you what I want to tell you now, to thank you. Oh, but that's absurd! Of course, I can't thank you. You know what you did for me, and you must know that I can't express my gratitude."

"Don't say any more," said Celia almost inaudibly. "I am glad that it is all right now: that you have no cause to fear—and that you've come back to England."

"Are you?" he said, with difficulty controlling his voice. "So am I; but I'm still more glad that I have been able to meet you so soon. You are looking—well." Poor fellow! He wanted to say, "more beautiful than ever; and I love you." "You are happy, I hope?"

"Quite," Celia replied, raising a face that was radiant. And at that moment she was happy indeed, suffused with a strange, sweet happiness which she did not understand. "I have got a splendid berth. But, of course, you know, or you wouldn't be here. Reggie told you."

"Yes," he said, glad to fall on Reggie as a subject for conversation. "He's a strange young man, but he appears to be a good friend of yours."

"Oh, yes, he is. Yes; isn't he singular? I met him at the Museum. Oh, long, long ago—And yet it isn't so long, though it seems so," she added, musingly, and more to herself than to him. "Yes; isn't he quaint?"

"But he's got a good heart," said Derrick, with a smile. Then he felt he could bring the conversation back to themselves. "I am so glad you are happy. I got your address—I can see you are wondering how I got it—from another friend of yours, Mr. Clendon, a remarkably nice old gentleman who was extremely kind to me. Of course, I went to Brown's Buildings the day I arrived."

She blushed and her eyes were downcast for a moment. Why "of course"? She pondered this, with a thrill of the heart.

"Tell me about yourself, what you've been doing," she said. "You won't think me curious? But, of course, I am interested——"

"Naturally, seeing that you saved me, set my feet on a new path," he said; and as he spoke, he seated himself on the bank beside her; but a little lower, so that he could look up into her face. "I've had rather a curious time, since we parted."

Then he told her, as briefly as he could, the story of his adventures. And she listened—well, as Desdemona of old listened to Othello; that is to say, her star-like eyes were fixed on his face, as if they were chained there, and she listened, sometimes her breath growing fast, sometimes with an exclamation of amazement, of fear. Her interest, her absorption were so intense that perhaps she was not conscious that imperceptibly he had drawn closer to her, so that his arm was touching her dress and his face was very near hers. Woman is never so charming to us men as when she is listening to the story of our lives; and, oh, what a sympathetic listener was this beautiful, dainty girl, with her wide-open eyes, her red, parted lips, her little sighs and murmured exclamations!

"Oh, it is wonderful!" she breathed at last. "It like a story in a book! I can see it all—you tell it so well; and yet I feel you are not telling half. And this Donna Elvira—what a good, kind woman she must be!"

"She is," assented Derrick. "I wish she were also a happy one; but I'm afraid she isn't. There is a kind of mystery about her—but I'm afraid you won't understand from my poor attempt to describe her."

"Oh, yes, yes I do!" said Celia. "You make it all so plain. I should like to meet her, to know her."

"I'll tell her so—when I go back," said Derrick.

What had happened? A moment before, the little wood had been all aglow with the rays of the setting sun, her heart had been palpitating with a sweet, delicious happiness; and now, all quite suddenly, the air had become cold, a chill had struck to her heart. Celia's face paled, she looked up at him and then away from him. With the toe of her dainty shoe, she traced a pattern in the moss at her feet; and still with downcast eyes, she said:

"You—you are going back? Of course."

"Yes; I must go back," he said, in a dry voice. "As I told you, I have only come over to do this business. I must go back soon."

"How—how soon?" she asked, scarcely knowing that she spoke.

"Oh, in a week or two, at longest," he replied, his eyes downcast, his voice barely above a murmur.

There was silence for a moment; then she forced a smile and, with difficulty raising her eyes to his, said:

"Of course, you must. Well, I am—am glad to have seen you, to have heard that you are prospering. I—I must be going back."

Again she made a movement, as if to rise; but he took her hand and gripped it tightly, almost fiercely.

"Not yet," he said, his voice choked and thick. "You can't go till I tell you——Oh, don't you know? You must know; something of the truth must have travelled from my heart to yours all these months. Don't you know that I love you?" he said breathlessly.

She sat quite still, her hand in his, her eyes fixed on the tree before her; her heart was beating so fast that its pulsations seemed to stifle her. But through her whole frame, through every nerve of her body, ran a hot flood of ecstatic happiness. His words were still ringing in her heart; mutely her lips were re-forming them: "I love you! I love you!" So great, so ineffable was the joy, that her eyes closed with the desire to shut out everything in the world but the one fact his dear lips had voiced.

"You know I love you," he said in a whisper. "From the first moment—no, let me be truthful, not from the first moment: you remember how angry I was with you; how I resented your dear presence, your interference?—but soon, very soon afterwards, you stole into my heart. And you have been there ever since. Oh, Celia!—think of it! I knew your name only a few hours ago—you are all the world to me, my saviour, my guardian angel. I can't live without you. I want you, dearest; I want you every hour, every moment. Oh, I know I'm a poor lot, of no account, a man with a stain still on his name, but I've got to tell you that I love you. I've thought of this hour of our meeting a hundred, a thousand times, in all sorts of places, in all sorts of circumstances. And now it has come! Celia, I love you, dear, I love you! Speak to me, dear! Oh, I know I'm not worthy of a single thought, a single breath of yours; but let my love plead for me, and—speak to me, Celia!"

She sat enthralled by that magic which has been omnipotent since this weary world of ours began, and will be till it ends. It was easy enough for him to say "speak," but ah, how difficult it was for her to obey, when her heart was too full for words! Instead of speech, she turned her face to him; and laid her hand on his, which held hers nearest to him. There was a thrill of a passionate love in that gentle touch; and Derrick's heart flamed up. He caught her in his arms, and their lips joined in that first ecstatic interchange of soul and heart. Presently, she lay on his breast, her face still upturned to his kisses, her eyes meeting his with the fullness, the fearlessness of a girl's first and perfect love.

Silence reigned in the little wood; a squirrel, which had been watching them from a distance, leapt noiselessly from a branch and stood and surveyed them with piquant interest; the good god Pan hovered about them and murmured his blessings on their mortal love. So long lasted the silence—the ecstatic silence which, indeed, is golden—that time lost its significance and they were caught up into the heaven of eternity.

At last, with a sigh, Celia came back to earth: that earth which his love had turned to a veritable Paradise.

"I must go," she whispered.

"Must you, dearest—Celia?" he asked, with all a lover's reluctance.

"Yes," she said, the word broken with a sigh. "I am sorry; but I must go. I don't know how late it is."

He took the watch from her belt—the very act was a caress—and looked at it.

"We have been here an hour. It seems only a minute. And we must part! That's hard."

"Yes, it's hard," she whispered, with a long breath. "But we shall meet again. Oh, I couldn't bear to think that we shall not meet again soon. You will come—will you come to the Hall?"

He knit his brows.

"I can't, dearest; I can't. Don't ask me why. God knows I want to tell you everything; but—but presently. You can trust me, Celia?"

"I'd trust you with my life, with all that there is of me," she said, with a simplicity that made him catch her to him.

"You must trust me, for the present," he said. "Let me think things over. I can't think now—I can scarcely realise that you are in my arms, that you are mine. Mine! Mine, after all this time of waiting and longing. Tell me once more, just once more, that you love me, Celia."

"I love you!" she breathed, her star-like eyes meeting his unflinchingly. "Oh, how strange it is! I don't even know your name."

He winced imperceptibly, and his lips drew straight. They had almost formed the words "Derrick Dene," but he held them back.

"Sydney," he said. "Sydney Green."

"Sydney," she murmured; and though Derrick hated the name on her lips, yet it sounded the sweetest music.

"You'll meet me to-morrow here, in the morning, Celia? I could not wait all day. Be here at ten o'clock."

"I will."

"By that time, I shall have thought things over; I shall be able to tell you——Oh, dearest, must you go? You seem to take my life with you."

"And I leave mine with you," she said, gravely.

"Celia! You've got my life and my heart in this little hand of yours." He kissed it.

"And do you think I shall not hold them? But I must go. Yes; kiss me once more—only once, or I shall never be able to leave you. I will be here at ten o'clock. It will seem an age——"

He gripped her to him, and kissed her; and he stood, with hand pressed hard against the tree, watching the slight, graceful form till it disappeared from his view.

It may be noted, by the student of human nature, that neither of them had spoken of the woman for whom Derrick had been ready to sacrifice his good name, his life itself. Perfect love means perfect faith, and they were so sure of each other's love and faith, that it may be said neither of them gave the other woman a thought; and if they had done so, Celia would not have been jealous of the past, and Derrick would have re-

garded the boyish passion of which he had been so completely cured, as something nebulous and unimportant. At that moment, he was capable of thinking only of Celia; the past was like a dream, his heart was in the present and future; and his happiness was alloyed by one regret only—that he had concealed from Celia his real name and his connection with the Heytons. But, as he walked on air towards the village, he told himself that such concealment would not long be necessary, that he would tell her the next time they met.

CHAPTER XXII

As happy as Derrick, Celia hurried back to the Hall. So suddenly had come her happiness, so swiftly and unexpectedly had her life been suffused by joy, that she was dazzled and bewildered, as one is dazzled and bewildered by the bursting of the midday sunlight through a bank of clouds. It seemed almost impossible to realise that he was back in England, near at hand, that he loved her, that he had held her in his arms; but the warmth of his kisses still lingered on her lips and helped her unbelief.

As she entered the hall, Heyton sauntered out of the smoking-room; the eternal cigarette was between his thick lips, his hands were thrust in his pockets; the smile, which Celia so much disliked, greeted her appearance, and his eyes roved over her with, the expression which always raised Celia's resentment.

"Hallo!" he exclaimed, with an offensive familiarity. "Been for a walk? By Jove! you look ripping, Miss Grant! Been enjoying yourself, to judge by the look of you! I wish you would let me come with you; I might have enjoyed myself too. I'm pretty well bored stiff; there's nothing to do here, and the old place is dull as ditch-water; gives me the horrors. But I say, you'll be late for dinner. Hurry up and come and dine with us, won't you?"

"Thank you, Lord Heyton," said Celia, "but I dine alone in my own little room."

"What nonsense that is!" he said, impatiently. "Here, Miriam"—turning to his wife, as she came languidly down

the stairs—"just tell Miss Grant that she's got to dine with us to-night; she'll keep us from going to sleep."

"Won't you?" asked Miriam, listlessly. "I wish you would; I'm sure Lord Sutcombe would like you to."

"Thank you very much," said Celia, as she passed on; "but I would rather dine alone. I've a great deal to do to-night and must not waste time over dinner."

"Oh, look here——!" began Heyton; but at the moment the butler advanced with a telegram. Heyton took it and looked at it, and his manner changed instantly. He stared at the telegram; his face growing pale, his teeth closing hard on the cigarette.

"What is it, Percy?" asked Miriam, as Celia passed into the library.

"Eh?" he said, with a start, as if waking up. "Oh, nothing! Yes, it is; it's dam bad news, I can tell you."

"Money again!" she said, with an impatient shrug of her shoulders.

"Yes, money; and a lot of it," he retorted. "Look here, Miriam, I'm in a hole, and a precious deep one this time. Hush! Here's the old man!" He broke off warningly, as the Marquess came into the hall.

He looked weary and careworn, and his shoulders drooped in the way that had become habitual with him of late; and he frowned slightly as he glanced at the cigarette between his son's lips; for he disliked its penetrating aroma as much as did Celia. Dinner was announced and they went in; they talked in the desultory fashion which was customary with them, and the Marquess, apparently lost in thought, did not notice Heyton's pallor and the furtive glance which every now and then he directed towards his father. As usual, Heyton did not refuse the butler's offer of wine, and, after awhile, a hectic flush rose to his cheek, and he began to talk with a strained and unnatural gaiety. Miriam, who had been watching him, presently stretched out her hand towards his glass with a significant frown; but her husband glared at her and, reaching for the decanter, helped himself. Suddenly, apropos of nothing,

Heyton, addressing the Marquess, said:

"Have you noticed that pendant Miriam's wearing?"

The Marquess raised his eyes and smiled at her.

"Very pretty, my dear!" he observed.

"A present from Percy," she said, fingering it. "I'm glad you like it."

"A wedding present," said Heyton, with a sneer. "Not much of a present; but it was the best I could afford. She's pretty enough to deserve a complete fit-out of diamonds, don't you think so?"

The Marquess looked up again, half curiously, as if he wondered whether there were any object in Heyton's remark; his lips moved as if he were about to speak; but he closed them again and his eyes went back to his plate. Miriam rose and went to the drawing-room, and almost immediately afterwards, the Marquess left the table, saying, as he passed Heyton,

"That port is rather heavy, Percy; don't drink too much of it."

The weak and vicious face grew red and, with a sneer, Heyton retorted,

"Oh, if you begrudge me a glass of wine——" But he spoke under his breath, and the Marquess apparently did not hear him.

Heyton finished the decanter and then, with a rather unsteady step, betook himself to the smoking-room, fell into a chair and rang the bell for coffee and cognac. He drank off the brandy, and took the telegram from his pocket. It was still in his hand when Miriam came into the room, closing the door behind her. She stood regarding him in silence for a moment, with the look of the disappointed woman in her eyes. Not for the first time did she realise the folly of her conduct; she had thrown over Derrick Dene for title and position; they were hers now, but to get them she had sold herself to a man whom she had learned to despise.

"Phew!" she breathed. "The room reeks of brandy." She went to a window and flung it open. "I should have thought you had had quite enough to drink at dinner——"

"You may keep your thoughts to yourself, my lady," he said, with a scowl. "What I drink is my own business. And, by George! you'd drink, if you had as much on your mind as I have."

"You'd better tell me about it," she said; "you'd better tell me what that telegram means. And—Percy, I want to know why you called your father's attention to my pendant. You had some meaning, some object."

"Oh, you noticed it, did you?" he said, with a sneer. "I would scarcely have given you credit for so much intelligence. Well, I had a meaning. I wanted to call the old man's attention to the fact that you, his daughter-in-law, had only a few trumpery trinkets to wear."

"Do you mean that you wanted him to buy me some, to give me a present?" she inquired, with a puzzled frown.

"No, not buy you some," he replied slowly, his eyes evading hers. "There's no need to buy any. I'm thinking of the family diamonds; there's any amount of them already; a tiara, necklaces, bracelets—and, I remember, a string of pearls as good as any in the country. What's the use of them, locked up in the strong room at the bank? Why doesn't he give them to you; they're yours; by right, as you might say."

She seated herself on a chair at a little distance from him and looked at him intently; her face had become flushed at his rough description of the Sutcombe jewels.

"What made you think of them tonight?" she asked.

"I've often thought of them," he answered, evasively.

"But you almost asked Lord Sutcombe to give them to me," she persisted. "He must have known what you meant; I could see it by his face. But you were foolish, Percy, to think that you'd get them that way."

"What other way of getting them is there?" he asked, sullenly.

"I don't know," she said. "You should have waited."

"Waited!" he repeated, with an oath. "I tell you I want those diamonds; and I must have them, and at once."

"*You* want them?" she said, as if mystified; then her face grew crimson for an instant, but paled again as she leant forward. "You mean—you can't mean, Percy, that you would *sell* the diamonds? Oh, I see what that telegram means; you've been betting again! You promised me you wouldn't. But a promise isn't much to you. You've been betting again, and you've lost a great deal of money."

"You've guessed it right the very first time," he said, with an attempt at a laugh; but the sweat had gathered on his forehead and he wiped it away with a shaking hand. "It's Skylark. He was a dead certainty; I got the tip straight from the stable; they must have pulled him; they must have sold me. But I've got to pay up; I've *got* to. Do you hear? If I can't find the money by Monday week, I shall be posted. I suppose you know what that means?"

"You'll be ruined," she said in a low voice.

"Cut by everybody; chucked out of every club, marked for life. Yes; sounds pretty black, doesn't it?"

"Is there no other way of getting the money?" she asked, wearily.

He shook his head. "If you knew anything at all, you'd know there isn't," he said, sullenly. "The old man has just paid some biggish debts for me. That was what the row was about the other night. He warned me that it was the last I'd have from him for some time, and he'll keep his word. Curse him!"

Miriam, accustomed as she was to his bad language, shrank.

"Percy! Your own father!" she whispered, with a shudder.

"Oh, don't go into heroics!" he said. "You'd curse everything and everybody, if you were in the plight I am. And look here, you've got to help me. You and the old man have been getting on better than I expected; if he hasn't taken a downright fancy to you, he's got used to you and treats you civilly. Can't you give him a hint about the diamonds? See here!" He leant forward, his hand gripping the table, the sweat gathering on his face again, his weak eyes bulging in his terrible eagerness. "I could raise money enough on the things to tide me over this bit of bad luck until

I struck a winner. Directly he'd given them to you, we'd go up to town; he wouldn't know whether you were wearing them or not. But there! if it comes to that, we could easily get them copied in paste; they imitate them so closely you can't tell the real from the sham. Fact. Why, half the women in London are wearing shams, and nobody's any the wiser."

She rose, her hand clutching at the lace on her bosom.

"I—I can't do it, Percy! Besides, it wouldn't be any use. It's strange how little you know of the Marquess; you, his own son! Why, even I, who have known him so short a time, know that to ask for them, to hint for them, would be of no use. They are the family diamonds; they're something more than jewels in his eyes—don't you understand that?—he will have to grow to like me a good deal better than he does before he gives them to me. It's no use, Percy. You must think of something else."

"There is no other way," he said.

He dropped back, his head sunk on his breast, his teeth gnawing at the projecting under-lip; and she stood looking down at him, though scarcely seeing him. Suddenly he glanced up at her, his lips twitching; a certain furtive gleam in his light eyes.

"Oh, well, never mind, old girl!" he said, with an affectation of concurrence. "Perhaps you're right. We'll give it up. Don't worry; after all, I dessay I shall find another way out. Here! you'd better go back to the old man. Go and play to him; he likes you to." As she moved towards the door, he called to her in a cautious undertone. "Here! Miriam, come back. Now I come to think of it, I'm sure you're right as to not giving him a hint. Don't do it; in fact, if he says anything about the diamonds, say that you'd rather not have them at present. You can say that we're likely to be moving about, and that you'd rather wait until we've settled down. You might lose 'em, don't you know."

Miriam looked at him, as if puzzled by this sudden *volte-face*; then, with a slight shrug of her shoulders, went out of the room. When the door had closed on her, Heyton rose and began to move about the room unsteadily. His narrow forehead was contracted, as if he were thinking deeply; his lips worked, his hands closed and unclosed in his pockets in which they were thrust, and he glanced from side to side furtively. So might a criminal look while plotting a coup more than usually risky and dangerous. Presently he came alongside the table on which the footman had placed the spirit-bottles and syphons. Heyton mixed himself a stiff glass of whisky and soda, drank it almost at a draught, then nodded at the reflection of himself in the mirror opposite him.

"I think I could work it," he muttered. "Yes, I think I could work it."

CHAPTER XXIII

Miriam went on to the drawing-room. The Marquess was sitting in his usual deep chair, his hands folded on his knees, his head bowed; he looked as if he were asleep, but he was not; he was thinking, at that moment, of the half-tipsy son he had left in the dining-room, of the thin, bent figure of the old man who had suddenly reappeared on that morning months ago at Sutcombe House. What a terrible tangle it was; what a mockery that he should be sitting here at Thexford Hall, while the real owner was living in poverty in London! His thoughts were almost too bitter to be borne, and the so-called Marquess crouched in his chair and stifled a groan.

Thinking he was dozing, Miriam went straight to the piano and began to play. When she had finished the piece, she was startled—for she had been going over and over in her mind the scene in the smoking-room—by the grave voice of the Marquess saying,

"Thank you, Miriam. That was very beautiful." He paused a moment. "My wife used to play that; it is a favourite of mine. Please go on, if you are not tired."

She played a nocturne of Chopin; and he rose and stood at the fireplace, with his hands folded behind his back. As she turned and looked at him, he said, with a smile,

"That is a pretty pendant, Miriam. I think you have not many jewels, have you?"

She started, and turned her head away from him.

"Oh, I have quite enough," she said, with a laugh. "You must remember, Lord Sutcombe, that I am a poor clergyman's fourth daughter, and that I am not accustomed to much jewellery."

"You are my son's wife, my dear Miriam," he said, with a slight smile. "And a lady of your position has usually quite a quantity of jewellery. Personally, I do not attach much importance to the decrees of fashion, but I suppose that it is as well to comply with them. Has Percy ever by chance spoken to you of the family diamonds?"

The blood mantled in Miriam's face for a moment; then left it paler than before.

"No," she replied.

"Ah!" said the Marquess. "Of course, there are some. Indeed, there are a great many, and some of them are very beautiful, very valuable; in fact, I do not think I should exaggerate if I were to say that some of the stones are priceless; not only in a monetary sense, but because of their size and quality. There are, too, historic associations," he added, thoughtfully.

There was a pause; Miriam drooped over the piano, touching a note here and there softly.

"Yes, some of them are historic," resumed the Marquess meditatively. "There is a necklace which belonged to Madame du Barri, and another which Queen Elizabeth gave to one of her ladies-in-waiting. An ancestor of ours was a son of hers. I think the time has arrived when the jewels should, so to speak, be resurrected; that they should pass into your possession."

Miriam's heart beat fast; but the flush of gratification did not rise to her face, for she was thinking of the base, the nefarious uses to which her husband would put these historic jewels.

"Indeed, they almost belong to you by right," said the Marquess. "They have always gone with the title."

His voice grew gradually slower, and presently he stopped and looked straight before him, as if he had forgotten her presence. Indeed, he had done so; for as he spoke of the title, there rose suddenly, like a cinematograph film thrown on the screen, the bent figure, grey face and piercing eyes of the real owner of the title. Not for the first time, he, the false Marquess, was giving away that which belonged to the shabbily-dressed old man who had refused to accept the position which was his by right of inheritance. The pause was a momentary one only, and the Marquess went on,

"I am a widower; fortunately, Percy is married, and the family jewels really belong to you. You shall have them."

Miriam moistened her lips; her heart was beating thickly. As a woman, she desired the jewels; as a wife, she must obey Heyton.

"Oh, how good of you!" she said, trying to keep her voice steady. "Indeed, it is more than kind of you, Lord Sutcombe. But—but I don't think I ought to accept them—now. They must be of very great value——"

"They are," he interjected, not complacently but with a sigh; for he recalled them as they shone on the neck and arms of his dead wife.

"And I feel as if they would be a great responsibility," Miriam continued. "Percy thinks of—of going abroad, of travelling for a time. Perhaps, when we come back and have settled down, you—you will be so good, so kind as to give them to me. I can't thank you enough."

Her voice broke; for weak and foolish as she was, she could not but think of the still weaker and more vicious man who had planned so base a use for the Sutcombe diamonds.

"Very well, my dear," he said, in a kindly voice. "We will leave them to their repose in the safe upstairs. I brought them down from the bank, intending to give them to you."

"Upstairs?" she said, in something like a whisper, a frightened whisper.

"Why, yes," he said, simply. "They are in the safe in the little room adjoining my bedroom. I have not seen them since my wife died," he added, with unconscious pathos.

Scarcely knowing why, a vague dread, a presentiment of evil stirred within Miriam's breast.

"Oh, ought they not to be sent back to the bank, Lord Sutcombe?" she said in a low voice.

"Perhaps they ought," he said, gravely. "You are thinking of burglars," he added, with a smile. "You need not be apprehensive; the safe is a remarkably good one; one of the best, I believe, and I carry the key about with me always. I have it on my watch-chain. I don't think the most modern and scientific burglar could break open the safe; at any rate, he could not do so without making a noise which someone in the house would hear. Oh, they are quite secure from burglars, believe me, Miriam."

"I am glad," she said, almost inaudibly. "Shall I play you something else."

"Do," he responded. "Where is Percy?"

"In the smoking-room, I believe," she replied.

He went to her and laid his hand on her shoulder.

"Percy is too fond of the smoking-room," he said, gravely. "Miriam, I do not wish to intrude—I have always held that no man has a right to interfere between his son and his wife. But—forgive me, Miriam—I am anxious about Percy. You, who are his wife, must have seen that—forgive me again—that he needs guidance. He is too fond of—what shall I say?—of pleasure, the sensation of the moment. I had hoped that his marriage would have wooed him from—from the self-indulgence to which he had yielded in early life. Miriam, I count a great deal upon your influence," he wound up lamely and with a deep sigh.

Her head bowed still lower over the keys, and she nodded.

"I know," she said. "I will do my best. But you know Percy!"

He sighed again. "Yes, I know," he assented. "There are certain weaknesses in most families which crop up, now and again, like ill-weeds, in some member; I fear that Percy—Don't cry, Miriam, we will hope for the best; and, as I say, I rely on you, I rely on you very much. You look tired, my child; it is time for your beauty sleep. I will go and find Percy."

She stretched out her hand with a sudden apprehension.

"No, don't!" she exclaimed, with a catch of her breath. "I mean, that I think he has gone to bed. He was very tired."

The Marquess nodded, as if he understood.

"Very well, my dear. Now go. But don't forget," he said, as he held her hand and kissed her on the forehead, "the diamonds are yours, whenever you would like to have them."

When she reached her room, Miriam sank into a chair and covered her eyes with her hands. She was weak and foolish, but she was not so weak and foolish as not to be touched by the kindness of the Marquess. She was glad that Percy had changed his mind about getting the diamonds, though she could not guess why he had done so. When the Marquess next offered them to her, she would refuse again to accept them until Percy had found some other way out of his difficulty. She knew that the diamonds were almost sacred in the eyes of the Marquess, not only because they were family heirlooms, but because his wife had worn them; and she shuddered at the idea of their falling into Percy's hands, the deceit and treachery which he contemplated.

She dismissed her maid when she heard Percy enter his dressing-room; she listened to his movements with a sense of uneasiness; he had already become indifferent to her, and a feeling of actual dislike of him was growing up within her. Presently the door between the two rooms opened and he looked in.

"Hallo! not in bed?" His voice was thick, as it always was at that hour of the night; but he spoke with affected lightness and smiled. "You and the old man been having a palaver, haven't you? Did he say anything about—the diamonds?" he added, casually.

"Yes," she said, without turning her head from the glass. "He offered them to me; but I refused them, as you told me to do."

He had been fumbling at his collar, but as she spoke, his hand fell to his side and he looked straight before him, with a curious expression on his face.

"That's right," he said, after awhile. "It wouldn't have done to have seemed too anxious for them, greedy. He'll think all the better of you. Let 'em lie at the bank a little longer, till we come back from the Continent."

"They're not at the bank; they're in the safe in Lord Sutcombe's dressing-room," she said, unthinkingly. Her eyes were still averted from him, and she did not see the sudden change in his face; it had grown absolutely white.

"Oh!" he said indifferently, too indifferently. "In the safe upstairs, are they? Then he meant giving them to you? Well, they're all right there. Don't you take them: I mean, put him off. Look here, I've thought of another way out of the mess I'm in, Miriam. After all, it would have been playing it rather low down to pop the things, to play tricks with them; they're the family diamonds, you know."

"Yes; your mother wore them," said Miriam in a low voice. "I'm glad you don't—want them, Percy."

"That's all right," he said, with a forced laugh. "Don't you worry yourself."

He closed the door and sank into a chair in his dressing-room. He was shaking, as if with ague; for the little plan he had formed in the smoking-room was now rendered of no avail.

The little plan can be stated in a few words. There is a certain fascination in forgery; it is so beautifully easy; you have but to write another's man's name, copying that man's handwriting, and the trick is done. Percy had tried his hand at the game already, and they say that a horse that once stumbles is certain to fall again. He had intended forging an order on the bank for the delivery of the jewels: and now they were not in the bank but here in the house. Within a few yards of him were diamonds and other precious stones, the possession of which would save him from ruin. The sweat broke out on his face, his lips grew parched, and he tried to moisten them with a tongue that was almost as dry. He knew the safe well enough, knew that even a skilled burglar would find it difficult, if not impossible, to break into it. The diamonds were within his reach, with only the door of that safe between him and them. It would have been far better for his purpose, if they had been at the bank!

Cursing his luck, the miserable man went on with his undressing.

CHAPTER XXIV

When Derrick left the wood—and how loath he was to leave it, for Celia's presence seemed still to haunt it!—and returned to the inn, he found Reggie still with his writing-pad on his knee. He glanced up, as Derrick sank into the seat beside him, and said drily,

"You look almost offensively happy, Green. I need not ask you if I am to congratulate you."

"Congratulate away," said Derrick, with so obvious an expression of satisfaction that Reggie nodded and smiled. "Have you been working all the time?"

"No," replied Reggie. "There has been an interlude. I have been for a walk. Green, did you ever meet an angel?"

"I have just left one," said Derrick, almost involuntarily.

"I beg your pardon. I forgot that there were two in this wicked old world of ours. Well, I've just parted from the other one. She was walking, with her wings folded, and a basket in her hand. It was heavy; and, after a time, I plucked up sufficient courage to ask her to let me take it. She would have refused, but the child she was carrying on her other arm was not very comfortable."

"There is a child?" said Derrick, with a smile. "I thought you had embarked on a love-story."

"There is a child," assented Reggie, gravely. "And it is a love-story," he added, still more gravely. "But the love is all on my side—at present."

"Oh, I see; a widow," said Derrick, not by any means lightly; for, to your lover, love is a sacred subject, and he is full of subtle sympathy for his kind.

"Very much a widow," said Reggie, with a touch of bitterness, and looking straight before him. "She not only permitted me, after much pressure, to carry the basket, but she allowed me to speak to her. She said very little to me—angels are not obliged to talk, you know; it is quite sufficient for them to exist. I carried the basket to the cottage," he went on in a low voice and dreamily, "and she said, 'Thank you.' When an angel says 'thank you'—But no doubt you have heard one repeat the simple, magic word and know its effect on you. To-morrow I shall be on the road at the same time, and, if Heaven is very kind to me, I shall meet her, and again she will be carrying a basket. You think I am very confiding, Green. Well, I feel that I've got to tell someone; just as you feel that you want to tell me about your angel."

Derrick smiled, and coloured.

"There's something weird about you, Rex," he said. "You'll be a great success as a novelist; you know human nature. Yes—it's strange!—I'm longing to tell someone of the great happiness that has fallen to me."

"Tell away," said Rex. "Of course, I saw, the moment you came in sight, that it was all right. You walked as if you were treading on asphodel, and you carried your head as if you'd bought the whole world. I'm very glad." He sighed and shook his head. "Yes, I'm glad, though I love her myself—in a way. But I'm going to be a brother to her, and therefore—if you'll permit me—to you, too. I hope you have made her very happy."

"I hope so," responded Derrick; "and I hope to make her happy all her life."

"You'll be married soon, I suppose?"

"Yes, if Celia will consent," replied Derrick, looking before him as if he saw a vista of ecstatic years stretching into infinity. "I will marry her as soon as she will have me, and I will take her to South America, where I have work—and friends," he added, as he remembered Donna Elvira.

"Of course, she'll go with you anywhere," said Reggie. "You're a lucky man, Green! But I'm sorry you're going so far away. I shall lose you both. You see, I include your honoured self, because, as I have said, I have already a sneaking fondness for you. May one, without being too intrusive, ask if it is necessary for you to leave your native land?"

"It is," said Derrick, quietly. "I've no place, no foothold here—and there are other reasons with which I needn't bother you."

"Oh, you wouldn't bother me; but I'm not curious. Or, rather, I am, but friendship sets a limit to my curiosity. Well, I must be going. I am to make an after-dinner call, by invitation, on a lady. Literally a lady—Lady Gridborough." Derrick turned his head sharply, and Reggie, noticing the movement, asked blandly, "Know her?"

"I've heard of her," answered Derrick, shortly.

"Delightful old lady," observed Reggie. "As she is a great friend of Miss Grant's, you'll come to know her, of course. She is very kind to me and asks me up to the Grange, that's her place, to smoke a cigarette when I've done my work; indeed, whenever I care to go. Sometimes we talk, sometimes I wander about the garden. She regards me as something between an orphan child and a freak of nature; to her, an author is a kind of imbecile which is to be humoured and cossetted. Well, so long! Shall I tell you what you'll do for the rest of the evening? Yes, I will tell you, whether you want me to do so or not. You will sit here and moon——"

Derrick reached for Reggie's empty tumbler and made a feint of throwing it at him, and Reggie went off, laughing.

If he did not sit in the same place all the evening, certainly Derrick "mooned," as Reggie had prophesied. The mention of Lady Gridborough had recalled the past, when he had been a favoured friend of the old lady's. He knew that she thought him guilty of wronging Susie Morton; it was just possible that she had heard of the forged cheque. He bit his lip with mortification and a dull anger, as the desire rose in him to go up to the Grange and clear

himself. But he could only do so by breaking the promise he had given to Heyton, by ruining Miriam's happiness.

He had suffered so much already for the sacrifice he had made, that it seemed to him an absolute waste of it to divulge the truth. Once again, there was Miriam, whose life would be wrecked if her husband were exposed. He must still remain silent, still bear the burden which he had taken upon his shoulders. Fortunately, there was a chance that he might persuade Celia to marry him very soon; they would leave England and the past behind them. She trusted him, would still continue to trust him; and some day, not to-morrow, as he had decided to do, he would tell her everything.

Long before ten o'clock the next morning, he was in the wood; and, as the clock struck, Celia came towards him. As he held her in his arms, indeed, at the very first sight of her, all his doubts and difficulties fled. At first they spoke but little; for there is no need for speech where perfect love exists. But presently, perhaps unconsciously, Celia led him to talk of his adventures; she had heard many of them yesterday, but she wanted to hear all again; she was insatiable. Every person he had met interested her.

"I seem to know them all," she said; "you describe them so beautifully to me. I should like to meet that funny old Mr. Bloxford and the circus people; but, much more than any of the others, the lady, Donna Elvira, who was so kind to you. I love her already!"

Derrick was silent for a moment; then he said:

"You shall meet her soon, if you will, dearest. Don't be startled, Celia. I'm going to ask you to do something, a great thing. I am going to ask you to marry me soon, at once. I want you to come back with me."

They had been walking slowly through the wood amongst the trees, his arm round her; she stopped, the blood suffused her face, then she turned pale. She was silent for a moment or two as he looked down at her yearningly, anxiously; then she said in a low voice,

"I will, if you wish it."

He drew her to him, and kissed her passionately, gratefully.

"You will, Celia?" he said, astonished at her goodness to him.

"Yes," she said, simply. "Does it seem so great a thing? No, don't answer. I feel mean; for, dearest, I'm only too ready. Oh, it's no use my trying to conceal my love. Think of the time we have been parted, all the months I've been thinking of and longing for you! Why should I refuse to marry you, now, this minute, if I could?"

He was silent, as she lay on his breast, her face upturned to his, her eyes, glowing with woman's tender passion and woman's glad surrender, meeting his fearlessly and yet with a little pleading in them, as if she were begging him not to think her immodest.

"I'm not worth such love as yours," said Derrick, his lips drawn straight. "I'm overwhelmed by it. You're too good for me to touch, dearest—and you're going to marry me, to be my wife!"

She laughed at him softly. "Don't put me on too high a pedestal," she said. "I shall tumble off some day and the fall will be so great. I'm just an ordinary girl, whose only merit is that she loves the best, the dearest man in the world. Such a lucky girl, dear!"

"All right," he said, with a laugh that was rather broken. "We'll leave it at that; it's too wild an assertion to contradict. Though the luck's all on my side, God knows. Now, let me think—it's hard to think when I'm holding you like this, when my heart's jumping and something's shouting in my ear, 'She's going to be your wife. Your wife!' I don't know much about the business of being married—I've never been married before, you see—but I fancy it's possible to get a special licence. I don't know how you manage it; but I'll find out. Oh, by George! I'll ask our friend, Reggie Rex; he appears to know everything, the human heart included. Dearest, I hope you won't mind: I told him about—ourselves, our happiness, last night. Not that it was necessary to tell him, for, with that weird penetration, acuteness, of his, he guessed it the moment he saw me, when I came back from you."

"I don't mind his knowing," said Celia. "I don't mind anyone knowing; I'm so proud, so happy!"

Derrick bit his lip and was silent for a moment; then he said reluctantly, hesitatingly,

"Celia, will you mind if I ask you, if I tell you that—that there are reasons why I want our engagement, our coming marriage, to be kept secret. Secret between us three."

She looked up at him with slight surprise in her eyes; then she said, after a momentary pause,

"I do not mind. I am sure there are good reasons——"

"Which I'd tell you, I want to tell you," he broke in, frowning; "but I can't. It's a question of honour——"

She put her hand on his lips. "There's no need to say any more. I don't want you to tell me. If it would help you, I will tell you that I guess it is something to do with that—that trouble which brought us together and separated us."

Derrick nodded.

"I understand," she said. "Dearest, shall we come to an agreement about all this? Shall we agree to forget it, to treat it as if it had never happened?" She pressed his arm and, of her own accord, drew closer to him. "Let us pretend that you and I met in the wood yesterday, for the first time."

"Would to God we had!" he broke out; then he went on, quickly, remorsefully, "No, no, I wouldn't lose that night, our first meeting, in 'the Jail.' That's far too precious a memory, Celia. It was then I fell in love with you, that you wiped out the past, that you gave me back life itself. No, I can't lose that. But we'll forget everything else—for the present, at any rate. Now, let's talk about our—wedding. I'll get Reggie Rex to help us, and we'll be married as soon as we can. I shall have done my business in London in a very short time, and we'll start for the ranch as soon as possible. The country is very beautiful, the house, the whole place, is charming; you will like the life——"

She smiled up at him. "Yes, I know.

But, Sydney, don't you know that I should like any place, if I lived in it, with you?"

Unconsciously, they had left the wood and were now standing by the gate on the roadway. It was all so still and solitary that they stood, hand in hand, looking at each other and lost to everything else in the world; they were so lost that they did not hear the sound of a carriage coming round the bend of the road; and Lady Gridborough's jingle was upon them before they had time to escape. In the little carriage were her ladyship and Reggie Rex. Celia was the first to see them, and with a faint exclamation and a burning blush, she gripped Derrick's hand, and looked round as if to fly into hiding. But they were standing in a little clearing, and there was no time to get back to the woods. As the jingle came up to them, Lady Gridborough put up her lorgnette and surveyed them,

"Why, bless me!" she said. "That looks like Celia Grant. It is! Who is that with her? Celia!" she called. "Celia!"

Then suddenly her voice faltered, the hand that held the lorgnette shook, her face seemed to stiffen and, in a low voice, she said to Reggie, who had pulled up Turk,

"Drive on! Drive on quickly!"

"Certainly," said Reggie, who had raised his hat to the pair, and was regarding them with a benedictory smile. "But what's the matter?"

"I—I know that young man," said Lady Gridborough. "What is Celia doing with him? She doesn't know——"

"Doesn't know what?" asked Reggie, as he persuaded Turk to resume his amble.

"That he's a very wicked young man; that he has no right to be in her company, to be standing there with her, all alone. Yes; he's a very wicked, unprincipled young fellow."

"Hold on, Lady Gridborough!" said Reggie, blandly. "I must tell you that you're abusing a friend of mine."

"A friend of yours!" said Lady Gridborough. "Well, he was a friend of mine once." She sighed. "He is one no longer; and, if you take my advice, you will

have nothing more to do with him."

"There is no person on earth whose advice I value more highly than yours, Lady Gridborough," said Reggie, as blandly as before; "and in most matters, I should accept it and follow it without hesitation; but, in this matter of my friend, Mr. Sydney Green——"

"Mr. Sydney—what?" broke in the old lady, evidently much agitated. "Oh, an alias, of course; yes, I'm not surprised that he should be ashamed of his own name. But, Celia, Celia Grant—oh, it is too sad! I must tell her, warn her."

"My dear Lady Gridborough," said Reggie, smoothly, "I'm going to ask you a great favour."

"What is it?" said Lady Gridborough, glancing over her shoulder at Derrick and Celia in a half-fearsome way. "I can't think of anything else but that young man and—and Celia Grant. Such a dear, sweet girl!"

"My favours concerns both the wicked young man and the dear, sweet girl," said Reggie. "I am going to ask you to refrain from uttering your warning; for two reasons. First, because Miss Grant is in love with him, and wouldn't listen to you—and wouldn't believe you, if she did listen to you; and secondly because, if I may use a vulgarism quite unfit for your aristocratic ears, you will upset the apple-cart."

"Apple-cart!" echoed Lady Gridborough, looking round confusedly. "What apple-cart? I thought for the moment we were going to run into something! You mean that you want me not to speak to Celia, to tell her what I know about your precious—Mr. Sydney Black?"

"Green," corrected Reggie, suavely. "Yes, that's what I want, Lady Gridborough; and I shall be eternally grateful, if you will consent to perform that operation which has hitherto been considered an impossible one to your sex."

"Operation!" repeated Lady Gridborough, staring at him. "What are you talking about now? What operation?"

"Holding your tongue, dear Lady Gridborough," said Reggie. "Though not fatal, it is always painful; but you really must perform it on this occasion—for Miss Grant's sake, to say nothing of mine."

As the jingle drove on, Derrick and Celia stood watching it in silence. She had seen the sudden change in Lady Gridborough's manner at sight of Derrick; the old lady's agitation had been too obvious, the cut had been too direct, to be mistaken. Celia's heart ached for her lover, and she could not bring herself to look up at him; but her hand stole into his and grasped it with loving pity and sympathy.

"You see!" said Derrick, with a touch of bitterness. "The man you are going to marry is an outcast and pariah, Celia. That old lady was once a friend. I was fond of her, am fond of her still, and she, I think, was fond of me; but you see how she regards me now. How can I ask you to marry me! I'll give you back your promise, Celia."

"Generous offer refused without thanks," said Celia, trying to speak lightly; then her voice grew grave and sweet, as she said, in a low voice, "Do you think it would make any difference to me if a hundred Lady Gridboroughs, if all the world, turned their backs on you? She does not know what I know; that you are innocent, that you sacrificed yourself, are still sacrificing yourself, for another person?"

"You're speaking about the forged cheque," said Derrick, moodily. "But there's something else. See here, dearest—God bless you for those sweet words, for your trust in me!—but there's something else. It was not because of the cheque that Lady Gridborough cut me just now—I'm not sure that she knows anything about it—but for something else she thinks me guilty of; something worse than forgery, something unutterably mean and base—Oh, I've got to tell you!"

"Not now," said Celia, resolutely. "If you were to tell me now, I should feel that you think Lady Gridborough's conduct had forced you to do it; and I want you to tell me, if ever you do so, of your own free will." She paused, then she put her hands on his shoulder and looked up at him, with all her soul in her eyes. "Dearest, don't you know that it is a joy to me to feel that I am trusting you, that

I am proving my love for you? Oh, let it go at that"—how soon she had caught his phrases! "And now come back a little way through the woods with me. And try to forget Lady Gridborough. Why, sir," she went on, with a tender, bewitching playfulness, though her eyes were moist, "you ought not to be thinking of any lady, old or young, but me."

When Derrick got back to the inn, he found Reggie at work on his masterpiece.

"Put that away for a minute or two, Rex," he said. "I want to talk to you. Do you know how to get married?"

"You catch your bride and bridegroom, dress them carefully, place them in a church, add a parson and mix slowly and carefully. There is also another way, much more expeditious and less trouble. You obtain a fresh, fair-sized special licence——"

"That's it," said Derrick, nodding. "Be serious, Rex, if you can. I want to know all about it."

"Quite so. And you've come to the right shop," said Reggie. "A novelist knows everything, or what's the use of him! I'll tell you all about it. And so you're going to marry your true love out of hand?" he said, when he had imparted the required information. "I don't blame you. If my angel would consent to marry me, I'd marry her the first available day, hour, instant. But why this haste on your part? I should have thought Miss Grant would have stipulated for the usual fuss and flare-up, bridesmaids, wedding cake, speeches, reception, et cetera."

"She ought to have them all," said Derrick, with a sigh. "But there are reasons why we should be married at once."

"One angel the less in England," said Reggie, with a sigh. "Well, you leave it all to me. I'll fix it for you, as the Americans say. By the way, do you know my friend, Lady Gridborough?"

"I did, but I don't," said Derrick, shortly. "At least, she doesn't know me now—as you saw. No, I can't tell you. Confound it all, I'm like a man in a beastly novel, a man 'with a secret,' a mystery."

"'Beastly novel!' I forgive you the blasphemy," said Reggie, "because I treasure you. A real live man with a secret is more precious than rubies in the eyes of a novelist. There, go in and get something to eat, if you can eat; I couldn't, if I were going to marry Celia Grant."

"And I can't—eat, I mean," said Derrick, and with something between a laugh and a sigh he rose and went into the inn.

CHAPTER XXV

Heyton slept badly that night and came down to breakfast after Lord Sutcombe and Miriam had finished theirs and gone out. He was in a bad temper, cursed the footman who waited on him, and when he had drunk a cup of coffee and made pretence of eating a piece of toast, mixed himself a glass of soda and whisky and went out.

He wandered about the park, and did not come in to lunch, but when he appeared at dinner, he was more than usually cheerful and talked to Miriam and his father in the aimless and futile way with which a man talks when he is engaged in the unaccustomed task of making himself agreeable. Both Miriam and his father noticed that he was more sparing of the wine than usual, and Lord Sutcombe, who thought that Miriam had given Percy a hint, glanced at her gratefully.

"Where have you been all day, Percy?" asked Miriam, masking her indifference with a show of curiosity.

"Oh, I've been mouching about," he said. "Looking round the estate generally." He fingered his glass and glanced across at the Marquess. "They seem to look after the preserves pretty well," he said; "but I noticed that there was a gipsy encampment down by the pool. Unpleasant sort of characters to have about you. I should clear them away, father."

"I know the gipsy encampment you mean," said the Marquess; "but they are pitched on that piece of common land; it is just outside the estate, and we have no power to remove them. Besides," he added, "I've a kind of liking for them; they do no harm; and they are, well, picturesque, don't you think, Miriam?"

"That's all very well," said Heyton, with a forced laugh; "but I don't know about their doing no harm. They're most of them thieves, I should say."

"We can spare a fowl or two," said the Marquess, with a smile. "And a broken hedge is soon mended."

"Oh, if it were only the fowls," said Heyton. "But I daresay some of them would fly higher than hen-roosts. For instance, nothing would be easier than to break into the house here; and there's plenty to tempt them—plenty of silver, I mean," he added, hastily and with a furtive glance at the Marquess.

"I don't think gipsies commit burglaries," said the Marquess, in his precise way. "They would find some difficulty in getting away with their booty. It would be easy to trace them."

"All the same, I'd try to get rid of them," said Heyton, doggedly. "I saw one or two of them, evil-looking chaps, lurking about the plantation."

"Looking for wood for their fires, no doubt," said the Marquess. "But I'll speak to the steward, if you wish it; though, as I say, they are on common land and it will not be easy to turn them off."

"Well, don't blame me when it's too late," said Percy, with a shrug of his shoulders.

Departing from his usual custom, he went into the drawing-room with his father and sat there, listening to Miriam's playing and singing; and it was he who suggested bed.

"I'm a bit tired; had a long tramp to-day," he said, yawning and stretching his arms.

"You ought to walk more, Percy," remarked the Marquess. "If you'll allow me to say so, I don't think you take enough exercise. You ought to ride; but perhaps you will when the hunting begins."

"Can't afford to hunt," retorted Heyton, with an unpleasant laugh. "Horses cost money."

"You shall have some hunters," said the Marquess, with a contraction of his brow. "I had thought of speaking to you about it. We will discuss it later on."

"All right," said Heyton, ungraciously. "Well, I'm off."

He went upstairs, and Miriam and the Marquess followed him soon after. Just as she was ready for bed, Heyton opened his dressing-room door and, looking in, said:

"I'm going to sleep in here to-night, Miriam."

He had often occupied the bed in his dressing-room; generally on nights when, if the truth must be told, he had drunk too much and was ashamed that Miriam should see him.

"Very well," she said, indifferently.

He closed the door and turned the key softly, took off his things and put on a thick dressing-gown over his pyjamas; then he sat down in a chair, with his hands thrust in the dressing-gown pockets, his head sunk on his breast, his teeth gnawing his lip. He was listening intently. Presently he got up, went to the bed and disarranged the clothes, giving them the appearance of having been slept in; then he went back to his chair and sat and listened again.

The faint noises of a big household retiring to rest grew less by degrees and then ceased; and presently all was perfectly still. He sat motionless, still listening, for another hour, two; then he rose and, opening the outer door stealthily, stopped, with craned head, still listening. The silence was unbroken, and with noiseless tread, he passed along the corridor to his father's door and, with his ear to the keyhole, listened again. He could hear his father's steady, long-drawn breathing, the breathing of a man in a deep sleep.

With a gesture, as if he were controlling his nervousness, Heyton tried the handle of the door; the door was not locked and he opened it and went in. The house was lit by electricity, and a small lamp was burning beside the Marquess's bed. Heyton stole across the room, in his felt slippers, and looked down at the sleeping man for a moment; then his furtive, bloodshot eyes went towards the small table beside the bed. There was a carafe of water and a glass, the Marquess's ring and his watch and chain on the table. The chain was an old-fashioned affair, with an extra ring, and on this ring were two keys, the key of the safe and a smaller one. Heyton knew that it was the key to the jewel-case.

His hand shook so much that, for a moment or two, he was afraid to touch the chain, lest it should jingle and wake the Marquess; with an effort, Heyton controlled the shaking hand, and, after some fumbling, took the keys from the ring; as he did so, his eyes wandered apprehensively from the things he was purloining to the face on the pillow; but in reality his movements had been noiseless, and the Marquess had not awakened.

With the keys in his hand, Heyton stole into the dressing-room adjoining, and closing the door softly, turned up the electric light. At sight of the safe, his courage rose, his nerves grew more steady; he had been careful to drink very little that night, and his brain was clear. He unlocked the safe and looked inside it. There were bundles of papers tied with tape and, at the back of them, a box covered with morocco leather. Heyton's breath came fast and his eyes glistened; he had seen that box once before, and knew that it contained the Sutcombe jewels. He took it out of the safe, closed the door and had got half-way across the room when he stopped suddenly; for it had occurred to him that, if he took the box, the Marquis, if he chanced to go to the safe, would miss it: it would be safer to empty the box of its precious contents and replace it in the safe. As he had guessed, the smaller key fitted the lock of the box; he opened it and, at sight of the diamonds and the other gems, he caught his breath, his eyes dilated.

There is a mystic fascination in precious stones and, gazing at them, Heyton yielded to that fascination and forgot for a moment, as his eyes dwelt on their flashing beauty, the need which had compelled him to steal them; but presently he released himself from the spell, thrust the jewels into the capacious pockets of his dressing-gown, locked the box and replaced it in the safe. As the safe door clanged softly to, he heard, or fancied he heard, a slight noise in the adjoining bedroom; the sound, actual or only fancied, struck a sudden terror to his craven heart and he sprang towards the door leading on to the corridor. The handle turned, but the door did not open: it was locked, and the key was not in it.

The noise in the Marquess's bedroom grew more distinct, and it had now resolved itself into the sound of footsteps. Livid with terror, with the perspiration standing out on his forehead, Heyton leant against the door as if powerless to move, powerless to stand upright. The door between the dressing-room and the bedroom opened; instinctively, Heyton stretched out his hand, found the switch, and extinguished the light.

"Who is there?" came the Marquess's voice. "What is it? Who is there?"

The voice came nearer; the Marquess was now in the dressing-room. Heyton knew that his father was standing still; that, in another instant, he would be calling for assistance. But the Marquess did not speak; he made a movement, and Heyton guessed that his father was returning to the bedroom to turn up all the lights there.

With a smothered oath, the wretched man stole forward, felt for the fireplace with his foot, caught up the poker and, feeling his way round the wall, reached the bedroom door. As he did so, the Marquess reached it also and actually touched his son. Heyton drew back a pace, swung up the poker and struck at the figure he could not see; there was a cry, a choked groan, the sound of a body falling to the floor; then a death-like silence.

Shaking in every limb, the poker still grasped in his hand, Heyton leant against the wall, his other hand clinging to it, as if for support. The clock on the mantelpiece seemed to tick a thousand times as he crouched there, staring, with protruding eyes, into the horrible darkness; then, with a gasp, as if he were suffocating, he felt his way round to the switch, and turned it on. The light fell on the figure of the Marquess, lying on its back, where he had fallen; his arms were stretched out, he was quite mo-

tionless, and a thin stream of blood was trickling from his forehead; it had already reddened his face and made a small pool on the carpet.

Heyton stood and gazed at this horrible sight, as if he were turned to stone. He was like a man who has been suddenly struck by paralysis; it seemed to him as if the whole of his legs and feet had been turned to lead, and that he should never again be able to move them, that he would be forced to remain there until the servants came and that— that horrible thing lying at his feet were discovered.

For some minutes he remained in this condition of coma, stupor; but presently, gradually, he recovered the use of his limbs, his brain began to work again, and he asked himself whether there was any reason for the terror which had obsessed him. Of compunction for the awful crime there was nothing in his mind or heart. That the man he had struck down was his own father, did not count; every fibre of his being was absorbed, to the exclusion of everything else, in the desire for his own safety. So gigantic was his selfishness, that the working of his mind was not disturbed by the enormity of the crime he had committed; he saw now that, as events had turned out, he had acted unwisely in taking the jewels from their box; and, alertly and with something like calmness, he unlocked the safe, replaced the jewels in the box and left the safe door open; he was actually turning away, leaving the jewel-case in its place, when his cupidity got the better of him and he took up the case, hid it under his dressing-gown, and went towards the bedroom door.

As he reached it, he glanced over his shoulder at the silent, blood-stained form lying on the floor; he wondered whether his father were dead or only stunned. For a moment, he wished that the blow had been fatal: he, Heyton, would be the Marquess; there would be plenty of money ready to his hand, there would be no need to steal his own jewels, he thought, with an hysterical giggle. But he could leave nothing to chance now. With another glance at the

motionless figure, he stole from the room and reached his own.

The unnatural calm which had supported him during the last few minutes had deserted him by this time, and, in closing the door, he did so clumsily enough to make a sound; the sound, slight as it was, struck him with renewed terror, and, in crossing the room, he stumbled against a chair and overthrew it; and let the two keys slip from his fingers. The sound of the falling chair was loud and distinct enough to fill him with apprehension, and he stood breathless and listened, as if he expected the whole household to awake.

There was a movement in Miriam's room, and he heard her voice calling to him softly.

"Was that you, Percy?" she asked, in the tone of one just awakened from sleep.

He was silent for a moment; it seemed hours to him—then he slipped into the bed, and, with a yawn, as if she had roused him from sleep, he replied,

"What is it?"

"I don't know," she said. "I thought I heard a noise."

"Oh, that!" he said, with another yawn. "I knocked over the chair by the bed, reaching for a glass of water. For goodness' sake, go to sleep and don't bother!"

Mentally cursing his wife, Heyton closed his eyes and tried to think. Strangely enough, his lack of imagination helped him; the imaginative man, in Heyton's position, would have conjured up all the terrible possibilities which environed him; but Heyton's mind was dull and narrow, and so he was able to concentrate on actual facts and actual chances.

Up to the present, he told himself, there was absolutely nothing to connect him with the robbery and the—murder, if murder it was. He felt sure that the Marquess had not seen him in that brief moment, when the old man stood in the doorway; if he had done so, he would certainly have spoken Heyton's name; there was nothing to show that the blow had been dealt by Heyton; with the selfishness of the baser kind of criminal, he had refrained from examining the motionless figure, lest he should be stained by the blood which flowed from the wound. No; the robbery would be laid to the charge of the ordinary burglar.

Then suddenly his mind switched off with a jolt; he had forgotten that the most damning proof of his guilt was in the cabinet opposite the bed, where he had thrust it. At that very moment he was actually in possession of the stolen goods; a minute search would be made, even his own room would not be exempt. He must hide the jewel-case somewhere. But where? Then he remembered having dropped the keys, and he hunted for them; but he could not find them. He was getting confused, obfuscated: he would search for the keys in the morning: perhaps, after all, he had left them in the dressing-room.

Throughout the remaining hours of that awful night, he lay pondering the momentous question, at one moment burning with fever, at another icy cold. The dawn broke, the sun rose, the room grew hot; and the heat gave him an idea. As the clock struck six, he rose, put on his boating flannels, and, with his bath towel over his arm, opened the bedroom door. He had actually forgotten the missing keys! Such lapses are common to the criminal.

Miriam was a light sleeper—as her awaking at the noise of the falling chair had proved—she became conscious of his presence and she opened her eyes.

"Oh, what is it, Percy?" she asked, petulantly and a little nervously.

"I'm going down to the lake for a swim," he said; "it's precious hot this morning. I left my white shoes in the room."

"No, you didn't," she said, impatiently. "I saw them with your other boots in the dressing-room yesterday."

"Oh, right!" he said. "Awfully sorry to have disturbed you."

He returned to the dressing-room, arranged the long bath towel over the jewel-case, and went downstairs. He was too early, as he knew, for any of the servants to be about, and he went through the lower hall and was unbolting the outer door when he chanced to glance at the window nearest it; it was closed by a common hasp, and was without bars. With a little nod of satisfaction, he opened the window noiselessly; then went out by the door.

He was about to go through the shrubbery, towards the little wood, at the bottom of which lay the lake, but it occurred to him that some of the servants might be getting up and that any movement of his should be open and free from secrecy. So he went straight across the lawn in the sauntering fashion of a man going for a bath and enjoying the fresh, warm air; but when he entered the wood, which was enchanted ground for Derrick and Celia, he looked round him cautiously; for it was just possible that one of the gamekeepers might be about; but there was no sight or sound of anyone, and when he had gained the centre of the wood, he stopped and looked around him, and presently, after waiting a minute or two listening intently, he hid the box under a bush and covered it with the leaves of last autumn. Then, with a sense of relief, for, light as it was, the jewel-case had weighed upon him like a leaden thing, he went to the lake, slipped off his things and had his swim.

He felt better after it; more of a man, as the poor fool told himself. There was nothing to connect him with the robbery, he had got rid of the jewel-case; it was well-nigh impossible that anyone should discover it; he could remove it when the fuss was over; indeed, perhaps there would be no need to deal with the jewels; the old man might be——

It was all very plausible; but he had forgotten to take into account that long arm of coincidence which so often upsets the plans of the most astute criminal. And yet, in this case, the arm was not so very long. For Derrick had acquired a habit of early rising during the experiences in South America; the circus people were always up soon after sunrise, and at the ranch most of the people were stirring at dawn, when the air was cool and fresh. That morning, Derrick, who had slept soundly, as your happy lover should sleep, rose and, leaving the inn, had sauntered along the road until he came to the gate where Lady Gridborough had seen him and Celia. Naturally enough, he passed into the wood; of course, taking the path on which he had walked with Celia. He was thinking of her, thinking of the future, of the joy that awaited him, and in that clear, sunlit air, with the song of the birds in his ears, the difficulties with which he was beset seemed very light and unimportant. The girl he had loved was going to be his; that thought was quite enough for such a morning. He had nearly reached the centre of the wood, when he stopped to take out his pipe and pouch, and he was about to strike a match, when he saw something white passing between the trees at a little distance from him.

At first he thought it was Celia, and, with a leap of the lover's heart, he took a step forward; then he stopped short; the figure was that of a man in flannels; and a moment or two afterwards, he had recognised Heyton. The disappointment was great; he had no desire to meet Heyton; the sight of him recalled the bitter past; and Derrick stood, frowning as he watched Heyton on his way to the lake. He saw Heyton stop and look round him, and then he lost sight of him, for Heyton was bending down in the act of hiding the jewel-case. When he rose, Derrick got a clear sight of the man's face, and something in its expression impressed Derrick curiously, painfully.

Nothing stops still in this world of ours; and men must go up or down. It was evident to Derrick that Heyton had gone very much down since he had last seen him. Heyton's face had coarsened, his lips had grown looser and more sensual, there were bags under his eyes; but it was not these grosser changes which struck Derrick so much, as the expression of the man's face; it was that of one burdened by some oppression of mind or body; it seemed to Derrick that the light, prominent eyes had in them a look of fear, the look a man wears when he is hunted and driven.

And why, just before he had disappeared, had Heyton looked round him, secretively, cautiously, as if he did not wish to be seen? It was ridiculous, Derrick told himself; but it seemed to him as if Heyton were hiding something. Half-unconsciously, he made a mental note of the spot at which Heyton had made that curious pause in his progress. But Derrick did not go to it; he wanted particularly to avoid Heyton—and Miriam, everyone connected with that wretched past which still hung over him like a cloud. So he returned to the road and went straight back to the inn.

Awaiting him, he found a letter from the engineers concerning matters which needed his immediate presence in London. He had just time to snatch a hasty breakfast, left word with the landlord for Reggie that he, Derrick, was obliged to go to London but would return by the night train, and reached the station just as the train came in. He was hot and, no doubt, looked rather worried; for there was no means of letting Celia know that he had gone, or of making an appointment with her. Of course, he pictured her wandering about the wood in the hope of seeing him, and acutely imagined her disappointment.

CHAPTER XXVI

Meanwhile, Heyton returned to the Hall; walking with a certain jauntiness which was not altogether assumed; for the disposal of the jewel-case had been an immense relief. Some of the servants were now about, and to her surprise, he wished one of the maids good morning quite pleasantly; to her surprise, because Heyton's manner to his inferiors was usually anything but a pleasant one; and, while all the household was devoted to the Marquess, and would have done anything for him, his son was unpopular. As he passed along the lower hall, Heyton glanced at the window he had opened: it had not been shut. He went up the stairs and, as he entered his dressing-room, hummed the latest comic song. The breakfast hour at the Hall was half-past nine; the Marquess was called at half-past eight, but Heyton's valet had orders not to disturb his master until he rang, and, more often than not, Heyton's bell did not ring until breakfast was on the table.

Heyton threw himself down on the bed and closed his eyes with the preposterous idea of getting a little sleep; but he lay and listened, and presently he heard Miriam's maid knocking at the bedroom door; then he rose and rang for his man.

"Early this morning, eh, Simcox?" he said. "Been for a swim. Feel jolly fit. Fact is, we all lie abed too late; I've half a mind to get up for a bath in the lake every morning."

The valet grinned to himself as he answered respectfully,

"Yes, my lord. Very pleasant in the morning."

When he had half finished dressing, Heyton called to Miriam.

"I say, Miriam, what about a drive this morning? We might go over to Teynsham."

"I don't know; I'll see," she called back listlessly.

"I'll wear a tweed suit," said Heyton to his man; "I'll have the new one. And, look here, you tell the tailor to give me a little more room round the waist. I suppose I must be getting fat, eh, Simcox?"

"Oh, not fat, my lord," murmured Simcox, remonstratingly. "More—er—comfortable."

When the man had finished with him, Heyton lit a cigarette and leant back in his chair—as if he were waiting for something.

He had not to wait long.

A cry rang through the house; it was followed by others; there was the sound of rushing footsteps and voices raised in terror; his door was flung open and Simcox stood on the threshold, his face white, his eyes starting; he gaped at his master speechlessly, and Heyton gaped back at him.

"Well, what the devil is it?" he asked at last, his face red, his lips quivering. "What do you mean by rushing in, in this—idiotic fashion?"

"Oh, my lord!" gasped Simcox. "Something's—something's happened. Oh, it's awful! It's the Marquess's man—Mr. Jenkins—he's just been to call his lordship and—and—oh, my lord, it's 'orrible!"

Heyton rose, gripping the back of the chair.

"What do you mean?" he demanded. "What the devil are you talking about?"

"Oh, my lord, the Marquess is dead!" stammered Simcox.

"Dead!" echoed Heyton, his face livid, his whole form shaking as if with palsy.

"Well, Jenkins thinks so, my lord. If so, it's—murder."

"Murder!" echoed Heyton, his voice again hoarse.

"Yes, my lord. There's been a burglary; the safe, the safe in his lordship's dressing-room, has been broken into. Jenkins found his lordship lying on the ground—there was blood——"

The man's voice had risen by this time and it brought Miriam to the door. She looked from one to the other, the nameless terror she felt showing in her eyes.

"What is it?" she demanded.

"Go—go away, Miriam," said Heyton, hoarsely. "Go back to your own room."

Disregarding his injunctions with a kind of contempt, she advanced and addressed herself to the terror-stricken valet.

"What is it, Simcox?" she asked. "I heard you say——"

"Yes, my lady, it's true," faltered Simcox, wiping the sweat from his face. "I helped Jenkins carry the Marquess into his bedroom. If his lordship isn't dead, he's as good as dead."

Swiftly, without a moment's hesitation, Miriam went past them to the Marquess's bedroom, thrusting her way through a crowd of horrified, gaping servants. The Marquess lay on the bed where they had placed him. The blood had ceased flowing, but it had stained one side of his face, had reddened a greater part of the old-fashioned nightshirt which he wore. He lay quite still, his eyes closed. She stood and looked at him, frozen with horror; then she became conscious that her husband was standing beside her.

"Is he dead?" she asked, almost inaudibly. "Who—who has done this?"

At the question, he drew back a little, and lifted his eyes from the reddened face to hers.

"What do you mean?" he demanded, almost shouted. "It's pretty plain, I should think. Didn't you hear what Simcox said? There's been a burglary; the—the safe's broken open——"

"The safe——?" she said, unconscious that she had spoken.

For a moment her eyes met his; then hers sank and she shuddered.

"Has anyone gone for the doctor?" she asked in a low voice.

"Yes, my lady," said Jenkins. "I've sent a groom for Doctor Scott; but I'm afraid——"

"Give me some water," she said tonelessly.

They brought her some and a sponge, and with a hand that was unnaturally calm, she wiped the blood from the old man's face and neck.

"Here, look here!" said Heyton, hesitatingly. "Do you think you ought to touch him, do anything till the doctor comes?"

She did not look at him, and continued her pitiful ministration. Heyton drew back from the bed, his eyes withdrawing themselves from his father's face slowly, as if fascinated.

"Has anything gone from the safe?" he asked.

"I don't know, my lord. I didn't wait to look," said Jenkins in a hushed voice.

Heyton went into the dressing-room and returned a moment later.

"If there was anything of value in the safe, it's gone," he said. "Look here!— Here, you, Simcox, what the devil are you gaping there for, like a stuck pig; why don't you send for the police?"

Simcox turned to fly, and almost ran into Mrs. Dexter, who was followed by Celia. Strangely enough Mrs. Dexter had been almost the last to hear of the calamity; a terrified servant had dashed into her room with the awful news. Celia's room was next to Mrs. Dexter's and she had heard Mrs. Dexter's cry of horror, and had darted out to learn what it meant. Mrs. Dexter went to the bed, gently and unconsciously putting Miriam aside, and bent over the motionless form.

"He is not dead," she said, in a whisper.

"Oh, thank God!" broke from Miriam's white lips, and she turned to Celia and grasped her arm. "Oh, I'm glad you've come; I'm glad you are here!" she sobbed. "I'm all alone—oh, I'm glad you are here! Do *you* think he is not dead?"

"Mrs. Dexter will know," said Celia, trying to control her voice. "Don't be frightened, don't get worried, Lady Heyton. Come with me!"

She took Miriam's hand and drew her into her bedroom. Miriam sank on the bed and covered her face with her hands; and for a while, there was silence; for Celia had no words at command. Presently Miriam dropped her hands from her face and looked straight before her; there was something worse than horror in her expression; there was a poignant, a vivid terror.

Celia found some eau-de-Cologne and bathed Miriam's forehead.

"You won't faint, Lady Heyton?" she said. "They will need you—you must try to bear up. He is not dead——"

"No, thank God!" murmured Miriam. "Why, it would be—murder, wouldn't it?" she asked suddenly, still staring in front of her.

"I—I don't know," said Celia. "I know no more than you do. It is a burglary, isn't it? I heard one of the servants say that the safe had been broken into."

"The safe!" echoed Miriam, in a toneless voice. "Yes, the safe—the diamonds. What is that?" she asked, with almost a scream.

"Carriage wheels: the doctor," said Celia, soothingly.

"Go—go and hear what he says," said Miriam, in a hushed whisper. "I—I want to know at once. I can't go back; I dare not!"

"No; stay here, I will come to you," said Celia. "Shall I bring Lord Heyton to you?"

"No, no!" responded Miriam, shrinking away. "No, no! Don't bring him here. I—I mean he should be there; there will be things to do——Oh, don't you understand! I don't want him here!"

"I understand," said Celia; "but you must try to be calm. There will be so much to do——"

"Calm!" cried Miriam, flinging out her arms. "Am I not calm? Do you think I'm not trying not to give way; that I'm not trying to keep sane? Go! Go!"

Celia went back to the Marquess's room. Mrs. Dexter and the doctor were bending over the bed; Heyton was standing at a little distance, watching them and gnawing his nails. Mrs. Dexter looked round as Celia entered.

"I want you, my dear," she said. "I want you to help me. He is not dead," she went on in a whisper; "he is still alive, though Doctor Scott will not give us any hope yet."

Celia assisted Mrs. Dexter in carrying out the doctor's orders; the Marquess was still unconscious; but though he looked more dead than alive, life was still present. After a time, there came a timid and subdued knock at the door. Mrs. Dexter signed to Celia to open it and she did so. It was Smith, the butler.

"The Inspector has come, Miss Grant, and is asking for Lord Heyton," he said in a tremulous voice.

Heyton turned at the sound of his name and went out.

"How is the Marquess, my lord?" asked Smith, who was deeply agitated.

"Oh, he's all right," said Heyton. "I mean, the doctor thinks he'll pull round. Here, don't make more fuss than is necessary, Smith; keep the house quiet and tell the servants to keep their mouths shut."

Smith looked at him with surprise; for Heyton's manner was scarcely that of a son whose father had nearly been done to death. The Inspector was in the hall and Heyton signed to him to follow into the library.

"This is dreadful news, my lord," said the Inspector.

"Rather!" assented Heyton. He was very pale, and his hair was dank with sweat, and his tongue moved over his lips thickly, with a restless, feverish movement. "Here, we'd better have a drink before we begin. I'm terribly upset. Only natural, eh, Inspector?—Own father, you know?—Bring in some soda and whisky," he ordered the footman who answered the bell.

"Not for me, my lord, thank you," said the Inspector, respectfully.

Heyton poured out half a glassful of whisky, made a pretence of adding soda, and swallowed the spirit.

"Absolutely upset," he said, wiping his lips on his handkerchief. "But there! I half expected it. I was telling my father only last night—or was it the night before?—about those damned gipsies on the common. I warned him; yes, I warned him."

"Gipsies, my lord?" said the Inspector. "You suspect them?"

"Who else am I to suspect?" demanded Heyton, with a sideway glance of his bloodshot eyes.

"That remains to be seen, my lord," said the Inspector quietly; "for myself, I don't think the gipsies have had any hand in this. I should like you to tell me everything you know about the affair, please, my lord."

"Certainly, Inspector," responded Heyton, promptly. "But, you see, I know precious little; in fact, I don't know anything. My man came bursting into my room this morning, and told me they'd found my father—well, as you know, lying in his dressing-room, badly knocked about; and, of course, I went straight to his room, and—that's all I know about it."

"Quite so, my lord. I should like to see the room at once."

"Come on, then," said Heyton. He was quite calm, and was quite proud of being so calm. The Inspector might look at the room as long as he liked; it wouldn't tell him anything of the truth.

They went up to the dressing-room, and the Inspector walked straight to the safe and began to look, not at its contents, but along the edge of the door. He nodded with a kind of satisfaction, and said:

"I've wired for a detective; he's more at home at this kind of case than I am."

He turned from the safe and examined the part of the floor on which the Marquess had fallen; then he caught sight of the poker and pursed his lips.

"That's what did it," he said, confidently. "The blood's still wet on it."

Heyton made as if to pick up the poker, but the Inspector caught his arm and stayed him.

"Beg pardon, my lord," he said, apologetically. "But you mustn't touch anything. We'll let everything bide as it is until the detective comes down from Scotland Yard."

He went to the window and examined it; but without touching it.

"Closed and hasped! Have you any idea how they got in, my lord; have any of the servants found a window or a door open?"

"No," replied Heyton; then he added, as if he had suddenly remembered. "Here, by George, that's strange! I mean about the window. I found one of the back windows open when I went down this morning for a swim."

"Oh!" said the Inspector. "I should like to see that window, my lord. But one moment! Was there anything of value—I mean, jewels or money or anything of that kind—in the safe?"

"Not that I'm aware of," replied Heyton, almost instantly; but he had had time to consider the question. "There may have been, of course. Not jewels, because my father kept the family diamonds at the bank."

"That's something to be thankful for, my lord," said the Inspector, with an approving shake of the head. "Quite the proper thing to do. There wouldn't be half the burglaries, if the gentry didn't leave their jewels about in the way they do. But there might have been money?"

"Oh, yes, there might," said Heyton.

The Inspector walked round the room cautiously, and presently went to the outer door.

"Is this locked, my lord?"

"I don't know," said Heyton; and, as if he had forgotten the Inspector's injunction, he tried the handle of the door before the Inspector could stop him. "It's locked," said Heyton.

"Tut, tut!" said the Inspector to himself, as if he were much annoyed by something.

"Come on," said Heyton. "I'll show you the window I found open." He was consumed by a feverish desire to get the Inspector out of the room.

They went down to the lower hall, the white-faced servants staring at them from coigns of vantage; and the Inspector glanced swiftly at the window and then at the hall.

"That's where they got in," he said. "Nothing easier. There is no door, I suppose, between the Marquess's room and the window here?"

"No," replied Heyton, moistening his lips as he stood behind the Inspector.

"And you are sure this window was open when you went out this morning, my lord? What time was that, by the way?"

"A little after six," replied Heyton. "It was deuced hot; I woke and had a fancy for a swim. There was no one about, and I opened the door, this door, for myself."

"Oh, it's plain enough," said the Inspector, nodding once or twice. "It's quite easy for them to slip this hasp back with an ordinary knife. The rest isn't difficult to guess. They must have made some noise while they were breaking into the safe; well, not 'breaking into' it, for they must have opened it with a key, because there wasn't even the mark of an ordinary chisel on the safe. You noticed that, my lord, no doubt?"

"I—I can't say I did," said Heyton; "I'm a bit upset and confused, you know."

"Yes, it was opened with a key," said the Inspector, "and that's the only part of the business that troubles me. That's a good safe, my lord; one of the first-class makers, and it couldn't have been opened with a skeleton key; in fact, with anything but the proper key or a duplicate."

"Oh?" said Heyton. "Where did they get it?"

The Inspector shook his head. "Of course, that's just the puzzle, my lord. I'm afraid we shall have to leave that to the Scotland Yard man."

As he spoke, he took out his whistle and blew sharply on it. A constable came to the door and saluted.

"Got your men placed, Brown?" asked the Inspector. "Just put another man on the drive, and give him orders that no man is to enter the lodge gates

excepting the detective, when he comes.
"

"What's that for?" asked Heyton, as if the question were inspired by his desire to understand everything that was being done.

"I don't want a lot of people tramping over the place," said the Inspector, rather evasively.

"Oh, ah, yes," said Heyton. "Well, I'll go upstairs again. Send for me, if you want me, Inspector."

He went upstairs, paused a moment outside the Marquess's door, then went on to his own dressing-room. He listened at the door leading to the bedroom; but there was no sound. He touched the handle of the door; but he could not open it, though he knew that Miriam was in the room, and that he ought to go to her. He could not. He rang the bell, and when the valet came, Heyton told him to bring some whisky and soda. But even the draught of almost undiluted spirit could not give him sufficient courage to face his wife.

For he knew that she would remember that she had told him the diamonds were in the safe. And that he had wanted them.

CHAPTER XXVII

Mr. Jacobs, the detective from Scotland Yard, arrived at the Hall a little after four. He was a short, comfortable-looking person, with a round, almost boyish face, a pleasant smile and a pair of blue eyes, with a frank and innocent expression; in fact, anything more unlike the conventional detective beloved by the fictionist it would be difficult to imagine. The Inspector had met him at the station, and had gone over the case with meticulous care; and Mr. Jacobs, smoking placidly, had listened—well, as you and I, dear reader, would listen to a tale which had no very great interest for us. If the truth must be told, the worthy Inspector was rather disappointed; he had expected the great man to display a hawk-like acuteness and to ask a number of incisive questions; but Mr. Jacobs asked none; he said merely, when the recital was finished,

"You have done everything you

could, Mr. Smith. Not a very difficult case, eh?"

"Not difficult!" repeated the Inspector, with surprise. "Have you got a clue already?"

Mr. Jacobs smiled. "Can't say yet," he replied.

As they drove up to the Hall, Heyton was seen standing just within the threshold, as if waiting for them.

"Lord Heyton, the Marquess's son," whispered the Inspector.

Mr. Jacobs nodded; he did not direct a piercing glance at Heyton's pale face and bloodshot eyes, with their swollen lids; in fact, he did not appear to notice anything, as he went forward, hat in hand.

A few words of commonplace greeting were exchanged; Mr. Jacobs expressed his sympathy in a low voice, devoid of any acuteness, and Heyton drew a breath of relief, as he led the way into the library; to him it seemed that the man from Scotland Yard looked rather stupid than otherwise. Mr. Jacobs took a seat, and Heyton, of his own accord, repeated, almost word for word, the account he had given to the Inspector.

"It's my opinion," he wound up, "that you'll find the man amongst those blackguard gipsies."

"Yes, my lord?" responded the detective, interrogatively. Then he went upstairs to the dressing-room. "I think I should like to be alone in here, my lord, if you don't mind," he said.

He took the key from the Inspector, and went in, closing the door after him. When he came out, his round, innocent-looking face was grave, but revealed nothing.

"Has the Marquess recovered consciousness?" he asked.

"Not yet, I am sorry to say," replied Heyton. "They are keeping the room very quiet, and my wife will tell me the moment my father comes to."

"I should like to know, when he does so, my lord," said the detective. "Is there anyone else with him—I mean, beside the doctor and the nurse?"

"Mrs. Dexter, the housekeeper, and a young lady, Miss Grant, a kind of secretary and librarian."

"Just so," said Mr. Jacobs. "Thank you, my lord. I don't use alcohol; but I should like to have a cup of tea, if I may: great tea-drinker."

He took his cup of tea with the Inspector in the morning-room, and while he drank it, he talked to the Inspector—of the country and the crops.

"I love the country," he said. "If I had my way, I would never put foot in London again. When I retire, Inspector, I'm going to buy a little farm—if it will run to it; and London won't see me again in a hurry. Beautiful place, this; and they breed a remarkably good class of cattle. I'm rather an authority on shorthorns; shall go in for some myself, if I can afford it."

To all this the Inspector listened with amazement.

"Anything you'd like me to do, Mr. Jacobs?" he asked, in a tone that verged on exasperation. "Is there anything else you'd like to see? That window in the lower hall, for instance?"

"Thanks; I saw it as we passed through," replied Mr. Jacobs, simply. "No; I don't think there's anything I want to see. Yes; this is a beautiful house; quite a show-place. I should like to see something of it presently; but one doesn't like to intrude at such a time as this." The Inspector stared at him. "But perhaps I might go through what I suppose you'd call the state rooms—and yes, upstairs."

"I thought you would have liked to examine the whole house without loss of time," remarked the Inspector, with an aggrieved air.

"Oh, presently will do," said Mr. Jacobs; "don't want to make myself a nuisance. We might walk round the grounds."

They went out, the Inspector still confused and aggrieved by what he considered the detective's lack of business method, and Mr. Jacobs gazed round him with approval and admiration.

"Beautiful! Beautiful!" he murmured. "Where's this lake Lord Heyton spoke of? I should like to see that. In my opinion, every place of this sort ought to have a bit of water: lends such a charm to the scenery, don't you think, Inspector?"

"Oh, yes," assented the Inspector, almost with disgust. "This way."

"Ah, this is the nearest way from the house, across the lawn, of course," said Mr. Jacobs. "I suppose this is the way Lord Heyton comes when he goes for his bath. Right across the lawn, eh?"

The Inspector nodded indifferently. It seemed to him that the detective was curious about everything unconnected with the case.

They went across the lawn, the detective still dilating on the charms of a country life, and entered the wood. If they had not followed exactly the line taken by Heyton in the morning, they had touched it now and again; and when they reached the edge of the lake, Mr. Jacobs looked round in a casual way and presently seated himself on the big stone on which Heyton had sat while he dressed himself. Mr. Jacobs obviously was delighted with the lake and its surroundings; and the Inspector would not have been surprised if the great detective had proposed a swim; but he stopped short of that eccentricity and they returned to the house.

They went into the state rooms, which received Mr. Jacobs' unstinted admiration, and were crossing the hall to the little sitting-room which had been set apart for him, when Celia met them. She was very pale, and her brows were drawn together by trouble and anxiety; for a great deal of responsibility had fallen suddenly on her shoulders. Though a duly qualified nurse was in possession of the sick-room, Mrs. Dexter and Celia were assisting her; and Celia had Miriam almost entirely on her hands; for Miriam was almost in a state of collapse. Celia had expected her to break down; but there was something in Miriam's condition which puzzled Celia. She seemed not only overwhelmed by grief and anxiety, but to be possessed of a nervous terror which expressed itself in an avoidance of her husband. Lord Heyton had asked after his wife several times that day; but Miriam had refused to see him, and once, when Celia ventured to plead with her, and to try to persuade her to allow

Lord Heyton to come into the room, Miriam had sprung at the door and leant with her back against it, panting, with absolute terror, and with a look of horror on her face which at once stopped all Celia's attempts at persuasion.

For a time, Miriam paced up and down the room, like one distraught, continually muttering, "Will he die? Will it be murder?" But at last Celia had succeeded in getting the hysterical woman to bed, where she lay, exhausted by her emotions. Celia was on her way to ask Doctor Scott for a sleeping draught, when she was met by the detective and the Inspector.

"Miss Grant, the librarian," murmured the Inspector; and Mr. Jacobs bowed politely.

"Pleased to make your acquaintance, Miss Grant," he said. "Wish it were in happier circumstances. How is the Marquess now?"

"Still the same," replied Celia. "He is not yet conscious."

"Dear me; dear me!" murmured Mr. Jacobs, sympathetically. "Now, my dear young lady, may I ask you a favour—I don't want to trouble the doctor, he's got quite enough to do; so have you, no doubt, for that matter; but you know what doctors are?—What I want you to do, if you will be so kind, and if you should be in the room and the Marquess recovers consciousness, is to just send to me in the sitting-room here and let me know."

"I will do so," said Celia, and she passed on to the morning-room, where Doctor Scott was giving some directions to his assistant.

So suddenly had the terrible blow fallen that she had scarcely time to think of her lover. It hurt her to imagine him waiting in the wood for her, on the chance of seeing her, and to know that she could not send a message to him, could not let him know. But she told herself that, no doubt, by this time, he had heard of the terrible tragedy and would understand. She could not afford much thought for him; her hands were too full; indeed, in addition to her other responsibilities, she had, in a measure, taken Mrs. Dexter's place in the house-

hold, and had to give directions to the still scared servants.

She sent down to the village for the sleeping draught which Doctor Scott prescribed for Miriam, and as soon as she could, went upstairs again. In the corridor, she met Lord Heyton, and he looked so ill, so careworn, that, for a moment, her dislike of him was outbalanced by pity. He nodded to her, and she was about to pass on; then she paused and said:

"Have you had anything to eat, my lord? Everyone is so busy and so confused, there will be no regular meals, I am afraid."

"Oh, that's all right," he said, glancing at her furtively, and then lowering his eyes. "I'm not much in the humour for meals, as you may guess. Has my father come to, yet? Look here, that officious fool of a nurse has shut me out of the room. I wish you'd—yes, look here, just let me know when he comes to. I shall be hanging about. I say," he added, with another furtive glance at her pale face, "you're looking pretty upset yourself. I suppose they've shoved everything on to you.—And there's Miriam! What's become of her?"

"Lady Heyton is in bed—and asleep, I hope, my lord," said Celia; and reluctantly and with a touch of colour, she added, "I think it would be better not to disturb her ladyship; she—she is very much upset; very ill, indeed."

He nodded. "Not to be surprised at!" he said. "I'm feeling pretty seedy myself. Here, will you come with me and have a glass of wine?"

"No, thank you, my lord," replied Celia; and, all her dislike of him active again, she left him.

About six o'clock the watchers by the sick bed noticed a change in the Marquess. His eyelids flickered a moment, his lips moved. Celia, who was standing nearest to him, bent over him and made a sign to Mrs. Dexter and the doctor, and they hastened forward noiselessly. For some time, the stricken man struggled for speech; then one word passed his lips, almost inaudibly,

"Percy!"

Celia looked at the doctor questioningly. He nodded, and she went out. She found Heyton in the smoking-room; there was a decanter of brandy in front of him and his face was flushed; but it went white as she said, as calmly as she could,

"The Marquess has recovered consciousness; he has asked for you, my lord."

He got up and steadied himself, with one hand on the table, looking at her with a curious expression in his face: in that instant, it reminded her of the expression on that of his wife; it was one of absolute terror. But it was only momentary; he nodded and went out of the room. Celia was following him, when she caught sight of a small part of the detective's figure, just inside the sitting-room; she had forgotten him, but as she went towards him he made a sign as if he understood; indeed, he waved her away.

Mr. Jacobs waited until Celia had gone; then he went upstairs softly; in the corridor, near the Marquess's door, he met the doctor, followed by Mrs. Dexter and the nurse, coming out.

"I beg your pardon," he said. "I was just going up to have another look at the dressing-room."

The doctor inclined his head. "Don't make any more noise than you can help," he said. "We have left the Marquess alone with Lord Heyton; you must do nothing to disturb them."

"Quite so; I'll go up presently," said Mr. Jacobs; and he walked down the corridor. But when the others had disappeared, he turned quickly and softly, and entered the dressing-room.

With the outer door open an inch, he watched and waited; and in a very few minutes Heyton came out of the sick-room. He was white as death, and he was shaking in every limb. The detective waited until he had heard Heyton's slow and heavy steps descend the stairs, then Mr. Jacobs went down, by the back stairs, to his sitting-room. He dined there, with the Inspector, and entertained—though that is scarcely the word—the amazed and disgusted Mr. Brown by an account of a visit Mr. Jacobs had paid to a big agricultural show

in the north.

After dinner, he smoked a cigar with an air of quiet and subdued enjoyment proper to the circumstances; and a little later on, he went for a stroll. The night was hot, and Heyton had gone on to the terrace; he had had some more brandy, and was trying to smoke; but his throat and lips were too parched to permit of his doing so, and with an oath, he flung the cigar away. It fell very nearly on Mr. Jacobs' Homburg hat.

"All right, my lord," he said, as Heyton muttered a sullen apology. "I was just taking a stroll." He went up the steps, and stood beside Heyton, looking at the view with obvious admiration; then presently, he said, "I was going to ask you if you'd mind signing a paper for me, my lord. It's just a little report for Scotland Yard; scarcely necessary perhaps, but still——"

"All right," said Heyton, dully. "Here, come in here!" They entered the library by the French door.

"A beautiful room: magnificent!" murmured Mr. Jacobs. He drew a paper from his pocket and spread it out on the writing-slope. "Just here, my lord, if you please; it's a kind of authorization from you to take charge of the case."

He handed Heyton a pen, and Heyton looked at the paper hazily and was about to sign, when Mr. Jacobs, in drawing the inkstand nearer, had the misfortune to upset it. The ink ran over the paper, and over Heyton's fingers.

"What the devil!" he exclaimed, angrily.

"I beg your pardon, my lord! I'm very sorry; very sorry; it was dreadfully clumsy of me. Dear, dear; it's all over your lordship's hand! Here, wipe it on this, my lord!"

In his agitation and embarrassment, Mr. Jacobs actually caught hold of Heyton's hand and pressed it on a sheet of paper.

"Tut, tut," he said. "I thought it was blotting-paper! Here it is! I really am so sorry—never did such a thing in my life before!"

"Damned clumsy of you!" growled Heyton. "I'm in a beast of a mess! Where's a cloth?"

"Pray take my handkerchief, my lord," said Mr. Jacobs, offering it.

At this moment, Celia entered the room. She would have drawn back at sight of the two men; but Heyton called to her over his shoulder.

"Hi! Have you got a cloth? The ink's upset——"

She ran to a drawer and took out a clean duster; and Heyton, swearing under his breath, wiped the remainder of the ink from his fingers.

"I'd better go and wash it," he said; and he went out of the room.

"Tut, tut!" said Mr. Jacobs. "It was my fault, Miss Grant. I was reaching for the ink, to bring it nearer his lordship, when my sleeve or something caught the corner of the desk here and, before you could say 'Jack Robinson,' the mischief was done."

He seemed so greatly distressed and upset by the accident, that Celia quite felt for him.

"Oh, it is not a very great matter," she said, soothingly. "There has been no harm done."

Indeed, it did seem to her a very trivial affair, compared with the awful tragedy in which they were moving. "I will get a cloth and wipe up the ink; fortunately, it hasn't run on to the carpet."

As she spoke, she took up the sheets of writing-paper and blotting paper between her finger and thumb, intending to put them in the waste-paper basket; but, with a kind of apologetic laugh, Mr. Jacobs laid his hand on her arm, and said:

"No, don't throw them away! Give them to me, if you will. I should like to keep them as a kind of memento, as a sort of warning for the future not to be so clumsy."

With a shadow of a smile, she gave the two pieces of paper to him, and as he took them he said,

"I've got my own fingers inked. Serve me right. I'll go and wash my hands. Really, I shall never forgive myself! No wonder his lordship was angry."

"Was he?" said Celia, absently. "Yes; he was. But you must remember Lord Heyton is very much upset; when one's nerves are on the rack, the least thing, trifling though it may be——"

"Quite so; quite so," said Mr. Jacobs, with a nod of comprehension.

He was still so much upset by the accident, that he forgot to wash his hands and went straight to his sitting-room, still carrying the two sheets of paper, the evidences of his inexcusable clumsiness.

CHAPTER XXVIII

That night, Inspector Brown confided his disappointment in the ways of Scotland Yard to the wife of his bosom. He was a conscientious man; and it seemed to him that, in the face of Mr. Jacobs' obvious incapacity, it behoved him, Mr. Brown, to follow the case with renewed energy. So far as the worthy Inspector could see, Mr. Jacobs was doing absolutely nothing, save eat his meals, smoke his cigar, and stroll about the grounds and admire the scenery. Therefore, the Inspector enjoined his men to keep a careful watch; and he himself, when not in Mr. Jacobs' company, patrolled the woods and, following the clue Lord Heyton had offered him, had visited the gipsy encampment and examined the members of the tribe. He came upon nothing to rouse his suspicions of them; indeed, he hit upon no clue whatever; but he still kept up a kind of patrol and scrutinised every person who approached the Hall.

If Mr. Jacobs was aware of the Inspector's renewed vigilance, he made no remark; and whenever they were together, and the Inspector wanted to talk of the case, Mr. Jacobs politely and quite inoffensively—in fact, he always listened most respectfully—led the conversation away from the subject. Once or twice, the Inspector was absolutely on the point of asking the famous detective why on earth he was lingering at the Hall; but his courage always failed him; for, notwithstanding the detective's boyish face and innocent-looking eyes, there was something about him which inspired a kind of respect in Inspector Brown.

After that momentary glimpse of intelligence, and his interview with his son, the Marquess had relapsed into unconsciousness; but the doctor, in answer to Celia's anxious inquiries, had told her that there was a chance, just a chance, of life.

As the great house settled into its nightly silence, Derrick's train was speeding on its way. He had got through Donna Elvira's business satisfactorily, and, moreover, following Reggie's instructions, obtained his special licence; therefore, his heart was light as he sat and smoked while the express tore through the silence of the night. He reached Thexford at ten o'clock in the morning, and went straight to the inn. Reggie, he was told, was out; and Derrick made a good breakfast and, naturally enough, was drawn towards the wood. It was a hundred to one chance that Celia should be there; but he decided to take the odds. The morning was hot; it was not at all unlikely that, puzzled and perhaps alarmed by his absence, she might go to the wood. On his way, it was also natural that he should recall his sight of Heyton on the preceding morning; and, having recalled that, it was also a corollary that he should remember Heyton's mysterious proceedings.

When they occurred to Derrick, he was not very far from the spot where Heyton had disappeared for a minute or two; and Derrick sauntered towards the place and stood looking round him. He was keen-eyed, and in some of his experiences in South America he had learnt a certain amount of bush-craft; and he had no difficulty in finding the exact spot in which he had lost sight, for a moment, of Heyton.

With a feeling that was scarcely one of curiosity, he examined the ground in close proximity, and presently, he caught sight of a portion of the fringe of a bathing-towel. He took it from the thorn on which it hung, and fingered it absently; and while doing so, he noted the mark of footsteps which had trodden down the bracken in front of a certain bush. Almost at the same moment, he saw a little heap of dried leaves beneath the bush, and, mechanically, he stirred them with his foot. To his amazement, the displaced leaves revealed a box covered with morocco leather. He stood and looked down at it with that sense of incredulity which comes to all of us when we happen upon something absolutely unexpected; then he knelt down and took up the box. It was heavy and, when he shook it, it rattled softly.

He stood with the box in his hand, staring at it, and wondering whether it was the thing Heyton had concealed, and what it contained. Also another most important question was agitating him: What should he do with it? Presumably, it was Heyton's property; and should be returned to him at once. But why on earth should Heyton come out in the early morning to conceal a morocco-covered box under a bush in Thexford Woods?

To say that Derrick was suspicious is to express inadequately the feeling that suddenly assailed him. He knew that the man was a scoundrel, and as unscrupulous as he was weak; a man who could forge a cheque, and plant the blame on another, is capable of anything; and Derrick scented a mystery, a base, ignoble one, with Heyton as its centre. He sat down on the trunk of a fallen tree, the box in his hand, and stared frowningly before him. He could find no answer to the enigma. That he himself should march up to the Hall and restore the box to Heyton, was impossible. After all, the affair was none of his, and, perhaps, the best thing he could do would be to put the box back in its hiding-place and leave things to work themselves out. He wanted to have nothing more to do with Heyton, or any business of his. Yes; the easiest and the safest plan would be to leave the box where he had found it and have nothing more to do with it. With this more or less wise resolution, he rose and had taken a step forward, when he heard a sound behind him, felt a hand fall heavily on his shoulder, and, turning, met the stern and agitated gaze of Inspector Brown.

"I arrest you for robbery and attempted murder!" said the Inspector.

His voice, for all its sternness, shook and his face was red and working; for this was the most important moment of Inspector Brown's life, and it was little wonder that he was agitated and strung up. While the great detective from Scotland Yard was doing nothing, here had he, the Inspector, actually discovered the criminal, caught him red-handed, so to speak!

"It is no use your offering any resistance," he said, brusquely. "Three or four constables are within call; you could not possibly escape. I've had my eye upon you for some time, my man, and have taken precautions."

This assertion was not strictly true, but the Inspector almost felt it was.

Derrick stared at the red face in a kind of stupefied amazement; at last he said:

"You mean that you are charging me with stealing this thing?"

"I do," replied the Inspector; "and you may as well hand it over to me without any fuss."

"I shall be delighted to do so," said Derrick, grimly.

He had not yet realized the full significance of the Inspector's first formal words; for the moment Derrick's mind was engrossed by the sardonic irony of Fate. Here it was again! There was something really monotonous in the way in which this peculiar phase of misfortune dogged him. Was he really going to be again charged with an offence he had not committed? He opened his lips to speak; to say where he had found the box; then he remembered the words "attempted murder," and instead of giving information—which the Inspector would certainly have received with incredulity—Derrick said quietly and with a sudden pallor,

"Did I understand you to charge me with attempted murder as well as robbery?"

"I did," responded the Inspector, sternly. "The attempted murder of the Marquess of Sutcombe."

Derrick did not start, made no exclamation, but the pallor of his face increased and he gave a little nod. If this box had been stolen, the man who had hidden it was, in all probability, the thief—and attempted murderer. Per-

cy—the Marquess's own son! Confused and bewildered as he was, Derrick had sense enough left in him to feel that he must hold his tongue.

"All right," he said, very gravely. "I should like to say——"

"If you'll take my advice, you'll say nothing," broke in the Inspector, in an official manner. "You must know as well as I do that everything you say——"

"Quite so," said Derrick. "Where are you going to take me?"

"To the lock-up at Fleckfield," replied the Inspector, much relieved in his mind now that he saw his prisoner was not going to offer any resistance, give any trouble. "You're quite right to take it quietly. As I said, we're surrounded by my men. What's this?"

"This" was Celia, coming through the wood and hastening her steps at the sound of Derrick's voice. She stopped dead short, at sight of the two men, looking from one to the other in surprise, but no alarm; then she advanced to Derrick with, "Sydney!" on her lips.

"Why, it's you, Miss Grant!" said the Inspector. "I'm glad you've come up—though this is no place for you." He paused and looked at her in a puzzled way. "But you know this man, you called him 'Sydney'?"

"What does he mean?" asked Celia, in a bewildered fashion, of Derrick. "Why does he speak like that?—Oh, what does it mean!"

"It means that the Inspector here is making a mistake, Celia," said Derrick gravely, but without any resentment. "It appears that there has been a robbery at the Hall——"

"You've heard nothing about it!" exclaimed Celia.

"No," said Derrick, quietly. "I left for London yesterday morning early; I returned this morning, saw no one, heard nothing of it."

"Oh, come now, you'd better keep silent," interrupted the Inspector. "Miss Grant, I met this gentleman"—he hesitated on the word—"with this"—he tapped the box—"in his possession. I know, from the description, that it is the missing jewel-case, and I have arrest-

ed him on the charge of robbery and attempted murder. How you seem to know him—I don't understand——"

Celia stood as if turned to stone for a moment or two; her eyes wandering from the faces of the two men to the jewel-case; then she broke out,

"Sydney, why don't you explain?—It's a mistake, Inspector, a terrible mistake! I know this gentleman; I—I am engaged to him, I am going to be his wife. It's—absurd to suspect him!—Sydney, where did you find the thing?"

"Now, Miss Grant," said the Inspector soothingly, before Derrick could reply. "Let me advise you, as I have already advised the prisoner, not to say another word. I am sorry, truly sorry that a young lady of your—position should be so intimately acquainted, should be——Dear, dear, this is very sad, Miss Grant! I think you'd better go back to the Hall. But please don't say anything to Mr. Jacobs; I will come back to him directly I have seen the prisoner locked up."

Celia was calm now; her momentary terror had given place to grief and pity for the man she loved. Not for a second did any doubt of his innocence assail her. With that almost divine intuition of true love, she knew, not only that he was innocent, but that this crime was in some way or other connected with the former one, that of the forged cheque.

"Yes, I will go back to the Hall," she said; "but you will let me speak to Mr. Green before I go?"

"Of course, I can't prevent you," said the Inspector; "but you must say what you have to say in my hearing, and, of course, I shall take note of every word."

Celia went to Derrick, put her arm round his neck and kissed him.

"I can wait, dearest," she said. "You will not let this—this weigh upon you, trouble you?"

He was silent for a moment, his lips working; but the kiss she had impressed upon him strengthened and nerved him.

"God bless you, Celia!" he murmured, very quietly. "Go now! One moment—is the Marquess dying?"

"No," she said, with a dry little sob. "He is very bad, has been dreadfully injured, but he may recover."

"Thank God!" said Derrick. "That is all I will say. Go back, now, dearest. I will write to you—if they will let me."

The two men moved on; but she stood, her hand pressed against the tree, as if for support, as if she were unable to move, her eyes following the two figures; and as she watched them, in an agony, she saw a third figure coming through the gate. For a moment she did not recognize it, then she saw that it was Mr. Clendon. She saw him stop in front of the other two men and she ran forward, calling his name, and, in another instant, she was clinging to him. The old man murmured her name soothingly, and she tried to control herself; but her voice was broken by sobs, as she said:

"Oh, Mr. Clendon, I am in great trouble. They have arrested him—the man I am going to marry——" She could get no further.

Mr. Clendon looked steadily, piercingly at Derrick; and Derrick, as if answering the look, shook his head slightly and shrugged his shoulders.

"Who is this?" demanded the Inspector, impatiently; for, naturally, he was anxious to get his prisoner under lock and key.

"I am a friend of Miss Grant's and this gentleman," said Mr. Clendon. "You need not explain, I have heard of the robbery. I am on my way to the Hall. The Marquess is—a friend of mine, an old friend. One moment," he added to the Inspector, "I want to tell this gentleman you have arrested—under a mistake, I am convinced—that I am assured of his innocence, and that I charge myself with his defence."

He held out his hand to Derrick as he spoke; the two men exchanged grips and looked into each other's eyes; and again Derrick was conscious of that peculiar thrill which he had felt when he first touched Mr. Clendon's hand.

"Thank you, sir," he said, quietly. "Will you please take care of Miss Grant—Celia? I should like you to take her away now."

"Come, my dear," said Mr. Clendon; and looking over her shoulder till Der-

rick had disappeared, Celia went with Mr. Clendon, her hand in his.

"Do you think you can tell me all you know about this terrible business?" he said, when she had yielded to the relief of tears and was calmer and more composed.

Celia told him all she knew, and Mr. Clendon listened with attention and in silence.

"Of course, he is innocent," she wound up. "Oh, Mr. Clendon, I'm so glad you've come; it is as if—as if you had been sent to me. A moment or two ago I felt as—as I saw him taken away—that I was left alone in the world; but I feel now that I have a friend——"

"I trust that you have, my child," he said. "Don't cry any more. Tears cost so much; and I am convinced that you need not weep for fear of your lover's safety. He has been wrongfully accused; I do not doubt that for a moment."

"You don't; I know you don't! But why?" said Celia. "The jewel-case—I know it was the jewel-case, because the bank has telegraphed to say that poor Lord Sutcombe took it from the bank, and he must have brought it here—it was in the safe, was stolen from it. And the Inspector said that he had found it in Sydney's possession. That looks so black against him. And yet—you are as convinced of his innocence as I am!"

"Yes," said Mr. Clendon, quietly, "I am convinced. I could not tell you why; let us say that it is because your lover's face is not that of a guilty man. Besides," he added, with the ghost of a smile, "a man does not walk about a wood with a stolen jewel-case under his arm—if he himself is the thief."

"Of course!" cried Celia, stopping short, her face lighting up. "No one would be such a fool—least of all Sydney," she added, more to herself than to him, "who is so clever."

"Exactly," said Mr. Clendon. "So you see, my child, you have nothing to be alarmed about. Here is the Hall!" He looked up at the noble façade with a curious expression in his face. "It is years since I have been here," he added, musingly.

"You have been here before, you know the Marquess?" said Celia. "Yes, you said so. How strange! Why, Mr. Clendon," she broke off, turning upon him, with a flush of gratitude, "I see now, I see now! It was you who got me the place here. And I never guessed it! Oh, how good you have been to me! And you hid it." Her hand pressed his.

The old man frowned slightly. "You have caught me, my dear," he said. "It was a great pleasure to me to be of assistance to you. But we have other things to think of," he added, as they passed up the steps into the hall.

The butler met them, suppressing the astonishment he felt at sight of the poorly-dressed old man in Miss Grant's company, suppressing it not only from the instincts of a well-trained servant, but because he knew, at a glance, that shabby as the bent figure was, the stranger was a gentleman.

"My name is Clendon," said Mr. Clendon. "I am an old friend of Lord Sutcombe's; and I have come down to inquire after him, to see him if it is possible."

"Certainly, sir," said the butler; and he led the way to the drawing-room. But Celia drew Mr. Clendon into the library.

"Stay with me here," she begged him. "I will go up to the Marquess's room and see if he is well enough to be told that you are here. I fear that you will not be able to see him. And you must have something to eat," she said, with womanly consideration.

"Thank you, my dear, I need nothing," he said.

As he spoke, the door was opened, none too gently, and Heyton stood on the threshold. He looked from Celia to the old man with what was intended to be a stare of haughty surprise; but was, in reality, a kind of sullen insolence.

"Oh? Who is this?" he demanded.

"A friend of your father's, Lord Heyton," said Mr. Clendon, before Celia could speak. "So old and so dear a friend that he is warranted in intruding, even at such a moment."

"Well, you are intruding, right enough, though you may be an old friend," said Heyton, thickly. "My father is very ill, dangerously ill, as you may have heard. This is no time for—for visitors."

"Forgive me," said Mr. Clendon gently, but with a calmness and dignity that impressed even the only half-sober Heyton, "but my intrusion is justified, as Lord Sutcombe will bear me out, when he knows I am here."

"Oh, well," said Heyton, with an insolent shrug of his shoulders. "I can't speak any more plainly. If you can't take a hint—but it doesn't matter; I'm quite certain that you can't see my father, even if he can be told that you are here."

"We will see," said Mr. Clendon.

Heyton looked at him for a moment, angrily and a trifle suspiciously; then he swung on his heel and went out.

"You must not mind," said Celia. "Lord Heyton is, naturally, very much upset. I should think he scarcely knows what he is saying to you."

"Very likely," assented Mr. Clendon gravely, and without any sign of resentment.

"I will go up now," said Celia; "and I will come down again to you directly."

"One moment," he said, staying her with a gesture. "Will you give me a sheet of paper and a pen and ink?"

Celia did so. Mr. Clendon wrote the letter "W" on the paper, folded it and handed it to her.

"Will you give him this, my dear? If he cannot read it, you may open it and tell him what is written on it."

CHAPTER XXIX

Celia went up to the sick-room. She saw at a glance that the Marquess's condition had improved; he was, of course, still dangerously ill, and very weak; but his eyes, as they rested on her, were perfectly intelligent and he smiled slightly as she bent over him. Then she turned away to Doctor Scott and told him of Mr. Clendon's arrival and desire to see the Marquess.

"I don't think he can do any harm, if he'll be quiet," said the doctor. "At any rate, there is not sufficient reason for refusing to show the paper to the Marquess."

Celia knelt beside the bed and conveyed gently Mr. Clendon's request for an interview.

"Mr. Clendon?" repeated the Marquess, knitting his brows. "I don't know him, my dear."

Then, slowly, she showed him the paper; but he could not read the letter on it and she told him what it was. A flush rose to the white face, and he nodded once or twice; and it seemed to Celia that the inclination of the head had in it something more than a consent to receive the visitor, an indication of some resolution, decision. She went downstairs, and told Mr. Clendon the Marquess would see him.

The old man rose, with the aid of a stick, and followed her through the hall; he looked about him, not curiously, but musingly; and he paused for a second or two before the portrait of the young man in hunting kit, the Marquess's elder brother; the pause was almost imperceptible, but Celia, remembering the scene between herself and the Marquess on the night of his arrival, noticed the pause; but the old man's face conveyed nothing and was as impassive as usual. She took him to the Marquess's room. Lord Sutcombe, at sight of his visitor, tried to rise; but fell back, stretching out his hand, murmuring,

"Wilfred!" Then he looked at the nurse and doctor. "Will you please leave us alone for a little while. This gentleman is——"

Mr. Clendon laid his hand upon his brother's arm and stopped him.

Celia went downstairs, and found Mr. Jacobs standing before the portrait of the Marquess's brother.

"Fine picture that, Miss Grant," he said. "He must have been a splendid fellow: great pity he died. Oh, yes, I know who it is," he went on, answering the question in Celia's eyes. "I've been making acquaintance with the family portraits: very fond of pictures; almost as fond as I am of cattle; but as I shan't be able to afford both, why——!"

At this moment Inspector Brown came hurriedly through the back hall; he was very hot and wiped the perspiration from his sunburnt face with a red ban-

dana.

"I've news for you, Mr. Jacobs," he cried, as calmly as he could. "Will you come into the sitting-room; will you come at once, please: most important!"

Mr. Jacobs looked at him curiously; then beckoned to Celia.

"You come too, Miss Grant," he said. "You know shorthand—I saw some scraps of paper in your waste-paper basket. You can take any notes we want. Splendid thing, shorthand. Wish I could do it. Now then, Mr. Brown!"—as he closed the door.

"Well, to put it in a word, Mr. Jacobs, *I've got our man!*"

Mr. Jacobs did not start or show any glad surprise, but looked steadily at Inspector Smith, and at the same time, seemed to be listening; they could all hear Lord Heyton pacing up and down the hall.

"Mind! I don't take any great credit for it, Mr. Jacobs. It was a fluke: just a fluke. I caught him red-handed; found him in the wood with the jewel-case in his hand. Yes, actually in his hand! He must have hidden it and dug it up."

Mr. Jacobs nodded, but said nothing.

"I've got him in the lock-up," said the Inspector, with an air of satisfaction which was pardonable in the circumstances. "He went very quietly—declared his innocence, of course—well, implied it. I've got notes of what he said. And I searched him."

Mr. Jacobs nodded again, and the Inspector drew from his pocket sundry articles.

"Not much money on him—there's some loose change and this five-pound note. Strange to say—a bit curious and suspicious!—he objected strongly to my taking the note: said that it was worth more than five pounds to him; in fact, he declared that he wouldn't part with it for five thousand and begged me to take care of it and let him change it back for gold." He smiled. Celia flushed hotly, her eyes glowed as they dwelt on the note, and she stifled an exclamation. She listened with parted lips, her breath coming fast. "Something in that, eh, Mr. Jacobs? Then there are some various letters; several of them from a lady in South America, invoices and letters about engineering. Seems to have come from abroad. And here's this packet. It's sealed, as you see; and I didn't care to open it by myself; thought you and I would open it together. May be important evidence, you know."

Mr. Jacobs took up the packet, turned it over, then placed it on the table and laid his hand on it.

"Shouldn't be surprised," he said, quietly. "And so you've got him in the lock-up? What's his name?"

"Well, he calls himself 'Sydney Green': an alias, I dare say."

Mr. Jacobs nodded once more. "Very likely, I should say; very likely. Well, I congratulate you, Inspector. You've done a good morning's work. Bit of a fluke, as you say; but you've been on the close watch, haven't you? And there's something more than luck in this. By the way, you didn't find the two keys—the key of the safe and the key of the jewel-box—on him?"

"No," said Mr. Brown, easily. "Of course, he's got rid of those; and, in another hour or two, he'd have got clear off with the jewel-box. I've got that locked up in my safe. So far as I can see—of course, you can't tell—it looks as if the contents had not been disturbed; in fact, as if we'd recovered all the missing property."

"Splendid!" murmured Mr. Jacobs.

"I suppose you'll go down and see him presently?" said Mr. Brown, almost showing his impatience and irritation at the detective's phlegmatic calm. Nothing seemed to move this man.

"Presently," said Mr. Jacobs, blandly. "There's a knock at the door. Please open it, Miss Grant."

Celia did so. Mrs. Dexter stood there. She seemed very agitated.

"Will you please come upstairs, Miss Grant," she said; "and—and, yes, you two gentlemen. Something strange, terrible, has happened."

Without a word, Mr. Jacobs signed to Celia to lead the way, placing the packet in his pocket as she did so, and they followed her up to the Marquess's room. He was lying back with his eyes closed; the doctor's hand was on his pulse. Mr.

Clendon was seated beside the bed, his hand on the Marquess's shoulder. Mr. Clendon looked troubled, but was quite calm.

"The Marquess has sent for you that you may hear something he has resolved to tell you," he said, in a low voice.

The Marquess opened his eyes and looked round; then they fixed themselves on Heyton, whom Mrs. Dexter had summoned, and who stood regarding the group sullenly.

"Yes," said the Marquess, feebly, but quite distinctly. "I want to tell you that this is my brother"—his hand reached for Mr. Clendon's—"my elder brother. He is Lord Sutcombe, not I. He disappeared and was supposed to have died. I knew some months ago that he was alive, but——"

"Yielding to my earnest entreaty, my command, my brother consented to conceal the fact," said Mr. Clendon, gravely.

"Yes, but it was wrong, Wilfred; and it was foolish," said the Marquess. His eyes went to his son. "I am sorry, Percy. I believed that he was dead; but I should have told you the moment I discovered the truth. Yes, I see now that it was my duty to have done so."

Heyton had stood staring at the two old men dully; his sodden brain did not realize at first the importance of the avowal; then the blood rushed to his face and he stammered:

"What's all this? What's the meaning of this cock-and-bull story? I—I don't understand. You don't suppose I'm going to cave in, accept this fairytale? I'm your son—I'm the next in succession——"

"Yes," said the Marquess, with a deep sigh, and a look at his son which Heyton understood and quailed from. "My brother is not married; you are his heir—after me."

"I did not say I was not married, Talbot," said Mr. Clendon, almost inaudibly. "I said that I had no son. But we will not dwell on that. If I could have had my desire, the truth, my identity, would have been buried with me."

"No, no," panted the Marquess; "even

if you had not come to-day, I should have told the truth, Wilfred. Would to God I had told it before!"

"Here, but look here!" Heyton broke out, with a kind of impatient insolence. "This is all very well. This old man comes here, makes a statement—gets you to make a statement—when, as everybody knows, you're not in your right mind—Oh, I'm not going to accept it!"

"There are proofs. You know, Wilfred," said the Marquess. "But I can talk no longer. Leave me with my brother."

They went, the doctor and nurse only remaining: the Marquess's little strength had been sorely tried, and the doctor was watching him closely. With a defiant air, Heyton swaggered down the steps. As he reached the bottom, a hand fell on his shoulder; lightly enough, but Heyton started and winced.

"Will you give me a minute or two in the sitting-room, my lord?" said Mr. Jacobs, blandly.

"Eh, what is it?" said Heyton, with an oath. "What do you want? I don't want to be bothered just now; got plenty of my own affairs on my mind."

But he followed the detective. Mr. Jacobs closed the door and stood, on one side of the table, looking at Heyton on the other.

"Yes, this has been a most upsetting business for you, my lord," he said. "You have had, and are having, a most trying time; this is the kind of thing which will break down the strongest man; and I'm about to take the liberty of offering you a word of advice." As he spoke, he took up a Continental Bradshaw which was lying open on the table. "In cases of your kind, there's nothing like a change of scene and air. You want to go right away: I mean, a *long* way.—I've been looking up one or two places where a man could hide himself—I beg your pardon!—I mean, seclude himself without fear of interruption or—interference."

Heyton stared at him; and as he stared, with a puzzled frown, his swollen face grew mottled, livid in places, red in others.

"I don't know what the devil you

mean!" he blurted out. "Why should I go anywhere?"

"For the sake of your health, my lord," said Mr. Jacobs, his innocent blue eyes fixed on Heyton. "You want a change—and at once; in fact, it is absolutely imperative." He leant forward across the table, patted the Bradshaw and dropped his voice as he went on incisively, "You can catch the night mail from Charing Cross. Book straight through by the Trans-Siberian, by way of Moscow and Pekin. When you reach Harbin, go right into the interior. There are mines there—anyhow, you can lose yourself. You understand, my lord?"

The sweat stood out in great drops on Heyton's face; he tried to meet the detective's eye with an insolent, indignant stare; but his eyes wavered and fell and he sank into a chair.

"I—I don't know what you mean?" he stammered thickly.

"But you will go?" inquired Mr. Jacobs. "In fact, I am sure you will."

Cur as he was, Heyton made a last stand; he threw up his head, swore a vile oath and struck the table.

"I'm hanged if I do!" he said.

"You'll be hanged, if you don't, my lord!" said Mr. Jacobs. Then, after a pause, he said, with a shrug of the shoulders, "I thought you'd have been sensible, that you'd have taken my tip without forcing me into particulars; but if you must have them—well, Lord Heyton, if you are here to-morrow morning, I shall arrest you for the robbery of the jewels and the attempted murder of Lord Sutcombe."

Heyton sprang to his feet; then sank back again with a hoarse attempt at a laugh.

"You must be a fool!"

"Well, one of us is a fool, but it's not me, my lord," said Mr. Jacobs, imperturbably. "I knew the truth ten minutes after I had examined the dressing-room. You see, the burglar who understands his business works in kid gloves; they leave no finger-prints. There were prints on the door of the safe, inside, on the poker—oh, well, everywhere; because, you see, when a man's engaged in this kind of work, he's naturally nervous,

his hands are sweaty. And these fingerprints were those of a gentleman's hands. Do you want me to go on, Lord Heyton?"

Heyton could not speak; his tongue seemed to cleave to the roof of his mouth; he felt as if his spine were giving way, as if all his strength of mind and body were ebbing from him.

"It's—it's ridiculous!" he stammered.

"No, my lord, it's quite simple, quite elementary. There were the fingerprints, on the safe, on the walls, on the poker. I could read them quite easily with a magnifying glass; and they never lie. 'Pon my word, Lord Heyton!" he broke off musingly, his mouth twisting into a smile, "I'm inclined to think they're the only things in this world one can rely on. Now, you'll see why I upset the ink over your hand." He took the two sheets of paper from his pocket and laid them on the table; and beside them he placed a silver print of the fingerprints in the room.

Heyton stared at them as if they were live things that could sting him.

"Another thing, my lord," said Mr. Jacobs. "I was in the dressing-room just after the Marquess recovered consciousness, and heard him charge you with the robbery. The evidence is quite conclusive. But there is, of course, what we call collateral proof. I found these two keys under the bed in your dressing-room. Of course, you intended throwing them in the lake, when you went down with the jewel-case; but you dropped the keys and didn't find them; there is always a little hitch like that— *it's the hitch in the rope.* I know you took the jewel-case the morning you went down to bathe, because I traced your footprints into the middle of the wood, where you need not have gone, if you had been going merely for a bath. I knew I should find the jewel-case just where you stopped; but I didn't want to discover it. I was waiting for *you* to go for it, which you would have done presently. Unfortunately for him, another man was in the wood that morning and saw you; and *he* went for the jewel-case. The Inspector has arrested him, worse luck. I say 'worse luck,' because

now we can't hush up the affair—and, you'll have to *go.*"

Heyton wiped the sweat from his face, his head sank on his breast; he was in a condition of coma; so stupefied, indeed, that it was only by an effort he could follow the detective's next words,

"There is only one other person—well, say, two—who suspect you, Lord Heyton. But she will keep her lips shut. She is your wife—fortunately for you."

He went to the sideboard, poured out some brandy and pushed the glass towards the wretched man.

"Drink that, my lord, and pull yourself together," he said, in a matter-of-fact way. "That's right," as Heyton stretched out a shaking hand and poured some of the spirit down his throat and some over his waistcoat. "Now, you'll want some money. Oh, I know! You wanted it badly or you wouldn't have played this idiotic game. In this bag is some gold. When you get to Harbin, you will find some more waiting for you. I'll take it upon myself to arrange all that. Don't take much luggage: just a change and a tooth-brush. Say you're going to town on business, any business you can think of that requires your immediate presence. And, mind! don't stop on the way; go straight through: you'll find the trains fit in. I won't add, 'Keep your mouth shut'; you'll do that; unless"—he nodded significantly at the empty glass—"you take too much of that. That's rather a weakness of yours, Lord Heyton: master it, or it'll master you. Now, there's no time to lose. I'll order a brougham for you. Come, pull yourself together. Man!"—his disgust, impatience broke out, for the first time—"try to think what you're running away from! It's a long rope, and it'll take you all your time and wits to get beyond its reach. And think of the risk I'm running; I'm compounding a felony. I—Harry Jacobs!"

Heyton rose, clutching at the table, chair; his quivering lips opened and shut; at last he cried hoarsely,

"Damn you!"

"That's all right, my lord," said Mr. Jacobs. "I'm glad I've roused your spirit. Here, pull yourself together—your face is giving you away. Upstairs and pack! The carriage will be waiting."

He held open the door; and Heyton, with a glance at him which meant murder, passed out.

Half an hour later, Celia saw Lord Heyton enter the brougham.

"Is Lord Heyton going away?" she asked, with surprise, as she saw the footman place a small portmanteau on the box. She hurried into the hall as she spoke, and it was Mr. Jacobs, who was standing there with Mrs. Dexter, who answered her.

"Yes, Miss Grant," he said. "Lord Heyton has been called away on most important business. Most unfortunate! But there was no help for it."

He waited until Mrs. Dexter had gone, then, with his eyes fixed on Celia's face, he said to her,

"Will you please tell the Marquess that Lord Heyton has gone? And you might say that his return is quite uncertain; in fact—er—he has gone abroad."

Celia's ingenuous countenance expressed her surprise, which seemed to satisfy Mr. Jacobs.

"Now," he said, briskly, "I'm going to see the prisoner, Mr. Sydney Green." The colour rose to Celia's face; but her eyes met Mr. Jacobs' steadily. "Have you any message for him, Miss Grant?"

"Yes," said Celia in a low voice and after a pause. "Will you tell him, please, that I will come to him, if—if I am allowed to do so?"

"You may go and see Mr. Green whenever you please, my dear Miss Grant," said Mr. Jacobs. As he turned away, he added, "By the way, perhaps you'd like to know I'm going to take Mr. Clendon with me. I beg his lordship's pardon—I mean, the Marquess."

Celia looked bewildered for a moment; then she sighed.

"Yes. I am rather confused. I am glad you are going to take him with you; very glad."

"So am I," said Mr. Jacobs, with his bland, innocent smile.

CHAPTER XXX

In the circumstances, Derrick was not uncomfortably lodged. The lock-up was an ancient, knock-down affair, and the Inspector had arranged that Derrick should occupy one of the rooms in the adjoining police-station. Here, Mr. Jacobs and Mr. Clendon found him, if not altogether resigned to the situation, at any rate not cast down or despondent.

"Well, here we are," said Mr. Jacobs, cheerfully. "I hope they've made you as comfortable as possible, Mr.—Green. I've brought a friend of yours with me, and I have a message from another friend of yours, Miss Grant. She says she will pay you a visit whenever you like to see her."

Derrick shook his head. "I don't want her to come here," he said. "But I'm very glad to see Mr. Clendon."

"By the way," cut in Mr. Jacobs, "I ought to introduce this gentleman by his right name, or, rather, title. You will be very much surprised to hear, Mr. Green, that Mr. Clendon is the Marquess of Sutcombe. It's a long story, but, with your permission, I will put it into a sentence. His lordship is the elder brother, who was thought to be dead, but has turned up—if his lordship will allow me the phrase."

"It is true," said Mr. Clendon, as we must still call him; and he made the admission with an air of resignation and a gesture of regret. "But we have come to talk of your affairs."

"Quite so, my lord," said Mr. Jacobs. "Now, Mr. Sydney Green—or shall I call you, Mr. Derrick Dene?"

Mr. Clendon started slightly and bent his piercing eyes on Derrick, who coloured and bit his lip.

"Yes, that's my name," he said; "but I don't know how you know it."

"My dear Mr. Dene," said Mr. Jacobs, blandly, "we people in Scotland Yard know a great many things. Just as an instance, let me tell you what I know about you. You were placed at an early age in the care of a worthy couple named Jackson, who brought you up and started you in the profession which I am sure you will adorn. Owing to a—well, let us say, a misunderstanding—you left England—er—somewhat abruptly, and went with a travelling circus to South America; in South America you left the circus and found employment on a ranch, owned by a lady named Donna Elvira——"

Derrick, frowning, stared at him and did not notice that Mr. Clendon had quietly sunk into a chair and, with his hands leaning on his stick, was looking fixedly at Derrick.

"You want to know how we came to know all this?" said Mr. Jacobs, cheerfully. "Well, we had the little affair of the forged cheque placed in our hands, and were following it up when a Mr. Brown, the Sutcombe family solicitor, stepped in and stopped us. You see, the bank refused to prosecute and we couldn't move without it. But, in the course of our inquiries into the business of the forged cheque, we naturally traced your antecedents, and it seemed to us—well, to put it shortly, that your history was so interesting it was worth following. I have all the notes here." He tapped a little book he had taken from his pocket. "You will want to know why I brought it down with me, when I was engaged upon another case and had little reason to expect that you would be arrested on this charge?"

"The question was in my mind," said Derrick, gravely. "Perhaps you'll explain."

"With pleasure," replied Mr. Jacobs, and his tone corroborated his words. "But perhaps this packet which we have, in the discharge of our duty, taken from you, will explain better than I can."

He took the packet from his pocket and laid it on the table. As he did so, he glanced for the first time at the old man, who was sitting so quietly, so immovably.

"Will you allow me to open it—or perhaps we will ask his lordship to do so?"

Derrick looked from one to the other and bit his lip.

"That packet is a confidential one," he said; "but"—moved by an impulse he could not understand—"I am willing that Mr. Clendon shall open it. It has passed out of my hands. I suppose I have no right to it," he added, rather bitterly.

"I made the proposition to save time," said Mr. Jacobs. "There is the packet, your lordship."

With a glance at Derrick, the old man took it and broke the seals slowly. There was no surprise on his face as he read the enclosures. Perhaps he had foreseen that which the packet contained. He read, in absolute silence, the two men watching him; Mr. Jacobs with a cheerful countenance, Derrick with an anxious regard; then presently, Mr. Clendon looked up. Now his face was working, his eyes were moist as he breathed, "My God!" and there was remorse, as well as a kind of solemn joy in the cry.

"You do not guess the truth contained in these papers?" he asked, in a very low voice, as his gaze met Derrick's.

"No, sir," said Derrick.

Mr. Clendon turned his eyes to Mr. Jacobs, but Derrick felt that the old man was addressing him.

"The lady who writes this letter, Mr. Jacobs, the Donna Elvira of whom you have spoken, is—my wife. We have been separated for years. The cause? Nothing that can cast a shadow of dishonour on her. I was wandering in South America when I met her; we fell in love, were married in haste. I was then a headstrong, hot-tempered, unreasonable youth; she—well, she was Spanish, and with a temper and disposition that matched mine. After many quarrels, we parted in anger. I went my way, a wild, desperate way; needless to tell you whither such a way leads. Wrecked in character and prospects, I decided to be quit of the world. I had thought of suicide—but God held my hand. Suffice it that I disappeared, that I concocted a false report of my death, and so made room for my younger brother, Talbot, to take the place in the world which I had rendered myself unfit to fill."

There was a pause, during which the old man strove for composure. Derrick began to tremble. He remembered Donna Elvira's strange tenderness to him, his strange tenderness towards her; and something vague and nebulous was growing out of the Marquess's words, a hope that, in its intensity, was more painful than joyous.

"I did not know," went on the Marquess in a lower voice, and with obvious difficulty, "that, when I left my wife, she was about to become a mother. I did not know that a child was born to me—a son. If I had known—well, the whole course of my life would have been altered from that moment. I should have gone back to her, should have claimed my child; perhaps it is because she knew that I should have done so that she concealed the fact from me. Be that as it may, I was kept in ignorance until this moment; and even now, she does not tell me, but—her son."

He raised his eyes to Derrick with something in them that made Derrick's heart leap, the tears spring to his eyes.

"Yes; you are my son," said Mr. Clendon, and he held out his hand.

Derrick, moving as if in a dream, took the thin hand and grasped it in both of his.

"Oh, is it true?" was all he could say, huskily.

"It is quite true," said Mr. Clendon. "The certificates are enclosed; there is a minute account of the way in which your mother placed you in the charge of these people; there are even periodical receipts for the sums she paid for your maintenance. As to your identity——"

"No doubts about that," murmured Mr. Jacobs, cheerfully. "Proved up to the hilt. Marquess, I congratulate you—and you, too, Lord Heyton."

Now, indeed, Derrick started.

"Do you mean that I——?" he stammered, overwhelmed by the significance of the title by which Mr. Jacobs had addressed him.

Mr. Jacobs nodded, as cheerfully as before. "Quite so," he said. "Your father being the Marquess of Sutcombe, you are, of course, Lord Heyton."

Derrick sank on to a chair, still holding his father's hand; and he was silent for a moment or two; then he looked up.

"This charge?" he said, almost in a whisper. "You—both of you—know that I am innocent?"

Mr. Jacobs nodded, and the father's hand closed tightly on his son's.

"Then," said Derrick hoarsely, "who—who is guilty?"

"Ah!" said Mr. Jacobs, with a shake of the head, his eyes fixed on the carpet. "Very difficult to say. I'm afraid it will turn out to be one of those undiscovered crimes with which the newspapers are always taunting poor Scotland Yard." He rose as he spoke, and reached for his hat. "Now I'll leave you two gentlemen together. By the way, Mr.—I beg your pardon, Lord Heyton!—I'm afraid you'll have to remain here for another hour or two; there are certain formalities which must be endured. For instance"—he smiled—"I shall have to take you before a local magistrate. Of course, we shall produce no evidence, throw any quantity of ashes on our heads, and apologize for the cruel mistake we have made; and the local magistrate, if he knows his business, will read me a severe lecture on my stupidity and set you free with an apology from all concerned. Now I'll leave you. You two gentlemen must have a great deal to say to each other. And I beg you to believe"—he spoke with deep feeling—"that I should not have intruded on this interview, if I had not considered my presence necessary."

He opened the door, but closed it again, holding the handle, and said, in a casual fashion,

"By the way, I am sorry to say that Lord Heyton—tut, tut!—the gentleman who was Lord Heyton—has been called away on important business. I am afraid he will be away some time; in fact, I have advised him to go on a long tour, when his business is finished. He requires change of air, a *long* change; in fact, I don't think England will ever suit him."

He spoke the last words over his shoulder and disappeared.

The father and son were engaged in a conversation that moved them both deeply; and a knock had been repeated on the door twice, before they heard it and Derrick said, "Come in!"

A policeman stood on the threshold.

"A lady and gentleman to see you, sir."

"I can see no one," said Derrick, trying to keep his voice steady; but his father made a gesture with his hand and Derrick nodded reluctantly.

There entered Lady Gridborough and Reggie Rex, who had obtained permission from Mr. Jacobs. Lady Gridborough was much agitated, and she was going with outstretched hand, straight to Derrick, but stopped at sight of the old man who had risen from his chair.

"Oh, I came at once!" she said, tremulously. "I couldn't stay away. Oh, Derrick, I am so sorry, so sorry. I might have known that you couldn't be so bad, so wicked as they all said! Will you forgive me? Oh, do say you'll forgive me for so cruelly misjudging you."

Derrick took the fat hand and looked, with a grave smile of more than forgiveness, at the good-natured, agitated face.

"Don't say any more, Lady Gridborough," he said. "It was my fault. I ought to have spoken—I see now what a fool I have been! My mistaken sense of honour has caused all this trouble; and grieved you very much, I see, dear Lady Gridborough. But how did you learn the truth—I mean discover that I had not wronged poor Susie?"

"It was Mr. Rex here," said Lady Gridborough, her face all smiles now. "He's an extraordinary young man, and has succeeded in doing that at which we had all failed—opening Susie's lips. How he managed it, I do not know! Perhaps he can tell you."

Derrick had got hold of Reggie's hand by this time, and was regarding him with a half-smiling interrogation; and Reggie was also smiling with that air of omniscience and supreme acuteness which sat so curiously on his boyish face.

"A future wife should have no secrets from her future husband, as you will be the first to admit, dear Lady Gridborough."

"'Future husband!'" echoed Derrick, with a surprise that was only momentary.

"Yes," said Reggie, quietly. "I have won my angel. I don't deny that it was difficult; but this last business of yours settled it. You see, Susie felt that, if she told the truth, and showed up the right man—or, rather, the wrong one; for, if

there was ever a 'wrong un,' it is——; but we won't mention names—Susie knew that she would be doing Celia a service; besides, Susie felt that she could face the world much more easily, if she had a great, hulking man beside her. And," he added modestly, "there were—ahem—other reasons."

"I am sure there were," said Derrick, warmly; and he wrung Reggie's hand. "I congratulate you—both."

"But how about this dreadful business of the robbery at the Hall?" said Lady Gridborough, suddenly growing pale.

"So far as my son is concerned, madam," said Mr. Clendon, in his grave voice which had grown very gentle, "you will be glad to hear that it has ended satisfactorily; he has been proved innocent of the crime laid to his charge."

"Oh, I'm so glad!" cried Lady Gridborough, delightedly. "But"—suddenly—"your son? You are his father? I didn't know—I thought his father was dead."

"So I was, madam; to the world; but I have returned from the grave to find my son," said Mr. Clendon.

"Well, I am glad!" cried Lady Gridborough. "You must both come and stay with me. Now, you won't refuse, Mr. Dene, will you?" She looked at Mr. Clendon pleadingly, and then with confusion and embarrassment, as they both remained silent.

"My father's name is not 'Dene,'" said Derrick, who felt that the explanation would have to come sooner or later. "He is Lord Sutcombe."

Reggie did not start; but, for the first time in his life, the young man looked nonplussed and discomfited; he regarded the father and son with a puzzled stare, then, with an exclamation, he cried,

"Of course, the *elder* brother! Then—then *you*, Green, are Lord Heyton?" He smiled as if he himself had conferred the title of nobility on Derrick. "Well, this knocks me out. No more detective novels for me! Realism is my line for the future. And yet, what a novel it would make!"

"You shall write it some day, Reg-

gie," said Derrick, with a smile.

"Some day?" retorted Reggie. "I'm going to write it at once! Come away, Lady Gridborough! This is no place for us," he added tactfully, and, taking her hand, he led the bewildered old lady out of the room, nodding, with a smile of intense gratification, over his shoulder at Derrick.

CHAPTER XXXI

The following afternoon, as the London evening papers were publishing what they were pleased to call "A Romance in High Life," Derrick and his father made their way through an excited crowd, which had gathered about the Court House. Affairs there had proceeded as Mr. Jacobs had prophesied; the magistrates had listened with amazement, not only to Mr. Jacobs' statement, but to the announcement which Mr. Clendon had made of his identity and his relationship to Derrick; and the worthy chairman, Sir Courtenay Comber, using almost the identical words Mr. Jacobs had attributed to him, had congratulated Derrick and informed him that he left the Court "without a stain on his character." Notwithstanding its satisfactory conclusion, the ordeal had been a trying one for father and son, and Derrick looked pale and somewhat worn as he grasped the hand of Reggie, who had been in Court, and had hurried after him to congratulate him.

"I've got a carriage here for you, round the corner," he said; "and I've succeeded in stopping them ringing the bells."

"I'm glad," said Derrick; "but why should they want to ring the bells?"

"Well, you see," explained Reggie, as he led them to the carriage, "Lord Heyton—I mean the other man—is not a great favourite; whereas, somehow or other, you have caught the popular imagination; besides, it has leaked out that you are going to marry Miss Grant; and she is tremendously popular. She has been very kind, in the do-good-and-blush-to-find-it-known way, to the poor people about her; and Susie has told a good many of Miss Grant's angelic kindnesses to her. Hence these tears," he added, as the people crowded about them and cheered heartily. "Where shall I tell the man to drive, my lord?"

"To the Hall," replied Mr. Clendon gravely. "Yes," he said to Derrick, as the carriage drove off, "the Marquess— I mean your uncle, Talbot, wants to see you, naturally."

"You have told him?" said Derrick. "Poor man!"

"Yes, I have told him; and, strangely enough, he welcomed the news. And yet it is not strange; for, alas! he knew the character of his son, knew that he was not worthy to bear the title. There is something more on my brother's mind than I am cognisant of. Some secret which worries him," he added.

Derrick remained silent. He dared not probe the mystery of the hidden jewel-case, of Heyton's sudden flight; but it was evident to him that Mr. Jacobs intended to conceal any knowledge he might have, and Derrick was only too thankful to concur in that concealment.

On their way to the Hall, Derrick and his father spoke of many things of the past and the future; and presently the old man said in a low voice,

"You will be married soon, Derrick?"

"The first moment Celia will have me," replied Derrick, promptly.

"I would like you to spend your honeymoon in South America," said his father.

Derrick understood, and he nodded and laid his hand on the old man's.

"And you, sir? Shall you go there—soon?"

Mr. Clendon shook his head. "No," he responded. "The chasm between us is too wide, has divided us for too long a time. But it shall be as your mother wishes. You will talk to her——We will leave her future and mine on the knees of the gods. But yours, thank God! is assured. How strangely Fate works! How little I thought, when I helped Celia to come to the Hall, that I was lending a guiding hand to the future of my son's wife. Derrick, that same fate has been very good to you."

"Don't I know it, sir!" said Derrick in a low voice.

They reached the Hall; and as they entered, they could not but be conscious of the stir of excitement there; the old butler and the other servants looked at them with an intense interest. As the two men stood in the hall, waiting the summons to the sick-room, Derrick looked round him eagerly; but it was not at the subdued splendour surrounding him; he scarcely noted the indications of luxury and wealth, the wealth and state to which he was heir; he was looking and listening for some sign of Celia; and he was so absorbed that he started when his father touched his arm and directed his gaze to a portrait.

"That is mine, Derrick," he said. "Do you see any resemblance to yourself?"

"Yes; I think—yes, I do," replied Derrick.

"I noticed it yesterday, directly I entered the hall, for the first time for many years."

The footman came down to say that they might go up, and they ascended the broad stairs, Derrick still looking about him and listening; but Celia did not appear. They were ushered into the sick-room, and the door closed on them; and they remained there for nearly half an hour; for the injured man had recovered something of his old strength, as if a burden had been lifted from his shoulders, and he was able to hear the story of Derrick's identity and to speak a few words of relief and satisfaction. When they left the room both Derrick and his father were much moved, and they went down the stairs in silence. Derrick stopped as they reached the hall, and again looked round him.

"You will find her in there," said his father, nodding towards the library; and Derrick, with a sudden flush and a brightening of the eyes, knocked at the door.

The voice that said, "Come in," made his heart leap. He turned the handle of the door and entered. Celia had heard his voice in the hall, was expecting him; she was standing by the table, her hand pressed on it, her face pale but her eyes glowing with the ineffable light of love.

"Sydney!" she murmured, all her heart in her voice.

He took her in his arms and, for a mo-ment, there was silence; then she raised her head and whispered,

"It is all right, Sydney?"

"It is all right," he responded. "I am here, as you see; I am acquitted; all is well. But, dearest," he hesitated apologetically, "you must not call me 'Sydney.'"

She looked up at him, her brows knit slightly; and he gathered her to him still more closely, as he went on.

"I've got the strangest news to tell you, Celia. You will think that you are dreaming, as I have been dreaming ever since I myself heard it."

"They have been talking, saying strange things—the servants, I mean—and Mrs. Dexter came in just now and tried to tell me—something; but she was too excited and checked herself; she said I should hear it from you! What is it, Syd——But I'm not to call you that? What am I to call you?"

"Derrick," he said; "it is the name that you shall always call me by; but the world will know me as Lord Heyton."

She started in his arms and, drawing back her head, gazed up at him in amazement; and she listened as he told her the wonderful news; at first with bewilderment and then with a gravity and a lack of enthusiasm which surprised him.

"You are glad, dearest?" he asked. "You are surprised, astonished, of course? It takes some time to realize. You are glad?"

"Are you?" she asked in a low voice.

Derrick shrugged his shoulders; then, as if he were ashamed of the gesture, he said quickly,

"That I have found a father—and such a father—yes. And I have found a mother too. Have you guessed that it is the Donna Elvira I have told you so much about? You are surprised; and no wonder. It is part of the strange story. I will tell you all about her presently. Of course, I am glad. I was all alone in the world—but for you—but for you, Celia! and the loneliness was hard sometimes to bear. But for the rest, the title and the estates and the other things, I welcome them only because you will share them with me. Celia, I'm not such an idiot as not to realize that I am coming to you as something more than a penniless adventurer, well-nigh nameless, a man of no account. If I had all the world at my command, the highest title a man could bear, I should only value them because I could lay them at your feet."

The tears welled to her eyes and, of her own accord, she drew his head down to her and laid her sweet lips on his.

"You are too good to me; I am not worth it," she said, brokenly. Then, with something like a start, she whispered, with a dawning fear and horror in her eyes, "And the other—Lord Heyton? And his wife! Oh, poor, poor woman! And she has borne so much already! She is lying there, upstairs, prostrated. Who is to tell her? Oh, Derrick, dearest, who is to tell her?"

"You," he said, gently. "No one can break it to her better than you can."

"Oh, must I? Oh, it will be hard for her."

"It will be hard, Celia; but no one can do it better than you. You will soften the blow. She will realise her debt to you, through me. Tell her that her future shall be cared for—but you know that I shall look after that. Celia, you, who are so quick, so acute, have divined the truth. It was for Miriam that I took on myself the forged cheque. I—cared for her once; I thought I was in love with her. I thought so until that night you came to me and stood like an angel of rescue between me and a shameful death. As to Miriam's husband——"

Derrick paused and, looking down at her steadily, laid his hand on her shoulder with an almost masterful pressure.

"—There must be nothing more said about him between us two, Celia," he continued, with solemnity in his voice and manner. "He is gone; let him go and take the past with him. But one word: Celia, it was Heyton who wronged Susie, it was Heyton who forged the cheque; it was because Lady Gridborough thought me guilty of wrecking Susie's life, that she cut me that morning when she passed us at the gate by the wood. She knows the truth now; for Reggie has got Susie to reveal it——"

"Reggie!" murmured Celia.

"Yes; he fell in love with Susie the first time he saw her; he has been telling me all about it."

"And Susie yielded! I can scarcely believe it," said Celia, with a note of delight in her voice.

"She yielded," said Derrick, with a smile. "Reggie is a wonderful young man; and has a way with him, as the saying is. He must have laid hard siege to Susie's heart—perhaps he won her through the child. Anyway, he has done so; and, in doing so, has cleared my name."

"I am glad, glad!" Celia murmured, giving him a little hug. "Yes; he is a wonderful young man; I saw that the first time I met him." She told him of that meeting in the British Museum Reading Room. "Oh, I can quite understand, now I come to think of it; with all her seeming coldness, Susie has a tender heart. I've found that out——"

"By the surest way, the revelation of your own," said Derrick. He looked round the room, as if everything in it were precious to him. "And this is where you have worked," he said.

"Yes," she nodded, also looking round; "and I have been very happy here—or should have been," she went on softly, her eyes on his, "if I had been able to keep a certain man out of my thoughts. But he was there all the time; I could close my eyes and be back at 'The Jail,' looking over the rails at his upturned face and hearing his voice. What a wonderful thing love is!"

"And yet so easy to understand," he said with a smile, as he caught her to him again. There was silence for a while; then he said, "We'll be married soon, Celia?"

She blushed and her eyes fell for a moment; then she raised them to his and whispered,

"Yes."

"My father wants us to spend our honeymoon in South America; wants us to go to my mother. You will go; you will not mind the long journey?"

She was silent for a moment; then, almost solemnly, but with an infinite love in her eyes and her voice, she murmured,

"'Whither thou goest, I will go . thy people shall be my people.'"

As Celia went to Miriam's room, can it be wondered that her step grew slower and, notwithstanding her own happiness, that her heart waxed heavy with sorrow for the wretched young wife? She found Miriam lying back in her chair, her hands clasped loosely in her lap, her face almost vacant of any expression; she seemed weighed down by the apathy resulting from utter hopelessness, from a knowledge of some evil from which she could not escape. She turned her eyes to Celia, and Celia's heart was made to ache by the look of dumb suffering in them, that look which the weak always wear when the world is going wrong with them.

Celia knelt down beside the chair, and took one of the nerveless hands.

"Are you better, getting stronger, Lady Heyton?" she asked, gently.

Miriam shook her head listlessly, and gazed out of the window; then she turned her eyes again slowly to Celia, and said, in a toneless voice,

"Is it true, what the servants are saying, that the Marquess's elder brother has been discovered, and that the Marquess, our Marquess, is no longer the master here? Marie came and told me something about it; but she was confused and rambled, and I could make very little of it."

"It is true," said Celia. "The elder brother is alive, is here in the house. He had been living in seclusion for years; the Marquess discovered a little while ago that his brother was alive; but the real Marquess did not wish to displace his younger brother. He was living in poverty, working for his living. I knew him at that time."

Miriam looked only slightly interested. "You knew him? That's strange."

"Yes; it is all very strange," Celia agreed. "It was Mr. Clendon—we still call him that; it is so difficult to remember that he is the Marquess—and I lived in the same building; we called it 'The Jail'; it was so prison-like." Her voice grew dreamy, as she spoke. "He played the violin in the orchestra of a theatre; I used to hear him practising; the music floated up to my room; how long ago it seems! It was he who persuaded Lord Sutcombe to engage me as librarian, here at the Hall."

"It sounds like a novel," commented Miriam, absently.

"Yes," assented Celia; "but it isn't any more wonderful and astounding than the occurrences one reads of in the newspapers almost every day."

"And there is no doubt? I mean, it is all settled; he *is* the Marquess?" said Miriam, still apathetically, as if no change, however revolutionary, could affect her.

"Yes, it is all settled, or will be very soon," said Celia. "The lawyers are coming down to-morrow; the evidence is quite complete." There was silence for a minute or two; then Celia, with her heart beating fast and heavily, said, in a still lower voice, "There is something else I must tell you, Lady Heyton. Mr. Clendon, the real Marquess, has—has a son."

She stopped to let this sink in, and Miriam's brows knit slightly; then she said, almost inaudibly,

"You mean that—that Heyton, my husband, is not the heir, is not Lord Heyton?"

"Yes," said Celia in a whisper. It seemed to her that Miriam drew a long breath of relief; but she made no comment and Celia went on, with still greater difficulty, "I must tell you who he is, Lady Heyton. I want to prepare you for a shock, and I don't know how to do it. You—you know him."

"I know him?" repeated Miriam, with dull surprise. "You mean I have met him. What is his name? Heyton, of course."

"That is his name, his title," said Celia; "but he has borne several names, has had a strange history. You knew him by the name of Derrick Dene."

Miriam did not start; but the pallor of her face increased, and her tear-swollen eyes fixed themselves with a kind of wan wonder and shame on Celia.

"Derrick Dene!" she echoed, faintly.

"Yes," murmured Celia; and, as briefly and gently as she could, she told Miriam of Derrick's recent experiences. Miriam's hands went up to her face; but they dropped into her lap again and she looked before her and said, in a stricken voice,

"I see you know everything. Yes, it was Heyton, my husband, who forged the cheque; I know it now: he is capable of—anything." She shuddered. "It was to save me from the shame and unhappiness of being a felon's wife that Derrick sacrificed himself. Yes; it was just what he would do." She glanced at Celia. "You know, of course, that I—I once cared for him; that we were to be married; I jilted him for a title, for money——"

"Don't say any more," pleaded Celia; but Miriam went on ruthlessly.

"I was a weak fool; I might have known that no good would come of such treachery—oh, yes, I knew in my heart; I knew that Derrick was worth a hundred of *him*. I sinned with my eyes open; no, I shut them; I was blinded by the thought, the prospect of being—what I am," she added bitterly; then, suddenly, she fixed her eyes on Celia's downcast face. "Derrick told you this? Then he knows you very well; you are a close friend of his; you are——?"

"Yes," murmured Celia. "I am going to be his wife—very soon. We met in 'The Jail.'" She did not, she could not tell how that meeting had been brought about; she wanted to spare Miriam all she could; but, notwithstanding her resolution, the next words slipped out unconsciously. "He was accused of the robbery of the jewels——" She bit her lip; but it was too late for remorse.

Miriam dropped back in the chair, her eyes closed and her lips became livid.

"He did not do it!" she gasped.

"No, no!" said Celia, quickly; "he has been proved innocent."

There was silence for a moment; while Miriam evidently made an effort to control her agitation.

"Who—who——? Have they found out who did it?"

"No," broke in Celia, swiftly and tremulously. "No one has been discovered. Mr. Jacobs, the detective, said that no one will be discovered. The jewels have been found."

"I know," murmured Miriam.

"There will be no more trouble," whispered Celia, soothingly.

Again there was a pause, then Miriam asked brokenly,

"Heyton—my husband?"

"He has gone abroad," said Celia, hanging her head; "he will be away some time."

Miriam's lips moved; she whispered, at last,

"I understand!—I must leave here—at once. I will go back to my people or hide myself somewhere in London."

"Oh, go back to your people," said Celia. "I—I want to tell you how sorry the Marquess, all of us, are for you, how deeply we sympathise with your loss; it weighs upon us all."

"It need not do," said Miriam, with a touch of bitterness. "I have always been a stranger and an alien here. Strangely enough, Celia, I have felt as if I—I have been walking on quicksand that might swallow me up at any moment. Oh, I have been as unhappy as I deserve. All the time, I have felt a sense of—of—oh, I can't explain; but it seemed to me as if my treachery to Derrick would come back on me. And it has! If you knew"—she shuddered—"but I can't tell you. I shall never open my lips—I want to go at once. Yes; I am quite strong enough. I want to go away from here—from you all. I want to be at rest, somewhere where I can try to forget. What a downfall! What a downfall!"

Celia, with the tears in her eyes, put her arm round the trembling form.

"Dear Lady Heyton," she murmured, "you must not give way. It may not be all as black as you think. And—and Derrick wishes me to tell you that your future—oh, how am I to put it!—that you will be well cared for; that you will have no need for anxiety about the future."

"Derrick!" breathed Miriam, ashamedly. "Yes, it is what he would do. It is like him to think of me, even in the moment of his own happiness. Oh, God, how ashamed I am!"

"You will not refuse—to let them help you, to let them look after you?"

pleaded Celia.

"No," replied Miriam, with a bitter laugh. "I'll take their charity thankfully enough. It's part of my punishment, I suppose. But I want to go at once. You seem to pity me——"

"Oh, Lady Heyton!"

"Then help me to get away. Send a telegram to my people to say that I am coming; tell Marie to pack——"

"Yes," said Celia, feeling that Miriam had decided on the best course. "I will see to everything. Will you lie down and rest, while I get everything ready?"

"Rest!" echoed Miriam, bitterly. "There cannot be a moment's rest for me while I am in this house. I have lain awake listening, listening——" She shuddered. "Go now. I'd try to thank you, if I could. You've been kind to me—Derrick's wife!" She pushed Celia from her and rose unsteadily. "Oh, go; I'm grateful, but the sight of you reminds me——"

With the tears running down her cheeks, Celia left her, to find Marie and send off the telegram.

CHAPTER XXXII

In the matter of an early marriage, both Derrick's father and he whom we have known as the Marquess, were on Derrick's side; indeed, the sick man was, if possible, more anxious than the others that the wedding should take place without delay.

"I want everything settled before—before I go, Wilfred," he said. "Something of the burden on my mind—not all! Ah, not all—will be lifted, if I can know that I shall, under Providence, leave the succession settled. You and I are old men, Wilfred—I am very near the grave. It is our duty to see, as far as lies within our power, that the future of the house is set upon a sound foundation. Your son, Derrick, will be a worthy successor; Celia—I need say nothing in her praise; she has won all our hearts, and she will lend a lustre to the title that will come to her."

A fortnight is not a long time in which to prepare the trousseau of a future Marchioness; but, with Lady Gridborough's enthusiastic assistance, Celia did her best; though, it must be confessed, she did not attach so much importance to this matter of the trousseau as it usually demands and receives from the bride elect; in fact, though Lady Gridborough has been described as an assistant, she bore the lion's share of the business, while Celia, as Lady Gridborough expressed it, in homely language, "gadded about, and mooned" with her lover.

She wanted a quiet wedding, but the church was full, and some ardent spirits had insisted upon decorating it, and an avenue of children, clothed in white and armed with flower blossoms to throw upon the pathway of the bride. Reggie was best man; and, consciously or unconsciously, had the air of one who had brought about the whole affair.

"If you had fixed the date a day later," he confided to Derrick, as he helped him into the regulation frock coat, and impressed upon him the solemn fact that the wedding ring was in the right-hand pocket of his waistcoat, "you'd have had to find another best man; for Susie and I are going to be married to-morrow at a quiet little church not a hundred miles from here. Ours is going to be really a quiet wedding: bride and bridegroom; parson, pew-opener and perhaps two sniffling children. We are going straight to France; address uncertain. And we're going to live there—that's one of the advantages of my profession, one of the precious few advantages; you can carry it on anywhere."

"I'm glad," said Derrick, as he wrung Reggie's hand. "No wonder you look so happy to-day: and I thought it was on my account!"

"So it is—partly," said Reggie. "You see, you're filling the bill so eminently satisfactorily. Between you and me, it isn't often that the hero in real life—in real life and out of fiction, mind you!—finishes up the last chapter looking absurdly happy in a frock coat and lavender trousers. You're the most satisfying 'hero' I've ever met with. And as to the bride—well, you wouldn't be married this morning, old chap, if I sat down right here and told you what I think of her."

"But you've told me already," said Derrick, laying his hand on Reggie's shoulder and shaking him affectionately.

To Lady Gridborough's intense satisfaction and delight, the sun shone brightly on Celia who, as the oldest inhabitant declared, was the most beautiful bride that had ever stood before the altar of the old church. One wedding is monotonously similar to another; and on this occasion there was nothing to distinguish Derrick's and Celia's, save the fact that the bridegroom had only just been acquitted of a criminal charge and had been discovered to be the heir to a marquisate; but the crowd which filled the church and gathered outside, felt these facts to be important ones, and they cheered the bride and bridegroom as they emerged from the church, husband and wife.

In the circumstances, it was not possible that there should be any festivities at the Hall—they would come later, all felt, when the happy couple returned from their honeymoon. There was an affecting scene when Derrick and Celia stood beside the bed of the injured man. But as he took Derrick's hand, and signed to Celia to bend down that he might kiss her, there was, plainly, an expression of relief in the dying man's wasted face. The great wrong had been set right; the elder brother restored to his own, his son, this handsome, erect young fellow, with the frank and honest eyes, established, or on the way to being established, as the heir.

The old man, lying there, a statesman and an aristocrat, recognized the responsibilities of his position, all that was due to the great family of which he had supposed himself the head; and that due was now being paid. As he blessed them both, his hand sought that of his elder brother, whom he had put in his proper place, and his eyes turned affectionately, restfully, to his.

Of course, Lady Gridborough and Reggie had been invited to the breakfast, which was disposed of somewhat hurriedly; for there was a train to catch. There were no speeches; they were not necessary; Lady Gridborough did most of the talking, breaking off now and then, sometimes to smile happily at Derrick and Celia, at others to wipe her eyes; for Lady Gridborough, at a wedding, was always hovering between smiles and tears.

They gathered in the hall, waiting for Celia to appear in her travelling dress; and presently she came down, radiant, blushing; but, before she went to her husband, she drew Reggie aside.

"I want to ask you to take a message from me to Susie," she whispered. "Tell her that I saw her in the church this morning; tell her that I shall always love her, and that some time—before long, I hope—we shall meet." Reggie, very red, and looking very happy, nodded. "And will you give her this as a wedding present?"

He opened the small case she slipped into his hand, and saw a pendant in the form of a ruby heart set round with diamonds. It was not a very costly gift, though doubtless it would seem so in Susie's eyes. But Reggie understood all it meant; the emblem of affection, warm and glowing; and again he could only nod.

Derrick's last word was with his father. The two men stood, with hands enclasped, looking at each other in a mute exchange of affection and trust.

"You will not be away too long?" said the father. "You are needed here." He glanced upwards towards his brother's room. "And I need you too, Derrick—my son that was lost and is found. " He paused, then he added, "Tell her that it shall rest with her."

Derrick gave the hand a pressure of comprehension.

As the carriage was starting, Celia's eyes wandered over the group gathered to see them off: Mrs. Dexter, as well as Lady Gridborough, between tears and smiles. Mr. Douglas, holding back Roddy, who was making frantic efforts to follow the carriage; but Derrick's eyes were fixed on his father.

In due course—how ecstatically happy was that course!—Derrick and Celia reached the ranch. On the steps stood Donna Elvira, his mother, awaiting them, with a kind of proud patience.

She had drawn herself up to her full height, was evidently fighting for self-composure; but, at the sight of her son, her hauteur melted, and, with a cry, she clasped him in her arms; but, the next moment, with a Spanish courtesy which swiftly melted to tenderness, she turned to the rather pale and trembling girl, and embraced her. With a hand of each in hers, she drew them into the house. There are moments too sacred for intrusion; such moments were those which passed between these three. At first sight, the Donna's heart had gone out to her son's beautiful young wife; and it was with a sigh that she said, after much talk had passed between them,

"Yes, you must not forget, dearest child, that you have a mother, and another home, here in the South. You will come sometimes? And for a long visit? The journey is so short nowadays, is it not? You will not forget altogether the lonely woman who has found a son—and a daughter?"

It was not until he and his mother were alone together that Derrick delivered his father's message; and he did so gently, tenderly, with his hand laid in hers. Donna Elvira was silent for a long time; then she said, in a low voice,

"We will leave it to time, Derrick. You say, in your language, that Time heals all things. And the wound is now almost healed. We will wait——Yes, we will leave it to time."

And with that Derrick had to be satisfied.

It was towards the close of their stay at the ranch that Derrick received a letter from his father containing the news of the death of him who had been known so long to the world as the Marquess of Sutcombe. The last days of the stricken man had passed in peacefulness and forgetfulness. He had never spoken of his son, had seemed to remember nothing of the terrible tragedy which had cast its shadow over all their lives; all his conscious thought had been of the brother whose place he had usurped, at first innocently, but whom now he had restored to his own. The letter closed with a hint that Derrick's father found the responsibility of his titles and

honours somewhat hard to bear; and Derrick knew that the old man needed him.

This letter brought their visit—already a long one—to an end, and Derrick and Celia started for home. Nothing shall be said of their reception; indeed, the most eloquent pen could not attempt to vie with the glowing periods in which the great event was enshrined in the columns of the local paper; suffice it that, after a progress through many triumphal arches, much cheering; some speechifying on the part of Derrick—which was by no means particularly happy but was received with delirious enthusiasm—the carriage conveyed them to the Hall, where Derrick's father and Celia's old friend stood, leaning on his stick, and awaited them.

"Thank God you've come back, Derrick!" said his father, fervently. "You and Celia are wanted here, very badly. You see," he added, with a touch of pathos, "I have been away from all this so long, I am so unused to everything——My dear, will you believe me"—he turned to Celia with a smile that had not a little pathos in it—"I sometimes long for the quietude, the—the bareness of 'The Jail'!"

"I know," said Celia in a low voice, and with a glance at Derrick beside her.

For she and Derrick, on their way home, had stopped for a night in London and had gone back to "The Jail." They had slept in her old room, and they had stood, hand in hand, in his, where first they had met, where she had come to him, an angel of rescue.

There were festivities enough now and to spare. The whole place seemed permeated by their happiness, and Derrick was wondering how long the rollicking would last and when he should be able to take up the duties which devolved upon him. One evening it chanced that he and Celia were walking through the village, on their way from Lady Gridborough's, engaged in earnest converse about those same duties; and, in the middle of a sentence, Celia broke off, and, catching at his arm, exclaimed,

"Derrick! Oh, Derrick, look!"

Derrick followed the direction of her

eyes, and saw a huge tent with a number of persons bustling about it. It was a circus tent; and, moreover, it was Bloxford's Mammoth Circus itself. He stopped and stared; then he laughed.

"Why, it's old Bloxford!" he cried, brightly. "Celia, this is a piece of luck. Think of his coming here—here, of all places! By George! how glad I shall be to see him; and I've an idea he'll be glad to see me! We'll go—no, not now"—stopping short—"I'll go to the show to-night."

"You'll take me, Derrick?" she said, eagerly. "I want to see him so badly."

Restraining the desire to go there and then, they had an early dinner and, on foot, made their way to the circus. The tent was crammed; the performance had just begun; Derrick and Celia got seats in the best part, and, exchanging glances of pleasure, they looked on. The whole company was there in force; and when Isabel rode into the ring on her black charger, Celia pressed Derrick's arm and whispered enthusiastically,

"What a splendid woman, Derrick! Oh, she's really grand! And how she rides!"

"Yes," responded Derrick, a trifle confusedly; for—well, while recounting his adventures to Celia, he had omitted any mention of the Isabel episode. "She is a great friend of mine. And so is that fine-looking chap who is going to do the trapeze act presently. There he is, standing by the entrance, where they come into the arena. His name is Sidcup: splendid fellow, isn't he?"

"Splendid," murmured Celia, admiringly. "How clever they all are!"

"Here, come, let's go round at once, now," said Derrick, as the performance came to an end and the band played "God save the King." He led her round to the performers' tent, and almost ran against Mr. Bloxford. Needless to say, he wore his fur coat. At sight of Derrick's smiling face and outstretched hand, Mr. Bloxford started and stared, in a bewildered fashion, then he recognised Derrick and, grasping the hand, shook it heartily.

"Why, dash my stars and stripes, if it isn't Sydney Green!" he exclaimed,

with so evident a pleasure that Celia's eyes glowed and she smiled upon him; and Mr. Bloxford, as if drawn by the smile, turned to her, and, sweeping off his hat, said,

"And I take it you're his young lady, miss?"

"I'm his wife," said Celia, with unabashed pride.

"You don't say!" commented Mr. Bloxford, his admiration eloquently expressed in his staring, Simian eyes. "Well, Mr. Green, you've taken the cake! Lor' bless my soul, what a picture you'd make in the high-stepping act! And you're well, and doing well, I should say, by the look of you, Mr. Green," he said to Derrick, who, indeed, looked absurdly happy and proud at that moment. "Well, you deserve it. Look here, ma'am, I could tell you a sight about this big gentleman of yours. You take it from me that he's a topper, a tip-topper. Here, just step in here, and I'll tell you how he saved the whole show from a wrecking out there in that darned dingo-land, Buenos Aires."

"I should like to hear it very much, Mr. Bloxford," said Celia, still glowing on him; "though my husband has already told me about it."

"Oh, well, you don't want to hear it from me; though, mind you, it was one of the coolest things I've ever seen done. Oh, he's grit all through, is that good man of yours."

"I know he is," said Celia, her face radiant, her smile fascinating and bewildering.

"But, look here!" he said. "The company will want to see you. Here, come along! I tell you, ma'am"—over his shoulder to Celia, as he led the way to the "Green Room"—"he is the most popular man we've ever had. And got a head as well as a heart; the best head *I* ever saw. Here, ladies and gentlemen," he cried to the medley group in the performers' tent, "here's an old friend come to pay you a visit. Here's Mr. Sydney Green, *and* his missis!"

They all turned and stared for a moment in silence. Isabel's face went pale, but not so pale as Alice's. Isabel was the first to recover. With a flush on her

face now, she came forward with her graceful swing and held out her hand, first to Derrick and then, after a momentary pause, to Celia; her hand was grasped warmly by both. An excited interchange of talk ensued; and presently, in the midst of it, Derrick felt a hand on his arm, and Sidcup, to whom he had spoken already, signed to him. Derrick went out of the tent with him.

"I can't tell you how glad I am to see you, Sidcup," he began; but Sidcup interrupted him with a nod and a smile.

"I wanted to get you away for a moment, to tell you that it's—all right," said Sidcup, colouring a little and looking just a trifle embarrassed, and yet with a tone of pride in his voice. "Isabel and I have fixed it up. Yes; we were spliced before we left South America. It's all right, old boy! Congratulate me!"

Derrick shook his hand until Sidcup winced, and they both laughed like a couple of boys.

"Congratulate you! I should think I do!" said Derrick. "I wish you could have heard my wife just now, expressing her admiration for yours. She is more beautiful than ever."

"Oh, well," said Sidcup, with a modest pride; "come to that, you've got a beauty too. Tell you what, Green, we're both of us deuced lucky men."

"You never spoke a truer word in your life," said Derrick; "and you, at any rate, deserve your luck."

They returned to the tent, talking as they went; and there, lo and behold! they found the future Marchioness of Sutcombe the centre of a laughing and talking group, the hearts of all of which she had conquered at first sight. For, consider: she was now a future Marchioness, but not long since she had been Celia Grant, living on a pound a week in Brown's Buildings—as she told them. Derrick tore her away at last, leaving the circus company ignorant of the exalted position of their guests; but, half an hour afterwards, they were astounded beyond words to receive an invitation to dine next night at Thexford Hall; an invitation from Sydney Green and his wife, otherwise, Lord and Lady Heyton.

That dinner is marked with a white stone in the history of Derrick and Celia.

One is reluctant to strike a discordant note, a note of squalid tragedy, in the harmony to which the lives of Celia and Derrick moved; but this record would not be complete without an account of the ending of the man who was known as Lord Heyton. Such an ending as his was inevitable. He died in a drunken brawl in a Chinese doss-house in Manchuria. For months before his death he had been a cause of trouble and anxiety to the authorities of the district; in such a place villainy and roguery have full scope; but poor Heyton never rose to the height of either. Small and petty offences only were those which came within his capacity.

For some time he had been connected with a gang of card-sharpers, living under an alias, and depending for his food and drink upon the small wits which Providence had vouchsafed him. It was during a dispute in one of the lowest doss-houses in the place that he met his death. There had been a quarrel, a scuffle, a death-thrust with a knife by a cold-blooded Chinaman, and it was not until the authorities had searched the body, that his identity had been discovered.

Derrick received the news of the death of Miriam's husband, the one-time recognised heir to the title and estate, from the British Consul; and he received the grim tidings with something like relief. His was the task to convey the tragic information to Miriam. Of that interview nothing shall be said. She also had received the account of her husband's death with something like relief; for, to her, he had been dead long since. At one point only did she shed tears; it was when she tried, in faltering accents, to express to Derrick her gratitude for all that he and Celia had done, and were doing, to render her life free from care.

The interview, painful as it necessarily had been, saddened Derrick; but his face cleared as, on his return to the Hall, he met Celia and took her in his arms; and, as her lips clung to his, he asked himself, as he had often asked himself in odd moments of his happiness, "What have I done to deserve my luck?"

***

CPSIA information can be obtained at www.ICGtesting.com
Printed in the USA
BVOW11s1103181114

375616BV00020B/462/P

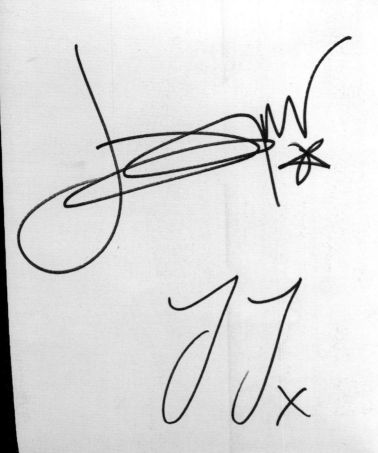

PUFFIN BOOKS
Published by the Penguin Group: London, New York, Australia, Canada, India, Ireland,
New Zealand and South Africa
Penguin Books Ltd, Registered Offices: 80 Strand, London WC2R 0RL, England

puffinbooks.com

First published 2013
001

Written by Sarah Delmege
Interviews by Martin Roach
Cover and internal photography © Elise Dumontet, 2013
Additional picture credits: pages 4, 10, 12, 14, 16, 18, 19, 20, 21, 23, 24, 25, 28, 34, 35, 38, 45, 46 © Shutterstock.com;
Pages 8, 23, 25 © Getty Images; Page 30 © iStock.com; Pages 16, 18, 19, 30, 45, 57 © Corbis.
Text copyright © UJ Music Ltd and Simco Ltd, 2013
Union J is a trademark owned by UJ Music Ltd under exclusive license to Simco Ltd, 2013
All rights reserved
The moral right of the author and photographers has been asserted

Printed in Italy

ISBN: 978-0-141-34949-7

THE OFFICIAL

Union J

ANNUAL
2014

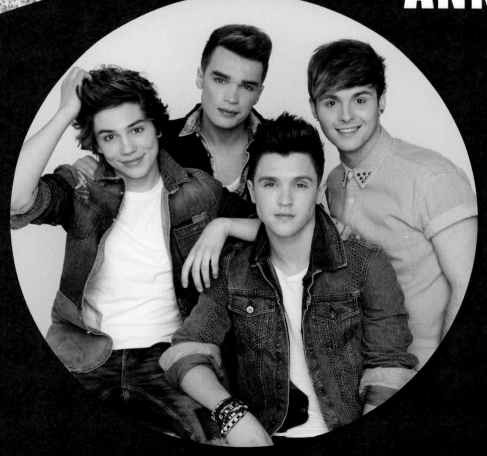

PUFFIN

Union J

INTRODUCING

Union J is one of the most exciting bands on the planet right now. They've taken the pop world by storm, lighting up the charts with their smooth vocals, down-to-earth charm and incredible talent. Their growing legion of devoted fans love their cheeky sense of humour, gorgeous good looks and, of course, their brilliant music. There's something special going on with this band. Something huge, in fact.

Amazingly, a year ago, Union J didn't even exist. Josh Cuthbert, George Shelley, JJ Hamblet and Jaymi Hensley were just four boys with dreams of making it big. Now those dreams have come true – beyond their wildest imaginings.

Union J

They are four of the most famous boys in pop and their journey has been an incredible one. They're young, they're talented and they've worked amazingly hard to get where they are. And more than anything the boys want to share their story with you. They know they couldn't have done any of it without their fans!

So here's the complete story so far of the fabulous foursome's rise to fame . . .

Up Close With
JOSH

Name: Josh Cuthbert
Born: 28 July 1992
Star sign: Leo
Home town: Ascot
Eye colour: blue
Height: 5'11

Star facts

- Josh is known as the 'funny one' in Union J.
- **He performed in the West End production of *Chitty Chitty Bang Bang* when he was fourteen.**
- His nan spent over £800 on tickets to see him in the show.
- **Josh has a sister called Victoria and a brother called Callum.**
- He can sing Enrique Iglesias' song 'Hero' in Spanish.
- **His favourite TV show is *Lost*.**
- His favourite cartoon character is Shrek.
- **If he wasn't a singer, Josh would have liked to be a footballer.**
- Before auditioning for *The X Factor*, he worked in IT sales.
- **Josh made it to Boot Camp once before a few years ago — as a solo artist!**

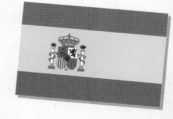

Up Close With
GEORGE

Name: George Shelley
Born: 27 July 1993
Star sign: Leo
Home town: Bristol
Eye colour: brown
Height: 5'10

☆ Star facts

- George taught himself the guitar (with help from his grandad).
- He has nine siblings: Tom, Will, Harriet, Cameron, Leo, Archie, Spencer, Annabelle and Louisa!
- His fave food is spag bol.
- He likes to watch *The Big Bang Theory* and his favourite character is Sheldon.
- Before auditioning for *The X Factor*, George was studying graphic design at Bath University.
- He designed the Union J logo!
- George likes being tickled.
- All he could think about when he auditioned for *The X Factor* was that he needed a wee!
- His favourite piece of furniture is his bed because he likes sleeping.
- George loves monkeys!

13

JJ

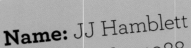

Name: JJ Hamblett
Born: 25 May 1988
Star sign: Gemini
Home town: Newmarket
Eye colour: brown
Height: 5'10

Star facts

- JJ used to be a jockey and he rode in more than 260 races!
- **His real name is Jamie.**
- JJ's biggest fear is elastic bands.

- **He loves peanut buter.**
- He prefers white sugar over brown sugar.
- **He sleepwalks and sleeptalks!**
- JJ has an older brother called Ashley.
- **If he had to be a vegetable, he'd be a sprout.**
- He likes having baths.
- **JJ is a quarter Norwegian.**

15

Up Close With
JAYMI

Name: Jaymi Hensley
Born: 24 February 1990
Star sign: Pisces
Home town: Luton
Eye colour: brown
Height: 5'11

☆ Star facts

- Before *The X Factor*, Jaymi was a part-time singing and dance teacher.
- **He has a boyfriend called Olly.**
- Jaymi is a massive fan of the Twilight saga.
- **He used to do ballet.**
- He's got seventeen tattoos.
- **Jaymi makes sure all the Union J boys are on time.**
- He can turn his feet 180 degrees backwards.
- **He did gymnastics when he was younger.**
- Jaymi has a younger brother called Aaron.
- **He has a pet dog, cat and fish.**

The Union J Journey

They're so close it's incredible to think that Union J hasn't been together forever. But a year ago Josh, JJ and Jaymi hadn't even met George. They were just four boys with one very big dream – to win *The X Factor* and become pop stars . . .

THE BEGINNING

Josh and Jaymi originally started a band while attending Sylvia Young Theatre School – but it wasn't until they added JJ to the mix to form Triple J that the magic started to happen. Eight months before *The X Factor* auditions, the boys began rehearsing and in the spring of 2012 they took to *The X Factor* stage in London . . . and wowed the judges at their very first audition. They performed Rihanna's hit 'We Found Love' with their own original backing track and the auditorium erupted as they finished!

'It's not just about the looks, which you have,' Gary Barlow said, 'it's the vocals – and you guys have incredible vocals.' They left the O2 arena floating on air. Meanwhile, George had applied to the show as a solo artist – and he too impressed the judges at his own audition. He performed a unique acoustic version of Britney Spears's 'Toxic', playing backing on his guitar. 'You have a great look and a great vocal,' Louis Walsh told him. An over-the-moon George was put through to the next stage.

'We loved George as soon as we met him.'
Jaymi

LOUIS'S SURPRISE

The boys could hardly contain their excitement when they arrived at the next round of the competition – Boot Camp. Both Triple J and George gave their all in their performances, but they were up against some tough competition and both were sent home. They were devastated. They felt they'd come so far – and all for nothing. But an unexpected series of events was about to change their lives beyond their wildest dreams . . .

Behind the scenes, one of the final groups, Rough Copy, had to drop out of the competition and Louis needed to replace them. He couldn't stop thinking about Triple J, who had come so close to getting through. He knew they were super-talented, but something was missing.

Louis thought about George. He'd liked him at Boot Camp, but felt he wasn't quite right on his own – could he be what Triple J were looking for?

It was a shock twist, but an idea all the boys were really happy with. Triple J and George had clicked straight away at Boot Camp. They had recognized the same drive to succeed in each other – and more, they genuinely got on! 'We loved George as soon as we met him,' said Jaymi. 'When we came out of the competition, we stayed in contact. We'd already bonded as people.'

19

UNION J IS BORN

As soon as Louis saw them perform at Judges' Houses, he knew the newly christened Union J had all the ingredients for pop success – and put them through to the live rounds. The boys were thrilled, but there was little time for celebration: the live shows were about to start. They put in some serious rehearsal time, but got off to a rocky start and were in the bottom two the first week, which shook them.

'Week one, we sat at the sound check and said, "We are the weakest link here," says Josh. 'Which we were.' The boys were worried, but Louis reassured them: he saw a fresh, talented pop act with a hunger for success. He told them he'd never believed in an act so much since JLS. 'That to us is incredible,' said George.

After listening to Louis, the boys were determined not to let the first live-show setback dent their confidence. 'Every time we've had a knock-back, we've come out fighting,' said Jaymi. 'We work well under pressure.' As the shows went on, the boys' performances got better and better, and the audience couldn't get enough of them! Everywhere they went, their excited fans grew in number. The boys even had to pull out of an appearance at a shopping centre because thousands of fans – or 'J Cats' as they were now being dubbed – turned up to see the band and there were concerns for their safety. Union J fever had truly erupted!

REAL PEOPLE

Right from the start, the boys were adamant that their fans should see them as real people. The boys wanted to be one hundred per cent honest about who they are – no one more so than Jaymi. He'd entered the competition wanting to focus on his talent, not his personal life, but as the show went on, he decided it felt right to let his fans know he is gay. "It's not a big thing for me," he explained.

'Every time we've had a knock-back, we've come out fighting. We work well under pressure.' *Jaymi*

'I came out when I was fourteen to my family and friends, and never had one piece of negativity. And if I can help just one kid out there that is enough for me.'

The J Cats responded with an overwhelming outpouring of supportive messages. Everyone was proud, inspired and grateful that Jaymi had the guts to come out and show the world how happy he is in his own skin.

'I'm so happy with how we've done. It's been a dream for us.'
Josh

FINAL FOUR

As the competition continued, week after week, Union J sang their hearts out. 'The aim of the game is to win it, and that's definitely what we want to do,' said JJ. They worked harder than they ever had before, and gave some spellbinding performances – eventually coming in fourth and leaving *The X Factor* in the semi-final. Ever professional, the boys left the competition with their heads held high, genuinely wishing all three finalists the best of luck. Josh spoke for all of them when he said, 'I'm so happy with how we've done. It's been a dream for us.'

A dream that was just beginning . . .

You a Union J Super-fa

do you really know the boys? Take this quiz and fi

1. Who has the most siblings?
2. What is JJ's real name?
3. Who loves to drink coffee?
4. Who once starred in *Chitty Chitty Bang Bang*?
5. Who is afraid of cockroaches?
6. Which member is from Ascot?
7. Who is a Pisces?
8. Which lad loves peanut butter?
9. Which boy likes to scoff Jaffa Cakes?
10. Whose grandad taught him to play guitar?
11. Which member had auditioned for *The X Factor* before 2012?
12. Who has the most tattoos?
13. Who loves chicken tikka masala?

14. Whose older brother is called Ashley?
15. Which two members were born in July?
16. Which boy really loves monkeys?
17. Who digs The Twilight Saga?
18. Which boy used to be a jockey?
19. Who thinks Boris Johnson, mayor of London, is awesome?
20. What was George's audition song on *The X Factor*?
21. Which band did Union J replace at Judges' Houses?
22. Which judge was their mentor?
23. Where did Union J come overall in the competition?
24. What was their final song on *The X Factor*?
25. What were Union J famous for wearing on the show?
26. What was the name of Union J's first single?
27. Who is George's celebrity crush?
28. Where would Josh take a girl on a date?
29. What is Jaymi's favourite movie?
30. What is JJ's favourite TV show?

ANSWERS
1. George
2. Jamie
3. George
4. Josh
5. JJ
6. Josh
7. Jaymi
8. JJ
9. George
10. George
11. Josh
12. Jaymi
13. Josh
14. JJ
15. Josh and George
16. George
17. Jaymi
18. JJ
19. Josh
20. Britney Spears's 'Toxic'
21. Rough Copy
22. Louis Walsh
23. Fourth
24. Taylor Swift's 'Love Story'
25. Onesies!
26. 'Carry You'
27. Demi Lovato
28. McDonald's
29. Avatar
30. Jersey Shore

SO . . . HOW DID YOU DO?

1–6 UNION FAIL
Anyone can gaze adoringly at Union J posters or sing along with their pop-tastic tunes. But a real J Cat needs to know EVERYTHING, from their birthdays to what they had for breakfast. Start reading this annual again from the beginning and get up to speed!

7–14 UNION OK
There's no denying you love these four boys, but to be a Number 1 fan you're gonna have to work a little bit harder! Start your swotting up now – hey, it's a hard job, but someone's got to do it.

15–20 UNION HURRAY!
You know so much about the boys that we wouldn't be surprised if you'd snuck into the studio and recorded everything they said! The boys know they'd be nowhere without fans like you, and they love you for it.

Life After The X Factor

Leaving *The X Factor* in the semi-finals wasn't as devastating as it might have been for Union J . . .

STAYING POSITIVE

'I'd had a feeling we were going to come fourth from the very start,' says Jaymi. But the band had seen *The X Factor* launch successful acts like JLS and One Direction, who also didn't win – and were pleased they'd made it as the last band left in the competition – it showed real staying power.

They were right not to be worried. The whole pop industry was interested in these four lads! Journalists were clamouring for interviews and every major record company wanted their signatures on a contract. Everyone who'd seen them had been impressed by their voices, work ethic and the way they could fill a stage with personality. It was obvious that Union J were going to be a very big deal indeed.

HARD WORK

After the show, the boys signed with record label RCA, knowing it could launch them to super-stardom – as it had done with Take That and JLS before them. 'We don't want there to be any limits on how big we can be,' Jaymi said. 'We would love to break America and tour the world.'

The press started paying serious attention as the band began working in earnest with the hottest producers, songwriters and stylists – and getting mobbed by fans wherever they went!

But Union J didn't get carried away. They knew that behind every big boy band is a lot of hard work. 'We wanted to prove we're worthy of the hype,' George explained.

After performing at the sell-out X Factor Tour in February, where they played to thousands of screaming J Cats, the band headed to the studio in March, where they worked with legendary writers Steve Mac and Wayne Heffner, who had penned JLS's 'Beat Again' and One Direction's 'Gotta Be You'. The boys were determined to get involved in every part of the process as

> 'We don't want there to be any limits on how big we can be.'
> Jaymi

they recorded their first album. 'It's massively important for us to get involved with the writing,' said Jaymi.

ALL ABOUT THE MUSIC

The boys adored every minute of being in the studio. Yes, it was a serious business, requiring long, often monotonous hours of work, but they embraced it – and it paid off. The result was a brilliantly crafted pop album, with a truly unique sound. 'Our album is very diverse,' explained Jaymi. 'We want to make our own sound and our own avenue.'

The release of their first hit single, 'Carry You' was extra special. It was the moment all the boys realized how far they'd come. 'If you'd told us at the beginning of *The X Factor* auditions that we'd have a record deal and would be releasing a single, we wouldn't have believed you,' said Josh. 'We've been through a lot in the short time we've been together,' added Jaymi. 'This song sums up how important it was for us to be there for each other.' The tune represented their journey, their bond and their belief in the future. The Union J story was just beginning . . .

Union J

UNION J REVEALED

We caught up with the lads for an exclusive chat! Find out what they had to say on some burning issues . . .

WHEN DID YOU LAST CRY? WHY?

JJ: 'I cried watching an amazing movie last week, *The Notebook*.'

Josh: 'Actually, the last time I cried was leaving The X Factor Tour in February 2013. We were at the airport and everyone was saying goodbye to each other. It had been such an emotional few months and Jahmene and I had a little hug and I cried then.'

Jaymi: 'The other night. I was tired and I just got a bit emotional.'

George: 'I last cried – in happiness – when we heard our finished debut single with our vocals on it for the first time. That was a really big moment for all of us: emotional, exciting, just brilliant.'

TELL US A SECRET ABOUT YOU:

Josh: 'I have hairy legs.'

JJ: 'Ooh! You're not supposed to tell people secrets!'

Jaymi: 'I don't know what to say! I'm not really into secrets. I'm really into being completely open about stuff!'

George: 'I'm not a big secrets person, but I would say I'm a massive geeky nerd!'

DO YOU HAVE ANY PHOBIAS?

Jaymi: 'Yes! I am claustrophobic.'

JJ: 'I hate creepy-crawlies, any kind, any insects – especially things like cockroaches.'

George: 'I have a phobia of moths. Horrible things.'

Josh: 'And I am terrified of wasps! Oddly, I also hate hay and dry grass, they're horrible. There's something about hay that I'm really terrified of. And bananas.'

WHAT WAS YOUR MOST RECENT DREAM?

George: 'I was running away from zombies with my family, and the only way that I could get away from these zombies was to fly. So it was a great zombie dream, but also my very first proper flying dream. I play a lot of computer games!'

Josh: 'It was really random.

We'd spoken about what it would be like having a Top 20 song in Belarus and then I had a dream about being Number 17 in Belarus and we were partying to celebrate.'

JJ: 'The band was at the Brits and we were sitting there watching the show and all that and then we won a Brit! What a dream!'

Jaymi: 'That's hard to say because I never really remember dreams. I'm sure I have them, but I never seem to recall them when I wake up.'

WHAT'S YOUR MOST EMBARRASSING MOMENT?

Jaymi: 'Falling over on *The X Factor* – it was one Sunday

night when we'd got through. That was really embarrassing as you can imagine.'

JJ: 'Once I was in a lift with a few old people and I always feel a little bit awkward in a lift; everyone just stands there silent, don't they? Well, someone farted and it wasn't me, but because I was the youngest person there they assumed it was me. And it wasn't!'

George: 'Well, during *The X Factor*, the week we got kicked out, we sang our farewell song and it was 'Love Story'. But I fell backwards off the stage and nearly landed on Nicole Scherzinger. Fortunately, Josh grabbed me just in time, but it was still really embarrassing.

All the fans love to replay that on the social networks!'

Josh: 'On The X Factor Live Tour, we all planned to sneak on to the stage during Chris Maloney's performance and join in on the dancers' routine. But as I went right to the middle of the stage, in front of a packed Belfast Arena, I slipped and fell on my bum, which was rather embarrassing. I'd hoped to take the mickey out of the dance moves, but ended up making a mockery of myself.'

WHAT'S THE ONE THING YOU CAN'T LIVE WITHOUT?

Josh: 'My Xbox and Fifa!'

JJ: 'I suppose I'm not a

massive fan of technology, but actually it would be my phone. I rely on that so much, so, yeah, I'd be lost without my phone.'

George: 'My MacBook.'

Jaymi: 'Telly. I am a telly junkie.'

IF YOU COULD COME BACK AS SOMETHING IN YOUR NEXT LIFE, WHAT WOULD IT BE?

JJ: 'The best racehorse ever to have lived. That's from my days as a racing jockey. All I ever wanted to be when I was a kid was a jockey and I raced professionally for five years, so I guess if I came back as an animal I would be a brilliant racehorse.'

George: 'I think it would be interesting to be an alien. Can you tell I play a lot of computer games?'

Josh: 'I would love to come back as a creature from the Ice Age. For some reason, every time I watch that movie, I want to come back as a sloth.'

Jaymi: 'Part of the royal family. A prince or maybe a princess.'

WHAT'S THE LAST SONG YOU LISTENED TO?

Josh and George: '"Pompeii" by Bastille!'

Jaymi: '"What About Us" by The Saturdays.'

JJ: 'One of the ones off Union J's debut album. We are in the recording studio loads at the moment, so it was one of our own tracks.'

IF YOU COULD HAVE ONE PERSON ROUND FOR DINNER WHO WOULD IT BE?

George: 'In the whole world? Well, it would make a lot of sense to ask Jamie Oliver because then I could ask him to cook!'

Josh: 'This is a bit random, but probably Boris Johnson, Mayor of London. He seems like the biggest "lad", he's really funny, quirky.'

JJ: 'If I could have anyone round for dinner, I'd ask David Walliams. I just find him hilarious. He's really funny so that would be a great night.'

Jaymi: 'Oh, easy, Beyoncé.'

WHAT CELEB DO YOU MOST WANT TO MEET?

JJ: 'It would be an honour to meet Simon Cowell. We haven't yet, so I look forward to that.'

Josh: 'Michael Caine, he's an amazing actor and he's been in some of my favourite films – that would be amazing to chat to him.'

George: 'I really want to meet Demi Lovato.'

Jaymi: 'Beyoncé.'

WHAT DO YOU DO ON A DAY OFF?

Jaymi: 'Chill, just relax.'

JJ: 'Depends. If it's just one day, I just relax, but if it's more time I will try to see my family as much as I can. I'm a very family-orientated guy so that's the first thing I'll try to fit in when we do get time away from our mad schedules. It's very important to do that, just go back to normality and freshen up and keep your feet on the ground.'

Josh: 'I like to chill out, or maybe go to the cinema and play Fifa, and see my mates.'

George: 'I spend time with my family and my best friends, but I also text the boys because I miss them.'

WHAT WOULD YOU MOST LIKE TO FIND IN YOUR CHRISTMAS STOCKING?

Josh: 'A number 1 single for Union J!'

JJ: 'A platinum album with Union J written on it.'

George: 'A pair of socks, because I'd find it quite interesting and ironic that there was a sock in a sock.'

Jaymi: 'Beyoncé! No, ha ha, let's say Beyoncé tickets.'

The Lives of Union J

Very Normal

They might be famous, but they're still just four ordinary boys . . .

DOWN TO EARTH

No doubt about it, these days Union J are fully fledged pop stars: they've conquered the charts, travelled the world and featured in countless magazines. And they've taken to it like naturals, whether onstage, in the studio, on the red carpet or chatting to their adoring fans. But despite their fame they've managed to remain the same down-to-earth, ordinary boys they've always been – the kind of guys you could imagine living next door. They might be huge celebrities, but none of them act that way. 'We're just four normal boys who love to sing,' says Josh.

FRIENDS AND FAMILY

The Union J lads are as unstarry as it gets and although they love every moment of their new lives, they've said the hardest thing about their job is being on the road full-time.

'We miss our families and our friends,' says JJ. Any chance they get, they go home, see their loved ones and enjoy some time out of the spotlight. And when the boys are travelling they make the effort to keep in touch with them through texts, video chats and email.

'Modern technology's the best,' laughs George.

BROTHERLY BOND

The boys also say it's their close bond with each other that helps keep their feet on the

> 'We're just four normal boys who love to sing.'
>
> Josh

ground, although spending so much time together does mean they have the odd argument. 'Sometimes we kick off,' says Jaymi. 'But like all close brothers we soon make up.' In fact, their occasional rows have brought the boys even closer; they know that no matter what happens they'll always have each other to lean on. And their healthy attitude means that no matter what craziness being in Union J brings them they'll embrace it all with good grace and a sense of fun.

HAPPY AND HUMBLE

As for becoming divas? The band insist that's never going to happen. 'It's just not our style,' says JJ.

Jaymi agrees. 'You have to be true to yourself,' he says. They might be four of the most famous faces in pop right now, but at heart Josh, JJ, George and Jaymi are just four best friends having the time of their lives and doing what they love.

'We're the luckiest lads ever,' says JJ.

'You have to be true to yourself.' *Jaymi*

'We're the luckiest lads ever.' *JJ*

33

Union J
in NUMBERS
Maths has never been so fun!

800 = the amount of £££ Josh's nan spent on seeing him in Chitty Chitty Bang Bang

11 = the number of songs Union J performed on *The X Factor* (not including survival songs)

14 = Josh's age when he appeared in Chitty Chitty Bang Bang

23 = the number of races JJ won as a jockey

9.5 = Josh's shoe size

34

9 = the number of George's siblings. He has six brothers and three sisters!

7631277

= JJ's X Factor audition number

13 = George's age when he got his first guitar

6.5

= JJ's shoe size

4 = the place Union J came in The X Factor

71145

= Union J's total height in cm

0 = the number of pet hamsters George owns

17 = the number of tattoos Jaymi has

1/4 = JJ is a quarter Norwegian

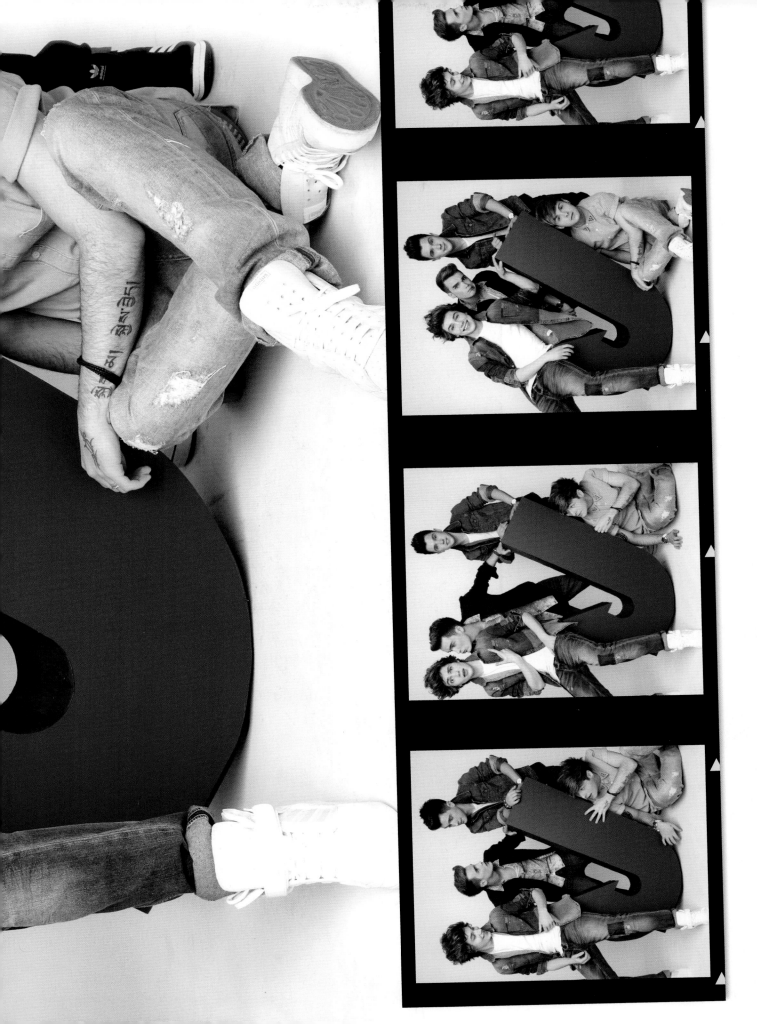

A-Z
of Union J!

You may think you know everything about Union J, but even their biggest fan can miss a thing or two . . .

A is for audition. JJ auditioned for the BBC series *The Cut*, but didn't get the part because he didn't quite fit the role they were looking for.

B is for brotherhood. These boys are so close they really are like brothers.

C is for Costa coffee. George worked part-time in the coffee store in Weston-super-Mare.

D is for *Deal or No Deal* – one of Josh's favourite TV shows.

E is for entertaining. These boys really know how to put on a show.

F is for Fifa. Union J's favourite computer game.

G is for George's grandad – who taught him to play the guitar.

H is for the song 'Hero'. Josh can sing it in Spanish!

I is for inventing. JJ and his brother once invented their own secret language.

J is for Jaffa Cakes – George's favourite snack.

K is for KEEP ON GOING no matter what. The boys never let setbacks keep them down.

L is for Louis. Their *X Factor* mentor believed in the boys' pop future from the very start.

M is for Marmite. 'Marmite on toast, peanut butter on toast, I'd just slap it on.' Jaymi really loves his Marmite.

N is for Nando's. The boys are all big fans.

O is for oldest member, JJ.

P is for **Putteridge High School** in Luton, where Jaymi went to school.

Q is for queueing. The boys will never get over how many fans queue to see them, whatever the weather.

R is for **Rough Copy.** If they hadn't dropped out of *The X Factor*, Union J wouldn't even exist. Can you imagine?!

S is for **Silvia Young Theatre School.** Where Josh and Jaymi first met!

T is for **Tom Cruise** – the actor JJ would like to play him in a movie.

U is for the boys' unique voices. We can't get enough of them.

V is for the boys' amazing videos. We love seeing their personalities jump off the screen.

W is for writing. The boys love penning songs and we love hearing them.

X is for *The X Factor* – thank goodness the boys entered!

Y is for youngest member. George is the baby of the group!

Z is for zzzzz. George's favourite piece of furniture is his bed because he loves sleeping.

JOIN THE *Union J* CREW

Tick all the statements that apply to you to see what part of the Union J crew you'd be . . .

- ○ You sing in the shower . . . it has the best sound quality!
- ○ You never leave the house without a slick of lipgloss.
- ○ You are always replaying the day in your head, creating different outcomes.
- ○ You love to put your own twist on your favourite songs.
- ○ You are always posting clips on YouTube.
- ○ You are fabulous at makeovers.
- ○ Your iPod speakers are practically cemented in your ears.
- ○ Your friends are always telling you off for being too nosy.

- Sometimes you pretend your bedroom floor is a red carpet.
- You love taking pictures of your friends.
- You are amazing at pulling outfits together.
- You have a loyal group of followers at school.
- Your parents joke that you could sing before you could talk.
- You spend your English lessons wishing you could style your teacher.
- You keep a diary every single day.
- In old family videos you always steal the scene.

YOU'D BE UNION J'S . . .

Mostly Red
BACKING SINGER

You were born to sing and be onstage. Your spine-tingling vocals would blend brilliantly with the boys' solid harmonies. You'd enhance any of Union J's shows.

Mostly Yellow
MUSIC VIDEO DIRECTOR

You see the whole world through a lens and know what makes a great visual story. Even more importantly, you're great at establishing trust with people: really important if you're going to get the lads to perform on-screen!

Mostly Blue
STYLIST

You've got an eye for style and know how to take any outfit from drab to fab! As their stylist, you'd understand that while trends are important to Union J their personalities still have to shine through in their clothes.

Pink
SONG WRITER

You're brilliant at getting emotions out of your head and on to the page. You'd help the boys craft even more delicious songs in pop and the fans will love you for it.

41

WHO'S YOUR UNION J SOUL MATE?

1. Your perfect dinner date is:
a) A fast food joint.
b) A meal in a beautiful setting.
c) A moonlight picnic.
d) On the sofa, in front of a movie.

2. Your style is:
a) Relaxed and casual.
b) Whatever you feel comfortable in.
c) A little bit alternative.
d) Something smart with a twist.

3. Your friends describe you as:
a) Caring and understanding.
b) Laugh-out-loud funny.
c) Fun and up for anything.
d) Always thinking of others.

4. What is the one thing you can't be without?
a) Your Xbox.
b) Your phone.
c) Your computer.
d) Your TV.

5. What do you love doing in your spare time?
a) Going to the cinema.
b) Spending time with your family.
c) Hanging with your friends.
d) Chilling out at home.

Mostly As: Josh

Relaxed and fun-loving, you have a happy, outgoing attitude to life. Your smile is completely infectious and together with Josh the pair of you would light up any room. Your friends know they can always count on you.

Mostly Bs: JJ

Your friends describe you as a riot a minute. Like JJ, you're confident and bold, but you also make everyone feel instantly at ease. All your pals know they can call you at any time with their problems and you'll always make them smile.

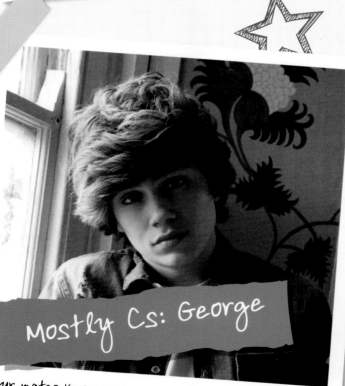

Mostly Cs: George

Your mates know you are sweet, innocent, random, cute and more than a little bit cheeky. Just like George, you have an adorably geeky side and aren't afraid to show it.

Mostly Ds: Jaymi

Just like Jaymi, you are amazingly kind-hearted and generous. You're always true to yourself and value honesty in your friends above everything else. You're incredibly loyal too, and are always there for your circle.

A DATE WITH Union J

EXCLUSIVE!

Find out what kind of boyfriends the boys would make . . .

What's the first thing that attracts you to someone?

JAYMI: 'Their smile.'

JJ: 'The very first thing is if I get along with their personality, that's a massive thing. And they've got to have a good smile as well.'

GEORGE: 'Gorgeous eyes and a cute face.'

JOSH: 'Easy answer: their smile.'

What qualities do you look for in a potential partner?

GEORGE: 'Someone who can make me laugh, make me happy and who I can be myself around, but is also really cute.'

JJ: 'Someone who is going to be with me for me, someone I can have a laugh with and someone who I am going to find attractive, obviously.'

JOSH: 'Someone who's caring, someone who's funny, down-to-earth and charming. Quite sort of flirty too.'

JAYMI: 'Someone who makes me laugh, who likes a laugh. Someone I get on with really well.'

What's the most romantic thing you've ever done?

JOSH: 'I once took a girl to Paris, the city of love and romance – that's OK, isn't it?'

JAYMI: 'I took my boyfriend to Rome for a romantic break.'

JJ: 'A few years ago I took a girlfriend on holiday to Mexico.'

GEORGE: 'I drove a girl to the beach spontaneously at midnight once, to look at the stars.'

What kind of boyfriend are you?

JAYMI: 'Lovely! Ha ha! I'd hope I am thoughtful. I really like to put his needs before mine. I never want to see him go without or feel like he isn't being put before me.'

JOSH: 'I would like to think I'm caring and understanding, and laid-back too.'

JJ: 'Caring, affectionate, I hope! I will do anything for a girl I like, literally. I am someone who likes to have a laugh and likes to make the girl laugh.'

GEORGE: 'I am honest, straight-up and hopefully fun, spontaneous.'

Who's your celebrity crush?

JAYMI: 'I can't say that! You should never say that. I might meet them!'

JOSH: 'I've got a couple, Kelly Brook or Jade from Little Mix.'

JJ: 'Michelle Keegan from *Coronation Street*.'

GEORGE: 'Demi Lovato.'

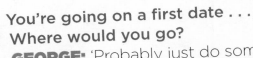

You're going on a first date . . . Where would you go?

GEORGE: 'Probably just do something crazy, like that time I went to the beach; just do something random, like a walk in the woods maybe, anything that was completely random. I wouldn't know what until it was the time, so I'd probably just invite them round for dinner and then think of something on the spot. Anything fun.'

JJ: 'I would take her to a place called Ely, which is down the road from where I live. It's beautiful, especially in the summer.'

There's a lovely bar and restaurant on the river with all the boats and stuff out there, and I'd take her on a boat.'

JAYMI: 'I'm quite a homely person so I'd probably invite him round to my house, just chill out and watch a film, have some food, just the two of us – a chilled environment. It can be very daunting to have a big first date so it's nice to just be relaxed.'

JOSH: 'McDonald's. Honestly!'

What would you wear? What would you like your date to wear?

GEORGE: 'Just whatever made us feel relaxed.'

JOSH: 'Slippers and a beanie. Both of us. I'm joking obviously.'

JAYMI: 'I'd wear something nice, slick, a little bit smart, a little bit suave! He should wear whatever makes him feel comfortable.'

JJ: 'Just casual stuff. I'd be myself, jeans or shorts if it was hot. Nice shirt maybe. And I would like her to wear anything she feels comfortable in.'

How would you make your date feel relaxed?

JJ: 'Just the flow of conversation really, make her relax, make her laugh, make sure she enjoyed herself.'

JAYMI: 'Make them laugh a lot.'

JOSH: 'I would offer to pay for her Big Mac! No, I'm joking. I would just chat away and see how we got on.'

GEORGE: 'Just try to be myself and be fun and smiley and happy and chatty.'

Would you pay or go halves?

JOSH: 'Of course I would pay.'

JJ: 'I'd pay.'

GEORGE: 'I would pay.'

JAYMI: 'Pay, always.'

It's the end of the night; would you go for a sneaky kiss?

GEORGE: 'Depends how the date went!'

JAYMI: 'I'd see how the date went.'

JJ: 'Depends how the date had gone really, but, yes, I'd go for a sneaky kiss if I felt it had gone well.'

JOSH: 'Yes, I would, definitely.'

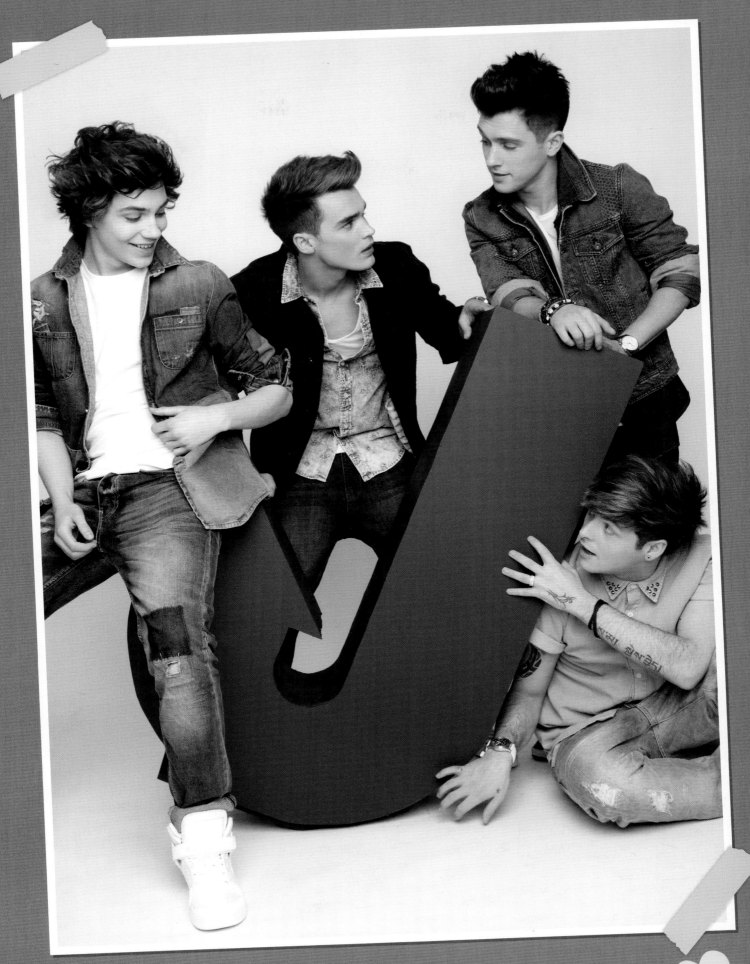

EXCLUSIVE! Union J FAST FACTS

GEORGE

- **What's your favourite TV show?** '*The Big Bang Theory.*'

- What's your favourite movie? 'The Lord of the Rings trilogy.'

- **What's your favourite meal?** 'Spaghetti Bolognese.'

- What's your favourite song? 'At the moment, it's our debut single, "Carry You"!'

- **What's your guilty secret?** 'I'd say girl bands. I'm a fan of Little Mix. I really wanted them to win when they were on *The X Factor*. Mind you, I was really into S Club 7 as well.'

- Who was the last person you called? 'My mum, to make sure she was bringing all my belongings so I can move into my new flat.'

JOSH

- **What's your favourite TV show?** '*Lost.*'

- What's your favourite movie? '*The Notebook.*'

- **What's your favourite meal?** 'Indian take-away, ideally chicken tikka masala.'

- What's your favourite song? "Wonderwall' by Oasis.'

- **What's your guilty pleasure?** 'Computer games. I spend so much time on my Xbox, especially playing Fifa. I've always been mad about football.'

- Who's the last person you called? 'My grandma.'

JAYMI

- **What's your favourite TV show?** '*Bones.*'

- What's your favourite movie? '*Avatar.*'

- **What's your favourite meal?** '*Fajitas.*'

- What's your favourite song? "Single Ladies" by Beyoncé.'

- **What's your guilty pleasure?** '*Glee!*'

- Who was the last person you called? 'My mum. I speak to her all the time.'

JJ

- **What's your favourite TV show?** '*Jersey Shore.*'

- What's your favourite movie? '*I Love You, Man.* It's one of the best movies ever – absolutely incredible.'

- **What's your favourite meal?** 'Fajitas probably. Or tacos.'

- What's your favourite song? "Use Somebody" by Kings of Leon. That will never get old, it's a classic track.'

- **Who was the last person you called?** 'My dad!'

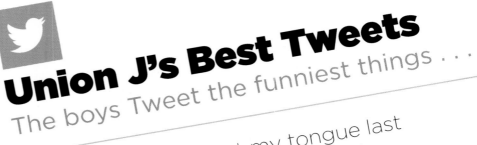

Union J's Best Tweets
The boys Tweet the funniest things . . .

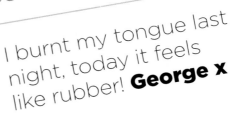

I burnt my tongue last night, today it feels like rubber! **George x**

I need to get a bigger bed because my cat Oreo takes the whole flipping thing up when I'm sleeping lol!!!! **Josh x**

Lovely day off, time for some lunch and housework haha :) **Jaymi xx**

Watching Paul the movie!!! I want an alien as a friend!!! **JJ x**

George just tripped over our bowl of shared apple crumble lol . . . he is such a thicket!!! hahahaha. **josh x**

50

Wow it's really raining atm. Had an umbrella up and a massive gust of wind nearly blew me off my feet!!! Felt like Mary Poppins haha! **JJ x**

Just seen an electric car! That is so cool lol!! I want one haha! **josh x**

I wouldn't date a fan? If I loved them I would! Simple :) **George x**

Last night at mummy's :(really excited to move but lil bit sad too. Love you mum. **Jaymi x**

I feel like finding a field and playing frisbee with my shoes off! **George x**

A Fine Bromance

No doubt about it, these lads are closer than close. The boys reveal everything about each other . . .

You seem to have a real bond; tell us about your friendship.

JOSH: 'Sounds cheesy, but it's a match made in heaven. There was a chemistry from the first minute we hooked up and that whole *X Factor* experience bonded us even more. We went through so many crazy experiences together.'

JJ: 'Union J is more like being with three amazing brothers. That's the relationship – it's really tight – we bicker of course, but we make up two minutes later. The way I am with the boys is exactly the way I am with my brother. It's very real, very close.'

GEORGE: 'The four of us are absolute brothers; we are just so close now. We get on like best friends, but we bicker like brothers. However, because we have that kind of tight relationship, we get over it really quickly and it seems to make us closer. I think we are the closest we can get.'

JAYMI: 'We are brothers, totally. It's a brotherhood; I love them like brothers. We are so close.'

Describe each other in three words:

JAYMI: 'George – smelly, clever and talented. Josh – sarcastic, hilarious and a gentleman. JJ – caring, a bit flighty and funny!'

JOSH: 'Jaymi – responsible, genuine and lovely. George – odd, caring and random. JJ – slow, affectionate and passionate.'

GEORGE: 'Jaymi – loving, caring and devoted. Josh – funny, cheeky, sarcastic. JJ – crazy, fun and immature.'

JJ: 'Jaymi – demanding (in a good way, sorry, more than three words!) funny and loving. George – geeky, funny and caring. Josh – sarcastic, funny and sensitive.'

Who's the bossiest?
JOSH: 'Jaymi.'
JJ: 'Jaymi.'
GEORGE: 'Jaymi.'
JAYMI: 'Me.'

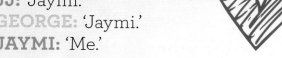

Who's the biggest troublemaker?
JJ: 'Josh!'
JOSH: 'Jaymi!'
GEORGE: 'Me.'
JAYMI: 'Me.'

Who's the funniest?
GEORGE: 'Josh.'
JAYMI: 'Josh.'
JOSH: 'The other three.'
JJ: 'Me! No, joking, Jaymi.'

Who's the most vain?
JOSH: 'JJ actually.'
JJ: 'Josh, I'd say. He probably said me, didn't he?'
JAYMI: 'Josh.'
GEORGE: 'I'd say JJ.'

Who has the most annoying habits?
GEORGE: 'JJ.'
JAYMI: 'JJ.'
JJ: 'Josh, actually.'
JOSH: 'Definitely me!'

Who's the messiest?
JJ: 'Josh. Easy.'
GEORGE: 'Josh.'
JAYMI: 'Josh.'
JOSH: 'JJ.'

Who's always late?
JOSH: 'Jaymi.'
JJ: 'That boy again, Josh!'
JAYMI: 'Josh.'
GEORGE: 'Josh.'

Who sings loudest in the shower?
JOSH: 'George.'
JJ: 'Jaymi.'
GEORGE: 'Jaymi.'
JAYMI: 'JJ.'

Union J
SHOW US THE WAY

The boys have certainly learnt a lot on their way to pop stardom . . .

DREAMS CAN COME TRUE

The boys have had many setbacks on their way to the top. But each time they've picked themselves up, brushed themselves down and tried again.

'If you really want something, then only you can make it happen.' George

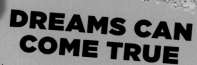

MUM'S ALWAYS RIGHT

The boys are all really close to their mums, who have supported them throughout their *X Factor* journey. 'I wouldn't be the man I am without my mum,' says JJ. The boys all credit their mums with giving them the confidence to make their dreams come true.

GIVE BACK

The boys have given money, effort and time to many charitable causes already, and use their fame to encourage their fans to think about how they can help the world around them. 'It's easy for us to forget how lucky we are,' says Josh.

EMBRACE YOUR INNER GEEK

Being confident is all about learning to love the skin you're in. 'I try to wake up every morning with a positive thought,' says George. Remember that you are young, individual and unique – just like George.

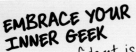

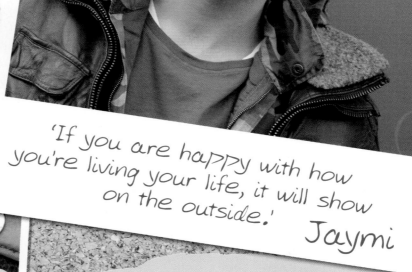

BE TRUE TO YOURSELF

The boys are determined to always be one hundred per cent real and true to who they are, and are determined to encourage their fans to do the same.

'If you are happy with how you're living your life, it will show on the outside.'

Jaymi

FAMILY MATTERS

JJ reckons he'd be nothing without his family. 'My family has been amazing,' he says. 'If I ever have down times, they're only a phone call away . . . I'm a real family guy.' Despite the many trappings that come with fame, the boys know what really counts in life.

Union J
L♥ve You ♥

Each of the boys tells us just how much they adore you lot – the J Cats!

Josh

WHAT DO YOUR FANS MEAN TO YOU?

'Oh, wow, they mean everything; without them nothing would be possible for Union J. We had all that support from them every week through *The X Factor* and we've had the same since. They are the twinkle in my eye!'

WHAT'S THE BEST PRESENT YOU'VE BEEN GIVEN? AND THE STRANGEST?

'The best present a fan has given me is a £10 iTunes voucher – that was really useful. And the strangest present? . . . a £10 iTunes voucher?'

George

WHAT DO YOUR FANS MEAN TO YOU?

'Our fans mean the world to us. I love it when we see fans that we have met before and we know their names; it's like having another family around us, another group of friends who we know are really loyal to us and support us. They are another group of best friends and we love seeing them as much as possible.'

WHAT'S THE BEST PRESENT YOU'VE BEEN GIVEN? AND THE STRANGEST?

'The best present is easy: someone paid for a star in the universe called Union J, and you can go online and look at the constellation where it is, and look at the actual star. The weirdest present is probably a bra that was thrown onstage.'

Jaymi

WHAT DO YOUR FANS MEAN TO YOU?

'Everything. Without them we would be nothing. That's short and sweet but absolutely true. One hundred per cent.'

WHAT'S THE BEST PRESENT YOU'VE BEEN GIVEN? AND THE STRANGEST?

'Aftershave. Always great. The strangest? Now you're asking! Someone sent me a pencil once. I was a bit confused by that.'

JJ

WHAT DO YOUR FANS MEAN TO YOU?

'Everything. Without fans we wouldn't be in the position we are – that's just a fact. We appreciate everything they have done for us, genuinely.'

WHAT'S THE BEST PRESENT YOU'VE BEEN GIVEN? AND THE STRANGEST?

'Probably the best is a teddy bear. I love teddy bears and we are always given those, which suits me. The weirdest present was a pair of boxers that were thrown up onstage once. The actual boxers themselves were quite good, to be fair. They had this monkey on there with some bananas.'

57

THE FUTURE

None of the boys could possibly have imagined how far they would come in such a short time.

'Our lives have totally changed,' says George, 'but we wouldn't swap it for the world.' The pressure is on to keep succeeding, which means that Josh, JJ, George and Jaymi's lives are full for the foreseeable future with a relentless schedule of recording, touring, interviews and photoshoots the world over. For the moment, they don't mind: they can take it all in their stride.

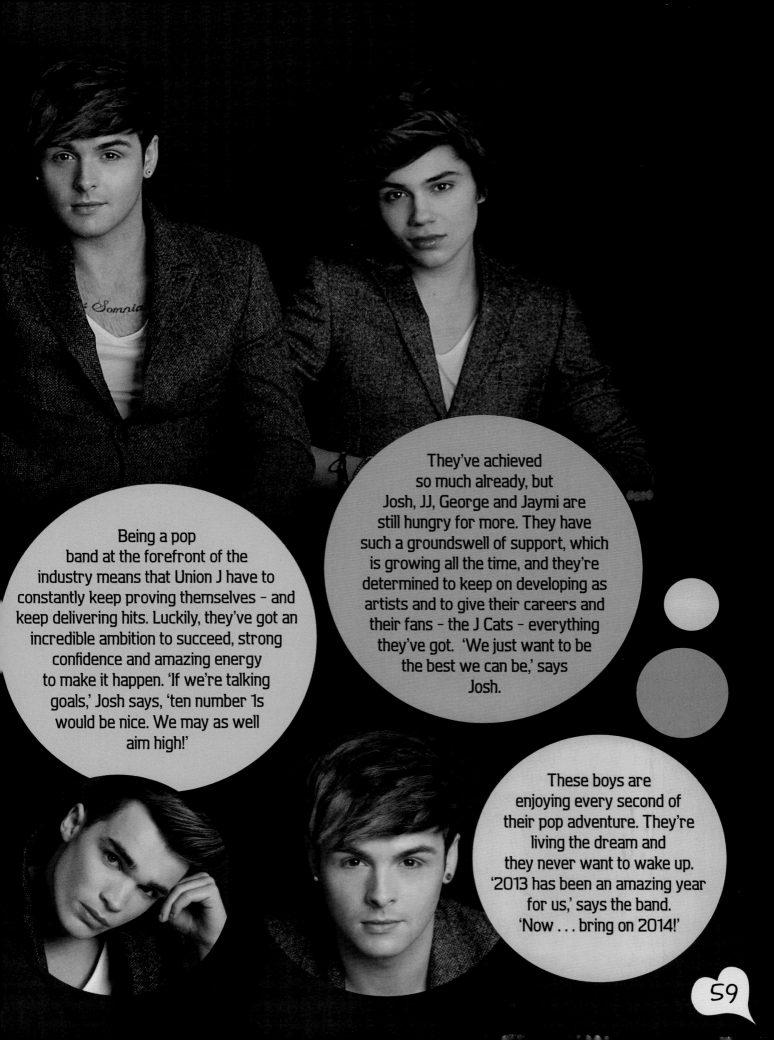

Being a pop band at the forefront of the industry means that Union J have to constantly keep proving themselves – and keep delivering hits. Luckily, they've got an incredible ambition to succeed, strong confidence and amazing energy to make it happen. 'If we're talking goals,' Josh says, 'ten number 1s would be nice. We may as well aim high!'

They've achieved so much already, but Josh, JJ, George and Jaymi are still hungry for more. They have such a groundswell of support, which is growing all the time, and they're determined to keep on developing as artists and to give their careers and their fans – the J Cats – everything they've got. 'We just want to be the best we can be,' says Josh.

These boys are enjoying every second of their pop adventure. They're living the dream and they never want to wake up. '2013 has been an amazing year for us,' says the band. 'Now . . . bring on 2014!'

'Hi, guys! Hope you are good and thank you so much for all of your support for everything we've been through so far. You mean the world to us and you make Union J World what it is. Hopefully we will get to meet every single one of you and give you all monkey hugs. You are amazing! See you soon hopefully.'

George

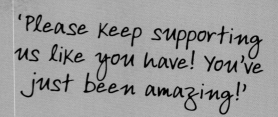

'Please keep supporting us like you have! You've just been amazing!'

Josh

'Thank you so much for everything you have done for us. You have really made our dreams come true. Everything we do, we do it for you, so we really hope you enjoy our careers as much as we will.

Jaymi

'Thank you for supporting Union J. I love you so much and keep supporting us, thanks again!'

JJ

61